PRAISE FOR J. TODD SCOTT

The Flock

"It's all here: doomsday cults, innocents and grifters, unexplainable phenomena. Heartache and regret. A chance at redemption. What sets *The Flock* above your average thriller is the absolute ring of authenticity from this twenty-plus-year career DEA agent. You got the real deal right here."

—Alma Katsu, author of *The Fervor* and *The Hunger*

"Scott lays out his short, propulsive chapters like a trail of breadcrumbs you can't help but follow. This one will keep you up late turning the pages."

—Brian Freeman, bestselling author of *Thief River Falls*

Other Works

"Mr. Scott, as it happens, has been a federal agent with the Drug Enforcement Administration for more than twenty years, which surely contributes to the authenticity of this convincing saga."

—*Wall Street Journal*

"Scott's twenty-year career as a DEA agent infuses his work with realism, and his writing chops will make readers wonder why he waited so long to launch his literary career."

—Associated Press

"The author exploits his decades of experience as a federal agent to create a powerful, real

—*Kirkus Reviews*

"Scott writes beautifully, dreaming up intriguing action scenes, which those who are focused only on thrills will wish kept going and going. But patient readers will recognize and appreciate Scott's end game: showing us a world where thieves, murderers, and sadists are everyday folk."

—*Booklist*

"J. Todd Scott's series reads like equal parts Don Winslow and Ace Atkins. Having spent twenty years working with the DEA, Scott knows his stuff, adding instant credibility to his stories, which are well written and hopelessly addictive."

—New York Journal of Books

"As addictive as the best crime show."

—*Newsweek*

"The poetic and bloody ground of [the west] has given birth to a powerful new voice in contemporary western crime fiction."

—Craig Johnson, *New York Times* bestselling author of the Walt Longmire series

"J. Todd Scott is the real deal."

—Michael McGarrity, *New York Times* bestselling author

CALL
THE
DARK

OTHER TITLES BY J. TODD SCOTT

CALL
THE
DARK

A Thriller

J. TODD SCOTT

THOMAS & MERCER

Published by Thomas & Mercer, Seattle

www.apub.com

Amazon, the Amazon logo, and Thomas & Mercer are trademarks of Amazon.com, Inc., or its affiliates.

ISBN-13: 9781662500411 (paperback)
ISBN-13: 9781662500428 (digital)

Cover design by David Drummond
Cover image: © rsooll, tuulijumala, Sergei Mishchenko / Shutterstock

Printed in the United States of America

For Lucy Catherine . . .
Take wing . . .

Little one, come to my knee!
Hark, how the rain is pouring
Over the roof, in the pitch-black night,
And the wind in the woods a-roaring!

Hush, my darling, and listen,
Then pay for the story with kisses.
Father was lost in the pitch-black night,
In just such a storm as this is!

High up on the lonely mountains,
Where the wild men watched and waited
Wolves in the forest, and bears in the bush,
And I on my path belated.

The rain and the night together
Came down, and the wind came after,
Bending the props of the pine-tree roof,
And snapping many a rafter.

I crept along in the darkness,
Stunned, and bruised, and blinded,—
Crept to a fir with thick-set boughs,
And a sheltering rock behind it.

There, from the blowing and raining
Crouching, I sought to hide me:
Something rustled, two green eyes shone,
And a wolf lay down beside me . . .

"A NIGHT WITH A WOLF"
By Bayard Taylor
(1825–1878)

BLACK MOUNTAIN

She talks to him all the time now without saying anything at all.

He *hears* her deep inside his skull, that dark hole behind his eyes.

She calls out for him, whispering his name, by the sound of a thousand feathered wings.

But right now, she's sitting two rows up, not even looking at him. He's been staring at her from the moment they went wheels up, even as she pretends to be too engrossed with the iPad in her lap, or her phone, or the glossy magazine with all the photoshopped pictures of surf, sand, and sun and impossibly blue skies far from here.

These indulgences are allowed only because they mean so much and so little. The iPad is restricted and constantly monitored, the phones contain no actual contacts—no friends to call or text—and the magazine is months old. The world changes so fast now that those out-of-date stories might as well be ancient history, little more than myths for a fairy princess trapped in a forest tower or deep asleep in a crystal coffin.

It could be argued that he is her only link to the outside world, her one true friend.

She once complained about this—no, she very much complained about *you*, he thinks—and although that betrayal should have infuriated him, would have once upon a time sent him into an oh-so-familiar frenzy, he bore it without complaint. Bore it with a smile.

Now he can better grasp subterfuge and subtlety, how to present one face while hiding another.

We both wear masks, he knows, because our true faces are so terrible . . .

He catches her stealing a look and grins amiably for her—another well-practiced gesture—only for her to turn away again just as quickly, staring lost and worried out the small window at the winter darkness all around and the scudding clouds and rolling mountains far below.

He keeps this safe distance for both their sakes, but that's getting harder by the day, even harder than ruling his emotions, keeping his placid mask on straight, his true intentions and temperament veiled.

From where he sits, he can still hear that incessant whispering, the beating of invisible wings: smell the tang of hospital soap on her skin, count every ticktock beat of her heart, feel the rising heat of each breath. Although they're not alone here, high above the winter clouds, they might as well be.

He only has eyes for her.

He checks his expensive watch and smooths out the odd crease in his shark-gray slacks. He stands, stretches, holding his gangly arms and switchblade elbows and big-knuckled hands in tight and close. He's too tall for this plane. Too thin, too pale, too awkward for polite company. He's all right angles and sharp edges, always folding himself smaller and smaller just to fit in, so as not to cut anyone in passing. A foolish man once joked that he looked like he'd been stitched together from spare parts, and although he'd laughed along at the time, making light of it like you're supposed to do, a month later he tracked the man down and left only spare parts behind—a few beneath the bed, some in the freezer, a handful arrayed in the bathtub like a pagan sundial—and he still wonders if anyone got that joke.

He's not so much at the mercy of those animallike rages anymore; his mask of calmness fits tighter now. But he learned long ago he can't change his fundamental nature either. Best he can do is keep it in check, control it when he can, and hide it long as possible.

Like her . . .

She doesn't fully comprehend that yet. He alone feels that sable energy radiating from her like dark feathers, like a dark and dying star. She swallows the light, and is slowly, surely, driving him mad.

The plane suddenly shudders, jostled hard by the unseen hand of the coming winter storm, and he senses her fear. Not of him, but of the storm itself. Ice and snow glaze the windows, gleaming cold as a knife edge, as the plane fights the weight and the wind. The squall's fury doesn't frighten him, but most scary things don't. If he checked his own heart rate now, it'd barely register above sixty.

He knows he shouldn't . . . don't touch her, don't ever, ever, touch her . . . but he bends himself into the seat beside her anyway and grabs one of her hands, trying to calm her, trying to reassure her. Although her skin crawls at his touch, he's glad she doesn't pull back.

It's okay, you're safe with me . . .

But she isn't, not truly . . . and neither is he.

When the plane lurches again, cabin lights flickering like fleeing shadows, he reaches for the gun he always carries as she suddenly grips his hand tight and gifts him with a tiny, terrible smile of her own.

. . . *i'll never hurt you* . . .

And the last thing he hears is the rustle of a thousand black wings . . .

It's not full dark yet when Maggie sees the burning plane crash.

A private jet, small and mostly white, one long dark stripe on the side, canted sharply to the left as it drops from the snowy heavens, leaving one wing higher than the other, like it's waving goodbye.

Light in its rounded windows, bright enough for her to count them, and still picking up speed even as it augers in toward the ground, falling from some unimaginable height.

Moments before, the sky was purple, dusted with snow and first flickering stars, the whole world cold and still and quiet, but more importantly empty. Just raw wilderness . . . wildness . . . in every direction.

Now alive with the ugly roar of this sudden falling plane and its one . . . two . . . three . . . four . . . windows on a side, arrowing at the earth, toward her.

Maggie imagines faces staring down, wonders what they see.

The lowered wing clips a red spruce, shearing the top off the big tree in an explosion of fiery sparks and conifer needles, balling up metal like paper. The impact shakes the whole plane, nearly tipping it back the other way, the growl of revving engines finally hitting her full in the face. Turbines desperately spin as high as they can, fighting to keep the small plane aloft, even as the mountain's pines and sycamores and elms reach for it, grasp at it, pulling it mercilessly toward the deep, dark heart of the wood.

The plane grazes a handful of dusky treetops, like fingers caressing skin, before the whole craft corkscrews over and over and both wings crumple and those four tiny, shiny, bright windows blow out and the plane comes apart in so much smoke and flame and so many jagged jigsaw pieces that Maggie can't tell anymore where the jet ends and the trees begin.

The following explosion, a crushing reverberation, lands like a second slap, knocking her to her knees.

It's the sound of trains colliding, a building falling over, a tidal wave crashing into that Outer Banks beach house she and Vann once owned. Almost immediately, that awful noise is followed by a fiery glow, blooming and blossoming like a garish flower in the wake of that final descent and impact. A staccato flash of light harshly illuminating the woods all around Maggie.

Illuminating her . . . reminding her too forcefully of swirling police lights.

The flash doesn't disappear altogether, fading instead to a silent, ghostly shimmering that turns the trees monstrous and menacing, that creates crawling shadows and eerie fractal patterns. A liminal faerie fire burning along the folding shovel now forgotten in her gloved hand. Glimmering, too, over the rifle she left against a tree while digging at the hard earth.

No . . . no . . . this can't be happening.

Not here. Not now.

Maggie once made a living off numbers but doesn't need to run any now to know the odds are near astronomical—maybe one in a million, even a billion—that a plane would crash down at the very same moment and over the one stretch of isolated West Virginia winter wilderness she is standing in, so close it nearly fell on her head, so close she can still feel the friction of its passage, the heat of its burning, beyond the trees.

But if there's any saving grace to this unthinkable, horrible moment or one thing she can count on, it's likely there's no way anyone survived that crash.

No way at all.

People will still come looking, though—sooner or later—scouring for wreckage and survivors, the inevitable bodies. But Maggie hopes to be long gone before then. She's gotten good at turning into a ghost, slipping through the shadows, fading out of sight. But it's still hard to completely vanish nowadays, even with serious planning and preparation.

And Maggie is nothing if not a serious planner. She's been planning this for 483 days.

But she never planned for a plane falling from the sky, and as with any similarly unexpected crash or tragedy, people on the run often leave plenty of telltale wreckage behind too.

Someone always, always, comes looking.

Sooner or later.

Maggie abandons the shovel and, using her dad's old nickel Wittnauer compass, searches for true north, deeper in the woods, higher up this mountain. A path through the oldest hollers where monsters still lurk, according to that book she left behind in Pullens, just before they cornered her.

There's still blood on her hands, gone black beneath her nails, that she didn't have time to scrub clean.

Now she does run a quick mental calculation, figuring she can still stay ahead of the fallout from Pullens, even outrun the search for the fallen plane. But safely escaping the coming Christmas nor'easter is getting too close to call, a dire winter storm predicted to blast the Monongahela over the next twenty-four to thirty-six hours.

At least if she's caught dead above the snow line, trapped up there in the dark and cold, she won't have to worry about running and hiding anymore. It might be months, years, before her body is found, if ever. And given all that's happened, all that she's done, a part of her is at peace with that. Finally, the lies, the chase . . . the hunt . . . will be over.

I'll just fade away, she thinks, let the snow cover me.

Safe. Peaceful.

No more memories . . . no more nightmares . . . just a black and welcoming silence.

And that's when Maggie hears a scream from the wreckage beyond the trees . . .

When Hudson Landry first heard that mysterious, unearthly scream, it terrified his sorrel, and all he could think of was the old stories of the White Thing of Randolph County, a creature once known and feared in times even further past.

It was long whispered that the White Thing was a cold-blooded killer, a monstrous wolflike beast, a pale vengeful ghost as large as a horse, unafraid of humans or any other living creature.

But in the cold, driving mountain rain, Hudson could make out no such monster, living or dead. Just the old trees crowding the path to the church, darkening his way. He told himself it was only the sudden October storm that made the night so black, that made the wind so fearsome, that made the air so cold. And as he fought to bring his scared mount under control, he laughed at his own folly.

When he would be found, days later, his own mother would not recognize him.

The White Thing roared from the woods on all fours, mouth agape, flashing jagged teeth the size of knives. It howled and snarled and bawled like a young girl in pain, like a dying child.

It fell on both horse and rider in a fury of blood.

It showed neither fear . . . nor mercy . . .

The White Things:
Tall Tales of West Virginia's White Monsters
Jim Collymore

Dark and Stormy Books
Pullens, West Virginia
2006

ONE

1

Ekker knows he makes people nervous.

It's the eyes.

Not that there's anything strange or unusual about them. There isn't. They are plainly, purposefully normal. It's the stare, though. Most people aren't used to being really looked at, really stared at, and it was Shakespeare who said the eyes are the windows to the soul.

Ekker doesn't care much for Shakespeare. And although he didn't believe in the existence of souls, either, until recently, the Bible does have something to say on the matter—

The lamp of the body is the eye. If therefore your eye is good, your whole body will be full of light. But if your eye is bad, your whole body will be full of darkness. If therefore the light that is in you is darkness, how great is that darkness . . .

So, maybe when Ekker looks at someone, really gives them a chance to gaze into his windows, all they see is . . . darkness. His darkness. Black, bottomless, impenetrable. Or maybe when he stares at them in that cool, unflinching way of his—stares until they succumb to the urge to blink and turn away—it's because they're afraid he'll truly see theirs.

"Theroux once said—"

Ekker cuts Brooking off with his eyes, and Jon Alexander Brooking's clearly not accustomed to anyone cutting him off. His overly tanned face goes white, like he's been slapped. "Do you want to talk *about* me,

Mr. Brooking?" Ekker asks, his accent plainly, purposefully impossible to place as well. "Repeat for me all these things and stories Theroux once told you. Or do you want to talk *to* me?"

Brooking only flashes Ekker a shark smile, all perfect, expensive teeth. Still trying to hide his anger, his frustration, still searching how to regain the upper hand.

They're sitting in Brooking's office, carved out of glass, as high up as anyone is willing to build in this city. Ekker knows Brooking is used to looking down on people no matter who they are; knows, too, that Brooking is surprised Ekker even agreed to meet him here. A man like Brooking dictates time and place for one reason only—to remind men like Ekker of life's center of gravity. But Ekker's weightless; there's nothing Brooking can do to him, nothing Brooking can bring to bear to hold him down; Brooking has no hold over him at all. Ekker can get up and walk out at any time, and if Theroux really told Brooking anything about him, he absolutely would've warned Brooking about that.

Ekker takes a long sip of Moroccan water from a crystal tumbler. More glass. Everything and the whole office itself cut from it, a hundred sharp angles and hues, all designed to make a statement. It's like a movie set, a child's idea of wealth and power. Ekker doesn't need to look into Brooking's eyes to look through him. He's as transparent as his ostentatious office.

Brooking turns a Breitling on his wrist with a hand that is big, solid, and delicately manicured. He plays tennis, plenty of tennis. Golf, too, at least twice a week. In that one small movement, Ekker sees all that and so much more.

Transparent.

Brooking smiles again, humorless, a smile as cool and clear as the water in Ekker's tumbler. Sometime in the last three to four hours, something bad has happened, and the truly powerful and dangerous men who employ Brooking want answers, want closure. Gravity itself has finally shifted beneath Brooking, and although he may not want to admit it—most of all to himself—Ekker is now the center of this new world order. Brooking needs Ekker, or he wouldn't be here.

Even when closure is a matter of life and death, a man like Ekker is never anyone's first resort. Brooking won't treat him as an equal, but unlike Theroux, Ekker isn't his employee, either, or his associate, or even an ally.

Ekker is a solution. Ekker *is* closure.

Brooking can't buy Ekker, can't own him, and Theroux would have told him that too. In the end, Brooking has zero control over what happens next, and Ekker's ultimate decision—yes, no—will have nothing to do with Brooking at all. And that deeply, deeply troubles Jon Brooking.

"We can only assume Theroux is dead," Brooking says.

"I assumed as much too," Ekker says, but he already knows Theroux is dead.

Or he wouldn't be here . . .

He smiles at Brooking and watches the sky turn dark shades of blue and black beyond all the glass.

"You . . . you aren't what I expected," Brooking concedes with a heavy shrug before reaching for a cell phone.

No, Ekker thinks, sipping the water turning blood warm in the tumbler. I am not.

After a brief, one-sided call Ekker can't hear, Brooking reluctantly leaves his glass desk and hands Ekker an iPad.

The iPad is alive with photos, documents—a hastily curated dossier—and Ekker skims through it with rapid-fire finger swipes. He doesn't linger on anything but takes it all in nevertheless.

When he returns it, Brooking hesitates before accepting it, as if expecting—assuming—Ekker would keep it, some sort of contract already between them.

It's not complete enough for Ekker. Too much has been left out, too much redacted, too many secrets.

"Theroux was managing the search," Brooking says. "He's been our eyes and ears on the ground for a while now."

"This is . . . managed?" Ekker asks, casually motioning to the iPad with his tumbler. "How long has he been out of contact?" He sets the glass down. "How many *know?*"

Brooking sits across from Ekker and puts the now-dark iPad on a small table between them. "Too long . . . and likely too many now."

Ekker checks his own watch, nothing expensive like Brooking's Breitling, just a bland Timex, and calculates the rate of ripples in this metaphorical pond. Tries to figure out just how far and wide this unique problem might've expanded, and if it's gone past the point of containment. No news reports yet out of West Virginia, but given Theroux's sudden silence, and the circumstances likely surrounding it, it's just a matter of time.

Brooking frowns at him, making the same calculation, revealing pale creases—laugh lines—that his overcooked tan can't quite cover. But there's nothing funny about what's unfolding now. "It's a goddamn mess," Brooking admits. "Theroux came highly recommended—"

"Like me?" Ekker says, sharp, cutting.

Brooking looks away, irritated at being interrupted but cagey enough not to take the bait, so Ekker lets him off the hook. If Ekker decides to get involved in this, neither will have time for useless sparring. "Theroux was good . . . once," Ekker concedes, "if a little old fashioned, conventional." More than likely, if the iPad files are any indication, Theroux just wasn't briefed thoroughly enough to be more creative. Not a mistake Ekker will make.

"Without Theroux," Brooking says, "we wouldn't know the half of it."

Now that he's gone dark, *the half of it*, as near as Ekker can tell, is bad and getting worse by the moment.

Brooking has a tumbler of his own filled with something dark and regal. It captures what little light there is in the room and holds it tight as a fist as he takes a long, serious drink. He's clearly agitated that this is spinning out of control so fast, that there are answers he desperately needs and doesn't have. Worse, there's nothing to do now but hope Ekker finds them for him.

Brooking hates him.

Brooking sets his tumbler down carefully to avoid the iPad, like he doesn't want to touch either anymore. "So, how does this work? What happens next?"

"You tell me a story . . . the whole story . . . and I listen."

"And then?"

"And then," Ekker says with a shrug, "I decide if there's anything next at all."

Brooking leans forward, clearly wanting to say more, even make an idle threat, implicit or otherwise, before changing his mind, reduced instead to spinning the Breitling futilely on his wrist again. Ekker understands in a way Brooking never will that problems like these are always just a matter of time, and even an expensive watch doesn't buy Brooking more of it, can't slow it down or roll it backward. Brooking can't rewind the reason he summoned Ekker here, or the failures he'll soon have to answer for.

Time runs the same, runs out, for us all. The clock is always ticking, and Ekker knows that as well as anyone.

Ekker has less than six months to live.

After a final mouthful of scotch to steady himself, Brooking says, "I'm not sure where to begin."

"Yes, you do," Ekker replies—an order now—as he locks eyes with the other man, pinning him down, until Brooking can't stand it anymore and looks away.

Tonight, Ekker's own eyes are faded blue, but tomorrow they'll be a different color altogether.

"Start at the beginning," Ekker commands. "Tell me about her. Tell me everything."

2

Marcus is dreaming again.

You wouldn't believe you could dream about fire this way, so bright and so hot and so goddamn *real*, but you can. So real you taste the bitter smoke itself . . . you're choking on it . . . so searing and unforgiving you feel the flames themselves racing up your hands, flying for your face, igniting your hair.

You're burning.

Shouts and echoes and the angry call-and-response of small arms fire.

You're screaming.

The stink of metal and sweat and blood.

You're boiling.

An actinic jolt to your heart that stops it dead in its tracks as superheated air throws you end over end, right at the sun.

You're falling.

Only to find out you can't fly.

You're dead.

Only to wake up later like you always do, hands clawing at your face, and realize for the hundredth or thousandth time that it was just the same awful dream . . . that nightmare . . . and no, you're not dead after all.

You're just a survivor.

But you're not whole, either, and never will be again.

That fire . . . so bright and so hot . . . made sure of that.

It burned you alive.

Marcus wakes with the shakes, realizing he nodded off in the front seat of his truck.

Five minutes only, no more than that, but these horrible little fugue episodes have become more frequent, more alarming. More real. Despite the dream . . . that nightmare . . . he isn't on fire, just the hot air blast from the truck's vent, working overtime to warm up the cab.

Cold outside and temps dropping fast, and his shirt is still cloying and damp, clinging to his old dog tags and his scarred skin.

He's got a fresh duty shirt in the back with SHERIFF M. AUSTIN hand stitched over the breast pocket and would love to change into it, even take a long cold shower, too, or send out for some of that good, strong black coffee at Mirabel's to wash away the taste of all that nightmare ash. But his chief deputy, Donnie Kornblue, is already jogging toward his truck, waving for his attention.

In the dusty snow and Marcus's spinning roof rack lights, Donnie is pallid, hazy, indistinct. A ghost who's seen a dead man.

God, Marcus thinks, I've seen so many . . .

And they all look the same.

☾

This dead man smiles up at him.

Wolfe County Sheriff Marcus Austin is the veteran of several counterterrorism combat tours, lost a best friend and left most of a leg in the Yakla district of Yemen's al-Bayda Province, and has firsthand experience with every sort of violence one man can visit on another. He's seen this sort of grim smile too many times before, an eerie mixture of horror and black-humored surprise, like the dead man finally got the joke, only to find the joke was on him.

Unfortunately, six inches of steel shoved through the heart is nothing to laugh at.

Marcus kneels close, sweeping his SureFire along the body, spotlighting the serrated knife above the bolster. Not a steak or common kitchen knife, not something someone yanked out of a drawer or grabbed fast off a granite counter—not that there's a ton of granite countertops in Pullens, West Virginia, anyway—but not a hunting or skinning blade either. No, this is a serious piece of work, a tactical combat knife, with one true purpose. And Marcus is staring at it.

Donnie leans over him, puzzling, too, over the dead man stabbed in the chest, lying faceup in a scrim of snow.

Donnie's been a deputy longer than Marcus has been the sheriff but has encountered far fewer corpses, maybe two that were the result of an actual homicide. "What the hell?" Donnie asks. "That's something right there, ain't it?"

"Yeah," Marcus answers, using a gloved hand to gently brush snow out of the man's face. Not a face he recognizes, but tiny Pullens gets its fair share of visitors, mostly backcountry skiers and hikers. Tucked in the shadows of Laurel Mountain near the Tygart Valley and Leading Creek, Pullens is the last light of civilization before the High Alleghenies and the Monongahela National Forest and Cranberry Wilderness. Not much, but way out here, it's all there is.

Marcus is careful not to disturb the body, but it's a futile gesture. This isn't a crime scene anymore, just a grave site. He won't be able to get an ME out of Buckhannon for a day or more but can't leave the corpse lying here behind the Briar Inn or framed by the back windows of the Big River Grill.

He and Donnie are going to have to move it themselves, and soon.

Over his shoulder, the bar's windows are lit with Christmas lights—haphazard bulbs, winking blue, green, red, and purple—but only someone looking out at just the right moment would've seen anything. Even then, it was likely too dark, easy to miss if it happened fast. And he figures this killing happened very fast.

The body's been out here a night at most. Hard to believe it lay out here a whole day exposed this way, knife pointing skyward like an accusing finger. But Andy Parsons claimed he stumbled on it only twenty minutes ago, and Andy's now sitting in the Big River, telling what he found to the few patrons—any one of whom could be the killer, come to think of it—and drinking three fingers of Four Roses, courtesy of the Wolfe County Sheriff's Office.

Donnie breathes into his cupped hands, even though they're wrapped tight in leather gloves. He tosses a longing glance back at the Big River's warm, muzzy windows, too, no doubt wishing he was in there sharing that Kentucky bourbon with Andy. Marcus hasn't taken a drink in five years. Donnie asks, "So, what do we do now?"

Marcus ignores him, still intent on the body, still working through the possibilities, and there are not a lot of them. Sure, the look, the clothes, say day hiker. R1 TechFace fleece and RailRiders Bushwacker pants pulled down over Rocky C4T tactical boots. Black merino beanie covering short hair. A bull neck with what might be the leading edge of a black-ink tattoo just visible near the carotid. Dark eyes open and unseeing, one bloodshot.

But the clothes are too expensive, too new, and not nearly sufficient to ward off the rapidly dropping temperatures either here or out in the woods. A winter storm, a big nor'easter, is aimed at them, and it's likely to be a blinding, cold, and very white Christmas. The last one dumped two feet of snow.

Marcus stands and stretches, testing the heavy weight of his Genesis X4 bionic prosthetic. It's as advanced as they come, waterproof and rugged, and the mechatronic left foot is adaptable and does a damn good job of replicating a natural, normal gait. Still, West Virginia's winter cold always seems to glitch the bionic's electronics, and trudging through fresh snowfall or navigating thick ice is never easy for even a practiced hiker, much less a ruined man with one leg.

Deidre hated when he talked that way . . . when he still thinks that way . . . so it's fortunate for them both she's not around to read his mind anymore.

Fortunately, too, there's not many places to track down a seasonal hiker or any other visitor to Pullens. A few Vrbo and Airbnb cottages out in the Cranberry, and the Briar Inn itself, its front porch twenty yards around the corner from the body and draped in gauzy Christmas lights too. Red and white like a candy cane.

"I'll ask over at the Briar," Marcus says, "find out who's checked in over the last forty-eight hours. Why don't you slip into the Big River, wring a real statement from Parsons before he's too drunk to remember anything. See for yourself if there's any unknown faces over there."

Donnie Kornblue smiles at that, clearly relieved, probably already imagining a heavy bourbon pour of his own, a Budweiser too. But the smile almost immediately flickers and falters as he stares at the dead man at their feet. "What about this poor guy?"

It's late, and downtown Pullens, such as it is, is sparse, mostly vacant. More Christmas lights now than people. This guy, their victim, could lie here quiet and undisturbed the rest of the night. Almost peaceful, Marcus thinks, and I haven't had a peaceful night in months.

Too many dreams . . . too many nightmares.

"Not like he's going anywhere," Marcus says, "but help me get him up in my truck anyway. We'll check for a wallet, any other ID."

Donnie grimaces, unhappy at the thought of putting even gloved hands on the dead man, but he grabs hold of the man's legs without complaint, while Marcus slides in under his arms.

It's only after they pry the body off the frozen ground that they discover the gun.

3

As unlikely as it sounds, the NTSB puts the odds of surviving any plane crash at about 95 percent.

Maggie knows you're more liable to die by poisoning or electrocution than in a plane. On the numbers alone, driving a car is statistically more dangerous. You could take a flight every day your whole life and never encounter a problem. But those are merely the universal odds, an aggregation of big data, all the runway slips and slides, the controlled landings, the near misses.

The "technically survivable" crashes.

Although airline manufacturers want you to believe that any seat is as safe as another, the numbers again suggest you're around 40 percent more likely to survive a crash if you're sitting near the tail, and royally screwed if you're in the first-class rows. While commercial airliners are nominally safer than private planes and jets, that's only because those smaller private jets are nothing but first-class rows.

She knows numbers, knows, too, just how easily they can be folded, spindled, and manipulated. That's why she's so pessimistic about the survivability chances of anyone on the jet she witnessed crash into the West Virginia wilderness. More than that, she felt it, the impact and flames and spiraling pieces. Most fatalities are fire or impact related, or from smoke inhalation, postcrash.

So, she's not surprised when the screaming stops before she gets to the crash site itself. She's relieved.

She's also not surprised when she discovers the first severed arm hanging from a tree. It's not even the arm that draws her attention.

It's the burning paper.

Infinite flecks of fiery paper, or maybe seat cushioning or insulation, drifting, dancing on the dark wind, churning amid the snowflakes. A miasma of floating ash and drifting hot smoke.

Bits and pieces of something bright and shiny—aluminum or tinfoil—all mixed up in the night air, too, reflecting and refracting and burnishing the falling firelight. It's like being trapped inside a wheeling kaleidoscope.

Like being in a snow globe. It's beautiful.

Her dad once gave her an antique snow globe, a gold-leaf dome so old the artificial snow inside was still made of bone chips. It was from Romania or Hungary or Poland, or so he claimed, and it held a tiny blonde girl with a great red scarf ice dancing away from a massive, feral, black wolf. Because of the snow globe's age, the girl's painted eyes and bow tie mouth had long disappeared, worried away, leaving her blank and expressionless. Blind and mute. But the wolf's eyes looked as fresh as if they had been painted on just yesterday, as ruby red as the skating girl's scarf, both menacing and piercing.

Even without seeing a face, Maggie assumed the girl was laughing, had to be laughing, wind in her hair and cold on her cheeks and wolf at her heels. One leg kicked high, so that a turn of the snow dome's bronze key would send her twirling en pointe, round and round and round.

Maggie loved that snow globe, like she loved all the weird gifts her dad unearthed. She'd shake it up and sit and study that frozen tableau for hours on end, that gothic wolf forever unable to catch the endlessly spinning, waltzing girl.

Dancing so delicately in a blizzard of bones.

She now grabs for one of the larger pieces of floating paper, a magazine ad that immediately turns black in her fingers, burned up and gone before she can read it.

The cold air is oily, slick, acidic. The stink of fuel and fire is full-on sensory overload, leaving Maggie breathless, her eyes tearing and stinging. But she clearly sees that severed arm caught in the crook of a red spruce, palm up, fingers wide, like it's beckoning her forward.

It's been sheared off midhumerus, an awful, ragged cut. And although it's too high up for Maggie to know for certain, she can almost make out the delicate hair—whatever hasn't been singed off—and the constellation of tiny, near-perfect moles near the elbow. The small rose or bird or fish tattoo on the casually bent wrist and even the coral nail polish.

The gold band on the ring finger.

Part of Maggie urges her, yells at her, to climb that tree, retrieve that wayward arm, and bring it down. But she can't do that, won't do that. She doesn't have time for respect or burials or grace. She should be running like hell the other direction, just like she planned.

That earlier scream still draws her, though . . . tugs at her . . . and she can't walk away from that.

She knows the numbers, knows the odds, but still needs to be sure. So, she moves onward through this bizarre snowfall of floating ash and paper, threading her way gingerly over bits and pieces of twisted metal and melting rubber, past the serrated slivers of painted steel embedded in the surrounding trees, beyond the flotsam and jetsam of shredded tree limbs and dead leaves and pine needles and boiling bits of glass and oil, until she finds the next body part—

A naked leg still wearing a cap-toe dress shoe, both blackened by ash . . .

Until she gets to the wide, burning clearing itself . . .

Until she finds the girl.

4

Marcus sits at his desk at the Wolfe County Sheriff's Office and spins the dead man's gun, a Springfield XD Sub-Compact, a weapon just as serious as the knife that killed him.

Marcus checked the mag, finding it fully loaded and unfired. Beyond minor trigger and rear-sight modifications, the gun might as well be brand new, just out of the box. Well oiled and well kept.

He also entered the gun's serial number into the ATF's National Tracing Center eTrace System—negative so far—and used the office's latent print kit to process what he now fears will either be worthless or, more likely, nonexistent prints. A perfect complement to the man's barren pockets and missing wallet and keys.

As far as Marcus can tell, neither this gun nor the man he pulled it from exists. It's as if both fell from the damn sky.

His earlier rundown at the Briar didn't turn up much either.

Torri Lampley, the Briar's owner, told him three of the inn's rooms were occupied. First one, a couple by way of Washington, DC; the second a more elderly couple up from Charleston to visit their nephew—Torri talked extensively to that pair earlier in the day, and both she and Marcus know the nephew in question—and the third, a woman, apparently traveling alone. In any other place, he might've needed warrants or subpoenas, but Torri was more than happy to share everything she had on her three guests, including the Washington couple's reservation and credit card information.

The lone woman—an *M. Roby* . . . NFI, no further information—checked in three days before, paying cash in advance for a two-week stay.

A possible red flag, but of what exactly?

Fortunately, the Washington couple proved easy to track down, still sharing a Goldeneye pinot noir in the Big River, just two tables over from Andy Parsons and Donnie. When Marcus and Donnie talked to them, they were at first sketchy, even evasive, but their nervousness had nothing to do with the mysterious murder. Both were young and recently married, just not to each other.

But the lone woman wasn't in either the Big River or her room, and despite Torri's willingness to slip him the key, Marcus wasn't prepared to cross that threshold yet, literally or figuratively. Having already threatened the integrity of whatever case he thought he was building with shoddy crime scene preservation and half-assed evidence collection, he still wanted to preserve the illusion of a legitimate police investigation. Instead, he pulled license plates off a handful of cars in the lot and left Donnie staking out the Briar itself, sitting in the inn's lobby, passing the time with Torri, drinking coffee, trying to stay awake. That was two hours ago.

Leaving Marcus alone now with the dead man and the dead man's gun. Both riddles, ciphers. Too many questions and not enough answers.

There are only two identifying marks on the dead man at all. The tattoo Marcus spied at first, proving to be some sort of tribal thing inked heavily on the man's left shoulder and down his left arm . . . and an old shrapnel wound on the same.

Once upon a time, artillery shrapnel was considered the most effective type of ammunition to use against troops out in the open. Nowadays, with micro wars and global terrorism on the rise, more and more blast injuries are a product of IEDs—improvised explosive devices—like the one that took Marcus's own leg. Marcus knows all about those injuries.

Knows all about the immediate barotrauma and rarefaction . . . *you're burning* . . . the blast-wind debris and penetrating shrapnel . . . *you're boiling* . . . the physical displacement and blunt trauma of flying into immovable objects so much bigger than yourself, like cars or buildings . . . *you're falling* . . . and the inevitable crushing and smoke inhalation.

Bang . . . you're dead. Most of the time.

But Marcus didn't die from his wounds, and neither did his tattooed stranger. And although Marcus isn't an ME or coroner, he's intimately familiar with those wounds and the scars they leave behind. Scars deep and eternal, scars that never fully heal. Intimately familiar as well with the stories scars can tell, and the one secret such scars do reveal about his dead man.

He was likely a soldier once too.

☾

After Marcus locks up the gun, he retreats upstairs and takes a long look out one of the big second-floor windows, studying tiny Pullens under the veil of night.

A blur of light, a hazy nimbus surrounded by a black ring of mountains.

He never thought he'd return here, never imagined he'd ever carry a gun of his own again. He's been the sheriff for two years and hasn't pulled his duty weapon once in that time. He doesn't hunt, doesn't even fish. Deidre questioned why he ran for sheriff, why he came home at all, just before she left him and went back to Virginia to teach at Norfolk State University. He didn't have a good answer then and doesn't have a better one now.

It might be easy to say he left a lot of himself *over there*, and coming home was a way to reclaim what he'd lost, to somehow ground or find himself again. But that's too easy, too simple. Marcus deep down suspects, fears, he came home because Pullens has always been small and safe, hemmed in and closed off by the rugged mountains and wilds. In fact, the greatest danger is all that untamed wilderness itself. With a population of less than two thousand, Pullens hasn't had a violent crime in five or six years. Hasn't been a murder in twice that long. Until now.

Marcus came home because he was done with the world at large. Had done enough, served enough, given enough, sacrificed enough. He ran for sheriff because the job was easy and available, and as a combat veteran and certified hometown hero, it was one of the few things he was truly qualified for. He took it because he hoped it would be quiet, uneventful—hell, just say it, boring—and before tonight, he'd been proven right.

In fact, it was so quiet, so uneventful, so isolated, that Deidre decided she couldn't take it anymore. Worse, she couldn't take him anymore either. She accused him of hiding out here, and she wasn't wrong.

Pullens is a damn good place to hide.

5

The girl is standing in a ring of fire, eyes open, staring but unseeing.

Maggie knows this because the girl doesn't flinch, doesn't acknowledge Maggie or the angular, wicked rifle in Maggie's hands as she approaches from the trees.

The girl just . . . stands there . . . hair singed and dancing with embers, face blackened by smoke, by blood.

A burning body at her bare feet.

Maggie circles once before approaching, taking it all in, figuring out just what the hell to do.

The plane has left a fiery smear through the trees, a ragged impact crater . . . no, a scar . . . thirty or forty yards long in the hard mountain earth. Wreckage and oil burn everywhere, air all fuzzy with that constant floating ash and paper. Plane pieces scattered like a minefield—twisted metal, unrecognizable detritus—and even more body parts. But none of that shocks Maggie anymore. Not as much as the sight of that lone girl, at least fourteen or fifteen, standing upright in the middle of it all. Clearly injured, although exactly just how bad is hard to say. Clearly in shock too. But more importantly, clearly very much *alive*.

Not impossible, Maggie knows, not even unlikely.

Crashes have a 95 percent survival rate . . .

But not a crash like this. This plane imploded on impact, was already burning, coming apart in the air, even before it hit trees. It shredded like the paper now blowing in the wind, torn into Christmas tinsel like the red and silver garlands that were decorating Pullens.

Maggie saw it, saw all of it. No, her initial instinct was right. No one could survive this crash. No one . . . no way. And even if someone did, they shouldn't be able to just up and walk away from it. But that's exactly what this young girl was doing when Maggie arrived. Her shoes blown or burned off, lost in the crash, but still, somehow, walking, with her hair on fire.

Maggie drops the rifle and closes the distance between them, scooping up loose snow and dead leaves to pat the girl's hair out. On instinct, she kicks what thin ground snow there is over the burning body at the girl's feet, too, but neither the body nor the girl reacts to her efforts.

The girl doesn't stop her or push away, doesn't resist, doesn't shirk away, even as Maggie checks her for serious wounds and then walks her a few more steps and sits her down out of the smoke and flames.

The girl is so thin, so delicate. The wind itself, or even Maggie's ragged breath, should be more than enough to knock her down. Touching her leaves Maggie's hands ashy, bloody again.

She knows you shouldn't move an accident victim like this—the internal, unseen damage could be serious, severe, still fatal—but Maggie figures all bets are off when the victim herself is conscious and moving on her own.

With the girl on the ground, out of the way, Maggie returns to the other body, still smoking, too, but no longer fully aflame. It's a man, tall and thin as well—near emaciated—arms spread, facedown, so Maggie can't see his features. His suit is mostly burned away, large swatches of it burned into him, melted like awful, bloody candle wax. But there's a leather belt clearly visible around his waist, and a bright-silver analog watch on his wrist, too hot to touch.

Maggie wonders if it still shows the time of the crash, that last eternal moment when the plane went down, and she was looking up at it.

The plane falling from the sky like a shooting star.

Like the girl, the man's hair was burning, too, but it's mostly gone now. Bare wisps of it remain, little more than ashes, tiny fading embers glowing in the blood haloed around his skull.

She can't bring herself to touch this man, won't dare turn him over. There's something so eerie and awful and off putting about the way he's lying there dead and unmoving, long fingers clawed deep into the earth, as writhing smoke snakes around his painfully thin body. She's afraid to flip him over, only to have him claw at her. To blink those awful, dead, torched eyes—fume-filled hollows seeing nothing at all—because she knows she'll finally scream.

She's been holding it in, but it's right there in her throat now. A hot torrent of tears, too, threatening with each new horror.

It looks like the man died crawling away from the crash . . . crawling after the girl.

Maybe he was her father, protecting her with his own body, his last bit of strength, his final dying breath.

Maggie wants to believe that as she turns away.

6

Walton Landry never sees the plane, just hears it.

A roaring, desperate whine, like the mountain itself is calling out to him. When you spend as much time out here alone as he does, you get to know the mountain's sounds intimately, all those longing whispers and desperate sighs of the deep wilderness, raw wind in the trees and cold rainwater working its way over rocks. Falling leaves and snow. The night—the very dark—telling itself secrets, a constant black susurration, like breathing.

In the wild, everything has a story to tell, even the dead and dying. You just need to listen.

At the first sound of the low-flying plane—a small commuter jet or other private craft—Walton abandons his big stone fireplace and races outside, trying to catch a glimpse of it. But at his age, north of seventy, he doesn't race anywhere fast enough, it seems, and he's too late to spy a goddamn thing. But standing out in the cold, wrapped in a plume of his own breath, there's no mistaking the echoes of it crashing.

He estimates the plane went down three, four miles north of his cabin. Still too far to see, given the tall trees, the leading edge of the old growth. There's no name for it on any map, but for years, he and Kell gave places and things out here names of their own, and they called that dark, tangled spur Kellan's Hollow, after his only son. It's the southern flank of about two hundred acres of yellow poplar and hemlock, chinquapin oaks, bitternut hickories, rhododendron thickets, and pine stands. Up in Kellan's Hollow, the trees are three or four hundred years old, and given the lack of skid trails and invasive species—other than old Walton himself—there hasn't been a significant human disturbance there since the War of 1812, if not longer.

Not a place to get lost, to crash and burn.

He doesn't bother telling all that to the new sheriff, Marcus Austin, when he makes the call a few minutes later. Just the facts: that a small plane crashed in the Cranberry Wilderness, at the foot of Black Mountain. But the kid's clearly distracted by other things, clearly disbelieving. He goes on and on about the FAA and flight plans and radio reports, as if Walton doesn't know all that, as if Walton hasn't heard what he heard.

As if Walton is too old and losing it.

Austin isn't a kid—hell, Walton thinks, he's a war hero—and he isn't even exactly the "new" sheriff anymore, holding the job for nearly two years since Walton himself abandoned it. But to folks in Wolfe County, truthfully to even Walton himself, Marcus Austin will always be the "new sheriff," least until Walton passes or Austin proves otherwise.

And as Walton angrily cuts short the satellite call with Austin—the Iridium an unwanted extravagance Kell bought him—the worst of it is not that the war hero doesn't believe him or dismisses him so easily out of hand. It's that Walton already started wondering months ago about his own sanity, about losing his goddamn marbles.

Worrying about truly going crazy out here alone, listening to the wilderness, and all the sounds he started hearing, or imagining, out in the dark. But Walton knows he didn't imagine the plane. Standing out again on his wraparound porch, he can still smell the smoke, the stink of jet fuel.

The scent comes and goes, and he'll lose it altogether if the wind shifts later tonight or in the morning, when the snow will really start coming down. If there are any survivors, Austin will never get to them in time, even if he does decide Walton's call wasn't a product of too little sleep or too much whiskey or just the addled ramblings of an old man. But Walton can.

He knows the land even in the dark better than his own liver-spotted hands, which don't shake as much when the weather's cold like this, the bone-chilling temperatures somehow steadying and strengthening his aged, brittle bones. But it'll be a hell of a hike, even for him, and one small mistake, any silly misstep, and he'll be just another body someone else is recovering.

Not that long ago, national parks and forests like the Monongahela were averaging thousands of search and rescue events a year. A SAR mission is difficult, expensive, time consuming, and not always successful. Walton knows it's hard for most folks to imagine anyone getting lost in the woods nowadays, what with GPS and cell phones and even satellite phones like his Iridium, but fools still do, all too easily and all the damn time.

They miscalculate distances, wildly misjudge their own capabilities. They don't pay attention or fail to rightly read their maps, if they have one at all. Follow game trails instead of hiking paths and take shortcuts that don't exist, or the weather just plumb turns on them.

They get caught out in the dark.

And mountains are the worst, the most treacherous, a wicked combination of tricky terrain and dangerous elevation.

The world seems so small and connected now, but out here in the woods and mountains, out here in the wilderness, it's still huge, still wild. Yet most people are recovered safe and sound, most of the time. Only a few die out here . . . and even fewer are never found at all, alive or dead.

Back in '05, they found Charlie Dance out in the Cranberry Wilderness during the national Rainbow Gathering, six days after his mama lost or left him, depending on who you believed at the time. In 2017, those Brafferton College hikers out of Williamsburg disappeared altogether near the Big Beechy Trail. Two young, pretty women, about to graduate, one even set to head off to medical school in Pittsburgh. They were lost for three weeks until the official search was called off for good.

Both sets of parents posted missing flyers for years after.

This plane wreck will be bad—all those dead, the injured—although no worse than the numerous fatal car crashes Walton's worked in his time. He can't imagine it'll be as horrible as when they finally found eight-year-old Charlie Dance.

Six days alone in the wilds.

So small and weak for his age even before that. No food, no water, and that god-awful sweltering summer sun hammering down on him the whole time.

Coyotes . . . or worse . . . tracking him.

In the end, it was the turkey vultures that pointed the way, and Walton didn't sleep well for about a month after that.

He forgets all sorts of things now—his truck keys, his dead wife's name, his favorite TV show, even what his boy, Kellan, looked like—but he can't seem to forget the bad things, the dark things, no matter how hard he tries. They never found those girls from Williamsburg, both just . . . gone . . . as if they never existed at all. No rhyme, no reason, and not a goddamn trace. But that not knowing, in its own forever-unfinished way, was certainly no better than the finality of finding Charlie Dance's savaged little corpse.

Eyes bloody, empty holes . . . eaten out of his skull . . .

Those are the kinds of things that happen in these mountains, out in the wild and dark.

Dead . . . or gone . . .

And after what happened to Charlie Dance, and his own boy, Walton still isn't sure which is worse.

Walton goes back inside and starts to get his gear together for a hike out to the crash site. But as he quickly packs, he leaves his front door open, letting in a handful of snow flurries and the biting cold.

Just in case the dark has anything more to tell him.

7

A few moments later Maggie finds the girl again, still sitting just as she left her.

Free now from the smoke and flames, she's reminded just how cold it is out here, how fast the temperature is dropping, and the girl is clothed in a black, long-sleeved T-shirt—ripped all to hell now—and similarly ripped jeans.

Her feet are bare, toes unpolished.

She should be shivering, freezing, but she just stares into the darkness, unblinking.

In the winter, at night, it routinely hits eighteen degrees in the mountains. But it's not just the raw temperature that's so dangerous; there's the windchill too. The looming threat of frostbite and hypothermia and a blanket of impending, blinding snow.

Maggie has a lightweight one-person NEMO Dragonfly tent and Disco sleeping bag. She's expertly layered, including an Arc'teryx Cerium LT Hoody, and even has a spare Patagonia fleece in her small pack and more wool socks. She's outfitted for a multiday solo hike and can afford to strip off a couple of things—she's taller and heavier than the girl, so they should more than fit—before searching for a suitcase that might've survived the crash. But the harsh reality is the girl isn't dressed to spend even one hour outside, and whatever Maggie can scavenge, or share, won't be enough to get her much beyond that.

No, she thinks, this isn't the plan, this isn't the damn plan . . .

If Maggie doesn't get her some help, though, find her some shelter soon, she'll have miraculously survived a plane crash, only to have the winter weather do her in. But she can't be Maggie's responsibility, her problem to solve. Maggie's got problems all her own, bearing down on her like a runaway train, like the Christmas nor'easter circling the skies.

No one knows Maggie's here . . . so no one will ever know if she leaves.

No one but you.

She rocks on her boots, thoughtful. Asks the girl a few questions but gets zero response. The girl's so silent, so still, Maggie checks to make sure she's breathing, and now that she takes a moment to look at her . . . no, she tells herself again, you don't have time for this, don't do this . . . she uses her small Maglite to really take her in.

Now that she has a better look at her, the girl's definitely at least fifteen but could be older. Her hair is blackened, singed off in sooty spots but was previously long, blonde, and straight, not so different from Maggie's hair now. She's dressed like any teenager, but there's no jewelry, no tattoos, no piercings. That doesn't mean she's not marked, however. Through the girl's ripped T-shirt, Maggie can make out . . . wounds . . . disfigurements . . . old surgical scars . . . twining around her like an ouroboros.

What the hell?

Maggie leans close, following the scars that crawl up the girl's abdomen to her neck, to her hairline, to her—

Eyes.

The girl's eyes are startlingly different colors, one blue gray like the sky over a winter ocean, the other a dazzling emerald. Both are bloodshot, bleary, and neither reacts to Maggie's light sweeping over them, but they're still beautiful. Amazing.

There's a word for eyes like that, but Maggie can't remember it, and doesn't have her cell phone to look it up. She left all electronics behind before entering the West Virginia wilderness, even before disappearing from New York. She's got no phone or laptop or a GPS to guide her, just her dad's old nickel compass, an even older sextant, and a USGS visitor map of the Monongahela National Forest.

Her memory and the plan she carefully crafted and knows by heart. A plan that this mysterious, wounded girl with weird eyes is not part of.

Maggie runs through her options, seeing in her mind's eye the Cranberry Wilderness all around her, the network of mining trails, streams, valleys, and hollows that crisscross Black Mountain and the surrounding hills. Kneeling next to the silent girl, she unfolds her USGS map, carefully annotated with a hundred hand-drawn notes that mean something only to her, a set of scribbled hash marks overlaying the National Forest System motor vehicle use guide on her topographic visitor map. The NFS maintains roads and trails open to certain vehicles during certain seasons, and four ranger districts service the area. There are more than twenty campground and cabin sites scattered across the Monongahela, but almost none within a half day's hike of here, and easily twice that long in the dark and coming snow.

She's purposefully been moving through the most forlorn parts of these woods, skirting civilization, cutting herself off from communication, avoiding all contact. Now that she needs some help, there's none to be found. She's got so few choices, no good ones anyway, and the bad ones are getting worse by the moment.

She doesn't have time for this. She doesn't have to do this . . .

But now that she's seen this girl, touched her, knows she's alive—that she somehow amazingly, miraculously, rose from the dead like Lazarus—Maggie's not sure she can just up and leave her. Her unseen injuries might still be too much to overcome, and the weather certainly will be. But abandoning this girl now would be tantamount to killing her all over again, and Maggie's got more than enough blood already on her hands. Too much.

Vann used to say—not kindly, not joking—that she had zero maternal instincts. He told her she was one truly cold, calculating bitch, but he couldn't love her any less because of it. *You're a shark, M,* he said to her, *a goddamn merciless apex predator.* And she proved him far too right for far too long. They were both perfectly, horribly, suited for each other.

But Maggie's not convinced there's any calculation that adds up to her leaving this girl alone out here, even given the risks, the exposure, to Maggie herself.

Turn your back and go, she thinks, just do it like you always do . . . like you've always done so many times before. The girl is in shock; she'll barely remember any of this at all.

At best, Maggie herself will dwindle to a distant dream . . . a shadow, a hint, a ghost . . . if the girl even survives the night.

All of this will be little more than snatches of a song the girl won't ever quite recall the lyrics to. And just like that, before Maggie even realizes she's made the decision—her booted feet suddenly moving of their own accord—she's scooping up her rifle and letting the darkness at the edge of the fiery clearing reclaim her.

Just go . . . go . . . go . . . and don't look back . . .

But . . . she does look back . . . to find the girl still sitting there unblinking, the last of the burning plane reflected in her unsettling, beautiful eyes. Rolling ocean in the left one, primeval forest in the right.

The only change is that the girl's hands are now moving of their own accord, too, her sooty fingers held out in front of her, held out low over the ground, dancing.

Maggie stops, afraid the girl is having a spasm, a fit or seizure, until she realizes the girl is only playing *music.* Running the keys on an invisible piano, slim fingers arching in the air, miming a song.

I'm only a song she won't ever quite remember the lyrics to . . .

Exactly what Maggie was thinking to herself as she grabbed up her rifle, a fleeting, final impression, just before she decided to leave the girl behind . . .

Maggie's darkest thoughts somehow now turned into the girl's silent pantomime, a virtuoso concert for two, as the snow starts to fall again.

8

"Well, I don't hear anything," Donnie says, shrugging, looking up at the starless night sky as if a plane might be there now.

"No, I know," Marcus says, trying without success to keep the irritation out of his voice. "Walton called me and said *he* heard a plane crash out his way."

"Sheriff called *you*?" Donnie says, like he doesn't believe it. "He really said that?"

"Yeah," Marcus answers, "he really said that."

Donnie nods, oblivious to his casual slight. Donnie worked for Walton Landry for years, so Marcus knows he still thinks of the old man as the *real* sheriff and isn't the only one around these parts who does. Donnie says, "So, what are you gonna do?"

Marcus doesn't answer, just puts his gloved hands deep into his coat pockets as the two trudge toward the Briar's parking lot. He was shocked, too, when Landry called him from a satellite phone—the last time Marcus used one himself was when he was in a combat zone in Yemen—and more shocked when the old man started going on and on about a plane crash.

He and Walton haven't spoken more than a handful of tense words about *anything* since Landry handed over the keys to the Wolf County Sheriff's Office, and the heavy gold badge that came with them.

This night is getting stranger by the hour.

☾

Marcus has all but given up finding M. Roby tonight.

She still hasn't returned to her room, and her car, a well-worn Nissan with New Jersey temp plates, is still parked out front, dusted with snow.

Earlier, when Marcus swept his SureFire past the Nissan's windows, it looked eerily, preternaturally empty. No fast-food bags or luggage or discarded sweatshirts in the back seat, no loose change, not even a crumpled ball of receipts in the center console. The temp plates came back to a used car lot in suburban Montclair, more than four hundred miles from here.

Marcus has no idea where the woman could be now, and the last of Pullens is shuttering for the night. Unless she's staying at someone's house, visiting a relative or friend, or hiked out alone into the backcountry—a sobering thought—she's vanished.

Their dead vic all but appeared out of thin air, and now M. Roby's disappeared *into* it. An hour ago, Marcus was imagining their dead man falling from a plane, making Walton's claim about hearing one out on Black Mountain even more curious. Marcus doesn't believe in coincidences, not really. He does, however, believe in all kinds of shit going wrong all at the same time—

Situation normal: all fucked up.

There are more than thirty airports and airfields scattered across West Virginia, and who knows how many tiny airstrips, legal or otherwise. The closest airfield to Pullens is North Central West Virginia Airport, running daily United and Allegiant commuters to Chicago O'Hare and Washington Dulles. But none this late, even with a weather delay. And Walton was insistent it was a *small* plane, a Cessna, a Learjet. But Marcus hasn't come up with anything. No one's got a flight plan for any kind of aircraft coming in or out of the area, the forest service can't confirm any sighting, and Walton's the only one who's claimed to have seen it.

He didn't even see it, just heard it.

Marcus will still make a call to the NTSB regional office in Ashburn, but he doesn't know what to call in. Walton holes up alone now in that ramshackle cabin of his out in the shadows of Black Mountain, and rarely comes into town anymore, and not recently. His wife passed away five or six years ago, but there was also some tragic issue with their son a year prior to Walton stepping aside as sheriff. Donnie's gently hinted that even before that, the old man was getting forgetful, difficult, and more than a little friendly with the bottle.

He doesn't want to write off Walton's phantom plane, but without more to go on, it's one more enigma like their dead soldier and the missing M. Roby.

For an otherwise-quiet Friday night in December, the mysteries are starting to pile up, just like the predicted snow. He warned Walton not to go stumbling around in the woods in the dark looking for . . . whatever . . . but it's even odds whether the man will listen to him. It's not a quick or easy trip to Walton's place, and although Marcus isn't inclined to send Donnie or another deputy out there to check on him at this hour under threat of the impending storm, he's even less inclined to go himself.

So, Marcus, what are you gonna do?

Not for the first time since taking over for Walton, Marcus wonders what the old man himself would do. He was Wolfe County sheriff for almost four decades and grew up in these mountains, can trace his family through three generations of coal miners, bootleggers, and outlaws. Marcus grew up here too—Clarksburg, though, not Pullens itself—and it's not the same, not even close. Walton is well past his prime, but there's still a sharp-edged mountain ruggedness to the man, a spiky aura that Marcus associates with the austere Hazara tribesmen he encountered in Afghanistan. Walton was never a soldier, but he would've been a damn good one, a hard son of a bitch with gray eyes and a black sense of humor you either appreciate or you don't, and who doesn't care either way.

Marcus and Walton are very, very different. But right now, only one of them is the sheriff. The real sheriff, with the badge and all the responsibility.

So, what are you gonna do?

"Go home, Donnie," Marcus says. "Wherever our M. Roby is, she's not coming back tonight. If we're not buried under three feet of snow in the morning, we'll get back at it then."

Donnie makes an uncertain waggle with his hand, pure guesswork. "Weather guy is still iffy on the storm. Moving slow as molasses, taking its own sweet-ass time. Fifty-fifty we really get slammed, or it may miss us altogether."

Marcus says, "I'm in no mood to shovel my ass out."

Donnie snorts, a small laugh for such a big man. "And the sheriff's plane?"

"What's your take?"

Donnie grows serious, thinking hard, before flashing Marcus that uncertain gesture again. "Fifty-fifty, too, I'd say." He blows out a heavy breath, watching it plume like a horse's tail, drift away white in the dark. He doesn't look comfortable, saying what he's about to say next. "Back in the day, I wouldn't even question it. Sheriff was steady as a sunrise, even after his Lottie passed. Sure, that was hard on him, hard on all of us who knew and loved her, but she'd long been sick, so we knew it was coming. She died on a Tuesday, warmest day that year, as I remember it. He buried her that Thursday, and damned if he wasn't back at his desk Saturday. He took himself up to that place of his on Black Mountain for a day to mourn, and that was it." Donnie snaps his fingers, pauses. "Not like what went down with Kellan."

"His son?"

"Yeah. Now, that was hard, too, but worse in its own way. They had a . . . tough relationship. Sheriff always pushing, Kell never giving an inch. Lottie used to say they were flint and steel. It took the kid a while to find himself, always into one thing or another, another misadventure, and the sheriff, well, he never had any use for foolishness, for indecision, for wasting time. Kell grew up hunting and camping these woods with his daddy, was a real natural at that stuff, gifted that way, so it was a real shock when he went missing up there."

"Up there?" Marcus has heard some of this talk around town, but this is the first Donnie's ever discussed it.

"On the mountain. Search parties combed the backcountry for two weeks, everyone figuring it had to be a freak accident, like he broke a leg or something. Maybe got snake bit." Donnie pauses, as if deciding what more to say. "But no confirmed sightings, and no official cause of death either. Not much of anything, really. Just . . . gone."

Marcus whistles. "Walton didn't take that well."

Donnie shakes his head. "Kept on going after the search parties stopped. All but moved to that cabin, where he lives now. Locked himself up there for a whole week alone that time, and then even when he came back, still didn't seem well or right, like a part of him was still locked away, or lost, too, out there on Black Mountain." Donnie shrugs, shaking off a dusting of light snow. "Hard to explain that kind of sad, I guess. What it does to you, how it affects you. How it gets inside you, like cold weather. He didn't want to step down, but he was older when Kell died, wearing more than a few of those years on his sleeve. He didn't want to forget his gun was loaded, or find himself parked somewhere, not able to remember how he got there. Once he made the decision, came around to it, there was no more fussin' or fightin' over it, he was done." Another finger snap as Donnie looks at Marcus, his expression unreadable. "And now here you are."

"Yeah, here I am."

"Guess maybe you get over grief," Donnie says, "but you can't get over gettin' old."

Marcus smiles at that. Donnie's got eighty pounds and more than twenty years on him and started wearing bifocals just last summer to read the paper and do the crossword puzzles. His face is as deeply lined and weathered as any of the ancient trees crowding Pullens. He's a well-liked fixture around the county and could've run for sheriff himself, stepped in after Walton stepped down, but had zero interest in it.

Marcus had a sergeant once who used to say not everyone's a captain, that you need plenty of soldiers too. And Donnie is nothing if not a loyal soldier.

"Guess I got to go out there to check on the old man then," Marcus says. "Plane or not, someone better see what he's up to."

Donnie raises his thick eyebrows at that. "Really?" He hems, haws. "You sure you don't want me to go too? Least I know how to deal with him." Donnie casts a furtive glance down at Marcus's prosthetic leg, hidden by his jeans. Marcus's injury never comes up, but Donnie and the other deputies, in their own silent, appraising way, never let Marcus forget it either.

Marcus shakes his head, tapping the badge on his chest. "Comes with the job and big paycheck, right?" Now they both smile, since Marcus makes just a couple hundred dollars a week more than Donnie. "You go on home. I'll see to him. Maybe if I do this tonight, it keeps us all from searching the woods for him tomorrow." Marcus imagines all those people searching for Kellan Landry, day after day. "None of us want that."

"True," Donnie says, barely hiding his relief at being let off the hook. Marcus's injury or not, his concern for Walton aside, he knows his chief deputy really, really, doesn't want to trek up into the mountains tonight. Donnie continues, "Just a word of warning then. Give the sheriff a call that you're coming. It's not that he doesn't like you, necessarily, it's nothing personal like that and never is with him. It's just he doesn't like much of anyone. Out there, out in the dark, it's easy to get confused." Donnie looks like he wants to add something to that thought, but instead he says, "He's like to have himself a whole damn hunting arsenal up there by now, and he's not much used to company anymore."

"I'll be careful," Marcus says, "give him plenty of heads-up."

Donnie claps him on the shoulder, satisfied, as they both start to turn from the Briar Inn to the sheriff's office, where their separate vehicles wait.

Flurries blur overhead and Christmas lights softly wink at their backs.

"Good deal," Donnie says with a grin. "I'd sure hate for him to blow the new sheriff's head off."

9

Walton moves slowly toward Kellan's Hollow, following a well-worn whitetail deer trail.

He's wearing his Nebo headlamp since his hands aren't free.

He's got a carbon trekking pole in one, and a semiauto Remington rifle in the other.

When he was younger, he used to hunt exclusively with bolt-actions, but that was when the only things to worry about were black bear and feral hogs. When he believed there weren't any worse things out here.

In the daylight, to most folks, this game trail would be unrecognizable, indecipherable. A thin vein beneath the pines and undergrowth, all but impossible to trace. But even in the dark, in the hazy nimbus of his headlamp, Walton reads the forest's skin like a map.

Not like his boy, though. Kell loved these wild places in the Monongahela, where maps don't make a difference. He explored it all, every inch, every dark crevice, until even this place wasn't wild enough for him anymore.

Walton stops, fighting for breath, fighting the exertion deep in his bones. He purposefully sweeps his head left to right, letting the Nebo's fifteen hundred lumens do some work. Snow twirls but it's otherwise still, quiet, silent. Just his own heavy breathing, the heavy beating of his heart. He's hiking east toward where the plane went down, tacking off a deep couloir to his left, hidden by rhododendron and hemlock and cow parsnip, both the latter deadly poisonous.

Walton's great-granddaddy, Cooper, used to claim the only way to kill parsnip was to put a silver nail through its root. Coop Landry believed all sorts of things like that; he was a natural woodsman and gifted storyteller with a hundred tales. Claimed he met "Devil Anse" Hatfield once and shook the man's hand and could recount every scary sighting of the White Things and the smoke wolves and Snarly Yow, the Phantom of Flatwoods, and the Mothman.

There are well-known show caves all over West Virginia, but his great-granddaddy swore there were innumerable other unchartered caverns hundreds of feet below Black Mountain and the Cranberry Wilderness. A whole dark world filled with forgotten things, Indian ghosts, and Confederate gold.

Three summers before Walton retired, some of Jules Wallace's dogs chased a bear down a hidden shaft near Staten Pike, getting stuck on a shale ledge about seventy feet down. The cave was previously unmapped, fuzzed with ancient lichen and a constellation of old bones, a secret midden for predators. It took Walton and his deputies and the fire department a full day to rappel all those terrified dogs out, one at a time, with that bear glowering at them the whole while from another ledge, a paw swipe away. Walton still remembers the feral, overpowering smell of that big animal, like hot sunlight and loam after a big rain, like fresh-spilled blood. Like the earth itself was breathing on him, trying to swallow him whole. The whole saga was a story even Coop Landry would've appreciated, with the governor himself calling in, wanting hourly reports on those damn dogs.

Walton didn't find any ghosts or gold down there. No treasure at all, just old, bleached bones, carrying weird teeth marks even bigger than a bear's.

But in 1928, one of the largest diamonds ever was pulled out of a pit in Monroe County. And although diamonds don't exist naturally in

West Virginia, Walton told Lottie Jane Anders just before she married him that he'd found a diamond in her all the same.

She was priceless to him, and he didn't know he could cherish a thing so much, until Kellan was born.

There's been a Landry by blood, birth, or marriage, hunting, trapping, digging, or bootlegging in these West Virginia woods since the Knights of the Golden Horseshoe Expedition in 1716. *Sic juvat transcendere montes.* And just like Coop did for him, Walton filled his boy's head with all the family stories of secrets and monsters and treasure, taught him to love and respect this land and its mysteries, when maybe he should've taught him to fear it instead.

Or maybe it wouldn't have mattered, and Kell would've loved the wilds all the same. It was in his blood, after all. In the end, it was just his daddy he couldn't stand.

Sic juvat transcendere montes.

Thus, it is pleasant to cross the mountains.

Walton realizes he's been standing too long, lost in his thoughts. He does this far too often now, getting turned around in his memories like those secret caves below his boots, astray in stories that happened long ago or didn't happen at all. Like those sounds he's been hearing in the dark, he's not sure which are real anymore.

Before he left his cabin, he grabbed his MyFAK My Medic, but all the first aid in the world won't do anyone any good if he doesn't get his ass in high gear and get there in time.

He's just plunging ahead into the dark again when the howling starts . . .

10

Damn if Marcus isn't lost.

He's got one hand on the wheel, steering over tree-hugged, snow-blown roads, while the other is balancing his phone, trying to use Google Maps.

There's an old paper map back at the office, hanging there since Walton himself was a deputy, even several decades before that. Yellow, stained, faded, done up in all that fanciful colonial cursive, like a relic from before West Virginia seceded from Virginia. Yet still mostly—surprisingly—accurate.

Still dotted, too, with Landry's pencil marks and personal notations, dozens of new roads and old landmarks and past searches.

Right now, Marcus would kill for it, because it'd be a hell of a lot more useful than his expensive phone, which is barely holding on to a signal. All these small trailheads and old logging and mining roads look about the same, and even when those last relics of civilization give way to the true heart of the Cranberry Wilderness itself, the terrain becomes all but unreadable, at least to a layman like Marcus. Donnie warned him.

Marcus did try to call Landry's Iridium before he set out, but when the old man didn't answer, that was just worrying enough that Marcus set out anyway.

Now he's futilely searching for the Hanging Rock Trailhead on the eastern edge of the Cranberry. Ten years ago, there was nothing out here at all, until some moneyed tech professionals out of DC and New York bought the last bit of available land for a handful of sprawling, eco-friendly homes, artfully blended into the mountain scape, done up in colors like *rock pearl* and *sweet sage* and *Indian smoke*. Marcus learned all about that on HGTV, and he's even since met a few of those folks, but not all of them, not enough. This is the very definition of "off the grid," and the rich always want to be off the grid, until the grid itself collapses, until the shit *really* hits the fan. Then they want the nearest authority—preferably one with a badge and gun—to come clean it all up.

It's possible one of those homes holds the secrets of the identity of their dead vic, or even the whereabouts of the Roby woman. Marcus will follow up in the morning if he doesn't drive into a ditch or a lake tonight.

There's off the grid, and then there's Walton's cabin, situated deep—and illegally—in a federal forest. Nowadays you can't so much as cut down a tree on fed land without serious fines or even jail time, but Walton's pine cottage has been a well-known secret around these parts forever. Marcus has never been out to the place himself, and has only a rough idea of where it is, based on Donnie's prior directions and his own time on these trails. But out here, a rough idea can mean being off target by miles, which might leave Marcus turning in circles for hours, least until dawn or Walton answers his goddamn phone again.

For the last twenty minutes, Marcus hasn't seen anything he'd recognize even in broad daylight, much less the dark, which is closed tight like a fist. Not so much as another lone set of bleary headlights. If he isn't truly lost, he's damn near close.

So, it's lucky that he's already slowing down, more intent on the tiny, illuminated map on his phone than making any headway, when something flashes right to left in front of him. Something low and fast, but heavy too. A solid white blur of haze and motion, of frantic, feral movement.

He barely catches a hint of it out of the corner of his eye. But because he is going so slow, has just enough time to react—a heartbeat, a little less—or he might have broadsided the thing or sailed hood-first into one of the big pitch pines looming around him.

Tossing the phone and grabbing the truck's wheel with both hands, he turns sharp, sliding to the right on the slippery pavement, fishtailing awkwardly. His Genesis is a technological marvel, but there are moments like these when the prosthetic's limitations are unavoidable, the full extent of his injury is inescapable. He feathers the brake, but his leg, the whole truck, is detached, an arm's length away. The natural tremor his body is expecting—that it craves—is absent. The haptic-feedback shivers that should be shooting all the way up his leg and the base of his spine are gone.

Instead, he feels he's floating, feels almost nothing at all.

He badly overcompensates, braking even harder, swerving more, sending the car into an ugly, counterclockwise spin.

Twelve o'clock. Ten o'clock. Seven o'clock.

Spinning faster, faster, faster.

Threatening to go wildly out of control, like—

Iferouane. Agadez. The Sahel. Four hours to hump to Mano Dayak airport under heavy, heavy fire. A long-ago firefight in Niger and drones flying into the night. Reapers loaded with Brimstone and Hellfire missiles.

Choking dust, hellish heat, buzz saw whip and crack of gunfire.

Gas fires in shadowy streets.

Burning rotors of a downed helicopter spinning and spinning and spinning in the dark, throwing embers and sparks in a way that's almost beautiful.

Spinning and spinning years later like his Wolfe County Sheriff's truck on an icy road in West Virginia.

Another one of those fugue states again, as detached from himself as he is from the old Dodge and the slick road beneath that. But just like in the Sahel, Marcus's muscle memory, his survival instincts, starts firing off, ready to take over, ready to take the wheel, slowing everything down as the panic takes hold. Breathe, *breathe.* He grips the wheel, leans into the spin, before fighting those well-honed survival instincts and letting go of the wheel altogether, letting the inevitable torque pull him forward.

Letting gravity or fate do its thing.

The night, the trees, blur by the windows.

Worst thing that happens is you die here, he thinks.

No, worst thing that happens is you don't. That you survive again but you're all busted worse, missing a few more jigsaw pieces of what you were before.

Deidre used to say in his darkest moments it was like he had a death wish, a *death regret.* His therapist told him it was just survivor's remorse or guilt, that Marcus couldn't or wouldn't forgive himself for surviving that later IED explosion. That he couldn't or wouldn't easily live with himself or what was left of the man he was afterward.

I didn't have the decency to burn to death with Yang or Mathers.

I burned alive.

The truck shudders once, twice, rotating off the road and slewing onto the shoulder, missing a big tree, narrowly missing a deep ditch, throwing up a shower of snow and gravel and pine needles. But there's no cliff face to fall from either. No oncoming truck to smash into, no cold, deep lake to tumble into and disappear.

Just that crazy clock-hand motion winding down at last—

Two o'clock. One o'clock.

Stop.

Leaving Marcus alone in the idling truck, his hands over his heart, breathing hard.

Still alive . . . again.

11

Walton follows the howls, plunging through the thicket in that direction, batting branches away with his trekking pole, holding his Remington high.

He catches a ghostly flash ahead, a sudden pale movement between the trees, angling his way.

Finding an exposed rock spur, a stony ledge thick with dirt and snow and strong enough to support his weight, he commands the high ground. He clicks off his headlamp and settles the Remington into his shoulder, letting it find that well-worn groove, as familiar as Lottie's touch when she was still alive.

He scopes the gathered dark in front of him, waiting for his night eyes to adjust, to resolve the shifting shadows, as the howling draws close, and something bleached the color of bone flashes and crashes through the barren winter undergrowth.

One of the *White Things*.

That's what Coop and others called the revenants they couldn't identify haunting these mountains, those entities and events they couldn't easily put a name to. Coop claimed to have seen them twice in his life, first when he was a boy, when his older brother Hudson was taken in a savage winter's storm. Then again when Coop was in his twenties, when he was fool enough to try and track and kill one to avenge Hudson's death.

Walton's granddaddy and daddy never saw one and never claimed to, and they didn't much believe in those kinds of monsters anyway. They said the White Things were nothing more than men's own failures and follies, the finality of bad weather or bad luck, the daily hardships of mountain living. They were the lies we tell ourselves, drink-fueled tales told to cover up other lies and tales, a way to bury mistakes and regrets, to recast fear as bravery, to somehow justify a bad decision or worse judgment. They were a good man's attempt to grapple with tragedy and even his own impending death.

They were sadness, desperation, and regret.

The White Things were always just men and their memories. The mountains were dangerous enough without monsters.

Neither Walton nor Kell saw any of Coop's White Things, either, not together, although they hiked and camped and trapped and fished and hunted all over these mountains. They saw all other manner of God's creatures, even a few they couldn't immediately identify. But no monsters, no ghosts, no revenants. Given all the dead and lost out here, that's saying something. They still found raw and wondrous beauty, though, and plenty of that.

The rising sun over Black Mountain, a pearlescent dawn.

Bald eagles on the wing, soaring over still water, reflected at themselves.

A gray-muzzled mountain lion moving low and slow through hemlock, eyes dark as oil.

A cliff face draped in saxifrage like a million tiny white stars just fallen from the sky.

The red tips of an Indian paintbrush glowing like match heads at dusk.

One winter when they were camping near an area Kell called the Black Eye Trail, they gazed out at the entire bowl of heaven, infinite stars in infinite shades of white and fire, the thick ghostly band of the Milky Way stretching across the horizon. They stared into the northern lights, the aurora borealis, a shimmering electric curtain of purple and crimson, billowing in the night sky.

Kell told him you didn't have to make up stories about a place like this to be amazed and mystified by it.

A fairy-tale world.

Walton used to believe Black Mountain had no more surprises or mysteries in store for him, until Kell disappeared. Until that terrible fruitless search for his boy took him into the mountain's blackest recesses, its most secret places. Until it took him so far into his own black depths that no human place—not the sheriff's office, not their old house in town, not Pullens—felt quite right anymore. Nothing . . . except this goddamn, cursed mountain itself.

That's when the scratching started outside his cabin on the darkest nights. That's when he found himself haunted, hunted, by a predatory breathing just beyond his light, a howl always just over the next ridge. Sometimes it was even worse than that, a full-throated keening, an unholy *scream*, a fearful mixture of wolf and big cat.

I'm waiting for you . . . always waiting . . .

It seemed to taunt him.

And what could that be but one of Coop Landry's White Things? The horrible thing that happened up there—that took his boy from him far too soon—finally, thankfully, mercifully, coming for him too.

Eyes adjusting at last, Walton puts the scope on the moving creature. It's slowed down now, gone silent, sensing him, smelling him. But it's not deterred. Still angling right below him, more motion than shape, a pale nimbus, a tenuous ghost, a—

Girl.

Walton blinks twice, swallows, wipes sweat from his eyes.

No, two girls.

One holding up the other, or more like dragging her forward. One kitted out for a hike, looking mostly ready for this kind of weather, while the other—younger—looking like she woke from a deep sleep and stepped outside a motel room for a moment and got lost.

She doesn't have any shoes.

Crash survivors. The plane.

These two girls—*two young women*, Lottie would've scolded—must've survived the crash he heard and are now searching for help. Searching for someone like him.

Walton abandons his ledge and crashes through the trees, appearing in front of the pair. When the older one realizes he's there, that he's armed, she raises a rifle of her own he somehow missed before, letting the younger girl in her arms slip to her knees.

"Drop the gun," she calls out, all the tension, the fear, taut as a cold wire in her voice. "Then don't make another move."

She puts the rifle's muzzle over his heart.

"Look, it's okay," he answers, raising the Remington slow and easy so she can see it clearly, although it's hard for either of them to see much in the gloom. Just shadows and hints. "If you go easy there, I'm going to put this down, just like you said." He bends forward, leaning the Remington against a tree where he can grab for it and snap a shot off, if it comes to that. Not exactly the command she gave him, but he hopes she doesn't get trigger happy because of it.

Instead, a bright light clicks on, blinding him, ruining his night vision all over again, as she paints his face with a flashlight.

"Dammit, girl, get that light off me," he barks, looking down and away, still surprised, and angry at himself, for not spying her rifle.

"Vann's people send you too?" she asks, steadier this time, her own face hidden behind the light shining in his eyes.

"*Vann?*" He racks his brain, comes up empty. "No, I don't know anyone by that name. My name's Landry. Walton Landry. I live up thataway." He gestures loosely, but slowly, deliberately, behind him. No sudden moves. "I heard the plane crash. I was coming to help."

There's a momentary beat, as if she's silently shaking her head. "No, that's not right. No one lives out here," she says, as much to herself as to him. The harsh light flits away, searching the thick trees crowded at his back, before finding his face again. "I was making for Chapel Creek Campground."

He raises a shielding hand. "Then you're heading the wrong way and you're about five miles off." Chapel Creek is a cluster of fifteen primitive campsites, little more than firepits, public tables, a public restroom. "Nobody there now anyway. Not this time of year, and not with this weather blowing down on us."

He can't see her but can almost *hear* her thinking, wheels turning, considering if he's telling the truth.

"Look," he says, pushing ahead, "are you hurt? Your friend there hurt? I've got a med kit here." He gestures at the bright-red MyFAK still slung over his back. "The crash? Are there others still out there?"

"No," she says, too quick, too final, too certain. "Just us . . . just this girl here."

It's an odd way to phrase it, ringing hollow. Walton doesn't know why this woman's lying to him, or exactly what she's lying about, but she is. "Then how about you let me get a look at her? Get you two out of the cold."

The light doesn't leave his face. "The crash," she asks, "anyone else know about that? Anyone else coming?"

Again, a strange question, although this whole conversation in the snow and dark is beyond strange.

"I don't know, miss," Walton says, unwilling to mask his own weariness and frustration anymore. He doesn't care if she hears exactly how tired he is of being interrogated. "Can't imagine so, not yet anyway." But he doesn't mention the call he made to Marcus Austin, the Iridium still back at his place, abandoned on his kitchen table. "Your plane went down over some hard terrain. If someone's looking for you, if you're expecting someone, it'll be a while. For better or worse, I'm all you got."

Another studied silence. Then, "I don't know how hurt this girl is. She's in shock."

"Hell, we're all in shock, right? Running into each other like this." He coughs, spits in the snow. "Let's just both take a breath here, okay? Least give me a chance to get mine. Probably can't tell, but I'm not spry as I once was. Poking around out here in the dark has damn near taken it out of me." He raises both hands toward her, palms out, so she can see they're still empty. All harmless. "And let's say we put that rifle down and get that light out of my face? We're going to be friends now."

A last silence, punctuated by his own heavy breathing and the murmuring wind between them, before the light finally slides from his face, pooling at his feet.

He spits again and nods a silent thanks.

Now he can see that the young woman with the rifle is kneeling next to the other one, brushing what looks like burned hair out of her eyes. Goddamn, he thinks, she's like to've caught fire. Like Walton's Remington, the burned, shoeless girl is leaning against a tree, thin legs folded beneath her. "I was calling for help," the woman says, and she sounds weary, too, even worse than him. Every word is heavy, an unbearable burden. "Just calling out over and over again, loud as I could, hoping someone, anyone, might hear me."

Those were the wild beast calls he imagined he heard, the howls that sent him running.

Not the challenge of some mystical mountain creature, the thing that took his boy once and his heart forever, only this scared young woman crying out for help.

"I don't even know who I thought I was calling for, who'd even come," she says. "I knew I was alone."

"Well," he says, drawing close, kneeling next to both young women. "I did hear you. Heard you clear as a church bell on Sunday. And I came."

12

A minute after his near miss, Marcus is out checking the road, spot-lighting the snowpack and gravel with his SureFire where his truck's still-bright headlights give way.

His tire marks are everywhere, fingerprint whorls in the snow, but if the thing he saw left behind any trace or tracks of its own, they're erased now, or lost in the dark like the thing itself.

Could've been a deer, a coyote, a bobcat. Even a bear.

Donnie, who used to hunt all year round, has told him black bears aren't hibernating in the winter like they're supposed to, something to do with the weather or the ready availability of food. Donnie claims he's spotted coywolves, eastern coyotes with old Great Lakes wolf or even local dog blood in them, lurking in the standing deadwood east of Pullens. Bigger than a regular coyote by twenty or thirty pounds, they're twice as fearless. But this thing was even bigger than that. Big and fast. It rumbled out of the darkness, broke free of the trees, lunged across the road in a hoary flash.

It was looking at me, Marcus recalls, staring right at me through the windshield . . .

Smoky gray and white, the color of ashen shadows, of soot and dried blood and old bone. A frantic origami of impossible arms and legs.

Arms and legs . . .

That's what Marcus knows he saw, what he tries to convince himself now couldn't have been possible, as he shines his light into the tall trees standing quiet watch on either side of the road, fat flakes tumbling down all around.

A victim, a wounded survivor, of Walton's plane crash?

No, that doesn't make sense. Couldn't be. But . . . those arms and legs . . . red eyes . . . staring through him. Considering. Thinking. Calculating.

Almost human.

Marcus figures it must've been his own eyes playing tricks on him, just one more trick this long, weird night had sprung on him, saving the best for last. Nothing more than a potent mixture of coffee-fueled exhaustion and frustration, the heavy adrenaline of that near miss.

Because whatever that pale thing was, whatever he thought it was, it was far from human.

If it was ever even there at all.

☾

After more fruitless searching, calling out futilely to the dark, Marcus abandons the cause and returns to his truck to see how much trouble he's in.

The truck lists hard to one side, like a ship stuck on a reef. He didn't entirely miss that roadside ditch the way he first thought, and although the old Dodge Ram is big and heavy, the one-two punch of angled ditch and slick snow—slicker and thicker by the moment—means it's going to take some finesse to get it unstuck.

He circles the truck, working out his options, only to discover he didn't miss that mysterious thing in the road either.

The Ram's hood is visibly crumpled in the right corner, a ragged metal scar, giving the truck an ugly sneer. Beneath his flashlight glare, the big old truck smokes, the idling engine rumbling in the cold.

Damn, there *was* something, he thinks, and I hit it.

He runs a hand over the damage, almost feels the weight of the thing in the crunched steel, the cracked passenger-side headlight, the ruined hood. Solid, heavy, and most certainly real. No trace of fur or hair that he can see, but it left a serious mark all the same. And a closer look does reveal a spot that could be blood, a nickel-size dark drop, that wipes away beneath his glove.

An animal that, even after that kind of impact, somehow leapt over the truck, kept running without breaking stride. It cleared the rest of the road and then vanished into the dark, into the cover of the far trees.

Staring at him the whole time . . .

On pure instinct, the kind of gut-level early-warning system that kept him alive in more than one firefight, Marcus slides a free hand to his holster, snapping the leather thumb break free in one smooth, easy motion. He doesn't draw the big Glock, not yet, but the heavy grip feels good in his hand.

He turns, slow, steady, aiming his flashlight back into the pines once more.

The old trees stand there garlanded in snow, still and quiet, shoulder to shoulder, like soldiers at attention. There's an ethereal, fable-like quality to them. Picture-book drawings. Shadows flicker beneath them as new snow falls all around, but there's nothing . . . no pale, ghostly animal there stalking him, no red eyes watching him.

C'mon, Marcus, get your shit together. There's nothing there.

Not anymore.

Just those folk story trees.

And if they saw anything, if they know more than he does, they're not telling.

13

The Mount Pleasant Tudor town house is worth $1.2 million, but money itself doesn't mean much to Ekker anymore. He keeps the place mostly unfurnished anyway, except for a low, slim couch, three Apple laptops, a bed.

That leaves plenty of empty space in twenty-four-hundred square feet, a muted expanse of exposed brick, antique brass, sandstone-colored walls.

Ekker tends to view his life as a tesseract of empty spaces like these. Cool liminal latitudes, an interstitial, ephemeral existence. He imagines himself occupying infinite, ambient possibilities all at once. Like, right now, he's standing in this empty brownstone in Mount Pleasant, but there are other versions of him—aliases—checked into hotels around Washington, DC, and Northern Virginia. A Motel 6 in Bowie, Maryland.

He's perfected the art of being everywhere and nowhere, and it's saved his life more than once. But not anymore, not now. All those various doppelgängers of himself, all his possibilities, have collapsed into one unassailable and unalterable reality.

He's dying.

☾

Knowing you will die is categorically different from knowing you are *going* to die.

Living with the specter of death is far easier than having it haunt you, and Ekker's haunting began last year with the sudden appearance of a ghostly presence, a roseate and black light. He was in Atlanta, another empty townhome like Mount Pleasant, when he woke in the middle of the night to a hazy, halolike glow hovering in the far corner of the room.

It was like lens flare, a spot of warp and sunlight in an old photograph, or cigarette burns on paper; a black hole, hovering there by a window, Buckhead reflected in the bare glass behind it.

At first, still groggy, still slow, he thought it was the glow of an intruder's flashlight, the gleam of a gun.

He retrieved his own SIG Sauer and rolled to an unsteady crouch on the floor, but the light didn't move, didn't react. And when he blinked, closing his eyes again and again, holding his breath, the light didn't dissipate either. If anything, the corona surrounding it got brighter . . . bright enough to warm his face. So bright, so hot, he raised his hand to his skin, only to find he was still cool to the touch.

Earlier that morning in Camp Biscayne, seven hundred miles away, he'd killed a man in an ornately tiled bathroom smelling of Florida sand and salt and Louis Vuitton Sun Song, garroting him from behind, lifting him off the floor, nearly decapitating him. The man's blood had seeped under Ekker's latex gloves, still beating-heart warm.

After that killing in Miami and the ethereal vision in Atlanta, he started seeing that black and reddish light—that fiery lens flare—in his left eye day and night, whether his eyes were open or shut. It was distracting, a wraith he couldn't ignore or avoid.

Worse, the light soon became the harbinger of piercing headaches, knife stabs that took his breath away, sometimes even took his knees out from under him. Short of full-on seizures, the episodes still left his face numb, his eyes glassy, his hands shaking.

Afterward, he'd taste metal too—his mouth full of it—like he'd just swallowed a handful of spent brass shell casings.

The eventual diagnosis was easy, the prognosis easier. Ekker's tumor, a grade 4 astrocytoma—a glioblastoma—was too far gone, too big, too deep. It wasn't a mere ghost, but a lethal living thing spreading malignant black wings inside him, a pulsing radiant maw behind his left eye. An insatiable hunger—a black hole—eating him inside, swallowing him whole.

There were experimental medicines and treatments that might gift him another handful of months and keep him functioning—that have, so far, kept him functioning—but nothing to stave off the inevitable.

He's dying . . .

And that hazy black light occluding his vision . . . his own winged Angel of Death . . . is a constant reminder now there are no miracles.

☾

He boots up one of the three laptops and, using his own considerable sources, double-checks the things Brooking told him.

Despite his warning to Brooking to tell him everything, Ekker can pick out the numerous holes in the man's story, more of those liminal spaces he's always been so adroit at moving through, at exploiting. If he truly wants or needs to know more, he'll have to find it out himself.

But Brooking's initial payment transferred successfully, as well as the additional backstop documents Ekker requested. The money itself is useless, a way of checking the boxes, keeping up the facade, since Ekker won't live long enough to spend it. This whole assignment is merely going through the motions, a futile waste of the short time Ekker has left. But that assumes time itself holds any value to Ekker. He has no friends, no family, no hobbies, no interests. Beyond his work, his unusual aptitudes, his life is as empty, as barren, as this town house and the four others he owns across the country.

This is all he is.

He took Brooking's money because much like a great white shark, propelled to swim endlessly lest it drown, if he stops doing *this*, he'll drown too. And although the world doesn't owe a man like him anything—he knows and accepts what he is and the horrible, unforgivable things he's done—he will not get cheated out of a single moment he has left.

I am a killer angel too . . .

Ekker doesn't believe in miracles, but Brooking's story suggests the world is still full of surprises, so he calls up the photo Brooking gave him, one of several, and studies her face again.

He appreciates this one the most.

It was taken surreptitiously from about twenty yards away, while she was looking up and to the left, smiling at something he'll never see or experience. A moment caught in time, now lost. She's young and pretty in a conventional way, but there's so much more to her than that.

It's her eyes.

Although she's flashing a warm, wonderful smile, it falls just short of her eyes, like a sudden drop in temperature, a change in the weather.

Eyes like a knife's edge. Sharp, bright, dangerous.

Thine eye be evil . . .

Deadly.

And if eyes truly are the windows to the soul, Ekker likes what he sees.

Ekker transfers her photo to his private cell phone and starts making his arrangements for West Virginia.

14

He should be dead; he knows that.

Instead, he remembers falling.

He remembers fire.

An unholy, unbearable pain. A scouring, a cleansing, burning him alive, stripping him to bare bone, until one thing remains, a ferocious, fiery animus.

A need . . .

She was gone when he came to, his pain still unimaginable, inescapable. But his need drove him blindly onward anyway like a wild, injured animal calling out for her, searching.

He ran, stumbled, crawled, as his dead skin sloughed off in thick, wet flakes. His burning blood dripping black, hissing in the snow beneath his bare feet.

As he stalked the night, shedding ruined skin and the old vestiges of what he'd been with each step, he became something altogether new. Altered, transformed, flayed, exposing sinew and bone . . . fang and claw . . . until he smelled winter colors on the air, tasted his own barely beating heart, heard the salty metal blood in his mouth.

His true nature finally bared to the world.

I am the eternal hunter, I am the night with fangs, I am the dark with claws . . .

He should be dead . . .

But he ran and leapt wild and free instead, like the great predator he always imagined himself to be. Unfettered, untouchable. The trees called after him as he pressed onward, ever higher. The mountain called after him, too, marking him. It whispered to him, the way *she* did. And when all his frantic strength was done, he came upon a dark, stinking midden, and sought the mountain's cold, black embrace.

Black Mountain.

C

He drifts in and out of consciousness now, sailing on tidal pain.

His hurt is so unfathomable, so deep, there is no bottom. Just limitless, lightless depths below him. A cave.

Even after the bloodbath in the sky, after she made him lose all control and he tried to shoot himself in the roof of his mouth but succeeded only in blowing his face apart, he held her as they tumbled and burned, held her tight and close, shielding her from the worst of it, still sacrificing himself for her.

And although he no longer hears her in his head, those thousand black wings beating behind his eyes gone silent, now the mountain itself is promising him in a thousand voices of its own both ancient and terrible that his sacrifice did not go unnoticed.

His willing offering of flesh, blood, was not in vain.

She lives . . .

Somewhere on Black Mountain. And the mountain, with all its primal power and eternal secrets and endless hidden paths, understands his need. It will show him the way to her, and all it requires, needs, is a sacrifice too.

Flesh, blood.

He howls at that, smiling in the cold dark of the cave, smiling just as he did at her before she tried to kill him before the plane went down.

Revealing now—

Fangs.

In the years after, no attempt to find the White Thing was ever successful, every effort to snare the beast ending in failure, even as landed men in Lost Hill still suffered brutal attacks on what livestock they held.

Even though men still disappeared in the mountains, leaving only blood behind.

"But where is this beast then?" asked Rufus Strange, one night at Tunny's Tavern while deep in his cups. "How has no man tracked this thing? How has it evaded us so well and for so long?"

All remained silent but for Cooper Landry, who still mourned the loss of his elder brother all those years earlier, when Cooper himself was not old enough to give chase. Now he searched the woods and caves for the beast long after others had given up, and to claim that nothing haunted the hills was an affront to Cooper and all others who had lost kin. But in all other things, Cooper was a temperate man and well thought of, so he only pulled a piece of plug from his jaw and spat the last juice into a bottle held tight in his fist. "Failure is perhaps our saving grace. No doubt we are fools to seek it. This mountain is its home and always has been. Yet pursue I will. I must."

A worrisome drunk, Rufus pointed a heavy finger at Cooper. "Vengeance leads you to chase it hither and yon with naught to show for it but bramble cuts. So, if it exists at all, it must surely be monstrous and very sly." Cooper ignored the veiled insult as Willem Cross added, "It is a grandfather bear only, Rufus, no smarter than coyote or wolf kin, and little more dangerous. Wily to be sure. But I don't fear this thing."

But Cooper only laughed and took a drink from the mug of dark liquor another good man handed to him. He regarded Rufus and Willem and all others before him. "We should be afraid, though. We should be."

The White Things:
Tall Tales of West Virginia's White Monsters
Jim Collymore

Dark and Stormy Books
Pullens, West Virginia
2006

TWO

15

Maggie was impressed when Walton Landry didn't flinch when she put her rifle in the curve of his back and told him no radio or cell calls, no sudden moves.

He didn't bat an eye when she tossed the rambling, rugged, two-story cabin, growing agitated only when she touched his photos, framed pictures of a wife and presumably a son.

She did find weapons everywhere, though, an arsenal that would've rivaled Vann's, as well as an old gold badge stowed away in a box on the rough-hewn mantel.

Landry was once a cop, and if she didn't believe her situation could possibly get any worse, there it was, heavy in her hand. She pocketed the badge and kept searching.

She also found his regular cell phone as well as a satellite phone, an expensive, late-model Iridium, forcing her to ask him again—point blank—if he'd made any earlier calls or raised an alarm about the plane. Again, he said he hadn't, even when she put her rifle in his face, right between his eyes.

Gray-blue eyes, the color of cold river water, surrounded by deep age lines like cracked stone, the shale and flint and glittering mica of a sun-weathered cliff face.

He didn't blink.

He just shrugged at the rifle in his face and told her to go ahead, shoot him, if it got all this goddamn nonsense over faster.

Then he asked if she wanted him to make them some coffee.

☾

That was an hour ago, after they got the girl bundled up in a pile of thick blankets next to the river-stone fireplace.

Neither she nor Landry could explain her obvious lack of crash wounds, nothing beyond a few scrapes and abrasions and badly scorched hair. While Landry looked the other way, Maggie got the girl out of her snow-wet, soot-covered clothes, revealing those old surgery scars again, as well as a newer constellation of contusions on her arms.

The gloomy cabin light made it hard to tell, but Maggie thought they looked like finger bruises, the lingering reminder of a strong grip, as if someone had held tight on to the girl . . . or held her down.

I know bruising like that, she thinks. I know how to cover it up . . .

The bruises were already going blue black, marring the girl's pale skin, as Maggie got her changed into one of Landry's son's old thermal tops and a well-worn T-shirt, some rock band, Breaking Benjamin. Their 2015 tour, *Dark Before Dawn*.

Dawn itself is still a few hours away as Maggie now sits next to the fireplace, next to the girl, finishing off her second cup of coffee. It's good—strong, simple, black—the way she always used to like it before Vann, the way her dad drank it. Vann took his expensive grinds with too much sugar and cream, softening it down to nothing. For a man who prided himself on toughness, that wasn't Vann's only weakness, though.

Landry's poured two fingers of something clear from a mason jar into a stoneware mug, then another two. He's perched on an old leather couch opposite, her rifle still angled between them. The fire's falling, turning the room rosy and close, almost safe, but he hasn't made any move to stoke it further, content to wait her out. She should be gone, long gone, back up the mountain, but needs to first decide what to do about Landry and the girl, and those decisions are best made from out of the cold and with some deliberation, where she can think clearly and get some answers.

The walls of the rough cabin are adorned with old pictures, deer and coyote and fox heads. A massive bear pelt, too, or what she guesses was a bear, hangs in the kitchen. A stuffed owl watches her unblinking from a mantel, black eyes like round mirrors, massive wings outstretched, its shadow embracing the room. The place is redolent with old smoke and cracked leather and something loamy, almost floral, but there are no touches around of the woman in his pictures, nor much evidence of the son, other than the clothes. If they're away on a trip, Landry hasn't offered that.

It's just the two of them . . . and the girl.

Landry sips his mug, says, "Look, I hope you understand, I can't just take your say-so on this."

"What say-so?"

"The plane. Your word there are no more survivors." He gestures at the sleeping girl with his mug. "That one there made it clear with barely a scratch, so who knows how many others did too? If I didn't worry you'd put a bullet in me, I'd already be back out there."

"She's the only one. I was there. I saw it."

Now it's Landry's turn to stare into her, those gray-blue eyes wintry. "But you weren't on that plane, miss, and we both know that."

She ignores the accusation. "Just call me Maggie."

He chuckles, an oddly comforting sound, given the knife-cut tension in the room. "And we both know that ain't your real name either. But look, that's fine, I like it all the same." He stands and moves to the window, pushes an old curtain aside, checks the dark outside. "So, miss . . . Maggie . . . it honestly don't much matter to me why you were out there or even what you might be running from." He finishes off the concoction in his mug. "Keep your secrets for now, I'm fine with that too. But I'm not fine letting folks die. I'm not fine leaving the dead"—he motions with his empty mug again, this time to the woods beyond the window—"out there." He turns back to her. "There's a storm bearing down, and every minute counts. You want a head start? I'll give it to you. You need supplies? Take whatever you can carry. Hell, I'll even lie about it later, claim I never saw you, if that makes any difference. But I am going back."

"You're a cop," she says. "Why lie to help me at all?"

"I was a sheriff. *The* sheriff for this county for a long, long time. Too long. But not anymore. And truth be told, you are not my kind of problem anymore either."

Maggie looks to the silent, unmoving girl. "Her?"

"Now, she is, no two ways around that. I'll just say I pulled her from the plane, all on my own."

"She might say different," Maggie counters, recalling the girl's phantom piano recital, her slim, ash-tinted fingers moving eerily over invisible black-and-white keys. It was that one gesture more than anything that stopped Maggie from leaving her out there. She still can't begin to guess what the girl will remember from all this, if anything, but neither can Landry. If he's truly serious about hiding Maggie's involvement, he's taking one serious risk after another.

He only shrugs. "And maybe she don't say a thing. But you walk out that door, I reckon you don't gotta worry about it. Then *we're* not your problem anymore either."

Silence settles between them, Landry's badge still heavy in her pocket. "And you really didn't hear any news about that plane?" she asks. She gestures at his phones, a nicked-up modern Motorola two-way and a vintage Panasonic shortwave radio—practically an antique—on a side table. Her dad would've loved it. "Nothing at all?"

Landry hesitates before shaking his head. "No, just the crash itself. But that won't last. And I can't not call it in, before too long. Who knows who else saw it, heard it, like I did?"

To Maggie, the true answer still might be no one; there was nothing out at the crash site, not a soul on their hike back here, not even the distant lights of a road or trail or passing car. Based on her planned route, Landry and his cabin shouldn't be here either.

He leans against the door, folds his arms, continues, "If you want to get gone so bad, I'd get going now. Although, honestly, it's probably safer if you wait to first light . . . even better if you give it until after the storm blows over, since you're like to just get all turned around again." His eyes are as wintry as the storm he's concerned about. "But I'm guessing that's just a little too long for you. I'm guessing you've been sitting there this whole time, chewing it over, worrying about just how little time you do have."

She smiles at that, drains the coffee going cold. "Am I that easy to read?"

"No," he answers, "but you do seem just that desperate. And I don't stand in the way of desperate people." He nods at his old badge in her pocket. "Not anymore."

Maggie has a hard time imagining this man Landry—badge or no—backing down from anyone, or any fight. Not in his prime, not now. But she also can't guess why he's so willing to let her leave—all but throwing her out despite his own warnings—unless it's not only her he's worried about. Unless it's someone else . . . unless he's expecting company.

He stands in front of the door, one gray-blue eye on her, the other on the window next to it. She stands, too, picking up one of his framed photos. "What about your wife? Your son?"

Landry stares at the wooden frame in her hand, as if wishing, willing, her to put it down. He's quiet. "My wife, Lottie, she's been dead and gone awhile now. The boy's not here."

Maggie can't guess the young man in the photo's age, can't guess when it might've been taken. There are hints of Landry in the man's hawkish face, the same straight nose and powerful stare. He's standing outside, his slim, suntanned torso bare, a long fly rod in hand. That arm is a gloriously colored tattoo sleeve, all eagles, fish, and flowers. She asks, "When's he coming back?"

"He's not," Landry says louder, too loud, without explanation, before walking over and taking the photo from her. His eyes are drawn to it, a lodestone, as he sets it gently back down where it belongs.

She and Landry are close now, close enough he can just grab her. Close enough he can be on her before she has a chance to get to her rifle, if it comes to that. He looms over her. "I really don't want to hurt anyone," she whispers, acknowledging that despite what Landry said a moment ago, they both know she is a problem . . . his problem . . . if he decides she's a threat to anyone who crosses her desperate path.

"I don't want you to hurt anyone either, Maggie," he says. "And I surely don't want to hurt *you*."

He straightens his son's photo, a ritualistic gesture, but one that buys them both a moment to step back from the high, dangerous ledge they've stepped out on. To both consider calmly what to do next.

"You've put me between the proverbial rock and a hard place," he says over his shoulder. "Between that young girl over there on that couch, and that plane out in those woods." Satisfied the photo's right again, he faces her. "It'll take me two hours or more to hike out there and back. In the meantime, she could wake any minute now, scared, alone, and who knows what else. She needs a doctor, Maggie, real help, more than either of us can give. I appreciate you got trouble on your tail, maybe even serious trouble, and like I already said, you don't have to tell me a goddamn thing about it. But you do need to tell me what we do about right here and now, because we're both running out of options and time."

The waning moment stretches between them, and Maggie can almost imagine wind against her face as they still teeter together on that high ledge neither of them wants to be on. A few years ago, she and Vann hiked Chimney Rock in North Carolina, three hundred feet up, on a crisp, Technicolor afternoon in late fall. From up there, wind tugging her hair—it was longer and far darker then—she could see more than seventy miles in every direction, the horizon a distant cerulean haze, a million autumn trees fanned out below, all crimson, gold, and amber.

Vann was ignoring the scene, of course, leaning on the surprisingly thin iron railing, working one of his phones like always, and she thought to herself—

Just push him . . .

She didn't, not then. But she's not sure that wasn't the moment she made her first fateful decision, setting into motion everything that came after, right up to this moment now, a moment just as serious, just as fateful, all because she pulled that girl from the plane crash.

All because I was thinking about music, and she started miming the piano . . .

All because Maggie couldn't bring herself to leave her out in the woods alone.

She should have, though. The girl's not safe with her. And neither is Landry.

And she probably should've pushed Vann off that rock too.

"You could just believe me about that crash," she says. "And let it go. I'm not lying."

He nods, unconvinced. "And you could believe I didn't make a call to someone before I hiked my old ass out there alone in the dark and found you." His eyes flick knowingly to the Iridium on the table next to her rifle, then back to her. "But I reckon that's a whole heap of trust too high for either of us to see over yet."

"Pretty high," she concedes, unable to mask her frustration, her exhaustion. Now that she's been sitting by the fire, out of the wind and cold, that initial adrenaline surge from the plane crashing and burning, too, she's worn down, every bone, every sinew, sore and tight. She prepped hard for this, as hard as she could in secret, but dragging and carrying the girl has taken it out of her, even with Landry's help.

It's a risk . . . *a whole heap of risk*, this Landry character might call it . . . but if all her planning didn't reveal this cabin, how likely is it the men looking for her will find it too? Vann once told her to never miscalculate their reach or resources—never, ever—but then again, he never appreciated or truly calculated her resourcefulness either. Still, for all her planning and figuring and preparing, she didn't account for this.

She decides, reluctantly. Says, "Okay, so rock and a hard place, what do we do?"

Landry retreats to the kitchen and grabs the mason jar, unscrewing the top. The acrid homemade alcohol hits her from across the cabin, burning her nose, her tired, bloodshot eyes.

This time, he doesn't even bother with the coffee. He takes a good long swallow, then offers her the jar. "First," he says, "I steal us both some more time . . ."

16

It's still dark, winter storm still threatening, still lingering like the old feral black dog that used to haunt the outskirts of Pullens, when Donnie Kornblue rolls back to the Wolfe County Sheriff's Office just before dawn.

Seems like he never left last night.

And because he woke Roberta both falling into and hauling his ass out of bed, she was none too eager to rustle him a pan of her famous cathead biscuits this morning. But now they're sitting warm on the other seat in the heavy bag she pressed into his hand before she went back to bed alone, likely to be breakfast, lunch . . . hell, dinner too . . . if this day goes down the way he figures it will.

Shitty, top to bottom . . .

It's days like these he wishes he wasn't the chief deputy anymore, where it might be nice if Marcus leaned on one of the other deputies a little bit more. It's not that Donnie doesn't want to be helpful or doesn't mind being the go-to guy every now and then; it's just sometimes he thinks he should've gone ahead and pulled the pin when Walton did. He'd always planned to, only to then stick around after both Walton and Marcus asked him to, the latter even tossing in a bit of a raise to sweeten the deal. But each new day really should be the last, if not one too many.

Everyone jaws about retiring after three bad days in a row, and as Donnie scans the blurry, steel-colored sky overhead, he figures he's chalked up number two.

He pulls into the office and parks alongside Marcus's truck, the damage from the tree Marcus claimed he hit clearly visible, even in the gloom. Donnie warned him about trying to drive out to Walton's place last night, but Marcus ignored him—again—and Donnie's not sure what being the go-to guy means if the guy going to you doesn't listen to a damn thing you say. If Sheriff Marcus Austin was just going to do his own thing anyway, he sure didn't need to pay Chief Deputy Donnie Kornblue an extra seventy-five dollars a month, before taxes, to ignore him. And he sure didn't have to get Donnie up this early again, either, after such a long, weird night.

Before going inside, Donnie runs his bare hand along the dent, knowing it wasn't a tree—despite what Marcus said when he called this morning—unless a knotted pitch pine just jumped off the side of the road and *bit* the truck.

Donnie's hit enough coyotes and deer in his day to know the marks they can leave in even good old solid American-made metal, and this wasn't either of those. But it was an animal of some kind, no doubt about that, and a big one. One with serious claws. He traces a ragged set of gashes and scratches in the hood and the side panel that could only be the handiwork of sharpened nails, spreading his own fingers to measure them.

He whistles. Wow, that's a big sucker . . .

Donnie's stares at his hand stretched wide between those marks, trying to imagine what it might've been. A bear, dummy, what else? You can still find black bears in every one of West Virginia's fifty-five counties. But that doesn't sit as easy as it should, doesn't sit right at all. Maybe it's just the odd, accumulated shit that happened last night: the dead guy they can't ID, the woman they can't find, the plane crash they can't confirm.

Or maybe . . . just maybe . . . it's the weird way his human fingers fit so neatly, almost *too* neatly, in those animal gouges. It's a shame that Marcus never got all the way out to Walton's place last night, because if there was anyone around Pullens who could identify a few strands of fur or some random-ass scratch marks, it'd be Walton.

Donnie can't begin to guess why Marcus would make up some bullshit story about hitting a tree but doesn't blame him for taking one look at his damaged truck out there in the middle of the night on that mountain and saying fuck all and heading right back to the safety of town.

He would've done the exact same thing.

☾

"Walton finally called me back," Marcus tells him when Donnie walks into his office, shaking his head at the offered bag of biscuits, even as Donnie pulls one out for himself and settles heavily into the chair opposite Marcus's desk.

"I'm not gonna tell Roberta you turned down one of these. That's like to break her heart. These here are award winners, six years running."

Marcus eyes the massive golden-brown biscuit, still dusty with flour, as big as Donnie's fist. "Jesus, that looks like a whole heart attack."

Donnie smiles. He'd like it better lathered in butter and some of Roberta's blackberry jam, wrapped around salty country ham, a big-ass fried egg, even four strips of pepper bacon, but Marcus wouldn't have appreciated the mess all over his clean white papers and folders. He was lucky enough to pry these out of Roberta. Ham or no. "Then I say it's a good way to go."

"I guess." Marcus pauses before adding, "I would've killed for one over there."

Donnie's come to figure out that *over there*, accompanied by one of Marcus's vague head nods, a certain faraway stare, means Marcus's time overseas, one of his many military tours. Marcus never talks about them much, nothing specific anyway, just those gestures and hints and long silences, and a lot more of the latter. But Donnie respects whatever he did over there, and everything he lost.

"Anyway," Marcus continues, "Walton rang while I was trying to get my truck out of that ditch."

"How'd he come across?"

"Well, not exactly sober, if that's what you're asking. Asked me if I'd had any reports about a plane, a crash, and said the weather was already bad out his way, getting worse. Admitted he'd poked around a bit but couldn't find anything, so said maybe he just had it wrong. Did tell me to call him again if I heard any different; otherwise he'd take another look at first light, just to be sure."

Donnie brushes biscuit crumbs to the floor and wheels around to eyeball the window, taking in the same leaden sky that greeted him this morning. "Light enough now, I s'pose."

"Yeah . . . if he's slept off the hangover."

Donnie laughs. "Oh, Walton doesn't get hungover. Does get meaner than a copperhead, though."

"Great," Marcus says. "I don't know, Donnie, there was just something . . . off . . . about his call. Honestly, the whole thing was weird."

"The whole damn night," Donnie agrees, fishing for another biscuit. "So, you get any kind of news about a plane?"

Marcus shakes his head, now making wider and wider circles on his desk blotter with a black pen. They look like dark eyes to Donnie, staring back at them both. "Nada, nothing. And by now, someone, somewhere, should be looking. There'd be . . . I don't know . . . something?"

"Sure, something," he agrees around a mouthful of still-warm biscuit. A walnut-size bit of lard in the White Lily flour and bacon grease in the fry pan is part of Roberta's secret. There's plenty about his wife that drives him plumb crazy, to be expected after thirty years of marriage. But the woman can still cook circles, no doubt about that.

"Sooooo," he says again, casting around the otherwise-empty, quiet office, "what's the five-alarm fire then?"

"Well, there's still our dead John Doe. We're going to check around for this Roby woman again, see where she's gotten herself off to. We'll start at the Briar, then canvass those houses near Hanging Rock. I got the idea when I was out that way last night." Marcus trades his pen for a stack of papers at his elbow. "Guess we'll get a warrant for her room, too, if we strike out everywhere else."

"Oh hell, Marcus, no need for that," he says, too fast, without thinking.

"No, we do it—" Marcus stops, catching the nakedly guilty look on Donnie's face, the unfinished warrant in his hand still hanging in the air. "Dammit, you looked already, didn't you? Last night, while you were sitting over there?"

Donnie carefully puts the half-eaten biscuit back in the bag. Some folks have a knack for lying, a poker face and all, but he isn't one of them. Roberta knows when he's lying from a mile away, like that little gambling thing he had a while back, and Donnie Kornblue hasn't won—hasn't even *played*—a hand of cards in five years. "Now, don't go getting hot at Ms. Torri. I just threw the idea out there, and bam, the next thing you know, she's got the key in hand."

"You know better, Don. You both do."

Sure, Donnie does. But he also knows that's how Walton would've done it. He wouldn't still be fussing around like this, wasting everyone's time, getting decent folks out of bed early for a bunch of foolishness. But it's also best he probably hold his tongue right now, though, give Marcus a moment to either simmer down or decide just how boiling mad he wants to get. Donnie's always suspected Marcus Austin's capable of one hell of a temper, one he works very hard to keep low and slow, like a perpetual pilot light.

For all his silence, all those things he doesn't say about his time *over there*, Donnie figures Marcus has dealt with his fair share of ugly stuff and hateful shit, and a lot of it has stayed with him. Donnie doesn't know how it couldn't, or how every time Marcus looks down at his ruined leg and his scars and the dog tags he still wears, he doesn't get furious all over again.

But now Marcus only looks tiredly at the useless affidavit in his hand, then back at Donnie, that heat, that slow-burn anger, simmering, threatening to ignite . . . but not quite.

Instead, Marcus just says "Dammit" again and tosses the warrant in the trash, before reaching for one of Roberta's biscuits, still shaking his head.

"All right, Deputy," he says, "tell me what we found."

17

Maggie, or whoever she is, wasn't lying about the plane.

But she wasn't exactly telling him the whole truth either.

Hiking now back to his cabin, dawn at his back, Walton can't get it out of his head, and won't for a long, long, time.

Death doesn't scare him, never has.

He's pulled bodies out of wrecked cars and semis, from fires and floods, bodies all swollen and glossy from heat, gases, and exposure, torched and torn and mutilated in every horrible way imaginable. He found an old woman in Beverly sitting upright at her dinner table, plumb mummified for two years, neglected—forgotten—by the remnants of distant family and friends. He once pulled a whole human head from a well, blue eyes still open, with a silver dollar under its tongue.

He carried what was left of little Charlie Dance out of the Cranberry Wilderness, clutching that boy's ravaged remains to his heart.

But nothing prepared him for the mess out there in that crash, the parts strewn here and there, bits and pieces of . . . life . . . so casually and randomly left fluttering in the trees, upended and exposed on the hard, snowy ground.

Magazines, glasses, an iPad, a ballpoint pen.

A torn shoe. A napkin. A gold wedding band.

A hand. A foot.

A gun.

The gun surprised him, a late-model H&K compact 9mm scorched and scored, but still loaded, still serviceable; it troubled him, too, in a way he couldn't quite put a finger on.

Five rounds . . . five missing rounds . . .

Maggie was right, though, no one else appeared to have survived that crash, no one he could find, even after he thought he might've picked out faint human tracks, heading into the trees. But with Maggie stomping around out there before him, as well as fresh snow still flurrying down, it was impossible to be sure.

It was impossible to imagine anyone surviving . . . including that girl Maggie claimed she found.

In the end, he fired off a flare and waited, watching the brazen red glow burn and drift on the wind. It twisted and twirled over the crash site, casting the ground below in molten lead, before eventually falling back to earth, like the plane itself had hours ago.

Maggie was right . . .

But that still doesn't mean she's telling the truth, not all of it.

Not even close.

☾

He finds Maggie dead asleep when he gets back to his cabin.

She's propped at the kitchen table, head resting on folded arms, his cell phone and the Iridium at her elbow, her rifle leaning against her. She doesn't stir when he comes in or even when he checks on the other girl and finds her asleep too . . . or faking it well. She's moved in his absence, though, shifting deeper beneath the pile of blankets, as if the cabin's dim fireplace glow, or the light of the slow-rising sun outside, is too harsh, too bright. Like she's hiding from it.

Walton leaves them both and heads upstairs to Kellan's old room to sit and think. It's silly but he does this sometimes, sitting on Kell's bed, looking out the window his son used to look out, surrounded by his boy's old photos and maps and drawings. It clears his head, and he needs to be thinking damn straight for the next few hours.

He stole them some time by calling Austin back again and waving him off, a decision less dire since there aren't any other apparent survivors to tend to. But search teams will be descending on them soon enough, and he can't keep the girl locked up here, not even until then. Walton wants to take Maggie at her word she doesn't have any personal connection to the girl, other than hearing the plane go down the same way he did, but that begs the question what the hell she was doing way out there in the first place.

Answers are likely to be found only down in Pullens now, and he needs to get the girl there anyway. Her folks and family will want to know she's alive, if they didn't perish in the crash.

Magazines, glasses, an iPad, a ballpoint pen . . .

"What'd you find?" Maggie asks, interrupting his quiet. She's leaning against the doorframe, still rubbing her red and tired eyes. Still has that damn rifle.

He shakes his head, his only answer. He watches her study Kell's drawings, visible in the watery morning light. When she tossed the place last night, moving fast in the dark, she probably didn't notice them.

"You do these?" she asks.

"No, my boy did," he says, remembering Kellan sitting cross-legged in this very room, on this very bed, with his sketch pad and pencils Lottie used to buy by the truckload from the Dollar General. "He had a way with things like that. Liked to catalog the trees, plants, flowers. A yellow-billed cuckoo sitting on a branch, a gray fox on the move, another sunrise, just like the one the day before. Silly, I used to say, drawing all this stuff, this old mountain. It's been here forever and ain't going anywhere. He could've just taken a picture if it mattered that much. But it meant more to him putting it all down by hand like that. Putting it in *here*." He lightly touches his head, his heart, and just as quickly is embarrassed by the gesture.

"I get it," she says, "and these are good, very good. I don't have a creative bone in my body. Clichéd, I know, but I was always more of a numbers person." She reaches out like she's going to take a picture but thinks better of it. A small thing, to be sure, but Walton appreciates it. "Tried music when I was younger, mostly just to make my dad happy. He thought it was cultured, a middle-class thing to do. He wanted to believe there's a budding artist in all of us."

"Was there?"

"No. I took piano lessons from about ten until eighteen, then I got rebellious, mouthy. I went off to college, and I haven't touched one since . . . well, not in years." It looks like Maggie's going to say something more before thinking better of that too. "I could memorize some of it by rote, scales, things like that. There's a certain math to music, which made sense to me. Despite all the lessons and the practices, I never had any real aptitude or gift for it." She comes and settles on the bed next to him, gun cradled in her arms. "Look, thank you for calling the sheriff earlier, before you went out to the crash."

She doesn't thank him for not snatching that rifle off her when he found her asleep, but he knows that's what she really means.

He says, "Not sure Austin bought my old drunkard act, but I appreciate you keeping watch on that girl down there while I hiked back. Seems even if we're both no-account liars, we can still strike an honest deal when it suits us." He smiles, then grows serious again. "She say anything, speak at all?"

"No, nothing."

"Doesn't matter. It's getting light now—woods will soon be crawling with folks looking for that plane . . . looking for her. They'll come looking for my help, too, and I'll give it to them. But if you tell me where you're heading, I can still help you. Point the best way, keep you out of sight."

"The less you know the better."

He snorts at that. "Hell, then I already know too much. Offer still stands, though, as does the extra supplies." He tries to imagine what could have this woman so determined, so serious, so scared. Tries to imagine what drove her to hiking alone through these woods in the winter and dark. "You didn't come all this way to kill yourself, did you? I reckon I can't just stand aside for that. This old mountain has enough restless spirits, too many haunts."

She considers the question, seconds ticking by slow, doing nothing to make him feel better about it.

Tell her about the sounds you hear, Walton, tell her about the shadows in the trees . . .

Tell her about the real dark out here and what it does to you . . .

Tell her about your boy . . .

But when she finally shakes her head *no*, Landry's relieved, standing and unpinning one of Kell's maps before sitting down next to her again.

"This shows our cabin, here," he says, using his finger to trace his son's faded pencil marks. "Move northwest, following this holler. Should see the ridgeline before long, even in snow. Stay below it, always keeping it on your left, always working your way up. There's some old grave sites—"

"Grave sites?" she asks. "Who's buried there?"

"Mountain people. My people, my kin." He taps the map, making sure she's focused. "From there, straighten out, due north. You'll fight through some tangles, but there's fresh water that way, not just snow melt, either, and caves, too, if you need to hunker down for a spell from the storm . . . or anything else." He lets that hang there. "But be careful in those caves, don't go down, don't go deep." She raises a questioning eyebrow, but he pushes ahead. "Once you get above the snow line it'll be hard, no help for that, so take it slow, take it easy, even if you are in a hurry. Stay the course, and you'll get over the back side of the mountain." He points to a smudged mark. "This here's Buckner Lookout, another place you can hole up for a bit, if you need to."

That puts her on a thin, wild peninsula hugging Virginia, an accusatory finger pointing at Maryland, where Walton figures she can rock-skip over a handful of small communities and landmarks: Capon Bridge, Gore, Lost Hill. None are drawn on Kellan's map, but she'll find them, if she gets that far. He hands the old paper to her. "Not much, I know, but it's something. Better than a fancy store-bought GPS. Those get screwy in the mountains, just like some folks do."

She takes the map and stares at it hard, as if memorizing it. Her hands are subtly shaking, and he notices she doesn't have a wedding band. "No, this is good, thank you," she says, sharing a long look with him around the room, at Kellan's things, all those childhood objects his son outgrew over time. Old dusty fly rods, winter flannels, cracked boots. A brightly colored horsehair blanket. A stack of books from that medical school in Huntington he never completed. Kell never lived out here full time, not until the end, but even before that, he spent more time on this mountain, in this cabin, than anywhere else. This pile of logs has been in Walton's family for a couple of generations, added to little by little—inch by inch, room by room, year by year—aging right along with Kell, who did much of that work alongside him. His son was twenty-six, last time Walton saw him. But he still sees him now in every corner, every pane of glass, every river rock, every log.

Maggie gently folds the map away, asks quietly, "Where is your son now? Did something happen?"

Walton knows she can see it in his eyes as he stares at his son's things. She can hear it in his voice, all the things he won't say.

Tell her, Walton, about the dark . . . tell her about your boy . . .

"No, not so much," Walton finally answers, standing abruptly, signaling they're done here. She doesn't belong in this room, and neither does he.

"Fine," she says, standing as well. "Fair enough. So, it's only fair to warn you that whatever you hear about me, whatever they eventually tell you about me, that'll all be true, okay? Every damn word of it."

She looks at him, won't look away. Her eyes are bright, green, hard, but not scared. Whatever scared her before, she's not afraid of the truth. He raises his hands. "Hell, I don't even know your real name." He surrenders before she protests. "And it don't matter much to me anyhow. You helped that girl downstairs, likely saved her life. I reckon that balances the scales a bit."

"Think so?" she asks. "You really think we can just make amends, balance some scales, set everything right?"

Truth is, Walton's not convinced. He never got the chance to set things right with Kell, so he's mostly decided there are no second chances, no grace or clemency or mercy. But he's not prepared to tell this woman that, and he's not the one to absolve her anyway.

"Don't matter what I believe, either, and—"

But she grabs his shoulder, stopping him, motioning him to be quiet. "Hey, wait, hear that?"

They stand in silence, listening, straining together.

"Goddamn," he says. "That's the front door . . ."

18

Torri Lampley keeps the Briar's rooms neat and warm.

Each one is unique, filled with furniture and fabrics and antique knickknacks she's collected across West Virginia, Virginia, and Pennsylvania.

M. Roby's room is lots of dark wood, centered by a big bed covered in a Kentucky quilt. She's got a view of the front of the inn, and a long, unobstructed look down Pullens's main street.

Most of the others have windows that face the mountains.

Torri says, "This is one of the smaller rooms. View's not as nice."

"Nice enough," Marcus says, staring out the frost-tinged window. Marcus went through army ranger sniper school in Fort Benning, and although he hates to think it, with these clean sight lines, a good shooter could nest here and take out the whole town, even without the help of a spotter. "You say the lady asked for this room?"

"She did," Torri says, "pretty much the only one she wanted, and she paid cash." Torri checks her green steno guestbook. "Still has another week or so on her bill."

Torri closes her guestbook. The Briar has a modern automated call reservation system, but Torri still jots things down in her big green book, and Marcus figures there must be comfort in that kind of familiarity, in old ways and memories. Torri was beautiful once—*a real looker*, as Deidre would say—who's grown gracefully into old age. Donnie told him she used to hold court on Saturday nights down at Gem's bar before that placed burned down, and all the deputies would buy her beers, beg her to dance. She's had three husbands—not a single deputy—and buried her last—the one who bought and fixed up the Briar—not long before Deidre left Marcus. There are five kids from those three marriages, fifteen grandkids, too, scattered throughout Kentucky, Ohio, and West Virginia, but none left in Pullens. All she has here is the Briar, its mostly empty, overly decorated rooms, but she won't give the old place up.

Marcus turns from the window to take in the room again as Donnie idly opens dresser and nightstand drawers, peeking inside, although they both know from Donnie's poking around last night that they don't contain much of anything.

No clothes, no personal effects, no luggage. No trash between the two cans in the bedroom and the bathroom.

It looks like M. Roby's fond of empty rooms, too, but they spend a few minutes searching in silence anyway. The woman didn't even break the seal on the water tumblers or the ice bucket or the fancy small lavender and peppermint soaps. If the bed was ever slept in, it's since been carefully remade. The only thing of interest is a well-worn book about West Virginia monsters abandoned on the nightstand.

"Oh, she didn't bring that," Torri says, catching Marcus flipping through it. "I picked that up at an estate sale in Century a few years back. A mining family. I find old books or magazines about West Virginia history or art or whatever and put them in the rooms. Better than a Bible, I guess. More likely to get read."

Marcus flashes by stories and crude drawings of a handful of West Virginia's infamous "monsters": the Mothman, the Ogua Monster, Sheepsquatch, Bat Boy. He grew up on those local yarns, everyone around here did, but they're just old wives' tales, older rural legends. The world's bad enough, filled with real thieves and murderers and monsters; there's no need to dream up more.

"How much did you speak with her?" he asks, leaving the book on the nightstand. He covered this ground with Torri last night, but never hurts to run over it again.

"Not much, just hi and bye, that sort of thing. She didn't strike me as too talkative. Not unfriendly, just, you know, standoffish."

"Young?"

"Well, not *old.*" Torri gestures at herself, flashing an almost-sad smile. "Blondish." She snaps her fingers, remembering. "Told me she'd lost her cell phone. It came up when we talked about driving out to Pullens, finding her way." She holds aloft her green book. "No number on her registration."

Donnie adds, "Roberta can't survive without her phone, always playing those damn games with the colored dots. Texting me funny dog videos. We don't even have a dog anymore."

Marcus wonders if Roby truly lost her cell phone or just dumped it. Service can be hit or miss in the mountains, but like the rest of the world now, most people in Pullens won't leave the front door without one. There were Nokia 105s even in those far-flung Yemeni villages, the cheap and expendable cell phones convenient trigger devices for IEDs.

But there is Green Bank, just east of Pullens, population two hundred or less. The community is the site of the Robert C. Byrd Green Bank Telescope and part of the National Radio Quiet Zone—thirteen thousand square miles of wilderness adjacent to the Monongahela— where radio, cellular, and Wi-Fi devices are outlawed. The NRQZ is a huge swath of rugged, remote forest, naturally protected like Pullens by the Allegheny Mountains, housing some of the most advanced technologies on earth, all pointed at the stars, listening.

Marcus has read about "electrosensitives" holed up out there in RFI-free tent cities and campers, seeking respite from the electromagnetic waves they believe are causing their illnesses. Roby could be one of those people, or nothing more than another rich ecotourist solo hiking or stargazing without the benefit, or the annoyance, of a cell phone.

He remembers the strange, jumbled figure that flashed across the road last night . . . arms and legs . . . red eyes . . . almost human . . . the thing he was too embarrassed to admit to Donnie that he'd sideswiped. Despite all the tight places Marcus has been in, he wouldn't want to be alone out in the Cranberry Wilderness, or on Black Mountain, without a way to get ahold of help.

"I don't know," Donnie says, summing up Marcus's thoughts as his chief deputy closes an empty closet door. "Seems dumb to pay a boatload for a room you don't use."

"Or . . . *calculated* . . . ," says an unfamiliar voice from behind, catching them all off guard.

Marcus turns to find a dark-haired man standing in the shadowed hall.

"I heard voices," this new stranger continues. "I hope you don't mind."

"No," Marcus says, surprised the man made his way up without any of them hearing him. And Marcus is about done with surprises. "If you're looking for a room, this one's taken. But I'm sure Torri, Ms. Lampley here, will be more than happy to help you down at the front desk." Marcus sweeps back his coat and gestures for Donnie and Torri to clear the room and head downstairs. Hopeful his tone, polite but serious, suggests to the stranger that he do the same.

That and the badge and holstered gun at Marcus's waist.

"Actually," the man says, ignoring the gun, not moving, "I'm here to see *you*, Sheriff Austin."

The man slowly, carefully, reaches into his coat and pulls out a credential wallet. He flips it open, revealing a small gold badge of his own, a bright shield crested by an eagle.

"I'm Agent Graham, FBI," he says, holding it high so both Marcus and Donnie can see it clearly. Then he smiles at Torri. "But I could very well need that room, ma'am. I might be here for a while."

19

Maggie catches the girl just a few yards off the porch, standing in the snow in stunned silence, hands covering her face, as if she not only doesn't know where she is, but can't even bear to look on it.

She left her blankets behind by the fireplace, wearing just those borrowed clothes . . . Landry's son's clothes . . . weak morning light filtering through the trees, illuminating her, stray snow twirling down around her shoulders.

Landry catches up a second later, but he hangs back, clearly unsure of what to do, so Maggie pushes her rifle into his hand and circles slowly around the girl until she's in front of her.

Maggie plants herself there, feet wide, arms outstretched, hoping to hold her in place and keep her from running for the woods again. But she doesn't grab her, doesn't touch her.

She doesn't know anything about kids, has never spent much time around them and never wanted or had any of her own—Vann wouldn't consider it, and given her own history and upbringing, Maggie couldn't imagine it—but Maggie does know what it's like to be angry, scared, and hurt.

Maggie saw the girl's scars and those bruises on her skin and knows how it feels to not want to be touched. How that dread feels like this thing you can't live with, yet the rage that follows feels like something you can't live without, because at least you know you're alive.

At least you feel something.

"Hey, hey, it's okay," Maggie says steadily, wondering if that's just the first of many lies she and Landry will tell this girl. "We found you, helped you. And that's all we're doing now."

The girl sways in place, so slender in her boy clothes, face still hidden by her hands.

"You were in an accident," Maggie continues. "A horrible, horrible, accident. I know you have a thousand questions, and so do we. But let's get you back inside where it's warm, where we can talk." Snowy silence settles over the three of them, and Maggie doesn't fight to fill it. She hopes Landry doesn't either.

Just give the girl a minute to breathe . . .

So many times, when things were at their worst with Vann, she just wanted, needed, a quiet moment to herself to think.

But the silence out here isn't empty.

Not just their shared breathing, or the wind, or even the distant snap and crack of snow and ice-caked tree limbs. But now, another sound, a . . . whisper . . . rustling and clawing at the edge of Maggie's consciousness.

The sound of a flock of birds beating their wings in time with her heartbeat . . .

She can't decide if it's emanating from the trees behind her, or somehow, the girl herself. And as if to answer, the girl lowers her hands, settling her two-color eyes on Maggie.

She's either been crying, or bleeding, or both. Maggie cleaned her off when they first got to Landry's cabin, but now fresh bloodied streaks course down her cheeks, her chin. Her whole face a frightening Kabuki mask, a horrifying crimson veil.

Bleeding from her eyes, Maggie thinks, trying not to gasp out loud. Oh my God, what's happened to her?

Landry hasn't moved off the porch yet, probably worried about spooking the girl, but seeing or sensing Maggie's reaction, he now steps forward, too, gripping her rifle tighter.

She stops him with a hand, trying to keep it from shaking, trying to compose herself.

"You're hurt. You're scared," she tells the girl, then hesitates, struggling with what to say next. "And I know what that's like. To feel like the best thing to do, the only thing, is run like hell and just keep on running until you're safe again. But I swear to you, you are safe here. We're not going to hurt you."

If Maggie's words are sinking in, striking home, it's almost impossible to tell. The girl's bloody face is impassive, red-rimmed eyes unblinking. So, when she does speak, it's such a jolt that Maggie nearly jumps out of her own skin.

"No one's safe," the girl says, her voice cracked, barely above the frantic whisper, that awful sonation Maggie imagined she heard a moment ago. "Not here, not with me, not *ever*."

The girl turns to walk back to the cabin, fixing that awful, bloody stare on Landry, who stands there, mouth open. "I don't want to hurt you," she says, still flat and emotionless, as cold as the air around them. "But I will. *I can*."

Then she walks past a stunned Landry into the darkened cabin.

20

When Marcus asked Agent Graham point blank if his sudden arrival in Pullens was due to their dead John Doe, the vanished M. Roby, or the mysterious missing plane, Graham looked surprised and asked—

"What plane?"

Sitting now in Marcus's too-hot office—Donnie making himself busy outside the door while still finding any reason to stare in and ogle—Graham says, "I truly don't know anything about a plane, but I can identify your John Doe, and probably fill in quite a bit about Roby for you. Obviously not her true name, but you already know that."

"I had my suspicions," Marcus says. "But I can't wait to hear this. Frankly, this whole thing's been a puzzle." He leans back in his chair, getting a better look at the man. "But honestly, I'm just as puzzled why *you're* here, Agent Graham. This is a local murder investigation, maybe a missing persons case, too, but neither worthy of federal attention. So, unless we're talking about a kidnapping, I can't imagine why any of it is an FBI matter at all. I sure didn't call for the cavalry . . . not yet anyway."

Marcus doesn't add that he never even got the chance to, the agent's lightning-quick arrival as unexpected, as sudden, as M. Roby's disappearing act.

But Graham simply smiles, a look that wears cheap on his face, almost drawn on. Marcus can't pin down his age, other than gray-flecked temples. He's clean shaven, not particularly tall, or heavy, or thin, or imposing. Not particularly . . . anything . . . really. He's appropriately dressed for the weather, with a dark cotton trail jacket over a thick henley and jeans, and, but for the badge and credentials he flashed—and his own leather-holstered gun—he could be a math teacher or an accountant out for a long ski weekend, not a federal agent. But as Marcus questions him, his plastic smile and pleasant but studied gaze tell a different story, give away the game.

Agent Carl Graham isn't used to being questioned and doesn't *particularly* like it.

"You're right, of course," Graham says, "all of it. Jurisdiction, local crimes. But I've been on that woman's trail for months, a significant criminal case that started in New York. She's been on the run, hiding, and I believe looking to disappear for good here in Pullens."

"On the run? Here? For what?"

Graham shifts in his seat. "Murder. *Kidnapping.*" He smiles again at his own little joke, if that's what it's supposed to be, then keeps ticking things off on his fingers, one at a time. "Embezzlement. Fraud. Conspiracy. RICO. Really, Sheriff, that's just the tip of the iceberg."

Marcus almost laughs at that. Graham makes it all sound so . . . serious . . . so ominous. This is Pullens, for Christ's sake. "Just how big is this iceberg of yours?"

Graham folds his hands in his lap, counting lesson over. "Let's say north of three hundred *million.*"

Marcus whistles at that. "All right, tell me what we're dealing with here."

And Agent Graham does.

21

With both Kellan and Lottie gone and his prostate problems flaring again, twice as bad, Walton's gotten into the habit of early to bed, early to rise.

Still, his sleep is too often uneven at best, an unsatisfying torture: a sliver of an hour here, a stolen minute there, the night broken by futile attempts to piss and bad dreams and—most recently—the sounds he's been hearing out in the woods, outside his door.

Whispering to him . . .

He hates the cold, empty side of the bed where Lottie used to sleep. Always on her side, her face always facing his. Her breath on him.

He gives up most mornings around four, just thankful to have another night over. At least the mountain can still be pretty at dawn, the sky catching unimaginable fire as the sun rises, the clouds full of smoke and embers, the tallest trees lit like matchsticks, piney tops aglow and burning. Not this morning, though. The sky's gunmetal gray, rotten and darkly curled at its edges like black ice. The mountain still holds last night close, like it doesn't want to let it go.

Maybe the mountain knows more than they do.

Walton lets Maggie get the girl settled again, while he gets her both coffee and water.

She ignores the coffee but greedily drinks the water as Maggie uses some of what's left in the old jelly jar to clean off her bloodied face for the second time.

There's no rhyme or reason for the crimson tears, still no obvious wounds.

A kind of stigmata, he thinks that's what it looks like. Although he isn't a religious man and never has been. And if she remembers any of those odd statements she made outside in the snow and cold . . . *I don't want to hurt you* . . . nothing in her demeanor now suggests it. It's as if they're dealing with two girls, the one from outside quickly locked away, hidden again.

But at least she's finally talking, her voice little more than a whisper, her eyes downcast.

She says she's fifteen or close to it and her name is *Luna*, but that doesn't ring a bell with Walton, nor evidently with Maggie. Getting answers from the girl is like pulling Jules Wallace's dogs out of that deep cave. There's a lot she either doesn't know or can't remember—maybe due to shock from the crash—or that she just won't tell them. The girl claims she was on a flight from Atlanta to . . . somewhere . . . a private charter arranged by someone named Dr. Jewell, and Luna's father, Leo. That name does seem to register with Maggie, who blinks at it but doesn't respond to Walton's obviously raised eyebrow, or pursue it with the girl.

She instead asks the girl how many people were on board.

"I don't know," the girl says. Her voice is still soft, damaged, like her throat's raw, like she's been yelling at the top of her lungs until she's hoarse, and maybe she has been. Maybe she was screaming the whole time as the plane went down, and like all of Walton's old memories of little Charlie Dance wandering alone in the Cranberry Wilderness, the idea is both unsettling and unforgettable.

"I don't know," the girl repeats, blinking again, before reaching for Maggie's arm, fingers digging in. "There's one, though. Roach."

"That's a name?" he asks, too loud, interrupting. He once knew a man named Harlan Bugg, but never a Roach.

The girl nods. "Did you find him?"

"It was . . . bad out there, Luna," Maggie says, struggling to convey just how bad. "I honestly don't know. We"—and she finally looks to Walton, including him—"believe you're the only survivor. I'm so, so sorry."

"Don't be," the girl says, with such fierce finality, such brutal honesty, it leaves Walton cold as the sky outside. The change in her is like a light switch, illuminating again for a moment the girl they saw out in the snow.

I don't want to hurt you . . .

But I will . . .

I can . . .

The girl continues, "Roach grabbed me. Trying to choke me, stop me."

"Maybe he was saving you," Walton offers. He read about a father who saved his daughter in a light plane crash in Michigan by hugging her close, least that's what the stories at the time claimed.

"He was *horrible*," she says, shuddering, as if still remembering this Roach's breath, his touch. "They all were."

Maggie makes a face that Walton assumes is supposed to be genuine, sympathetic. "Honestly, it's a miracle," she says. "I saw that plane, Luna. All the wreckage. I was shocked to find you alive in the middle of it, and I still don't know how it's possible. But I do know this . . . you must be one tough young woman." Maggie smiles, but the girl seems to shrink from the compliment. He can see how Maggie is picking her way ahead carefully with this strange girl, trying to understand what happened to her, what they're dealing with. He wonders if Maggie had kids of her own once, or still does, somewhere. "Do you have any idea what happened up there? Was the plane having trouble? Bad weather?"

The girl shakes her head. "It was me."

"What?" Walton asks, interrupting again, not sure he heard her right. "You? What does that even mean?"

She said this Roach character was trying to choke her . . . stop her . . .

The girl reaches for the coffee now, cradling it in both her hands. She stares deep into the dark liquid before taking a long sip, savoring it.

"I *wanted* the plane to crash," she says. "And it did."

22

"Her real name is *Mia*, Mia Rade." Agent Graham flips around an iPad he's produced from a messenger bag, laying it flat on Marcus's desk. "Husband, Vann Carter Rade."

"Neither mean anything to me," Marcus says, pulling the tablet closer, putting eyes for the first time on M. Roby—

Mia Rade.

He's not sure he ever had a concrete image of the woman in mind, but this isn't it.

This woman is dark haired, lithe, sheathed in a dark-blue or black single-breasted suiting blazer over cream pants and gold-strap high heels. A very tailored, very expensive look, although it's easy for Marcus to imagine her possessing a mile-wide closetful of similar clothes. Deidre owned two nice suits, and he could barely stretch to buy her those.

This woman looks like she stepped out of a perfect magazine spread. Not a woman driving a beater Nissan with New Jersey plates across West Virginia. Not even close to the woman Torri Lampley loosely described.

"Obviously, she's changed her hair color and style several times since this was taken," Graham says, reading his mind. "And this photo is several years old, too, included in a professional prospectus put out by her and her husband."

"A prospectus? For what? A business?"

"Exactly. Mrs. Rade and her husband were joint partners in an exclusive boutique financial services firm. Specialties included creative accounting and tax avoidance."

"Money laundering, you mean," Marcus concludes.

"Exactly," Graham says without hesitation. "Ms. Rade took her Harvard MBA to BlackRock Financial, where she first met Vann. He's a bit older than her, daddy figure, but they worked together well at BlackRock, made each other rich, became close, became intimate, before setting out their own shingle. She's something of a wizard with numbers, a real magician. She was the brains. He was more a pitch man."

"Used car salesman. I know the type," Marcus says, still studying Mia Rade's photo, trying to imagine either her or her husband in Pullens, and why. "But they wouldn't be the first rich people to help *other* rich people avoid taxes or hide their money." He slides the iPad back to Agent Graham. "That's six months in a low-security facility and a fine, maybe even a hefty one. But that's nothing. I watch the news."

Graham darkens the tablet with a touch. "Not just rich people, Sheriff. The Rades' select client list was primarily international, carefully curated, and highly discreet. The sort of clients who don't make the news . . . and are not interested in US legal remedies."

Marcus takes that in. "Drug dealers, then? Cartels?"

"Broadly," Graham answers, lighting the iPad again, now shuffling through a kaleidoscope of photos. "What do you know about cryptocurrency?"

"Again, only what I see on the news," he says, shrugging. "It's hard to be a savvy investor on a West Virginia sheriff's salary."

Graham laughs. "Honestly, I don't understand it all either," he admits, although Marcus suspects that's far from true. "Not the numbers, not like Mia Rade. Not even the crime itself, all the funneling and the embezzling. But the hiding? The *running*? Well, that I understand completely."

Over Graham's shoulder, Marcus catches Donnie shadowing the door for the third time now. Marcus waves him off. "So, they ran off with a bunch of someone else's money?"

Graham spins the tablet for Marcus's benefit. "In a manner of speaking. *A lot* of someone else's money."

The image now is a news article, more shiny pictures of the beautiful Mia, including her husband. Marcus glosses over most of it—Saint Kitts and Nevis . . . high-yield investments . . . crypto bubble . . . Ponzi . . . offshore . . . CambionXCG—focusing instead on Vann Rade.

He's a thick man who wasn't always that way, a man now wearing his wealth . . . someone else's money . . . everywhere. It's not just the suit, the watch, the haircut. It's his very *skin*, that perfect gold leaf tan, the slick extra weight from one too many steak and bourbon dinners fighting a winning battle against the once-a-week personal trainer. Too much time on a boat in the sun-drenched Caribbean or somewhere like it.

Marcus knows it's a cheap shot, the kind of quick-trigger judgment you should never make, more so if you carry a badge and a gun for a living, but he doesn't like Vann Rade.

He's also not the body they found in the snow outside the Big River Grill.

"Where'd the money go? What about him?" Marcus points at Vann's smiling news clipping.

"Vann Rade is *dead*, Sheriff Austin. Tragically. Suddenly. Unexpectedly. And unfortunately, according to the lone witness, his wife, he was also the only person on earth who knew where the money went. Thousands of crypto investors out their savings, many their *life* savings . . . not to mention a handful of exceedingly concerned foreign clients who found themselves shortchanged in the middle of very complex, very delicate, transactions."

"The cartels," Marcus says, and now, glancing again at the accumulated articles, he remembers this story. High-flying, high-society couple who defrauded little old ladies and widowers and pension funds. Echoes, too, of that blonde woman who started her own blood-drop company, the one they made all the movies and TV series about. Her downfall was even more public and dramatic, almost biblical, but even she didn't go on the run. "And Mia Rade was an accomplice in all that?"

"Accomplice . . . or mastermind?" Agent Graham shares a knowing shrug. "She was the numbers guru, after all. But she's always maintained she doesn't know anything about the money, just as she's steadfastly insisted that Vann's death was a mere accident."

"You think otherwise?"

"If I didn't, I wouldn't be here," Graham says. "Vann Rade was an extremely unpleasant individual, and Mia Rade wasn't . . . isn't . . . much nicer. She has a complicated backstory, to say the least. But fraud and embezzlement, even murder, aren't my only reasons for tracking her to Pullens, West Virginia."

"Then why?"

Agent Graham stands and stretches, staring out Marcus's window to the town and the mountains beyond, to gathered clouds and threatened snow. "To help her, Sheriff Austin. To protect her. Despite everything she's done, I'm here to save her."

23

"Bullshit," Landry says to Maggie as she stands outside with him for the second time this morning in the cold, shaking off the things the girl Luna told them. "That girl saying she crashed that plane. That she somehow killed them people on board."

"Sure, bullshit," Maggie says. "But *she* believes it. Or wants us to."

Landry's eyes narrow. "Do you?"

Maggie hugs herself, watching the trees. She doesn't know what sort of trees they are, but they're thick and close, old, and tall and gnarled, frosted silver with new snow. They're like Landry himself, implacable, looming over her. She doesn't want to believe anything. "This isn't my problem, remember? She's conscious and okay, I guess. More or less. So, I'm gone."

But she was bleeding from her eyes, Maggie . . . you can't say you didn't see that . . . you can't pretend that didn't just happen . . .

And that's not good enough for Landry either. Not anymore. "That's bullshit too," he says, all but pointing a finger at her. "You just going to up and leave now?"

"Yes, I am," she fires back. "Look, when she was going on about how no one is safe around her, all that weird shit? Maybe it's true, maybe it isn't. But you both are in real danger, grave danger, long as I'm here. That is *not* bullshit."

"Girl ain't even sure of her own age. Doesn't know her last name. How is that possible?" Landry changes tack. "What was that about her daddy?"

Maggie sighs, rubs her eyes. Her bare fingers are frigid, frozen, the dropping temperature working its way beneath her skin. She thought it was cold last night, but at least she was warmed for a while by the burning plane. If this ice storm really hits, she can't imagine how dark, how cold it'll be on the mountain. "I don't know anything about her father either. But I might've heard of him. Leo . . . Stier . . . or is it Stauder? Staller?" She and Vann moved in certain small, rarified circles, met only certain kinds of people. They were never friends or associates, just clients or accomplices. Victims or grifters. Assets or debts. "Owns some hush-hush biomedical firm in Atlanta. Big pharma . . . or something. Look, I just remember a lot of money at stake." But Maggie pauses, remembering other things, too, things she can't unsee from last night or again this morning, not long before she chased Luna out into the snow. She says it out loud, although it weirdly feels like sharing a secret. "Scars."

"Come again?"

"Luna, the girl. When I first found her out at the crash, I saw she had these . . . scars . . . all over her. Surgery scars. Significant ones. I saw them again when she was changing clothes. Bruises too." Maggie recalls all her own attempts to hide small scars, cover up fresh bruises.

"What the hell from?"

"Jesus," Maggie says, "I don't know. And unless you're a doctor now, what difference does it make?" Luna mentioned a doctor too . . . Dr. Jewell. "Just call this in again like you've been wanting to, tell everyone you found a survivor. We had a deal."

Landry nods in a solemn way that suggests he didn't hear a thing she just said or doesn't care. "You know, I been thinking on this all morning, on my long, lonely hike out there and back. Can't seem to quite get it out of my head. Not now, not since that girl finally spoke up."

"You don't have to share this with me. In fact, I really, really don't want you to."

Landry ignores her again, now watching the trees as well. "Last year before I gave up the badge, 'Demon' Tinsley lost his dog, Pie Crust, near Hagen's Point."

Maggie throws up her hands, laughing out loud, futile and frustrated. "This is ridiculous. Now *you're* making shit up."

"No," Landry says, "this is the Lord's own truth, and Demon's God-given name was actually *Ben*." He leans against the old, spotted planks of the cabin, doesn't seem anywhere near as affected by the razor-edged wind, the seeping cold, even as his breath hangs thick and white in the air between them. "But his mama was calling him her little demon from the moment he broke out of the womb. Boy grew into a man with a temper like an Ohio Blue Tip match, and had the rap sheet to prove it, near as long as my arm. Mostly penny-ante stuff, drugs and bad checks and breaking and entering and the like. But as much trouble as he could get up to and as mean as he often was, that dog of his, that old Aussie heeler? Well, she was sweet as she could be."

"Okay, I get it," Maggie says, resigned to hear him out. "Pie Crust."

"Yes, you do. Now, I'm partial to cherry myself, but my old chief deputy's wife makes a hell of a pawpaw pie. Damn good vinegar one too." Landry smiles at her. They both know he's holding her in place with his story and taking his own sweet time doing it. "Anyway, Demon's been laying low, dodging an active warrant out of Beckley. Haven't seen hide nor hair of man or dog for months. But then Pie Crust gets lost on Hagen's Point, and here Demon comes, stomping into my office, begging me to throw the cuffs on him. Says he'll do his time, even offers to double it for all the trouble he's caused, just long as I gather up some folks to find that animal."

"There's a point?" she asks, but already knows where Landry's going with this.

"That dog wasn't missing an hour, and Demon's in my face, hollering for a search party. Willing to go to jail, just to get her found." Now Landry drops the homespun, folksy facade. She's not even sure it is a facade, not fully. But he's all cop now, former or not. And she's dealt with numerous cops and agents in her life. "That plane out there's been crashed for what? Eight hours, more? A whole *plane*, Maggie, filled full of *people*, including that girl inside. And you don't find it . . . funny . . . least curious . . . there hasn't been a single report about it? The new sheriff here, Marcus Austin, he's green, no doubt about that. But he's also diligent, thorough, conscientious. A war hero. And if he'd heard something, anything at all, he'd be blowing up my phone right now. Hell, he'd already be here. So, no calls, no reports, no media, no forest service alert, no searches. Nothing. That just doesn't make any damn sense, particularly if that girl's daddy is important, and even less if he's got loads of money, like you say. Fact is, this should be all over the goddamn news, nonstop. Missing young white girls get found, you know that, and right or wrong, that's 'cause people always come looking." He pauses, letting that sink in deep, just like the cold. "You're so worried someone's out there looking for you? Then why the hell isn't someone worried about finding *her*?"

Maggie's got to admit, Landry's good. He's probably gotten his fair share of confessions, and who knows how many sins he's heard, or how many he still carries. But she also knows he's right about Luna. The apparent lack of a search for the girl or panic over the missing plane has crossed her mind, too, more than once. A dozen times. But all she can say is, "I don't know."

"Well, I know our so-called deal doesn't hold much water anymore. It *can't*."

"You can't stop me from leaving," Maggie says, keeping her voice low, serious. "Please, please, don't try."

"No, I reckon I can't. And I won't. But I also reckon I'm about tired of them idle threats. You really planning on shooting both of us now? Me and that girl?" Maggie stays silent, looking at her boots. "I want you to stay. I want you to help me until we can figure this out, until I get more help."

"No, not happening."

Landry sniffs, like he's smelling the air itself. His eyes are dark now, like ocean waves. "You do not want to hike into the teeth of this storm, and it is coming on all fours, mark my words. I can smell it, taste it, feel it in my bones. That sky is going to turn blue, black, then blizzard white. It'll be beautiful, and it'll kill you just as dead. This mountain will eat you, girl." He blinks, his sea-swell eyes softening a little. "Just . . . let me make another call, one more call, to someone I trust. Let me get an idea of what's going on here before you run off hell to leather. And I think you need to know just as much as I do. Hell, maybe more."

Maggie groans, frustrated and flickering like she's just swallowed one of those Ohio Blue Tip matches he was going on about. She's so irritated, conflicted, her skin's on fire, fury just below the surface. But some choices are like gravity, weighing you down, pulling you inexorably forward, until you're falling before you even know it. "I'm not some two-bit drug addict like your friend Demon. And that girl, Luna, isn't some missing dog."

"No," he agrees, "you're a serious woman in serious trouble. I get that. But don't think I don't got some blood on my hands too."

"Not like me, not the same," she counters.

"Blood's always red, Maggie. It's always the same."

Maggie shakes her head. "Do you just sit out here in the sticks and dream up a country parable or saying for everything?"

He flashes a thin, cryptic smile. "Stick around a little while longer and find out."

Maggie searches the sky, watches it change colors, the sun struggling to break above the smoke-gray clouds.

That sky is going to turn blue, black, then blizzard white. It'll be beautiful, and it'll kill you just as dead . . .

She says, "Dammit, make your call. We can check the weather, too, see if this storm's really coming or not."

"Oh, it's coming," Landry says. "No two ways about that."

Maggie brushes windblown hair out of her eyes. She's still not used to this color, this length. "So, what did happen to Demon? To Pie Crust?"

"Demon? Oh, he did his eight months over in Tygart regional jail, then got himself shot in a bar fight over in Morgantown, about a week after his release. A forty-five hollow-point to the heart and"—Landry snaps his fingers—"he was dead just like that, before he hit the ground. No time even for his life to flash before him, if you believe in that sort of thing."

She stares. "But . . . the dog? You found *her*, right?"

Landry's eyes are even softer now. Not gentle, but . . . sad. "No, we didn't," he says. "We looked high and low, though, with Demon . . . Ben . . . a grown man crying the whole time, like a little kid. Crying all the way to Tygart. Grief like that, well, it makes us all little kids again, I guess. Waking up for the first time to just how shitty and unfair the world can be."

He motions out to the woods, the crowded trees almost trembling beneath the snow in the air. "Sometimes things do get lost up here forever, Maggie, no matter how goddamn hard we look."

24

She knows they're outside talking about her, deciding what to do with her.

She's used to that.

She can almost *hear* their dark thoughts, all their bad feelings and fears. Hazy, weightless impressions, forever circling her.

. . . ben . . . jail . . . maggie . . . heart . . . grief . . .

She's not supposed to do this, to concentrate this hard. Dr. Jewell taught her that bad thoughts and feelings are like birds: we can't stop them from flying around us, but we don't have to let them nest in our heads. But when she's really scared or tired, when she's weak, or when she goes too long without Dr. Jewell's meds, those birds swell in number, grow too loud, too raucous, too insistent.

. . . things do get lost up here . . .

Black wings beating again and again.

She can't even hear herself think then, and the only thing that quiets them, or better yet drives them away, that keeps all those wild, dark thoughts from roosting behind her eyes, is *fury.*

The only thing that gives her peace sometimes is to set them free.

☾

They've gone quiet out there, listening for her now.

Wondering if she's sleeping, or hurt, or faking.

She could chance another run for it, like she did earlier, the way she's tried a dozen times before, but she has no idea where she is, and even a couple of minutes out there in the snow, out in the cold, out in the dark, were more than enough to remind her she won't get far.

She's trapped . . . again.

Not behind sterile white walls or hospital bars but a barricade of snow-whitened trees and rocky hills and deep ravines. A bleak, unforgiving sky. A wintry, frozen prison, as inescapable as Dr. Jewell's lab. And something else out there in the wilds too. A presence. Something she's never felt before, circling, circling, circling. Stalking. Something far older, so ancient, so massive, so monumental, she doesn't dare let it nest in her head.

It flies on bat's wings.

It's so strong it scares her. And although she's gotten so much stronger, too, this past year, so much so even Dr. Jewell finally understood she might not be contained, whenever the dark thoughts do overwhelm her, whenever she's forced hard to drive the black birds away, to really scream out in anger, the effort can still leave her weak, tongue tied, burned out. Helpless.

At least there are no constant cameras here, no monitoring day and night, no med regimen to quiet or calm or dull her. No Roach to sit close by with the gun he kept holstered beneath his left shoulder, just for her.

. . . it's okay, you're safe with me . . .

All it took was letting her guard down for one moment, letting one of his stray, dark thoughts alight on her. All she wanted was for him to stay away from her, to stop smiling his awful smile at her.

She wanted him—wanted them all—to crash and burn.

The last thing Roach said was her name before she told him to put the gun's barrel against his smiling teeth—

Luna . . . Luna . . .

She now sips the warm, bitter coffee the uncertain old man poured for her and lets it warm her, waiting for feeling to return to her cold hands, numb feet.

Waiting for her next best chance.

25

Donnie's trying to get an ear—again—on the conversation between Marcus and that FBI agent when his cell phone starts buzzing.

Reluctantly, he retreats to his desk and takes the call, surprised, relieved, to find Walton on the other end.

"Sheriff, damn good to hear you," Donnie says, and means it. "Now, I don't want to breathe a bad word about Marcus, not at all, but it's been a hellacious twenty-four hours. A hell of a lot for anyone to handle." He glances toward Marcus's office, lowers his voice. "Just saying . . . it might be nice to have an experienced perspective here . . . an old hand, as it were."

When Walton asks him to run it all down for him, not leave anything out, Donnie does.

Minutes later, just as Donnie's getting to Special Agent Carl Graham's sudden appearance at the Briar, Walton abruptly cuts him off, his voice echoey, distant. "This is important, Donnie. Is Marcus on his way out here again right now?"

"Oh no," Donnie answers. "No, that was last night, when he went up the mountain and got all turned around in the dark and hit a tree, or so he said to me. Before you called him back and told him there weren't no need anyhow. See, he was going to follow up with you later this morning when we were done with Ms. Torri. But then, you know, as I was just saying, the FBI showed up and—"

"FBI? For the plane?"

"No, don't think so. Still no word at all about that. Nothing. FBI guy didn't seem to know anything about it either." Donnie spins in his chair. "And Marcus did check. Seems the FBI's only here for that murder." Donnie tries not to make it sound like he's giving away secrets. He's glad to tell all this to Walton, though, to unburden it, figuring the sheriff still has a right to know about anything going on in Pullens or the Wolfe County Sheriff's Office, and that Marcus will probably tell him all this anyway. But he doesn't want Marcus to get all spun sideways if he finds out Donnie shared it first. "And when's the last time we had one of those? Poor guy gave up the ghost on the Big River's steps. Stabbed right in the old ticker."

Donnie makes a gesture toward his heart he knows the sheriff can't see.

"Just so I understand, Don, just so I'm crystal clear, you're telling me the FBI arrived this *morning* . . . for that killing *last night?*"

"Well, yes . . . no. I mean, I guess that is about the size of it." Whenever Walton calls him *Don*, Donnie knows he's serious, just like Marcus. And now that Walton's put it that way, saying it out loud like that, the agent's appearance and timing does seem a bit . . . off. "I mean, sure, the murder, or this woman we've been looking for, too, who Marcus thinks might know something about it." Donnie rolls awkwardly in his chair to steal another glance toward Marcus's office, where both men are still talking. "Honestly, Sheriff, I don't know much more than that. Marcus is jawing with the man right now behind closed doors."

Walton is silent on the other end. Silent like he's thinking hard on what to say next . . . or even harder on what *not* to say. Donnie adds, "So, what about that plane? You get out for another look? Find something?"

"Yeah," Walton says, reluctantly. "Looks like we might need to rustle up a real search, unfortunately."

Donnie whistles, low and slow. "Damn, now that is a shame. I'll let Marcus know soon as he's free. We'll get it all in motion."

A pause . . . until Walton says, "Or maybe just have him call me first?" More silence. Finally, "How's Roberta doing?"

Donnie smiles to himself. "Same as always. Sour first thing in the morning but sweetens up as the day wears on. Just like sun tea." He laughs. "She whipped up a mess of her cathead biscuits, so you know, it's all good."

"And I bet you still got a sack of 'em right there on your desk."

Donnie eyes the heavy bag weighing down a pile of empty folders. "You know it." And as much as he appreciates Walton asking after Roberta, he gets the sense the sheriff's marking time, like he's making up his mind on something. All these weird questions, the weirder silences after. Walton's never been one to hold his tongue about anything, but it reminds Donnie of those dark weeks after Kell disappeared, when it was hard to pry a word out of him.

"Say, you okay, Sheriff?" Donnie desperately doesn't want to press, to push, but he's concerned, wonders what's going on, what he might be missing. Wonders, too, if this is how Marcus felt last night, and that's why he headed into the mountains alone. Not that he was so worried that Walton was drunk and out of his head, but that Walton was stone-cold sober and still acting this way.

"Anything else I can do?" he asks. But he only gets another mute beat, not a *yes*, but not a *no* either. "If you want, I can run there right now and beat them bushes with you. Honestly, probably should, before the storm smacks us."

His questions are followed by more of that unnerving silence, this time so long Donnie Kornblue can almost count it out like that country song about counting down shots of whiskey.

Until Walton finally says, "You know, I think I could use a hand, if you're willing to check on a few things for me, before heading this way? Now, if you can't break free, I understand, I truly do. I don't want you getting sideways with Marcus . . . Sheriff Austin. Or Roberta."

"No, no. We're all good," Donnie says, mostly relieved, although all that quiet on the other end still hangs heavy between them, like the sheriff's still weighing something out over there.

Walton's never been one to be indecisive either.

"Fine," Walton says, "that'd be a big help then. A really big help. Grab a pen to jot a couple things down. And let's make sure you save some of them biscuits for us too . . ."

26

Landry doesn't say anything to Maggie for several minutes after ending his call with his former deputy.

He stares stubbornly at the Iridium before handing it to her, then silently busies himself in the small, earthy kitchen ripe with old leather and rough wood and stale coffee grounds, the whiskey or moonshine or whatever it was he was drinking earlier.

Briskly moving unused plates and coffee mugs and tumblers from the counter to the standing sink to the counter again in a futile attempt to make some sense of what's happening, to impose some sort of order.

Ignoring her.

Maggie recognizes those empty gestures, all that wheel-spinning futility. Vann used to call it "shuffling deckchairs on the *Titanic*," and in the end, when the dark water was rising around them both, that's all she felt like she was doing every day: going through the motions, keeping up appearances, smiling and lying in a failed bid to hold it all together, even as the boat—their life, her life—foundered and sank below the waves.

A storm I caused, she thinks, and my boat wasn't the only one that went down.

Luna is perched again on the couch watching the fire Landry kicked up before he reached out to Deputy Donnie in Pullens. If she was paying attention to the call, there's no sign of it, although Maggie's caught her stealing glances their way, those bicolor eyes reflecting curiosity, concern, flames.

I wanted *the plane to crash* . . .

"What do you know about the FBI?" Landry asks. She heard it all the same as he did when he spoke to the deputy—Landry holding the phone so she could listen in, their heads pushed together, nearly touching—but isn't sure she has the kind of answers he wants, even less sure he wants to hear the ones she does have. "Is that who you're running from," he continues, rubbing at a coffee mug with a dish towel, "the FBI?"

"It's more complicated than that."

He blinks slow like he's trying to bring her into focus, see her again for the first time. "Then why don't you make it real easy for a dumb backwoods hick like me."

"No," she says, ignoring his sarcasm. For all his homespun affectations, Landry's no country bumpkin, and he's not good at playing dumb. "I can't."

"Try hard," Landry fires back, gripping the mug until his knuckles go white. "Or how about that dead man on the street? Your handiwork too?"

"He was going to hurt me," she says. "He was *hunting* me. And I have no idea how he found me." And she still doesn't, not given all the precautions she took, all the contingencies she made. She spent years preparing for this. In some ways, her whole life, only to have it all come undone in a matter of hours. She should've abandoned Black Mountain when they caught up to her in Pullens, but she was already too invested, out of options and alternatives, the dark water already too high. She was lucky to escape there, just barely, holding out hope that everything she'd put in place, everything she'd long set into motion, would still allow her to slip away one more time.

But that was before the plane, the girl, and now this angry old man.

"Does he have a name?" Landry asks, not bothering to wait for a reply. "Was he a fed too? Any kind of cop?"

She laughs, bitter. "No, not even close." Although Maggie understands that Landry's calculus about her changes significantly if he believes she's running around killing cops in Pullens or anywhere else. He carried a badge too long to turn his back on that, and he won't. "I don't know. His name isn't important, probably bullshit, would be an alias anyway. He isn't important."

"I doubt that. But everything with you is a big ole secret, isn't it," Landry asks, but it's not really a question. He regards her, mug still in hand. "Too complicated to explain, too dangerous to share. Yet you're damn sure all the sudden about this man you put a knife into."

"He *was* dangerous . . . a killer."

"Seems to me, so are you, Maggie," Landry says with a shrug. Now quieter, "So are you."

"I had to," she says.

"And my experience is most people who say they *had* to are just looking to square something they were *going* to do anyway." Landry finally puts the polished mug down, flashing an eye-catching logo on the side, an enigmatic black wraith with a red face and yellow eyes set against an outline of West Virginia, the words HOME OF THE FLATWOODS MONSTER scrolling above. "How many others?"

Again, she doesn't know how to answer that. "I hope the last," is all she says.

Landry nods, not agreeing, but because he clearly never expected any better answer. "How many others like that one are still on your trail?"

"As many as it takes to find me."

Landry blinks, the first time she's seen something like real concern or worry cross his face. "Well, that deputy, Donnie Kornblue, is a good man. A man with a wife, and I've known both for thirty years." Landry crosses his arms. "Roberta sent him out this morning expecting him to come home tonight, and so do I. Asking for his help likely means getting him sideways with Sheriff Austin, and it absolutely means putting him dead in the middle of . . . *this*"—Landry raises a weathered hand, gesturing first at Luna, then at Maggie—"whatever this turns out to be. But neither of you are leaving me many good options here. So, guess I kind of had to . . . too."

"Don't you dare put this on me," she says, fighting to lower her own voice again. "Because you can put her in your truck right now and drive her to town and hand her over to the *real* authorities. You can still wash your hands of both of us."

"Maybe," he counters, "but I won't, probably for all the reasons you haven't immediately lit off again either." He points toward the front door. "Despite all your warnings, your threats, you're *scared* of what's out there, and look, you have every good reason to be. You don't know what you're walking into anymore, don't know the lay of the land now, if you ever thought you did." He leans close. "Last night blew it all to hell, and I'm not just talking about some damn plane. You say you're pretty good with numbers, but the odds are tilting against you, aren't they? And there's no way you ever counted on her . . . or me."

"Now you're going to tell me we need to count on each other?" She rolls her eyes. "No, that's too easy."

"I'm telling you I tried grabbing a tail number off that plane and couldn't find one. Sure, it was too dark, too much wreckage. But I had no trouble finding *this* . . ." He raises his Carhartt flannel, revealing the grip of a scorched gun. Seeing it leaves cold fingers on her neck, the way Vann used to put his thick hand there, gripping, squeezing until her eyes watered, whenever he wanted to make sure she was paying attention.

I told you . . . he'd say . . . *I fucking told you . . .*

"Yours?" Landry asks, and she shakes her head *no*. She never thought to check Landry after he went out to the plane, never thought to pat him down. He could've pulled that gun on her anytime, even now, but he just drops his shirt, hiding it again.

It's not like he's putting a hand to her neck, but he's making sure she's listening to him now.

"Donnie said he and Marcus still haven't got any word on a lost plane. So, we got a plane no one is missing, and a girl no one is looking for." He lowers his voice. "A girl you say has been all cut up, operated on. Who in the hell would do such a thing? Why would they do it? Surgery or no, it's clear she's not entirely well." He gently taps the side of his head. "And we both can agree on that. So, was she kidnapped . . . or is she on the run? A victim . . . or something else? Whatever's going on, she's rightly scared, too, and I want to know *why*. I want to know exactly what the hell is going on in my town and on my mountain. I want to know what *I'm* walking into . . . just like you do . . . before I just start handing her over to anyone."

Maggie recognizes Landry could as easily be talking about handing *her* over. But he didn't breathe a word about her when he was on the phone with Deputy Don, and knowing now he's been armed all along, she's not sure it had anything to do with her standing over his shoulder, listening in.

"You still didn't need to bring your deputy friend out here."

"I got to secure that plane crash and deal with this girl. And when you do bolt, I got to see you off, make sure you get free and clear and don't bring any more of your trouble down on my head, or find the need to hurt anyone else just to cover your tracks. All in all, I reckon another pair of friendly eyes and ears ain't a bad thing. For both of us."

That's a lot of *got to's* and *have to's*, but she doesn't throw them back at him. "You're worried about that FBI agent in town."

"Shouldn't you be?"

She lets that hang between them. "Do you think he's here for me . . . or her?" Maggie looks to Luna, who is still curled by the fireplace, eyes now closed.

"I have no idea. You?" Landry asks.

Maggie takes up the mug he was scrubbing, staring into the eyes of the cartoon monster. Back in Pullens, back at that inn, there was a book in her room about West Virginia myths, rural folklore. She imagines Landry's got a thousand such stories always at the ready, like the one about dead "Demon" Tinsley and his lost dog, Pie Crust.

He said something about noises out in the dark last night, and it's clear he doesn't want her on the mountain on her own. Not only because he's worried about her running headlong into hikers or cops or rangers or federal agents, but because he's afraid *for* her.

For the first time, she wonders if Landry's not entirely well, either, getting senile.

If being alone out here has gotten into his head.

"My real name is Mia," she says, setting the mug down. "And I don't think that man in Pullens asking all those questions is any kind of real FBI agent at all."

27

He wants to wait and move again under the cover of darkness but won't have the chance.

She's awake now, too, alert.

He hears her out there, oh so faint, oh so far away.

Her idle thoughts gnaw and scratch and scrabble at the inside of his ruined skull, clawing like a flock of birds to escape. Her whispers are like grit or dust, like salt or sand, getting into everything. Not loud enough to silence the mountain, nothing can do that now, but always there all the same. Consistent, insistent, persistent.

She's a stitch in his side, a thorn in his paw, a needle in his eye, a knife in the heart.

He smells her on the cold wind, can track her. The mountain will show him the best way, all the pooling little shadows and dark hollows, the hidden lees, the briary passages.

He'll move beneath the mountain's skin like hot blood.

He crawls into the morning over a pile of bones, and what little sun there is burns his night-sensitive eyes, so he keeps them closed tight. He tells himself he doesn't need them now, not all the time.

He sits on his scorched haunches like an animal, picking at his skin, scenting.

Despite the distance, he can breathe her in, chew on her. Now that he's free of the cave, her thoughts are clearer, although she can't sense him yet. She's strong but unfocused and doesn't have the mountain's help. There are others with her, though.

He tastes their fear, too, the dread palpable and bloody and metallic between his teeth. They move around her like bluebottle flies buzzing in constant circles, and when he finds her, he'll swat them away, snap at them, swallow them whole.

He doesn't have to control his rages anymore. Doesn't have to pretend *anything*.

He stretches and lets the cold caress him. The air is good on his blackened skin, exposed bone. He shakes, and the winter wind takes what's left of his hair, blowing it down the mountain like loose thistles. Yesterday, when he still cared about such things . . . *when I was still human* . . . he kept his thick blond hair slicked back with Baxter of California hair pomade. Now, his naked skull is shiny and slick, natural, and unadorned. Probing with ragged nails, he finds his skull is longer, shovel-shaped, feral.

The old mask is gone for good.

But a part of him, a part deep and untouched and still clinging to what little humanity he had before the crash, nearly recoils.

I am dead.

I died in that plane, in the fire, in the crash, and none of this is happening or is real. This can't be real. I shot myself in the head, and this is my sick mind dying.

This is hell.

But that small voice is just as quickly overwhelmed by her skittering thoughts, drowned out, too, by the mountain's serenade, a chamber orchestra of wind and cold and snow.

No, I've been given a great gift. And if this is hell, then there are worse places . . .

I'm finally free . . .

He doesn't know whether to laugh or cry, so he just howls and then he's on the move.

He runs, chasing the wind.

28

Lying on the slab at Kohr & Red Mortuary on the eastern edge of Pullens, the dead man's no different this morning than last night, except now he has a name.

Three names, in fact—

Ivan Kruger. Carlos Botero Lutz. Weiland Theroux.

Agent Graham admits there may be others, even dozens, but those are the three he knows.

Marcus is starting to wonder if *anyone* involved in this thing is who they say they are, and when he muses that out loud—just before sliding Kruger or Theroux or whoever the hell he was back into the mortuary's small freezer—Graham just laughs.

Marcus didn't think it was all that funny, and he wasn't trying to be.

Minutes later, after he's done with the dead man for the second time, Marcus warms up his truck again as Graham paces outside Kohr & Red, making calls.

Graham keeps looking to the sky as if the agent expects the clouds overhead to rip open any moment, dump a fury of snow on them. News reports still say it's coming, and despite what the agent told Torri Lampley about keeping a room, he probably doesn't want to get snowed in, courtesy of the Wolfe County Sheriff's Office.

If Mia Rade isn't here anymore, there's no need for Graham to be here either.

When he finally slides into Marcus's truck, slipping his cell back into his coat pocket, he says, "I'll have someone claim the body."

"Good." That means less paperwork for Marcus, frees him from ordering an autopsy—mandatory in any homicide—or worrying about getting the dead vic transported to the state police in this weather. "You say this Theroux guy was a—"

"A problem solver, a specialist, hired by some of Vann and Mia Rade's clients." Graham studies the mountains. "Clients exceedingly desperate to know what happened to their money, and willing to expend even more to find out. Clients who now believe, rightly or wrongly, that Mia Rade is key to that. That man in there wasn't the first to come looking, Sheriff Austin, and, until I find her, won't be the last." Graham flicks a knowing look at Marcus's covered leg. "Many vets are finding such work, selling their skills to the highest bidder."

Marcus doesn't know what to say to that, or what Graham's implying. Duly elected county sheriff is a far cry from hired gun or mercenary, even in a small town like Pullens. Although maybe Agent Graham doesn't see a whole lot of difference. "Did you serve?"

"No," Graham says. "Law school, Notre Dame, then straight to the Bureau. I appreciate your sacrifice, though. I've worked with rangers before . . . although I understand you were quite highly *specialized* too."

Marcus turns in his seat, the truck warming around them. "You run a background on me?"

"I did, although much of it's redacted. A lot of black ink, even for someone with my clearances."

"Trust me, not as sexy as it reads, even if you could read it." Marcus watches snow twirl down, flakes the size of pennies. Little snow, big snow. The promised storm does seem to be picking up. "But honestly, why look at all?"

Graham shrugs. "My job to know who I'm dealing with. Like yours."

Marcus doesn't buy it. "No, you were fishing to find out if I had any direct connection to that dead man in there . . . or your Rade woman."

Graham shrugs a second time, smiles, caught. "I'm trying to understand why Mia Rade ended up in Pullens. Her history is . . . unusual . . . but there's nothing in it to suggest any connections here at all. If she's getting local help, I don't see it." Now it's Graham's turn to count the flakes, to stare up at the cold, gloomy skies again. "These clients I mentioned aren't only interested in their lost funds, although that's not an insignificant consideration. You see, when Rade disappeared, she was already in preemptive negotiations with us, offering to trade everything she knew about her less-reputable clients for reduced sentencing and witness protection. That woman is carrying a lot of dangerous and valuable secrets in her pretty head, the least of which might be the whereabouts of missing money."

"If she was cooperating with you, helping the FBI, then why up and run?"

Graham looks at him. "Now, that's the several-hundred-million-dollar question, isn't it?"

Marcus figures it is. "Okay, what next?"

Graham considers. "Ask ourselves what her options truly are now. Theroux caught up to her here, made his move—"

"Yeah, that didn't turn out so well," Marcus interjects.

"No, it did not. And I have no doubt killing him and leaving his body in public was *not* part of the plan. But she didn't pick Pullens on a whim. She doesn't work that way."

"What you see is what you get," Marcus says, waving at the quiet snowy town, the pine-clad mountains rising in a dark ring around them. "A whole lot of nothing."

"Why'd you come back then, Sheriff?"

Marcus hesitates, stalling, not comfortable admitting to the FBI agent that *nothing* is exactly what he wanted when he returned to these mountains. "Peace, quiet, solitude." He points out the now breath-fogged windshield, north, east, west. "Pullens is surrounded by a million acres of empty wilderness. National forests, federal preserves. You go any direction, and soon enough you're falling off the face of the planet."

"Cell service that bad?"

"Ten miles outside of town it's hit or miss. A mile beyond, it's a swing and a miss altogether." He describes Green Bank's big telescope, the NRQZ. "It's like a hole in the world out there."

Graham takes it all in. Asks, "Know how many people go missing a year, Sheriff?"

"Too many, probably."

Graham nods. "Half a million people just up and . . . vanish. Sure, a lot of those just up and walk away from their miserable lives. But many more drop through that hole in the world in the kind of woods just like those surrounding Pullens. It's so easy to walk into the trees, turn around, disappear." Graham retrieves his phone, scrolls through it. "If you really wanted to get lost, fall down a dark hole, there are few better places."

"Oh shit, the *plane*," Marcus says, all but snapping his fingers. "The damn plane. Walton's plane."

Graham seems unimpressed. "You mentioned that earlier, but there aren't any missing flights. I checked all the local and regional airports before arriving here. I checked them twice."

"I know, I did too. Nothing last night, nothing this morning either. But Walton Landry, former sheriff, swore he heard a plane flying low over the Cranberry Wilderness. Thought it might've gone down near Black Mountain, where he holes up."

"The mountain? Someone lives out there?"

"He has a cabin, like a family hunting lodge, held together with dual fuel generators and a handful of solar panels. Probably not even legal. Hell, I know it's not legal. But Walton was a law unto himself here for a long, long time. Untouchable. Something of a local legend." For reasons Marcus can't explain, he doesn't admit to Graham that he tried to drive out to see the old man last night. Doesn't admit to the thing he saw in the woods. "Look, he's old, senile, and definitely likes the bottle. But he sure seemed certain last night, least at first. Only to call later to say maybe he had it all wrong. Cells really don't work out that way, but he has a forest service radio. And a satellite phone."

Graham stares at Marcus hard, unblinking. "Could you land a plane there?"

"I'm . . . not sure," Marcus answers honestly, shrugging off a fleeting vision of night clouds and roaring wind and desert sand, pinpoint city lights far below. He's jumped out of both planes and helicopters but has never flown either. There's a moment when you first push free from the jump door when you're terrifyingly weightless, almost ephemeral, lost in the air, heart in your throat. It hammers away, ringing in your ears, as you count each beat, falling. He never wants to experience that again. "Hard for me to imagine, though, unless you put it down on a road, and there aren't many of those, not paved anyway. Even fewer straight enough. It's all thick tree cover and gravel and mud switchbacks." Marcus remembers his own truck levered into that snowy ditch. "Maybe it's not impossible, but it's damn close."

"Helo?"

"Less impossible," Marcus concedes.

Graham nods, rapid-firing a message on his phone. Marcus watches him type, wonders who he's notifying or giving orders to. Asks, "You think Mia Rade tried to fly out of here?"

Graham keeps typing. He must have a partner, a team, somewhere, but it begs the question why he arrived alone, and leaves Marcus wondering if *he* should ask for another look at the man's badge, or maybe make a call of his own to whoever Graham answers to. But the agent finally glances up, replies, "Your former sheriff heard something last night, and Rade is MIA this morning. I'd say it's worth a look."

For what seems like the hundredth time, Marcus surveys the sky, how the snow is holding the morning light close. It's too dark out there, getting darker. "Look, we don't want to get caught up at Walton's when this storm breaks over us. I'll call him, let him know—"

"Let's not do that," Graham says, cutting him short, a tone that suggests it's not even close to a suggestion.

"Why?" Marcus tries to read Agent Graham's eyes, what looks like fresh, cold calculation there. Suspicion. "You really believe Walton Landry is *helping* this woman?"

Graham hides his phone away again. "You suggested the man's got a very personal sense of the law . . . of right and wrong." Graham says it from behind that sterile, plastic smile of his, reminding Marcus of winter at the beach, barren boardwalks and deserted sands. "Best-case scenario, they've never met, didn't know each other until last night, when something happened out there on that mountain. Maybe her little disappearing act worked . . . or more likely, it didn't. The plane or helicopter she chartered malfunctioned, crashed, leaving her a damsel in distress, lost in the woods. *His* woods. He found her, or she found him, told him a sob story, or she didn't bother telling him anything at all. Mia Rade can be very convincing, very charming when the situation calls for it. She's adept at changing her colors. Play it out any number of ways, but it all comes down to this . . . is he the type of a man who'd help someone like that, no questions asked?"

Marcus replays Walton's odd calls last night, all his strident dealings with the man for the twenty-four months before that.

The stories Donnie still shares about him.

It's just he doesn't like much of anyone. Out there, out in the dark, it's easy to get confused . . .

"Yeah, he's exactly the type," Marcus admits, and then angrily slams the big Dodge into gear before Graham even tells him to.

29

With Marcus and the FBI agent over at the mortuary, Donnie's free to run NCIC, NamUs, and a few other database checks Walton asked him for, including an ATF eTrace query on a gun serial number.

Walton didn't go into *why* he wanted these things and didn't say out loud that Donnie needed to keep them all under his hat, but Donnie got the message loud and clear anyway.

He doesn't like keeping secrets, but long as Marcus is joined at the hip with the fed, it's probably for the best. It's not that *he* doesn't trust FBI agent Graham; it's just that he trusts Walton's gut instincts more, and Walton's hackles are up.

Back in the summer of '21 they rode over to Coalton to serve an outstanding warrant on Forrest Gantry, and even before they got out of Donnie's truck, Walton told Donnie to get on the horn and call for backup. Walton took just one look at Forrest's rusty trailer shadowed by bent pines, smelled something on the hot breeze that day—that summer was twice as hot as hell—or spied a furtive movement or caught a glimpse of a shadow or maybe even saw a ghost lurking around the trailer's tinfoil and broken mini-blind-covered windows, and he just *knew* that Forrest was still reeling from a twenty-four-hour meth- and fentanyl-fueled bender.

Knew Forrest was lurking in there with two loaded shotguns, seeing all kinds of bad ghosts himself.

Instead of walking up and knocking on the door, likely getting both sawed in two by Forrest's old Remington over/under, Walton instead had them hang back by the truck until some support arrived. All the while, Walton went on talking up Forrest through the bullhorn, telling him another of Walton's endless stories, suggesting he fix himself up a frozen pizza and take a damn drink of Johnny Drum and cold cola and calm himself down.

Told Forrest about hunting whitetail on Black Mountain's western face with his boy, Kellan, and that he knew just how badly Forrest missed his own young son, Colt, who Trudy Gantry hauled up to Beckley to stay with her mom, 'cause Forrest had gotten so strung out and violent.

Walton stood there exposed and defenseless in that infernal summer sun, hat in hand, and just . . . talked . . . even as Clarksburg PD SWAT quietly took up positions in the trees around the trailer. He talked until the afternoon shadows got thick and long and twisty, and the mountain took on that smell it does when the sun starts to go down, all wet moss and black loam and dark flowers blooming. He talked until he was hoarse and tongue tied, his left side numb, and didn't *stop* talking until Forrest came out of his own accord, tossing both scatter guns on the ground, hands up high above his head.

Those are the sort of instincts Walton's always had, call it his gut or his intuition or a sixth sense. Roberta claimed he had the second sight, and one time, deep in his cups, Walton hinted it was the mountain talking to him, telling him things. But it was always just Walton's way of *knowing* . . . knowing when to stop, look, listen. Knowing when things were sour or the air itself didn't smell right. Knowing when a bad situation might be talked down, or when no amount of jawing was going to make a damn bit of difference.

And if Walton feels something's off about this FBI agent, well, that's a feeling Donnie would be a fool to ignore.

It's saved his life more than once.

☽

He can't make heads or tails of the information he's turned up, but after twenty minutes, he prints out what he's got, shoves it in an old accordion folder, and, a few minutes after that, is rolling out past the Big River and the Briar under heavy, busy skies the color of a cat's-eye marble, heading toward Black Mountain in what's become a thick, driving snow.

It'll be a race to beat the storm.

One of the files Walton asked Donnie to check was the "Peerless fugitive report," even asked him very specifically to check it twice, and although it took a bit to puzzle that out, it finally came to him. There is no such thing. But the Wolfe County Sheriff's Office issues only one kind of handcuffs, stock Peerless chain-links with a nickel finish. Walton should have an old set lying around his cabin somewhere, but it seems he wants more . . . at least *two* other pairs.

Both sets now tucked deep in the accordion folder, hidden by the fresh printouts.

Donnie has no idea what Walton's got himself into up the mountain, or how—or even *if*—it ties back to FBI agent Graham. But he can't leave the sheriff up there alone, storm be damned.

Marcus's truck isn't parked over at the mortuary anymore, but Donnie doesn't try to raise him on the radio. Once he's well on his way, and just before cell service gets sketchy out by the Hanging Rock Trailhead, he'll fire off a text to Marcus, letting him know what he's up to.

He really doesn't like keeping secrets . . .

But by then, it'll be too late for Marcus to summon him back.

30

Walton doesn't have TV or internet out at the lodge, not even a computer.

He can tell Maggie . . . Mia . . . doesn't believe him, but it's true.

Since moving out to Black Mountain full time, he's never seen the need for it. He gets all the news he cares for when he grabs a pastrami and rye for lunch once a month at Roy's Diner in Pullens or heads into Beckley for the odd supply run.

Out here he's got Kell's Iridium, his old cell phone—doesn't even get halfway-decent service until he's out on the road headed down the mountain—and his forest ranger Motorola LMR two-way, which without full-time dispatch isn't much more reliable than his cell and suffers from numerous dead spots as well. Last night, after he first heard Luna's plane crash, he got a half hour of static and frustrating silence from the LMR while trying to raise a ranger.

Even that old shortwave is pretty much for show now. He hasn't lit it up in years.

Most of the time he has little more than candle or gas lamp light, conserving the small amount of juice he gets off his generator and the off-grid solar panel system Kell helped him install.

He spends too much time in near darkness.

When Maggie asks him what he's supposed to do when there's an emergency—like right now, she adds—he tells her he just makes do. Most of the time, out here in the wilderness, out in the dark, that's all you can do.

He also tells her since he met her as a Maggie, he's going to keep right on calling her that. It just seems more natural to him, like everyone always calling Ben Tinsley "Demon." Sometimes a name just fits better, fits right, like the worn stock of a hunting rifle or an old flannel jacket. Whatever this other woman Mia did, whoever she was before she showed up on his mountain, that's in the past. And for now, he's still willing to try and put that past behind them both, if she is.

Maggie seems genuinely relieved at that.

☾

The girl is a different story.

Walton pulls a chair up close to her, arms on his knees, hands laced together like he's praying.

"I know you're awake over here," he says. "I know you been listening to us this whole time. It's not polite to pretend otherwise. Without that nice woman over there, you'd be froze dead, like a Popsicle. Without me, you would've both ended up as ice pops."

As if on command, the girl opens her eyes, and Walton is struck by just how weird, how beautiful, they are. Each is different, mysterious, pretty. In the darkened cabin, they almost glow, like the tapetum lucidum sheen of a big wolf's stare. Bounties were paid out on gray wolves in West Virginia throughout the 1800s, with the last recorded gray gunned down by hunters in Randolph County in 1897. But once upon a time, there wasn't a corner of West Virginia where wolves didn't run, breed, hunt. For a while, Kell was involved with Fish and Wildlife to relocate some North Carolina red wolves into the Monongahela, but nothing came of it before he disappeared.

The girl's eyes, fixed hard on him, are imposing. A wolf's stare. If she was in shock or overwhelmed or scared before, there's no sign of that now.

Her eyes stalk his own, like she can see right through them, right inside his head.

"But . . . I guess it ain't so polite to talk about someone like they're not here either," he continues. "So, here's the thing, as I see it. We need to get you off this mountain, get you home, wherever home is. But Maggie over there's got a bit of trouble on her hands, and although it's got nothing to do with you, it does rightly complicate things for all of us. Folks are going to have questions, they're going to want answers, about what's happened up here. When we do get you to town, your story, the *only* story, is that I found you on my own. That's all you can or need to remember, no more, no less. Deal?"

The girl flicks those wolf eyes toward Maggie, standing with her arms crossed, then nods.

"But I still gotta ask," he says, pushing ahead, "if you know why the FBI might already be here poking around? Maybe something your daddy's involved in, or something or someone on that plane? Maybe this Roach character you talked about?" Walton waits for a reaction but doesn't get one, the girl's face stoic behind her eyes. "Or is this all just about *you*, girl?"

"I don't know." Her voice is a whisper.

He presses. "You're going to have to do better than that. How come no one's tearing up this mountain looking for you? Where are they? What kinda man puts his own flesh and blood on a plane no one else seems to know about, flies her around under the cover of darkness, and then . . ." And then Walton trails off, not even sure what he's suggesting. He doesn't want to badger this poor, delirious girl, but every attempt to conjure an answer that makes any damn sense, to see beyond her magical eyes—one wilderness green, the other mountain gray—brings him right back to that burning plane wreckage, body parts strewn in the snow, and her standing outside the cabin, blood sheeting down her face.

"A bad man," Luna says, ignoring Walton, focusing instead on Maggie.

"Is he *hiding* you?" he pushes. "Is that what's going on here? What about your mama?" The thought has occurred to him that the girl might be caught in an ugly tug-of-war between parents. He saw it time and again while serving a hundred Wolfe County warrants over the years over child custody issues. The scale and means here are different: this girl's daddy might have plenty of money, but the impulse is the same, estranged parents and ex-spouses fighting tooth and nail because they love their kids so much, or because they hate each other even more.

"I don't know her," the girl says. "I just don't."

But Walton also knows sometimes the relationship between a son or daughter and a parent can be just as complicated, even more so if one isn't around all the time or not in the picture at all. That's a heart-size hole to throw a lifetime of love and anger into, hope and expectation and disappointment. Growing up is already a struggle between fear and freedom, a push and pull as timeless as the tides, and just as strong. Least that's the way it was between Walton and Kell, and Walton was *always* around, ever present, demanding, overbearing.

Walton talked and talked but never about anything that mattered, never about the darkness . . .

Lottie warned Walton he was suffocating Kell, until his boy showed him just how much.

"Sorry to hear that, I am," Walton says, and he means it. "I'm asking because you're gonna get asked this all over again soon enough. So, just like we need to get our story straight here, you might want to get your story straight too." Now the girl's eyes really do glimmer, awareness arising. "That's right, you understand. There's a plane full of dead people that no one's rightly looking for yet, that no one's even come to claim, except for maybe one lone FBI agent. That's suspicious enough and hard to explain, but then . . . there's you." He reaches out, pats her crossed leg beneath his blanket, as she jerks back hard from his touch. "Young girl, apparent survivor, sole survivor, whose only explanation is that *she* crashed her daddy's plane. Now, I'm willing to chalk that up to fear, to shock, to trauma. Hell, I'm willing to forget I heard it at all . . . if you're willing to forget our friend Maggie over there too. Either way, though, I reckon you better square up nicely what you're going to say, if not to us, then to them."

"They hurt me," she says, getting louder, growing agitated.

"I gather that. Someone has hurt you bad, I don't doubt it. Maggie saw the scars. I can't imagine anyone doing that to you, much less why. But I'd like to know about it. And I'd like someone to answer for it."

"No!" the girls shouts, and Walton takes it like a sharp slap to the face, a fierce energy, a fury. Those eyes of hers shimmer and shine in the dying firelight, burn hot like campfires themselves, making Walton slide back in his chair.

A noise uncoils like a black snake between his ears, a feral slithering or scratching, a whispery breathing like a *voice*.

No, it sounds like birds, a murder of crows, flushed from a tree canopy . . .

Not exactly what he's been hearing in the dark outside his cabin, but close, too close.

"Explain that to me," he fights to get out, even as his vision goes muddy, his breath catching as those birds flap wildly in his chest. Everything below eye level screws up tight, his body winces, numb, until he can't feel his arms, his legs. He almost reaches for the girl to help hold him up, to keep him from falling over, even though he doesn't want to touch her.

Jesus, Walton thinks, I'm having a goddamn heart attack . . .

"Tell me—"

"No, Landry, that's enough," Maggie says, even as the girl whispers—

. . . *i know what happened to your son* . . .

"Enough." And it's Maggie again, cutting them both off, one hand on his shoulder, another on the girl's. She's put herself between them, shielding her from his questions, breaking that electric tension between them. "You want answers? Fine. But not like this. Not now." She kneels next to him. "You're willing to let my past lay. You need to do the same here."

He stands, pushing back from the girl, from Maggie, rubbing his face in his hands, to make sure he can still feel both.

Concern wings over Maggie's face. "Hey now, are you okay?"

He coughs, spits something thick and bloody on the planks between his boots. Lottie would've thrown him out the door by his ear for spitting on her floor like that. "You get that?" he asks Maggie. "Any of it?"

Maggie shakes her head, but her eyes, and the way she does it . . . slow, halfhearted . . . hints she's got more than a small idea of what he's talking about. Even if she didn't just bear the full brunt of the same furious burst he just did, she experienced it or already has.

"She said something about Kellan, about my boy."

The girl watches them both, now impassive.

"No, she didn't," Maggie says. "She didn't say anything."

Walton has no clue what's happening, or what happened out there in the woods between these two before he came upon them. Has no idea what secrets they now share, other than the obvious hurts inflicted on them, and the hurt they've seemingly dealt out to others.

The crashed plane . . . the dead man in Pullens . . .

Even after Lottie's passing, those coal-dark days after Kellan's disappearance, he didn't feel this alone . . . no, old man, you mean this scared . . . but that's all he feels now, an awful fear corkscrewed up in his gut, where those crows the girl unleashed have come to rest.

Just admit it, Walton, this young girl scares the hell out of you . . .

"I need to go outside," he says. "Gotta clear my head."

"We were just out there, and it's cold," Maggie says, concern still flitting in her eyes. "It's practically snowing sideways out there now."

Walton shuffles to the window to find Maggie's right, the white snow is thick, busy, and hazy, sticking to the glass. It reminds him of wolf fur, already deep enough to run your hands through. Or feathers . . . a million bird feathers.

Even if Donnie is lucky enough to get to them, he won't be leaving. None of them will.

As if on cue, Walton makes out a Wolfe County Sheriff's truck rolling slow through the snow and trees toward them.

31

Marcus and Graham didn't talk much on the ride out to Landry's cabin, not the usual cop bullshit and banter, the back-and-forth that used to define the rhythm of long deployments, where you might find that you're stuck with someone for hours on end in a Humvee or an M1296 Dragoon or a foxhole.

Graham was too intent on messaging on his original cell phone for as long as they had service, then switched to another phone—sleek, black, unidentifiable—as they made their way up the mountain in driving snow.

Marcus was too intent on not getting lost a second time.

☾

Snow curls around them now, like a giant white hand holding on to the truck.

Marcus takes it slow as he winds them through thick woods on what used to be a logging road.

Walton's cabin flickers between small breaks in the trees, there and gone again like a magic trick, the rambling log-and-stone structure feathered by freshly fallen snow, gray smoke hovering over it from an unseen chimney.

It's pretty, picturesque, like a West Virginia postcard. Like a gingerbread cottage in one of those old tales.

"Like I said, this place has been in Walton's family for generations," Marcus offers, squinting. "He's added onto it through the years."

"Looks that way," Agent Graham says, intent on their all-too-brief glimpses of the cabin, sizing up what little he can see. "Let's hold up here, give it a moment before we walk up."

Marcus stops the truck, letting it idle. He can see the porch, the front door, a slice of frosted window to the right of that, the glass darkened by blinds or curtains. He turns in his seat, checking the woods around them. "No vehicles, nothing." He rolls down the window, both men catching the smoky hint of burning logs and the storm's cold bite. Otherwise, silence. "Looks to be home, though no idea if he's alone."

"Where does he park his truck or horse and buggy or whatever?" Graham asks, following Marcus's gaze.

"Out back, I think. He once talked about having a bass boat, so maybe that's stored there too? Look, I've only been up a couple of times. I have no idea what he's got stashed all around."

"Power?"

"Dual fuel generator. Propane, gas. Some solar panels. He could have a coal-fired furnace."

Agent Graham glances at the trees. "Trail or game cameras?"

"If it were me? Absolutely, what with the whole *Deliverance* vibe going on. But I'm sure he's not too worried about something creeping up on him out here."

"Except us," Graham says, flat and humorless.

"But we're not creeping," Marcus says, closing the window, breath pluming. "Hell, we're not even *trespassing*." Without waiting for Graham's say-so, Marcus shifts the truck into drive again.

The tires crunch loudly.

"This is federal land," Marcus says, "and you're a federal agent." He thumbs at Graham's FBI badge, hidden by the other man's coat. "So, let's just get up there and get this over with."

32

Landry tosses the binoculars he was peering through the window with and orders Luna to get dressed warm for leaving, then tells Maggie to go back upstairs, wait in Kellan's room.

She protests, asks, "Isn't that just your deputy friend?"

Landry shakes his head and silently mouths *Too soon* before flashing two fingers.

Two fingers. Two people.

One more than he was apparently expecting. But Maggie only whispers to Luna, "These men are here to help. They'll get you home safe. Just do everything Mr. Landry tells you."

But she also finds herself wanting to tell the girl so much more than that, more than just good luck or goodbye. As fast as Maggie herself wanted to get gone and away from here, if that moment is now, then right now is suddenly feeling far too soon as well.

You have nothing to offer her, Maggie thinks. Not a damn thing you can do.

Except that she wasn't a whole lot older than Luna when strange men came to her door, too, telling her they were there to help, that everything was going to be okay, only to learn that nothing would ever be quite okay again.

Her dad was gone, he was *taken*, and then she was adrift and alone . . . until Vann.

She hesitates, unsure if she dare leave Landry downstairs alone now, much less Luna alone with him.

Until Landry snaps his fingers to get her attention.

"Get your gear ready," he barks at her, "take the MyFAK and make sure you have that map I gave you. You can watch from the window up there," he says, pointing above their head, "but keep your eyes open. Wide open. If the girl and I leave with these folks, wait thirty minutes, then head out yourself. But if I take my hat off, there's a trapdoor in the kitchen, hidden beneath that old rug by the sink. A tunnel. Follow it out and don't slow down for me, her, or anyone else. Don't slow down for a goddamn thing."

She remembers a knotted pine door tucked in the back corner of the uneven kitchen, opening out to a ramshackle mud porch. Remembers, too, an ugly, unassuming rug, tattered and faded by who knows how many pairs of boots and how many hunting seasons.

The thought of crawling down some cold, dark hole unnerves her. "Did you *dig* that? Where's it go?"

But Landry just glares at her. "Out."

If it comes to it, she should be able to slip down the stairs again and through his secret door without being seen from either the front room or the front of the cabin. Landry's truck is parked in back, next to a flipped-over jon boat and a rambling toolshed, all surrounded by what would be thick, knee-high grass in the summer but now is little more than snowed-over brown stubble and knotted winter-dead foliage.

She figures his hidden passage pops out back there . . . somewhere.

"If that happens, I'll wait at your cemetery. It's not on any other map—no one else should know about it," she says, recalling Kellan Landry's delicately hand-drawn images, and leaving no room for debate. "Thirty minutes."

Landry looks ready to argue anyway, but with one eye out the window, leaves it at, "Not a minute more, then, hear me?"

"I hear you." She smiles at Luna, projecting confidence she doesn't feel, as Luna watches them both in studied silence with her amazing eyes. "Thank you for this," she tells Landry. "Thank you for everything."

He smiles, too, but it's mostly sad, defeated. "Don't thank me. If I had any sense, I'd cuff your ass to that damn chair over there and save you and the rest of us a bunch of misery." Now it's Landry's turn to hesitate, his liver-spotted hands worrying against each other, turning red. "It'll be dark up there, on the mountain. Dark." He motions vaguely out to Black Mountain outside and beyond. "Don't let it get to you." Although to Maggie it sounds more like *Don't let it get into you.* "Don't be afraid to light a fire."

Even out in the wilderness a fire could draw unwanted attention, and if search parties are already combing the woods looking for the plane, for Luna, or for Maggie herself, any fire would be bright as a signal flare. Landry knows that as well as she does.

Don't be afraid to light a fire . . .

Yet, right now, she's more afraid to leave this old man and Luna behind.

They both turn at the sound of the truck crunching to a stop outside.

"Go," he says, an order this time.

She sprints toward the stairs, turning back long enough to whisper-yell, "Hey, what *hat?*"

But by then, Landry has shoved a well-worn Carter Roag Coal Company baseball cap on his head and stepped out the door.

33

The storm is finally getting its hackles up, snapping and howling at Donnie's windshield.

He can hardly see a thing in his headlights, just a twisting, wind-blown pallor threatening to whiten out the world.

The last big nor'easter iced them in for five days, flash-freezing power lines and dumping a foot of snow on Pullens. Terra Alta, sixty miles away as the crow flies, got twenty-two inches. No crows flying in this mess, though, he thinks. Anything with half a brain is hunkered down, waiting this out. But here he is, right in the teeth of it, still fifteen miles out and might as well be forever away from Walton's cabin.

He never even texted Marcus like he planned, too distracted by the storm rolling in. But Marcus hasn't reached out to him, either, so he has no idea where he and Agent Graham have gotten themselves off to in this mess. It's easy to imagine them wrapped up in the warmth of the Big River, enjoying a coffee or even a little Four Roses, although in their brief run-in, the FBI agent didn't strike Donnie as the type to tip one back on duty, if ever.

Donnie's never really credited himself with Walton's gut instincts, or Marcus's cop intuition, but he'd be lying if he didn't think that after last night's events, the agent's arrival this morning, and now this god-awful storm today, the world wasn't conspiring to whip up a bad feeling even his cast-iron stomach can't ignore.

There's also all that stuff Walton had him track down: the gun e-Trace query for a private security contractor and those articles about that hospital or whatever in Atlanta, all wrapped around two pairs of Peerless cuffs in the folder next to him.

Hey, Walton said, *run that Peerless report for me . . . do it twice, okay?*

He can't make heads or tails of it, has no idea what Walton's gotten himself into and, by extension, what Walton's gotten *him* into, but this ferocious storm is likely the least of it.

Call it what it is, this is gonna be a damn blizzard before the day's through . . .

That's what his own gut is telling him anyway, so he isn't surprised at all when two dark SUVs loom out of the squall at his back, driving way too fast, crowding him to the shoulder, pushing him aside. He momentarily hits his emergency lights, blue-and-red spinners bright but muted by the gloom—like a hand covering a candle—but still throwing just enough light the winter storm around them takes on a circus tent glow, letting those assholes know they're riding the ass of a cop. But even that doesn't back them down much.

Instead, they quick-flash bright lights of their own, headlight wig-wags blinking back and forth like glaring eyes. Donnie gives them the finger but lets them pass, the two black SUVs—riding tight on each other's bumpers too—sliding past and disappearing again behind the white veil ahead.

He tells himself it's got to be more feds, Agent Graham's people, but like everything else over the past twenty-four hours, something about it doesn't set quite right. His gut is now rumbling, innards churning, and he knows he's not hungry. He's still got the rest of Roberta's biscuits in the back for Walton.

He's been taking it slow and cautious because of the snow—Roberta would accuse him of ambling along, like he's wont to do, and Walton used to say his chief deputy had two damn speeds, slow and stop—but those other feds were truly driving to beat the devil, like they were racing to a fire, and despite the storm, Donnie can't see any flames up ahead. Not yet anyway.

He curses under his breath and flips his emergency lights back on and gives his old truck some gas.

34

Walton doesn't like the look of things one bit.

Not the blowing snow, now getting thick in his beard and lashes, or the biting cold, or the sky itself. An unnatural color, both dark and slick, reminding him of the inner curve of a shell or the inside of a cave wall. The clouds all shimmery, too, aglow with the same greenish hue as the girl's eyes flashed inside.

He doesn't like the look of the FBI agent standing next to Marcus Austin's truck, either, the way he stands there so quiet and still while his eyes are busy cataloging everything.

Calculating.

He's measuring distances with those eyes, looking for what he can't see, and not just what he can. To anyone else they'd be ordinary, unassuming, unreadable. But Walton knows them.

Cop eyes . . . which are just another kind of wolf's eyes too.

The agent's bare hands hang loose and relaxed, but they're not. They're carefully, strategically placed. He's carrying a duty pistol high on his right hip, hidden beneath his unbuttoned jacket—unbuttoned despite the cold so he can draw it smooth as a snake—and likely a holdout piece in the small of his back or hanging close to his heart in a shoulder holster on the opposite side.

He's taken a bladed stance so he can use the open door of the truck as cover and keep decent visibility to the woods to his right. His eyes have already flicked past Kellan's window upstairs, noting it . . . *ranging it* . . . and he's mentally paced off a running start to both the porch and the tree line, depending on how this goes.

That's the question, Walton, how's this going to go?

For all the agent's faked disinterest, he doesn't seem in a hurry. In Walton's experience, men in a hurry give off a brittle, jangly vibe, a high-tension vibration, and dangerous men in a hurry practically buzz and hum like a goddamn power line.

But slow, patient, dangerous men are a whole different matter altogether.

It's also tough to gauge Austin's own read on the situation. He's out of the truck too—they rode together in Walton's old official Dodge, a small detail that bothers Walton, although he can't say why—but hasn't yet made a move up the steps to the porch. Walton doesn't know if Austin's fancy prosthetic sticks or slips or gets unwieldy in the snow—he's never seen the man struggle with it—but it'd be tough enough to dance around out here in the woods and weather on two good legs, much less one bad one.

Austin *does* give off the vibe of a man in a hurry, though.

He's eyeing the storm, and Walton, and the cabin, and everything else. He's blowing into his gloved hands, tired, distracted, a man who just wants to get this over with and get home. But if this turns as ugly as the weather itself, he won't be any less dangerous. Walton's heard a few of the things Sergeant Marcus Austin did overseas, all secondhand accounts to be sure, but he should know his way around a gun, or once did. But it won't matter if Austin never has a chance to draw it.

I don't think that man in Pullens asking all those questions is any kind of real FBI agent at all . . .

Walton thinks Maggie is about to be proven right about that, although he still isn't sure what to think about Maggie herself, or the girl, who, truth be told, put the creeps on him hard. Despite Maggie's insistence otherwise, he can still hear her voice in his head . . . *i know what happened to your son* . . . although it's a fair question if he truly heard it at all. He hinted for Donnie to bring some spare irons in case he decided to just cuff everyone and let the West Virginia State Police figure it all out. But passing off a problem has never been his way, even less now with Donnie MIA and Austin rolling up unannounced with this supposed agent in tow.

If Kell were here, if he'd been the one to come across those two scared women out on the mountain, he wouldn't have let Walton abandon them anyway.

Kell had a soft spot for the lost and injured, the scared and forsaken, no matter their nature. When he was fifteen, he once got bit something terrible while tending to a furious, injured coyote, and Lottie rushed him in a mad panic all her own up to Davis Medical Center, convinced he was going to get rabies.

In the end, he didn't, but the shots Kell had to get to stave it off hurt something fierce, and Walton held his hand through every one of them.

No, Walton's pretty sure now this man slowly eye-fucking him *isn't* with the FBI or any other law enforcement agency, and Walton doesn't like the look of him at all.

Walton raises an empty hand, flashes a toothy grin, and says, "Now what brings y'all all the way out here?"

35

It's been a few months since Marcus has seen the old man, and Walton Landry's seen better days.

Despite his thick Carhartt coat, he's gotten thinner, if that's possible, although his beard is even fuller, wilder, grayer. The dirty baseball hat on his head sits awkwardly on his crown, his chapped hands fidgety, rubbing against each other in constant motion. Stooped over, he looks almost pained, and although some of that is him leaning into the rough wind, it's more that age and time itself seem to have worn him down.

Last night, Marcus worried Walton might be losing it out here, and he'll argue now on first glance he's already lost it. No matter what comes of this little talk with Agent Graham, Marcus will need to address Walton wasting away alone out here in his dark and battered cabin, which looks ready to fall around his ears.

But—

His *Now what brings y'all all the way out here?* did sound spry enough, though—Walton's always had a deep, sonorous voice—and his eyes aren't overly cloudy or hazy. Still bright, alert, perceptive. Marcus can't imagine Walton playacting this crazy old coot routine, or why he'd feel the need to, but he's not downplaying it either. But Agent Graham also isn't buying it. He's wearing that forged smile of his, both Graham and Walton staring over Marcus's hood like Old West gunfighters sizing each other up before high noon.

It's too cold for this nonsense, Marcus thinks. If we don't get gone, we're going to get snowed in here for a week. And the last thing Marcus wants is to get trapped with these two.

"Sorry to show up like this," Marcus says. "Probably should've called first." He shoots a loaded glance of his own toward Graham. "Just wanted to follow up on last night's call about that plane. FBI agent Graham here also has some questions about a suspect he's looking for, who might be wrapped up in a killing in Pullens." Marcus shrugs to signal what he really feels—

It's been a long, long twenty-four hours.

"Some kind of fugitive?" Walton asks.

"Something like that," Graham says before Marcus can. "On the run . . . dangerous."

"Can we come in for a few?" Marcus asks. He wants to bat away the snow flurrying between them, clouding his vision. "It's bad out here, Walton, and getting worse. Give us five or ten and we'll be on our way."

Walton gestures vaguely to the cabin at his back, or the woods beyond. "Place not really made up for company."

"We're fine," Graham says, coolly amused. "And we're not exactly company."

"You got any kinda badge?" Walton asks, walking off the porch, crossing his thin arms. "Any kind of warrant?"

"Jesus, Walton," Marcus says. The storm is a foggy haze, frigid breath, coming in fits and starts, the trees dark and quiet and reminding Marcus of the roadside pines last night, that thing he saw in the woods. "We just want to talk. You called me first, remember?"

"Sure. Say, you hear anything about that?" Walton is looking to Marcus as he asks, but the question is directed at Graham. "At all?"

"No," Marcus concedes. "No plane. But Agent Graham here thinks his fugitive might be connected somehow. Thinks you might have really heard something."

Walton scratches his thick beard. "Likely was just confused about all that. Fell asleep last night to the radio, too into my cups." Walton mimes taking a drink. "Haven't laid eyes on anyone today other than you two. So, guess me and your agent friend here are both wrong." Walton waves them off. "Sorry to waste your time on a bunch of nonsense."

"How about I show you this photo anyway?" Graham asks, although he doesn't move to produce his iPad, doesn't make any attempt to flash Walton the magazine-spread picture of Mia Rade the way he flashed her to Marcus. He doesn't move, period. "Maybe someone you recognize from around town . . . or saw hiking the last couple of weeks?"

Walton snorts, then glares, eyes raptor-like beneath thick salt-and-pepper brows. "Don't need to see her because I don't see anyone, ever . . . which is mostly the way I like it."

Silence settles between the three men like the snow thickening on the ground.

Graham now shakes his head, sad and slow. "I never said *her*, Walton." More silence, more snow, as Walton flicks a look back and forth between Marcus and Graham, a trapped defiance. "I never said who I was looking for . . . *at all*."

Marcus isn't sure he heard Walton right but also doesn't like the way *Walton* just rolled off Graham's tongue like an implied threat, a level of unearned familiarity from someone Marcus hadn't laid eyes on, either, until a few hours ago.

Walton already spoke to Donnie . . . that's all . . . that's how he knows . . .

He turns to Graham. "Let's watch that, Graham. *Sheriff* Landry's carried a badge longer than both of us put together. He's earned the right to have a respectful conversation. And like I said before, that's all this is . . . a conversation."

But for the first time since rolling up, the old man does look confused. Old. Walton's hands fidget again. "Funny, must've heard it wrong then, I guess." He goes for the hat on his head, revealing a thin scrub of haggard hair, quickly flecked by thick cold flakes. He scratches at his forehead. "Not just my goddamn eyesight going bad."

The gesture is slow, deliberate—almost echoing Graham's head shake—but so much more pronounced, so obvious, it causes Marcus to focus on the cabin again.

Walton's also stepped clear of the porch, now visible to all three windows facing them.

In Sadr City, in Fallujah, every open doorway, every window, was a mortal threat, every dark opening like a freshly dug grave. Marcus has had a thousand hours of urban terrain and combat training, and there was a time his hands would pop cold sweat just standing near an open door and the uncleared room beyond, but that sharp instinct has gotten dulled by the emptiness and expanse of rural West Virginia.

A threat . . . a signal . . .

A movement or shift in the second-floor window, more hint than substance, but real enough, dangerous enough. "Graham—" he starts, motioning to the upstairs window, but the agent clocked it two heartbeats ahead of Marcus.

He's moving forward, drawing his gun.

"Dammit, Walton," Marcus shouts, unsure whether to get Graham to stand down, cover the agent, or take cover himself.

He decides to go for Walton first and knock the old man on his ass before he does something truly stupid.

Before Marcus can get to him, bright lights burn through the trees . . .

36

The last day Maggie saw Vann alive, he punched her in the throat.

They were sailing the Outer Banks on the forty-seven-foot single-sail Catalina that Vann had to have, the one he'd bought on the cheap from a desperate investor and renamed *Cambion's Hand*, after CambionXCG. It took him months to learn to sail the temperamental craft, and even then, every time they took it out on the water, it precipitated a battle of wills between Vann and that vessel as he fought and cursed the rigging, the mainsail, the jib. An outing meant to be relaxing and fun was more often tense and miserable.

She hated that boat.

She hated even more Vann's insistence that she always wear that expensive black Valentino bikini, no matter the weather. Hated that he wanted to show her and that boat off in equal measure, both meaning about the same to him. That he used both as an excuse to drink with abandon, and that she in turn drank to escape his breath and his eyes and his hands, so the entire time they were turning drunken circles in the cold blue of the Atlantic, trapped together on a boat neither truly liked with a partner neither loved anymore, all she could dream of was jumping overboard and slipping beneath the shifting surface, letting the tides take her farther and farther out to sea.

Not that Vann wasn't perpetually ruthless, or uncaring, but the sailing excursions made him fragile and mean, his entire body tense like his clenched jaw.

He didn't hit her for the first time on *Cambion's Hand*, not even close, but it was the last time.

They were belowdecks in the galley, Vann pouring his third or fourth Blanton's of the morning, and although she can't now remember what he said, or what she said in response—she'll never remember either—she can still vividly recall the look he gave her—sly, predatory, pissy—and the way he carefully, gingerly, set down that Lismore Connoisseur Diamond tumbler—realizing later he didn't want to spill the Blanton's or break the Waterford—and then just as carefully wrapped his thick knuckles in a dish towel—realizing later, too, he didn't want to hurt his hand or leave a visible mark—and punched her in the throat.

She never had a chance to tell him wait or stop or don't or I'm sorry. Never had a chance to wonder, does he know?

The curling overhand shot took all the air out of her, doubling her over, an entire constellation sparking and wheeling in front of her eyes. She couldn't suck a single breath back in, and as she spat blood and heaved and coughed, she thought she was going to choke to death then and there. She figured he'd crushed her windpipe, a reasonable "Vann solution" to her ever talking back to him again.

It's still hard for Maggie . . . Mia . . . to recognize the woman curled on the galley floor of that boat. A woman who had everything, everything material anyway, but was weirdly hollowed out, an empty husk, lying there spitting up blood, desperate for air.

A woman whose whole life was an empty stage, everything in it, including *her*, little more than a prop.

A woman who was a thief and a liar and even worse, and who probably deserved to die.

But for all the times she'd thought about leaping into the water or drowning or taking too many pills, she realized she didn't want to die like that, not with Vann still standing over her, momentarily unwrapping and unclenching and rinsing off his stinging hand, before coolly returning to his bourbon in the Waterford crystal with the big rock cube that hadn't even started melting yet, because everything had happened so fast.

She didn't want to die on his fucking boat . . . their fucking boat . . . in the time it took him to finish a drink.

Why then? What was it about that moment, not the worst but certainly not one of the finer ones, that pushed her so far?

Why had it taken so long?

That was the last time Vann Carter Rade hit her and the last day she saw her husband alive.

☾

But today she just wants Landry to give the two men out in the snow whatever it is they want.

One of them is clearly the new sheriff, Marcus Austin. A lithe Black man who's been doing most of the talking so far, or at least most of the gesturing.

The other's a blur, a hole in the winter air, opposite Austin.

The snow's whited this man out, and since he's been angled away from her this whole time, she hasn't been able to get a good look at his face and can only guess it's the so-called FBI agent.

What she can't figure out is why Landry hasn't handed over Luna to them yet.

Why he's still just . . . talking.

Whatever is going on down there has been taking an eternity, though, far longer than the blink-and-miss punch that put her on the galley floor of *Cambion's Hand* two years ago, a moment—not unlike that knock on her door when she wasn't much older than Luna—that changed her life immediately then and irrevocably ever after. She hasn't been able to hear a thing the three men have been saying, just murmurs rising and falling and rising again—a sound reminiscent of waves, of wind—but even with that, she's sensed the underlying tension down below.

Staring out Kellan Landry's window, all she's been able to do is silently pray, please, please don't take your hat off . . .

Please, please, please . . . just give those men what they want . . . whatever they want . . . even if it's me . . .

But it's right around her fifth or sixth silent please, when she's gripping the glass tight enough it might crack and her breath is messily fogging the window, that the baseball hat comes off like a part of her always knew it would, and she finds herself staring at Sheriff Austin.

He's looking up right at that moment . . . that moment between when Vann hit her and she was lying there, struggling to breathe . . . and they lock eyes until the snow erases everything between them and the moment closes like a curtain on an empty stage again and things *really* start to speed up.

Austin now shouting and running, and the other man with him, that hole in the air, suddenly present, flickering into existence below her, crouching like it's the most natural movement in the world and drawing a dark gun she can see so much more clearly than the man himself even as Landry rushes, stumbles, off the porch to throw himself at Austin.

Nononono . . .

And now Maggie is in motion, too, grabbing up her gear and random clothes and fleeing back down the stairs, to Landry and Luna.

37

Donnie tries to sort out what the hell is going on as his truck slides to a stop in front of Walton's cabin.

Agent Graham is down on one knee, aiming his gun at, well, Donnie's not sure.

Other than Walton or Marcus, or Donnie himself, there's no one else, not that he can see.

As he made his way up the logging track to Walton's cabin, he never spied those black SUVs from earlier again, or any other cars, for that matter.

Walton is up near the cabin's sagging porch, grabbing, or fighting with Marcus, or it's the other way around, and Marcus is the one tackling the sheriff.

Christ on a cross . . .

They're puzzle pieces he can't fit together, letters in a crossword he hasn't figured out yet. He doesn't have near enough pieces, not enough letters, to spell out what the hell is going on.

Before he was running silent through the woods, emergency lights on, though, painting the trees electric red and blue as he went past, but now he gooses his sirens, loud, a bid to get everyone's attention. It works.

Graham waves at him to back off, waves at him to pull back.

At the first piercing wail, Walton near jumps out of his skin, and that alone almost breaks Donnie's heart. For the only time he can remember, Walton looks surprised. Worse than that, he looks scared, and that look, far more than Agent Graham waving a gun around like a lunatic, gives Donnie pause.

Marcus turns at the siren, too, giving even a surprised, scared Walton enough of an opening to knock the younger man on his ass.

Walton's scared look is still almost enough to prompt Donnie to throw his truck in reverse and hightail it back up the trail, but he won't leave Walton, and can't leave Marcus, not until one of them makes sense of all this for him. On instinct, he grabs the folder Walton asked for, realizing a moment too late he should be drawing his gun instead.

He's still stumbling out of the truck into the whipping snow when something black and fast and furious brushes by his cheek, gentle but menacing. It goes by so fast, soundless beneath his sirens, he almost doesn't recognize it for what it is.

For the oddest reason, he imagines a bird . . . *a small black bird* . . . winging past his face.

It's only when his driver's side window shatters, then the big windshield spiderwebs and buckles, that he figures out someone is shooting at him.

38

When she was really scared, like when Dr. Jewell was putting her under again for another surgery, or she was just waking up from the last one and her whole body was still a raw, open wound, Dr. Jewell would say—

Let me tell you a story . . .

That was their code, their secret sign, tacit permission for her to leaf through Dr. Jewell's mind.

Dr. Jewell would close her eyes then, breathe slow, try to relax—she later learned it was a form of mindfulness meditation, something Dr. Jewell claimed she wanted to teach her too—and slow her flurrying thoughts and perceptions down like birds taking roost in trees, bedding down for the night.

All her thoughts, good and bad. Memories too. Hopes, fears. Feelings.

It was like she was reading over Dr. Jewell's shoulder, the older woman's life an open book, a few pages at a time. She knew it was Dr. Jewell's way of building trust and rapport, a tactic or technique, just like she knew Dr. Jewell spent just as much time using an alternative-meditative technique to keep that book closed and her out of her head.

Like she also knew that for all the . . . *fear . . . regret . . . imsosorry . . . thiswillsoonbeover* thoughts and instincts and feelings Dr. Jewell was willing to share, the smell, too, of her coffee in the morning or the duck-like bark of her long-dead Corgi, JoJo, or that time at Amherst when she drank too much and kissed her Latin professor through a haze of tequila and weed—things she will never experience herself—there was also no way Dr. Jewell was ever going to let it be over.

It was never going to end, never stop.

There would always be more surgeries, more fear, more endless *hurt*, until she was used up. Until she was nothing but another one of Dr. Jewell's fleeting thoughts, too, one of her old memories.

Despite Dr. Jewell's smarts and theories and techniques, the doctor never fully understood that she *knew* Dr. Jewell was lying, and it didn't take any special trick or ability or tactic or technique to figure that out.

All she had to do was look into Dr. Jewell's eyes.

They were all lying to her . . . all of them . . . and that was never going to stop either.

☾

The woman, Maggie, is grabbing for her, telling her to *comecomecome*, as a siren starts up outside.

. . . mia . . . vann . . . a boat . . . water like blood . . .

It's going to be okay, the woman, Maggie who's really Mia, tells her, but she knows she's lying, too, just like Dr. Jewell.

Fear is rolling off her in waves, like the ocean Maggie/Mia was just remembering.

She's never seen the ocean, not for real.

And the siren outside isn't louder than all the other sounds inside her head, all those fresh thoughts like a flock of angry birds, twirling and whirling. Cawing and crying. They batter behind her eyes, trying to escape, and even pressing her hands to her temples doesn't make them stop or go away.

It never does.

But there's one louder than all the rest, one worse than all the others. She thought he was dead in the crash, but he's out there now circling, drawing closer.

Roach.

She doesn't know how that's possible but doesn't have time to dwell on it, either, as Maggie pushes her forward, ducking through the living room, keeping low of the windows, running them both to the kitchen, to the rug, to the hole beneath.

Maggie's got her rifle and is grabbing up her pack and telling Luna to stay close, keep moving, don't stop running.

. . . don't stop . . .

Maggie throws back the rug and the trapdoor, revealing a dark, dank, dirty hole rimmed in concrete and wood, and Maggie doesn't want either of them to go down there . . . *oh no i can't do this i can't do this* . . . until all the windows shatter and small bright metal objects start ticking, clicking, bouncing all over the floor.

Then she and Maggie are falling down the hole together.

39

When Walton grabs him, all but punches him in the side of the head, Marcus figures the old man finally has lost his last few marbles.

He's not the only one.

There's Donnie Kornblue suddenly rolling up out of nowhere and that ghostly figure in the window upstairs—Mia Rade, more than likely—and Agent Graham waving his gun around over there.

Donnie's truck siren going full throat, too, so that Marcus can't hear himself think. He doesn't want to hurt Walton, but he's got to get this under control before someone does get hurt.

He pushes Walton off him, wrestling with him, but the old man is surprisingly strong, all wiry sinew, clinging to him. "Dammit, Walton," Marcus spits out, struggling, close to just breaking down and hitting the old man in the face, right between his eyes. "Get off me." But Walton doesn't let go, using instead what little weight he's got to weigh Marcus down, a dead fall, pulling them both to the ground.

"Get down then," Walton breathes into his ear. "Get down before you get yourself fucking killed . . . before you get us *all* killed."

40

Just as Donnie drove up, Walton saw men moving through the trees.

Two of them, flanking right to left, trailing in the truck's snowy wake. They were at Marcus's back, using the big vehicle for cover, and even if Donnie had one eye on his rearview—which Walton doubted— he wouldn't have picked them out, either, against the trees and storm.

Marcus couldn't see them at all.

They were dressed the same, hell, at distance, might as well have been the same—one man and his shadow—right down to the scoped long rifles raised high in their hands.

Walton was sure this Agent Graham had summoned them on some secret signal, even before Marcus spied Maggie up in the window, which he clearly did, at just about the same moment he saw right through that silly hat signal, which was what prompted Walton to leap for him in the first place.

Not just to buy Maggie some much-needed time, but also to keep Marcus out of the line of fire.

Walton now guesses if there are two men in the woods, Graham has more stowed around, maybe a lot more, maybe already moving in tandem on the cabin. The agent must *really* want Maggie bad.

Walton figures things are about to go from bad to worse, and he's right.

41

Several things happen almost at once—

When Walton tells Marcus to stay down, the soldier in Marcus heeds the warning and stops struggling with him.

Together, they roll to their knees as if they practiced it, and now Marcus can also see the armed twins bearing down on Donnie.

Together, they watch as one of the men—shadow twin to the left— raises a long gun and opens fire on Donnie. The gun's silenced, the truck's wailing siren and the wind covering what little sound it still might make, but Marcus picks out the distinctive flare of repeated muzzle flashes against the snow.

The old truck buckles under the incoming rounds, tires exploding, windows shattering, the light bar on the roof cracking. Donnie stands in the middle of it all, stunned, staring down at something clutched in his hands—a folder, by the looks of it—as if he can't make sense of it.

"What the fu—?" Marcus starts, even as he draws his own duty Glock, taking a bead on the first shooter.

"I'll go for Graham," Walton yells, and then runs low toward the agent to intercept him . . .

☾

Maggie bursts out from under the jon boat with Luna behind her, right into the arms of a waiting man.

There are two of them, two heavily armed men who don't look much different from the one she stabbed in Pullens, both moving stealthily through the trees to the back of the cabin, launching what she assumes are more of those smoke grenades or incendiary devices through the cabin's windows.

Pop. Pop. Pop.

The metal cylinders spin through the air, trailing sparks.

Her sudden appearance, their focus on the cabin, and the howling storm slow the men's reaction. But there's still not enough time for Maggie to drop back down the hole again, to do much more than watch the two men raise their weapons toward her and brace for the heavy impact of their bullets.

To try frantically to drive them away with the only thing at her disposal—

Her rifle.

Maggie pushes Luna down and raises the Weatherby and starts shooting . . .

Donnie finally draws his gun, too, but like Maggie, it's too late.

He's shot in the right leg, through and through, blood spraying out on the snow. Then the stomach, the left arm, but it's the one just above his heart that puts him down.

The last should've killed him instantly, but it miraculously ricochets off one of those sets of Peerless cuffs hidden in the folder he brought for Walton.

A dozen loose papers flutter and fly away into the storm . . .

Walton stumbles toward Graham, drawing the scorched gun he retrieved from the plane, and then swings it like a hammer at the agent's skull as hard as he can.

Graham's quick, though, dodging the worst of the blow, and on the backswing he wrenches the blackened gun from Walton and hits him in the throat with it.

Walton didn't want to kill the man, but it doesn't appear Graham is too concerned about killing *him*.

He's about to go for his little Southern Grind Jackal Pup—he always carries a hunting or survival knife on his belt—and stab Graham in his leg, or anything else he can reach, when Donnie appears, a bloody, dying apparition.

He's trying to say something, his eyes locked on Walton, when Graham shoots him in the face.

Donnie all but falls on Graham then, his bulk driving the agent to the ground, the way Walton pulled Austin down moments before. As Graham struggles beneath Donnie, Walton kicks the agent's duty gun from his hand and then kicks him twice in the head to keep him down.

He then turns and runs for the house.

☾

Marcus doesn't have a full-on PTSD flashback but can't seem to wrap his head around how all the battles he left behind *over there* are now suddenly *here*.

Seeing Donnie go down in a blur of white paper and blood, only to rise again and stumble forward, even as Walton fights hand to hand with Agent Graham, brings the world into immediate, bloody focus.

It's a cliché to say he was ever good at one thing, but this is it. The gun is natural in his hand. Marcus leans low, takes a deep breath, settles in, and starts walking rounds into the two men stalking them from behind.

Just like riding a goddamn bicycle . . .

He catches one of those bastards who shot Donnie Kornblue in the throat, dropping him in a spiral of arms and legs. The man's dead before he hits the ground.

Marcus cleanly dumps his mag in the snow at his feet and reloads in less than two seconds and resights on the other . . .

☾

He's circling downwind, scenting the girl, breaking from the trees, and angling toward the cabin, when he runs pell-mell into the old man.

He claws and rips into him, throwing him aside in a looping spray of flying blood and torn flesh, still focused only on her . . .

He can smell her, taste her . . .

He sees her, she sees *him*, and he smiles and howls.

☾

The cabin's windows blow out, raining glass and black smoke.

It's one dull thud after another, twice as loud in the small confines of the cabin, making its insides glow hot and white, and surprising Maggie so much she nearly drops her rifle.

But right after there's another sound above the detonating grenades, something higher pitched, an awful keening.

A howling.

And then Maggie realizes it's only Luna screaming . . .

☾

Pascal Bisek knows the exact moment things go sideways.

They're making their approach on the back of the cabin when that shitty canoe or boat they never had the chance to properly check suddenly flips over to reveal a hidey-hole and a young girl . . . who the hell is that . . . but even more importantly, their target, Mia Rade, all done up in hiking gear, carrying a hunting rifle.

He's about to swap out the flash-bang and tag the Rade woman with 20 ccs of surgical anesthesia—a potent cocktail of propofol, ketamine, and dexmedetomidine—when Rade starts shooting wildly at them, and the girl . . . still don't know who she is . . . starts screaming holy hell, and his nose starts bleeding.

Not bleeding. Gushing.

That's when things go sideways . . .

Like he got hit in the head with a claw hammer, claw end first.

Like his forehead is being split open and someone is pouring fire behind his eyes, or worse, a flock of flaming birds, crows, or ravens, scratching at the inside of his skull.

The girl's screaming is a thousand burning bird wings.

Then Bisek is all of twelve again, and awful Uncle Stepan is leaning over his bed whispering, *you got this comin'* . . . and Bisek, both then and now, can only cry and agree *i am a bad person . . . i've done so many bad things . . .*

And although he's willing to do about anything to make this horror show stop, up to and including shooting himself in the head, he groans and cries and shoots his partner, Rico Tancredi, in the heart first.

☾

Marcus ducks as the flash-bangs go off in Walton's cabin one after another and then someone screams and he can't concentrate because it sounds and feels like a low-flying chopper is doing an exfil in his head, his teeth rattling so hard they hurt.

He tries to gag up the sound behind his eyes—Graham just did— but his mouth is empty, dry, chalky.

He struggles to stand, to keep shooting, and then mercifully throws up, too, in the snow at his feet.

☾

Walton doesn't know who or even what it is that attacked him . . . oh, you know what it was, Walton, a White Thing . . . but he's still crawling away from it, crawling for his life, when that weird sensation hits him behind his eyes, that electrical-charge jolt, and it nearly knocks him flat again.

Austin must feel it, too, because his eyes are rolling back in his head, showing whites. His gun hand quivers, shakes, his whole arm bouncing in the air. But he doesn't let it go. It's the girl . . . Walton thinks, if he can think at all. Oh my God . . .

He remembers that horrible devil mask, blood running down her face.

Screws now turning in his head, the air itself turning him inside out, and if there's any upside to it all, it's that the jolt stops Agent Graham dead in his tracks as well.

Why do I hear birds?

Oh, Kell, I hear birds coming to carry me away . . .

The agent is just getting up when he suddenly reaches for his head, too, falls back to his knees again, and then throws up a fountain of black blood, as the girl's scream from behind the cabin carries over the roof and rises above Donnie's abandoned truck siren into the storm-racked sky.

☾

Maggie's stomach is seasick queasy, the snow-choked morning air itself almost seeming to waver and turn to cold, dark water in front of her eyes, as Luna screams and one killer turns on the other.

. . . i'm back on that boat and vann is there and he's sliding beneath the waves and . . .

And she's struggling to keep shooting and then scoop up Luna and carry her away as the other killer, bleeding from his nose, his eyes, struggles to remember how his gun works and the whole ridiculous, horrible scene might be funny if Maggie wasn't so sure she and Luna were about to die.

All she can do now is scream herself—*pleasenononono*—and shield Luna's body with her own as the man finally regains his senses and shoots the girl again and again to make it stop and save them all.

As they waited in the boughs, the chilly wind blowing, Rory Tinsley, a loyal third cousin to Cooper Landry on his mother's side, turned to Cooper and said, "What if it was no beast at all that took Hudson and all those others? No mortal creature?"

"True, that is what many believe, even our own kin. That the White Thing is no earthly monster, but instead a ghost, the lost spirit of a dead man," Cooper answered and then patted Rory's shoulder. "A ghost story." Cooper paused, listening to the wind, to his cousin's tremulous breathing, before tightening his grip on his musket. "I've heard it said Indians believed that the ghosts of the restless and vengeful might take the form of animals." Both Cooper and Rory had found artifacts of ancient tribes once native to the area, bits of pottery, small, ill-formed beads, and even black bear and wolf masks.

Rory only gripped his own musket tighter. He loved his cousin but thought as many others did that Cooper's obsession with the thing had salted his own good reason. "My ma says that is why the White Thing might take comfort in graveyards and cemeteries. That is what her own ma told her."

"Then perhaps that is where we must hunt next," Cooper agreed, smiling at his cousin to bolster his spirits.

"But how do we kill a ghost?" Rory asked plaintively, his eyes still wary and afraid. "How do we kill that which is already dead?"

The White Things:
Tall Tales of West Virginia's White Monsters
Jim Collymore

Dark and Stormy Books
Pullens, West Virginia
2006

THREE

42

FBI special agent Carl Graham, a.k.a. Ekker, comes to in blood and snow.

He flutters to consciousness already in motion, rolling to his left, looking for a weapon, looking for cover. His memories are a kaleidoscope of dark, whirling pieces he can't grab hold of. An image here, a sensation there.

. . . black wings beating at me . . .

Porter and Mosley moving in on that fat hick deputy from the trees, and Walton Landry and Marcus Austin fighting up by the cabin, and the Rade woman staring down at them all from the cabin's upstairs window.

Landry attacking him.

Shooting the fat deputy.

A girl's scream and then . . . *all those black wings.*

A black feathered *light* cleansing everything in his head, a synaptic discharge, a black hole flare, a collapsing star around the Angel of Death hovering in his vision. A light so dark, so deep, so furious, it even drove his angel away.

It's still out there somewhere, winging and waiting overhead, ready to swoop in and lodge itself in his head again. But as Ekker blinks and spits and coughs blood, tries to get his bearings, his vision is clear for the first time in months, no cigarette-burn hole in his left eye, no spent-brass metallic taste in his mouth other than fresh blood and vomit.

Now he remembers gunshots, one after another, and throwing up.

Remembers . . . thinks he remembers . . . Landry kicking him in the head.

Ekker remembers who he is and why he's here and searches for a gun.

Ten minutes later Ekker is already feeling better, but the overall situation hasn't improved.

The snow is coming down thick now, like Austin predicted. Out front, Porter is dead, and Mosley badly, fatally, wounded. Either the fat deputy, Kornblue, got off a shot or two before he launched himself at Ekker and expired, or Austin took out two of his men alone.

Ekker retrieves Mosley's gun and ejects all the rounds but one, and despite the man's meager protests—he might be praying—Ekker puts the SIG firmly beneath the man's jaw, holds his head upright and tight, and blows the top of his skull off.

Out back, Tancredi is dead too.

Bisek sits in a daze next to him, sprawled against an overturned bass boat, both his sidearm and long gun covered in fresh snow. Blood freezing around his eyes, his nose.

Something went at his face . . . or he did that to himself . . .

Ekker spies the escape hole beneath the boat and eyes the distance to the cabin, checking the angle and dispersion of bullet holes, Tancredi's wounds, and a rough set of quickly disappearing tracks in the snow. Ekker concludes Bisek turned his gun on Tancredi, even as Tancredi was trying to incapacitate and take down Mia Rade. The contours of the scenario almost make sense, but not the *why*. Not even close.

Did Bisek experience that dark, feathered light too?

Ekker makes sure Bisek isn't further armed—he doesn't resist—and then leaves him in a fetal heap so he can sweep the whole cabin. He follows the hole back inside, up through the kitchen, searching all the rooms. Smoke hovers and small fires burn here and there, ashy residue from the multibang-flash and thermobaric devices his team launched into the small space. He ordered them not to be overzealous, but it's clear they didn't take that order to heart.

He catalogs everything—blankets by the fireplace, abandoned mugs scattered around, weird drawings in the room upstairs—even his own face when he catches sight of it in a bathroom mirror.

Blood near his eyes too. Dark stains of spit and blood around his mouth. Bruises going black and blue up the side of his head, where Landry kicked him hard.

He then retreats outside, where there's nothing else to find, no Mia Rade or anyone else, and stands there for a long time, staring at the bodies, the cabin, the snow. The papers blowing around the yard, a handful freezing solid beneath Kornblue's body.

He didn't register the mountain's cold before, but does now, as the storm sweeps in, deep, dark, menacing. The sky's the color of the bruises Landry left him with.

Landry and Austin aren't dead yet. Neither is Mia Rade. That much is clear. They might be badly wounded, might even die before the storm and cold finish them off. But there *was* someone else here, too, an unexpected variable . . . a girl's scream . . . too high pitched, too young, to be Rade, just before the dark light descended on him.

Ekker is certain that girl was the source of that black-winged light.

He has no idea who she might be, or why she'd be out here. Landry's son is dead, and there are no records of a marriage or any grandchildren. Maybe Landry was telling the truth all along, and there was a plane crash? But Ekker checked that, as did his tech, Feiser. He had complete dossiers compiled on everyone and everything he possibly could've accounted for.

He'll also have to make a call soon and account to Brooking what's happened here.

That won't be pleasant, or easy, with the few answers he has. And he prides himself on always having answers. Significant work and back-stopping went into this effort to scoop up Mia Rade without a lot of questions and even less bloodshed, and he failed on both accounts—spectacularly—especially after criticizing Theroux for these same failings.

The storm gives him cover, an excuse, if he wants it, as does the unexpected appearance of this young girl, if she even exists at all. But he doesn't believe in excuses, doesn't want to justify what did or didn't happen here to the likes of Brooking, and for the first time in months, with his angel gone and his vision clear, he has time on his side. He only wants answers.

Ekker pulls the Silynx earbud from his pocket and slips it in, keying an open channel to Feiser, and then walks to Deputy Kornblue's body and starts pulling frozen papers free.

43

For the second time in as many days, it's a miracle the girl isn't dead.

Maggie was sure Luna *was* dead, shot dead right before her eyes, after the man in black brutally opened fire on his partner and then took aim and fired on them. Knew for certain when the screaming girl—turning all their legs to jelly with those emanating shock waves—collapsed in a sudden heap against her, almost knocking her over.

The girl's falling body didn't affect Maggie's aim, though; it may have even helped, nudging her own rifle exactly where it needed to be, had to be, closer to the man's heart.

That's the second man I might've killed in as many days too . . .

If her shot didn't hit or kill him—a distinct possibility—it did distract him. As she was grabbing up Luna's lifeless body, or what she thought was her lifeless body, the other man was clawing at his face, at his freshly bleeding eyes.

She heard other shooting and shouts from the front of the house, but in the midst of the snow, wind, and blood, all she could think to do was fireman-carry Luna's lifeless body into the trees as far as she could until she collapsed.

Second time, also, that she somehow carted the girl from a scene of death, of carnage.

Only after Maggie was shielded from the cabin, once the sounds had died down at her back, did she catch Luna's breath on her face.

Only after she'd put her down, frantically searching for a heartbeat, did she find the red-winged dart protruding from the girl's slim neck.

Drugged, not dead . . . a miracle . . .

Although, standing alone in the woods with the girl comatose and the sky darkening and the snow turning sideways into her face, it doesn't feel like one.

☽

As she huddles beneath the pines and watches the sleeping girl, Maggie asks herself *why*—

Why carry her away at all? Why drag her from the cabin if you really thought she was dead? Was it misplaced loyalty to Landry, an old man you barely knew? Motherly instinct to a girl that's not even yours?

Or was it Luna's scars and bruises, the sort of scars and injuries Maggie herself once had to hide?

Sitting in the wet, gray snow, blinking away hot tears she neither summoned nor wants, Maggie can't answer that, and doesn't even know if there is an answer.

But now with her adrenaline gone and cold, frigid reality settling in, she does know there's no way she's going to carry Luna off this mountain. No way she's going to get them both to safety. She was lucky to get as far as she did the first time—wouldn't have made it ten steps farther without Landry's fortunate appearance last night—and must admit to herself that Landry and Sheriff Austin and anyone else who might've been willing to help her probably just died back there at the cabin.

Because of me . . .

She doesn't even have her rifle anymore. It's just her and Luna . . . and the men Jon Brooking sent after her. Men drawing closer by the moment, stalking them both, if she doesn't get moving again.

She's just getting Luna pulled into her arms when one of those men slips in beneath the shadowed boughs, gun drawn.

She doesn't have time to run, barely has time to react, so she does the only thing she can: she throws herself headfirst at him, kneeing his groin, striking his face, clawing his eyes.

If they still want her alive, maybe he won't kill her outright . . .

But her attacker seems just as shocked by her maneuver, and they tumble together in the snow, throwing up plumes of thick powder, rolling to an awkward stop, where he's finally able to lever himself on top and use his weight to pin her down.

"You sonofabitch," she says, still going for his eyes.

"No, hey, stop. Just *stop*," the man whispers, trying to still her hands. He's breathing heavy, his breath close and warm on her face, voice slow and measured. "That's twice I've been jumped today." He pushes her away, still sitting on his ass, raising his own hands in surrender, showing her he means no harm.

His gun is somewhere lost in the snow behind him, difficult for either of them to grab.

"You're alive," Maggie says, less a question than a statement.

"Makes two of us," Sheriff Austin answers, flicking a glance over her shoulder to a sleeping Luna. "Three?"

Maggie nods. "How'd you—?"

He holds up a hand, quieting her, his voice still barely above a whisper, although it doesn't matter with the rasping wind. "We're still not safe. Far from it. In fact, we need to get far from here."

She asks, "Landry?"

Sheriff Austin shrugs, uncertain. "Don't know. I didn't see him, and I didn't have a chance to stay and find out. Things got . . . bad."

She doesn't know this man at all but can tell that final choice back there at the cabin, whatever decision he had or didn't have or couldn't make, still bothers him, and will for a long time, if there is a long time.

Sheriff Austin stands and moves closer, before awkwardly kneeling next to her. It's painful the way he inches along, a constant struggle to stay upright and balanced, less to do with any injuries or snowdrift and storm wind and more to do with the high-tech prosthetic blading out from beneath his pants leg. He says, "That girl there, is she okay? Hurt?" But Maggie also hears the unasked question in his voice—

Can she walk?

Maggie doesn't know what their options are if neither Sheriff Austin nor Luna can move on their own. "They drugged her, a dart of some kind. I don't know what it is, or how long she'll be out." She pauses. "It was meant for me." Then asks the next question, knowing the answer. "You don't have your cell phone, do you?"

"No, was in the truck when I got out at the cabin. Still there." He looks to the windblown trees. "Probably not much use out here anyway." Focuses back on her. "You did good, getting this far, but we got to keep moving. I'll take her from here."

She tries not to look at his leg. "Where?"

"Not sure we can go back to the cabin, and circling back down to the trail we followed in is . . . dangerous . . . if they're still searching." He peers through the trees again, all the swirling snow. "I don't have any idea where we are or how to get back to the road, and this cold is going to kill us before I find it. But if Walton is still out here somewhere, wounded or not, I can't leave him." Sheriff Austin looks back and forth between Luna and Maggie. "Gotta be honest, I don't have a fucking clue."

Maggie says, "Maybe I do."

44

Marcus follows the woman who calls herself Maggie through the snow.

They don't talk much, both focused on getting higher up the mountain, someplace Maggie's aiming for. He carries the girl Luna in his arms, and although she's not heavy, they still need to take frequent breaks so he can rest, so he can adjust her weight and adjust his prosthetic, and so Maggie can consult the compass in her pack and a small hand-drawn map she claims Walton gave her.

It's only when they stop for those few precious moments that they share a few words, too, fill in each other's stories, as best they can. He tells her about the dead man in Pullens, the arrival of FBI agent Graham, and the missing Mia Rade from New York. She tells him about the plane crash in the woods, the girl she found miraculously alive—Luna—and Walton finding them both lost and nearly dead on the mountain.

Neither talks much about the shoot-out at the cabin or how either of them escaped.

When there's nothing else to say, they lapse into silence, and start walking again.

☾

They now pick their way through a rocky gorge shadowed by large trees, like moving through a tunnel. Down here, the storm's taking a breather, too, and although gentle snow continues to twirl down, the wind isn't half as bad, not anywhere near as cutting.

The world inside this frozen gorge is twilight, starless, painted in muted greens and grays. Maggie is a shadow in front of him, slowly moving over knee-breaking stones and exposed pine roots, pointing him the way and where to step.

If those men from the cabin take the high ground above them, they won't stand a chance, not that they honestly have a prayer anyway. He has two rounds left in his Glock, and although he grabbed an AR-15-style long gun off one of the men he put down at the cabin—the latest-model SIG Sauer MCX-SPEAR—it's got half a clip left, if that. Call it fourteen rounds.

Maggie doesn't appear armed, although he's betting she's got something more dangerous than a compass and camping gear stowed in her pack.

He's been watching her close, trying to square the picture of the woman Graham showed him with this one. Although she hasn't admitted it, this Maggie is Graham's Mia Rade, of that Marcus has no doubt. Hair's different color and length, and she's carrying a few more pounds—more muscle—but the hiking clothes fit her as naturally as the expensive suit in the photo ever did.

He wouldn't have imagined *that* Mia Rade as an outdoor enthusiast, but even if he wasn't carrying a comatose girl on a prosthetic leg through a snowstorm, he'd have trouble keeping up.

Even he's got to smile at that.

A grim smile, death's-head to be sure, but a smile all the same.

☽

After ten minutes more on the mountain, he finds the first gravestone.

It's a black, smoothed-over stone poking up at an odd angle, like a rotted tooth jutting up out of some sleeping giant's jaw.

As Maggie/Mia drops her pack a few yards in front of him, he starts counting other old gravestones littered all around. One has a rough-hewn angel taking wing over it, escaping for a sky he can't see due to the overhanging trees, and he gently lays the girl next to it before sliding down himself next to another marker, a simple square etched with a date: 1928. "What the hell is this place?" he asks.

Maggie folds her map away, waving at the stones pocking the snow. "An old family cemetery."

"Walton's?"

"So he said. I told him if we got separated at the cabin, I'd wait here for him. Thirty minutes."

Marcus flashes the tritium glow of his watch in the gloom. Most people don't wear watches anymore, but he still religiously sports his old military Marathon Navigator in desert tan and feels incomplete without it. "That would've been forty minutes ago, easily. Maybe more."

She says, "I know. But still thought it was worth a try." She leans against her own gravestone, stares skyward.

"What's the rest of your plan?"

Maggie laughs. "There's no *plan*, no scheme. Landry was only trying to help me—"

"Get away?"

"Yeah, get away," she says, bitterly. There's resignation there, too, a sense of futility or finality that she doesn't try to hide, and that Marcus can feel in every word, each as heavy as the gravestones around them.

"How much did he know about you?"

Maggie drops her gaze sharply, pins Marcus with it. "How much do *you*?"

"Just what Agent Graham back there told me."

Maggie shakes her head. "Really think that man was an FBI agent?"

Marcus picks up snow and crunches it in his gloves. Thick, wet, and getting deeper. Although he's desperate to rest, to sleep for a week, they shouldn't sit here long, and if they're forced to, he'll need to scope out a spot to bed Maggie and Luna down and set a perimeter if he can. Dig in deep or take a high spot in a tree. Sixteen rounds between two weapons, not even the same caliber. That's all you got, soldier, got to make each one count. Just like that bloodbath back at the cabin, how it all came back and felt so natural to him, old habits die hard.

He says, "I'm not sure who that man was, but he told me your real name is Mia Rade, and that you're on the run from some very bad men. He claimed he was here to help you."

"Did any of that back there look like help to you?"

"It went to shit so quick I don't know what that was. I'm just telling you what the man said, which is more than you." Marcus rises from his gravestone and checks the girl's pulse, strong and steady. He thought her fingers might've moved, her eyes fluttered, but he's not sure.

Marcus carries the SPEAR at low ready and moves to Maggie and sits down in front of her. "So, are you Mia Rade?"

Maggie shakes her head again. "Does it matter now?"

"It does to me. Just answer that . . . just the one question. And look me in the eye."

The moment lingers, Maggie searching the sky, the snow, the trees, before finally settling on him again. "Yes, I'm Mia Rade."

"Okay then, Mia, it doesn't matter. Not now. Not anymore. But *Maggie*, we need to figure out how we're getting off this mountain alive, because that's all that does matter. We can assume there's several men tracking us, as many as a half dozen, and FBI or not, they're likely well equipped, highly skilled, and given what happened back there, extremely motivated. We got lucky at Walton's cabin. We won't again. The only advantages we have are a surprise head start, the storm overhead, if that doesn't kill us first, and whatever your plan was to get off this mountain. I'm assuming you had one."

"What about her," Maggie says, pointing to the sleeping girl.

"What about her?"

"Come on, Sheriff, you must've felt it. Back there, at the cabin. We didn't just get *lucky* . . ."

Marcus hesitates. "I don't know." He stops a second time, uncertain on how to start again. "The shooting started, flash-bangs started going off inside the cabin, and then I started flashing back too. Look, I did several combat tours . . ." He still doesn't know how to say these things, not even after all this time, and could never say them out loud to Deidre. But this Maggie woman says it for him.

"You thought it was PTSD? Combat related?"

"Something like that. I have . . . weird moments. Lost moments. Kind of tune in and out. Nothing like what happened at the cabin, but then again, it's been a while since I've had someone shooting at me."

"That makes two of us," Maggie says, with the barest hint of a smile. "But I've never been in real combat, don't have PTSD, and I still felt *something*. And whatever it was, it started with her. Luna."

Marcus is nowhere near to conceding that or even understanding it. His episodes, his fugue states, have been powerful in the past, near crippling. Different from what took hold of him at the cabin, but not dissimilar. "What's that mean? How so?"

"I don't know that I can explain it exactly either. But sometimes there's this . . . aura . . . around her. I felt it, so did Landry." It's clear to Marcus that Maggie doesn't have the words for it any more than he's ever had the words for his own episodes. "Like a pulse . . . an electricity . . . an energy. Like the air itself is alive, almost *dangerous*. And I think it hurts her too."

"Okay, what do we know about her?" he asks, nodding in Luna's direction.

"Less than you and I know about each other," Maggie answers. "Landry was trying to find out about her, though, about the crashed plane I pulled her out of. He called that deputy of yours—"

"Donnie. Donnie Kornblue." Marcus can't shake that fleeting image of the stunned look on Donnie's face as the bullets flew past him. "That's why he was there." Marcus cut Donnie out of his dealings with Graham, thought he was saving him some hassle, and got him killed anyway. "All those damn papers blowing all around."

Circling skyward like bloodstained birds.

"Guess we'll never know what he learned," Maggie says.

"But maybe they will." He doesn't have to tell her who *they* are. "Donnie's dead, and with each passing minute, we have to assume Walton is as well."

"Maybe they caught him?"

He last remembers Walton on the move, heading toward the cabin. Remembers him kicking the living shit out of Graham. Remembers the old man getting tangled up with someone else near the porch, another one of Graham's men. He says, "Walton's not the sort to go quietly—"

Now a new voice, whispered and up close, "And you two don't know shit about how to keep quiet."

Both Marcus and Maggie turn to find Walton crouched near the girl, looking wild, feral, bloody. But alive.

Jesus, Marcus thinks, I didn't hear a thing.

Ignoring Walton's admonition, Maggie cries out, something between anger and joy, and runs to hug him, search him. She runs her hands over his chest, his face. "You're hurt."

"I'm above ground and breathing," Walton says, pushing her away. "And I aim to stay that way. Aim to keep us all that way."

Marcus joins them. "I'm glad you're here, Walton. Glad you're okay." There's so much more he wants to say, about what happened at the cabin, about Donnie, but Walton just nods and waves at him to kneel again. Walton's eyes are on the sky, the trees, the gravestones. His eyes *are* gravestones, bruised and black. Marcus can't tell how badly he's hurt, or even what hurt him, but he doesn't look good.

"Did you lose them back there?" Marcus asks.

"Yeah, I lost that bullshit FBI agent and his crew. The men you brought here." Walton makes it sound like an accusation, and it every bit is. "But that's not what I'm worried about."

"Then what?" Maggie asks.

"There's something else out there," Walton says, dark eyes still on the trees. "Something out there stalking us . . ."

45

It was a White Thing.

That was Walton's first thought when he caught it slipping through the trees. One of West Virginia's monsters. One of the things that got Cooper's brother, Hudson.

One of those things in the mountains that took his boy.

It came at him big and fast, stank like oil and burned skin. Bone white, striped black and red, either flayed skin or open wounds. It crouched like a man but ran or loped like a wolf. Moved tree to tree, smart or wily enough to seek cover.

Even in the frigid, snowy gloom, something bright shone on its left wrist . . . a manacle or a chain or cuffs . . . the same left arm that swung at him, that knocked him down.

It caught him before he got to the porch and bowled him over and went at his throat and his eyes with its bare hands or claws, and he was barely able to get it off him. It mewled and breathed and formed humanlike words, but it wasn't asking for mercy, grace, or help. It mouthed one thing—

Luna . . .

It wasn't much interested in him at all.

It seemed drawn by the girl . . . drawn to her . . . and even as it choked him out and tried to bash his head open on the exposed porch planks, its animal impulse to get to her gave Walton the opening he needed to fight it off.

He wasn't weaponless, still had the Jackal Pup he'd almost drawn on Agent Graham, and he was able to work the small blade loose from its horizontal sheath and get a few good jabs in on the thing, low to the rib cage. He was seeking its heart, and he felt the sharp toothlike blade go in and out, in and out, deep enough to score off bone. The thing howled in his face and kicked him free and let go.

Then it was gone inside . . . inside his cabin . . . his home.

He would've given it chase, would've chased it to hell and back for the trespass, but rifle rounds were picking their way toward him, chewing up the porch, shattering the windows he'd put in years before by hand. The fusillade kept him low, left him belly-crawling off his own damn porch like a worthless snake, slithering for cover. He wanted to get to Donnie but couldn't crawl far or fast enough, not exposed like that, not in the cold and snow and not with bullets raining down.

He shouldn't have kicked the agent's gun away; that was so stupid. The kind of stupidity that gets you killed. He was about to scramble on all fours into the woods, and that's when the girl started screaming.

A few seconds after that was when he saw Kellan.

His boy, feathered in twilight itself, waving at him. Guiding him forward, silently showing him the way. He was a shadow in shadow, looking just like he did the last day Walton ever saw him alive, not a day older, and every bit as beautiful as Walton remembered.

Oh, Kell, I hear birds coming to carry me away . . .

And then all the girl's screaming and the gunfire stopped, and all that was left was Walton's labored, desperate breathing.

His sobbing.

☾

He doesn't tell Austin or Maggie about seeing his dead son, doesn't tell them how his boy may or may not have ushered him to safety.

But he does tell them about the thing that attacked him.

"I thought I saw you fighting with one of Graham's men, but I didn't see anything like that, nothing like what you just described," Austin says, looking to Maggie for support, even if a flicker in his eye suggests he saw *something*. "You?"

Maggie shakes her head but seems even less sure. "It was crazy. I'm not sure I can tell you what I saw or didn't see."

"I'm not looking for you to agree with me," he says. "I'm just saying what happened. And unlike those other men, I'm not so sure it was even there for you, Maggie. This was . . . something different." He can't help but look to the girl, and the others follow his gaze. "I hoped I'd put it down for good, but it's been on me since I got away. Slow, steady, but there."

"And you brought it here?" Austin asks. "How do you even know?"

Walton glares. "You may be a war hero, but I'm a hunter. I know how to track something, and I sure in the hell know when something's tracking *me*." Walton touches the bruises and rake marks on his neck, makes sure both Austin and Maggie see them good and clear. "It's out there. And I figured if it was stalking me, it would just as soon find the likes of you two, if either of you had survived that Alamo down below."

"Thanks," Austin says. "I can take care of myself."

"You're *welcome*," Walton shoots back. "Then I can just—"

"Stop, please," Maggie interrupts. "It's fine, you did what you could, what you had to, like we all did. But we're here now. Together. Safety now in numbers, right?"

It's a strange admission for a woman who only hours earlier was desperate and willing to light out on her own.

Austin raises a long gun he must've grabbed off one of Graham's men, says, "I'd feel a lot safer with a couple more of these and another two hundred rounds of ammo."

On that, Walton doesn't disagree, even though they'll never be able to shoot their way off Black Mountain, and that's assuming the mountain doesn't take them first. He's wounded and the other two are shivering. Before long, as night falls, none of them will be thinking clearly.

"Here's the deal," he says. "Temperatures are dropping fast, even another two or three degrees and our brains are gonna be nothing but static. This isn't even a full-on blizzard yet, but the storm we already got spitting down is going to both slow us down and snow-blind us. Our eyelids are gonna freeze shut, and we're like to freeze to death if we don't shelter, and soon. But this squall can help us too . . . if we're smart. If we keep moving, use as much daylight as we can to put some distance between us and that FBI agent and his men, and then bed down for the night." Walton eyes Maggie's pack. "You still got your gear in there?"

Maggie nods. "Everything you gave me as well."

"Good." He keeps his eyes on Maggie. "That Graham character will need to call in the cavalry now if he's serious about seeing this through, although I reckon he's already got some help close by. Still, it'll take him time to rally it all, and if we can steal ourselves some more, keep up our head start, let the storm slow him down, no one should be able to catch us here. No one knows this place as well as I do, 'cept Kell." Maggie raises an eyebrow, questions, but he ignores her. He turns to address them both. "Not gonna lie, though, we're up against it. I'm busted up, you"—he looks to Austin's covered leg, doesn't want to make an issue of it but has got to acknowledge it all the same—"ain't gonna win any footraces, and right now, that young girl is nothing but deadweight. We don't want to shoot it out with these people, we can't, but I can get us off this mountain. I will. But it's gonna be painful near every step of the way, and you're gonna have to do about every damn thing I say, the second I say it. No lip, no questions."

Austin glares but finally shrugs. "I'll do my best to keep my lip zipped." And if Austin is being a smart-ass, Walton is fine with that, long as he does what he's told.

"Leave me," Maggie suggests. "Take Luna and go. They're only after me."

But Austin isn't done yet either. "What about this man out there tracking you . . . now tracking us? What are we going to do about that? Are you both sure no one else survived that crash? Are you willing to bet our lives on it?"

Maggie looks to Walton. "You saw that scene."

"I didn't see anything alive," he replies, "not so much as a single body . . ."

At that, Maggie starts. "Wait, you didn't see that burned guy? Facedown, like he was clawing at the dirt?" Maggie's visibly upset by the memory, and although he knows she said *clawing*, it just as easily could've been *crawling*. "He was right there where I found Luna." She laughs, almost crazy. "He was still wearing a watch, for Christ's sake. He was definitely dead, though. Burning. But he was there."

That thing that attacked him—

Even in the frigid, snowy gloom, something bright shone on its left wrist . . . a manacle or a chain or cuffs . . . the same left arm that swung at him, that knocked him down . . .

He doesn't know which is crazier: that someone else somehow survived that crash and then attacked him on his porch, or that a dead man did.

A White Thing, one of the mountain's ghosts or monsters.

But before he can answer, before he even knows what to answer, the girl speaks up—

"It was *him.*"

She says it again, her tongue still thick from whatever was used to knock her out.

"It was him."

46

He lost her again and suffered mightily doing so.

He'd wanted to use the chaos of the shooting to make his move but wasted too much time on that old man, who proved more formidable than he first appeared, although the mountain warned him.

The wounds the man gave him would kill most, but not him, not anymore.

He crashed through the cabin, but before he could find her the cabin itself exploded in white-hot light that sucked all the air from his lungs and a crush of brutal, unforgiving noise and then she started screaming, too, releasing again all the furious birds in his head.

They beat their wings and scrabbled and clawed and cawed, and he wanted to tear his eyes out. Not even the mountain could shield him that close from her fury.

The agony and his injuries drove him back into the woods, where he waited to die, but when he didn't, when he picked up the old man's trail moving west from the cabin . . . moving up . . . he started after him.

☾

He lopes now through a cold veil.

The snow curls around him, hiding him. A deep, lost part of him remembers a time when he was ten or eleven and his family, now all dead, visited a cold place like this, sitting in that old car and staring out a glass window too glacial to touch, watching snow fall on tall trees in the dark.

Streetlights and flurries glistening and twirling in their light, like moths or fleeting jewels or flecks of windblown glass.

He no longer recalls the name of his mother or his father or what became of them, other than that they are long dead. It's possible he had a sister once, too, because a young girl's face beckons at the edge of these memories, but every time he tries to summon it, it's *her* face that appears.

She's gone quiet and still in the aftermath of the cabin. Unconscious, drugged, but very much alive. Her thoughts flutter brightly out there for him to follow.

Just like—

Moths or fleeting jewels or flecks of windblown glass . . .

He scoops up the frigid snow, licks at it, uses it to stanch his wounds.

And continues to climb.

47

Ekker sits in the sheriff's cold truck and takes stock of his assets.

Bisek is next to him in the front passenger seat—Ekker was still wary about putting the man at his back, given what happened to Tancredi—but appears finally to be shaking off whatever afflicted him.

Unfortunately, he's not particularly helpful either. He can't fill in the blanks on what happened at the cabin. Or how—exactly—Rade got away. He does recall a young girl with her, though, a teen or close to it, but all he can say about her is she whispered to him, called out his name, and the world turned upside down. He mentions someone named Uncle Stepan, and his eyes go dark.

Ekker doesn't know what any of this means, but given what he experienced, too, he's unwilling to dismiss it out of hand. He can't dismiss anything; he's prepared to use everything at his disposal, and that includes Bisek, no matter how broken he still might be.

In World War II, the Nazis distributed Pervitin, the Japanese Philopon, and the Allies Benzedrine, all methamphetamine-based stimulants to get soldiers back into the fight. In Vietnam, it was dextroamphetamine, so-called pep pills, and it left a whole generation of veterans with raging substance abuse problems. The designer pharmaceutical cocktail Ekker hits Bisek with is more elegant than any of those, but just as addictive, twice as powerful. It still has numerous potentially unpleasant side effects, too, including burning away Bisek's brain fog as well as most of his short-term memory.

He's conscious, stable, and very angry. And that's good enough for now.

☾

Hindsight is a perfect science, and in hindsight, Ekker should have called up a bigger team.

Bisek. Tancredi. Porter. Mosely.

Local extraction and delivery. Hands-on support.

Feiser.

Logistics and tech and signal intelligence.

But Ekker came to the same conclusion that Theroux did: Pullens was small enough that any significant outside presence would draw too much unwanted attention, both from Rade herself (if she was still even bedded down in the town) and any local law enforcement (if things got loud trying to find her), so better to follow in Rade's footsteps as quiet as possible until the last-possible moment, aiming for low-profile infiltration and exfil. Ekker, however, decided to extrapolate off Theroux's failure and make Pullens's size and remoteness an exploitable asset, turning Pullens's small, rural, and woefully unprepared sheriff's office into an unwitting force multiplier for his own small team via the Agent Graham persona. A good plan almost necessitated by Brooking's insistence on Ekker bringing Rade in *alive*.

That stipulation is what derailed Theroux's efforts as well. In the end, his attempt to go in too small, too soft, is exactly what got him killed. The delicate balance of putting hands on the woman without injuring her too badly, if at all. The unnatural hesitation you force on a killer when you order that killer not to draw blood.

None of that matters, though, if Rade *isn't* the primary target anymore, and that's why he's decided to forgo alerting Brooking. He doesn't want Brooking getting antsy, doesn't want him interfering. That's also why Ekker's decided not to call in further external reinforcements, even if he easily could. Between the storm lurking overhead and the nonexistent cellular service around the mountain, he's limited to Feiser's mobile network array and their satellite comms, not to mention the time it'd take for another prepped team to get on the ground here.

After what he's experienced at the cabin, the disappearance of that black angel in his eye, Ekker doesn't care what happens to Mia Rade anymore. She'll still be Brooking's problem if she survives the next twenty-four hours, which Ekker is planning she won't.

She's merely a means to an end now, a vector for his new target.

The girl.

C

The papers the dead deputy brought start a story without an ending.

There *was* a plane crash, somewhere likely close to here, but the plane had nothing to do with Rade at all. The girl was on the plane, and somehow survived its descent. And either Rade or Landry found her, and no doubt found themselves just as curious about her as Ekker is now, prompting Landry to reach out to Deputy Kornblue.

It's telling that Landry went to his prior chief deputy rather than Sheriff Austin. Assuming both survived—and Ekker's going to assume so—it speaks to an interesting dynamic between the two.

There's not much left of Kornblue's work and there wasn't much to begin with, most of it windblown down the mountain or bullet riddled. But between the eTrace queries and what look to be a (real) FBI report and at least one news article, a handful of those words or phrases catch Ekker's eye—

Conrad Stoll, a.k.a. Colm Roach. Leo Stier. Tesseract.

It's not actionable intel, nothing he can use yet, but it's a start.

Right now, the girl, Rade, Landry, and Austin are all somewhere on the mountain above him, cold and exhausted and probably wounded. Either together or separate. Landry knows the lay of the land, and Austin might still prove dangerous if he gets his combat senses dialed back in and his hands on a gun. The black, silent redactions in Austin's military record speak volumes, as do Porter's and Mosley's fresh corpses.

Rade is the unknown variable. She's proven resourceful time and again. The last two years have hardened her, and Ekker appreciates that, even admires it. That's what drew him into this before. *Her eyes.* He knows her complicated history, the things she's done and what she's capable of, and not everything FBI agent Graham told Sheriff Austin about her was a lie.

How much is she willing to personally risk?

Another telling dynamic, like the tension between Austin and Landry. If the plane wasn't for Rade, then why was she up here at all? What was she doing?

Why here?

He circles back to the question that brought him and Austin up here to begin with—

Where was she going?

Headlights bloom wearily in the window behind Bisek's head, shining on Ekker's face.

It's Feiser, and it's time to start hunting again.

48

As Walton roots through Maggie's pack, taking stock of her gear and getting both her and the girl ready to set out again, Marcus keeps watch from fifteen yards away, tucked in beneath the overhanging branches of a canted pine.

The tree's so low and twisted it's about to fall over on him, but it keeps the wind and lightly blowing snow out of his face and affords him mostly unobstructed views of two cardinal directions on their position.

White snow. Gray gravestones. Black trees.

Sky the color of granite, of unwashed stone.

The stolen long gun is heavy in his hands. His hands are cold, and they're going to get a hell of a lot colder. He and Walton aren't really dressed for an extended winter hike, nor is the girl, done up in a mishmash of castoffs from Maggie and from Walton's dead son.

Every few minutes Marcus takes his eyes off the storm and watches her, trying to make sense of her relationship to the other two. When she came to and said, *It was him,* both Walton and Maggie knew exactly who the girl was referring to, even if they couldn't agree on what it meant.

Another plane crash survivor, a man named Roach or . . . something else.

Donnie used to say that Walton was as well versed in West Virginia's unique lore as anyone in the state. Not just the "real" history, but all those old campfire ghost stories, too, like those in Ms. Torri's bed-side book back at the inn. As evidenced by this backwoods cemetery spread out around Marcus, all these cracked markers and stones and the winged marble angel taking flight, the old lawman's family has been here a long, long time. Marcus has no doubt such stories were passed down again and again.

Walton's own son vanished up here, and more than once. Donnie suggested that whenever Walton got into a bottle, he'd hint that he was haunted by more than just Kellan's untimely disappearance and the mystery around it. Marcus isn't sure what's worse: armed federal agents or mercenaries hunting them or being stalked by a West Virginia ghost story.

His own experience last night—

It rumbled out of the darkness, broke free of the trees, lunged across the road in a hoary flash . . . smoky gray and white, the color of ashen shadows, of soot and dried blood and old bone. A frantic origami of impossible arms and legs . . .

But he didn't hit a myth or ghost. Whatever it was left a dent in his truck, blood on the metal. He touched it, felt it.

Despite the haunted trappings of these woods, this isn't a folktale, a fairy story. It could have been this man, this Roach, another crash survivor. But what are the odds, he asks himself, the luck of surviving a plane crash, only to be run over by a truck?

If any man somehow survived both things and then crawled through the woods to attack Walton in the middle of that firefight— still a big *if* that Marcus isn't ready to accept, no more than he's willing to accept that the girl gave them all a case of PTSD, like a virus—then that's a man Marcus doesn't want to face. Might not even be right to call it a man anymore.

Although he can't begin to guess what might motivate such a man, he agrees with Walton that his appearance has more to do with the young girl with the weird eyes and burned hair than Mia Rade. If he's still out here on this mountain stalking them, it's because she's here too. This whole mess might have started with the Rade woman, but it'll end with that girl.

Those eyes are something . . .

Hard to shake, harder to forget.

He and Deidre never seriously considered kids. She had a rough upbringing in Norfolk that didn't plant the desire, and after Marcus saw some of the shittiest sides of a world that didn't seem fit to bring a child into, nothing he'd seen after had much changed his mind. It was the one thing they could always agree on, even when they couldn't agree on much else.

He doesn't recall if the Mia Rade from Graham's reports had children, but it's hard to imagine she would have up and left them, not if danger was close on her heels, and Graham was telling the truth. This Maggie didn't leave the girl behind at the cabin, either, and she had every chance.

But Marcus assumes now that nearly everything Graham told him was a lie, anyway, including the man's name. Marcus was duped, played for a fool, and Donnie Kornblue is dead as a result. The way things are going they're likely all to be dead before night falls.

The cold holds him and he scans the white snow, the gray gravestones, the black trees.

He's not particularly afraid of dying.

But just let me see that sonofabitch one more time, he thinks. Just give me one chance to return the favor.

49

Maggie shrugs when Landry finds the ten-inch-long, wicked-looking serrated knife in her pack.

He holds up the sheathed blade, asks, "A Tom Brown Tracker T3?"

"Yeah, I guess. I found it used at a pawn shop," she answers. "I bought a couple different ones."

"I reckon," he says, not commenting on the one she left buried in a man back in Pullens. "My boy swore by 'em. He had several too." He tosses the Tracker to her. "Put it on. Won't do you any good otherwise."

He continues cataloging her pack: UCO Stormproof Sweetfire Strikeable Fire Starters, Titan Stormproof Match Kit, HART day hike safety kit, Black Diamond headlamp, NEMO Dragonfly tent and Disco sleeping bag. Spare clothes and socks. An extra SureFire and batteries. His MyFAK emergency kit and her dad's compass and sextant and her trail map with her handwritten marks.

Five thousand dollars in tens, and twenties, tightly heat sealed. Another thousand in smaller denominations and $100 bills, all in a ziplock baggie.

Two sets of car keys, the first still sporting the ring and tag from that used car lot in New Jersey, the second a simple key fob, blurry and indistinct in its own heat-sealed pouch.

She can recite everything and doesn't protest or resist as Landry goes through it all. They were all a means to an end anyway, and if any of it can keep even one of them alive for another day, another hour, that's all that matters now.

"How's she doing?" Landry asks her, nodding at Luna. The girl's stayed conscious, but she's slipped into one of her waking catatonic states again. Like shock, but not. Breathing steady, eyes open, staring, but it's anybody's guess what she's seeing.

Maggie knows if Luna survives this, it'll be a long time—maybe never—for her to unsee what's happened here.

Landry looks up the mountain, lost in thought. It's getting tough to talk and hear over the wind; the snow's now hardened, too, tiny freezing tears pelting them, and it's going to get worse when they start moving again. Maggie can barely reason, her brain freezing. She wonders when they'll all start seeing and hearing things. Landry wouldn't let Maggie or even Marcus examine his wounds, but he took some of the moleskin, gauze, and butterfly closures from her HART kit, as well as some Wound Wipes and Tribiotic from the MyFAK. He dry-chewed a handful of Cetafen and Proprinal, but didn't take all of it, figuring he'll need more later, or one of them will.

He holds up a second dart they pulled from Luna's clothes, an ugly wasplike stinger with blood-colored fletching. The tiny microfiber feathers are hot and bright against the cold and snowy backdrop, impossible to ignore. This one somehow never burrowed its way through Maggie's borrowed merino, stopping millimeters from Luna's skin.

"What do you know about this?" he asks.

"Nothing," she answers truthfully.

"They clearly still want Maggie alive, Walton," Sheriff Austin—Marcus—says from over her shoulder. Earlier, he'd taken up a position a little ways off, but now he's returned to their little redoubt. He kneels and exchanges Landry his wicked-looking rifle for the dart, turning it over in his gloved fingers. "Graham said Maggie was cooperating with the FBI, against the interests of some very dangerous men. He was there to bring her in safe." He holds up the dart. "Willing or not, apparently."

J. Todd Scott

218

Landry snorts. "Looks to me like your Graham was one of those dangerous men. A wolf in sheep's clothes."

Marcus says, "Hey, fuck you. He isn't *my* anything. The man had a badge and creds. I had no reason to assume he wasn't who he said he was, and least he was telling me *something*." Marcus points at both Maggie and Walton. "If you'd been honest with me from the jump, we might not be in this mess."

"You'd have handled it then?" Landry fires back.

"We wouldn't have gotten Donnie killed . . . I can tell you that. And we did, Walton. We did." Marcus looks like he's going to throw the dart out into the snow but thinks better of it. Instead, he tosses it back to Landry. "We both got to own that, however long we have left."

Maggie can see the pain in his eyes, the anger. She says, "And we can't do this now. Either of you."

"But he ain't wrong, though," Landry says. "We gotta own it."

"I could say the same thing too," Maggie concedes.

Marcus nods. "Then we all have debts to pay to that fucker Graham."

Landry lets that settle between them before he hands the rifle back to Marcus and turns back to her. "Remember when we talked up in Kell's room, I told you the best way to cross over the mountain? That's what you and Marcus and the girl here are gonna do right now. Start heading up that ridgeline."

"No, wait. What about you?" she asks.

Landry's already grabbing up some of the things he's taken out of her pack, as well as the dart. "I'll be just a few minutes behind. I'll catch up. Promise. I'm going to thieve us more of that head start I talked about, throw Graham off our scent."

She doesn't know if Walton really means the *other* thing stalking them . . . whatever attacked him outside his cabin.

But it's Marcus who balks. "Then what, Walton?" He turns to her. "Look, I know you had a plan here, some way to disappear, something better than hiding in a damn cave. Graham believed it and I do too. Whatever it is you had up your sleeve, we need to know about it, and we need to know it now."

Landry looks at her. He's trying to hide it, but he winces in pain. "He's not wrong about that either, Maggie. Moment of truth here. And we're running out of moments."

She takes the Tracker blade she's been holding and clips it horizontal to the belt at the small of her back, the same way Landry carried his own. It's like a heavy but gentle hand, pushing her forward.

"Lost Hill," she says. "I was going to Lost Hill."

50

Once Maggie and the others are out of sight, Walton does his best to clear traces of their presence from the cemetery.

The snow blurring down will do its work, too, sow confusion if nothing else, but he knows it's largely a futile gesture. If Graham is determined, Walton's stealing them moments at best, and like he told Maggie, they're fast running out of those.

Walton can't remember the last time he came up here and sat with these old gravestones, certainly not since Kell disappeared. When Walton was young, and his great-grandfather Cooper was alive, he'd bring Walton here in the summer, when the trees were so green they were black, and they'd sit among these markers, and Coop would drink some clear shine and whittle and share an apple with Walton and fill his head full of stories.

Coop told Walton not to be scared, not up here. His kin's blood and bones and spirits were in this place, soaked through and through, and it was sacred in a way. Protected here in the heart of this widening circle of gray rocks and toppled monuments, at least for a little while.

That's why he was comfortable hunkering down here with the others, at least for a little while too. But unless his dead ancestors were ready to rise out of the cold ground here and help them, they couldn't stay here forever. This place isn't sacred or powerful enough to ward off Graham and his men, not their darts, nor their bullets. Not forever.

In the end, the mountain itself also proved too much for his own boy, who spent many of his summers in this cemetery, too, with Walton.

If his son is still up here somewhere, he's not lying peaceful in one of these graves.

☾

About fifty yards west of the old graveyard, Walton finds a spot on the lee side of a pitch pine and tosses down an unopened Cetafen pack.

Another fifty yards from that, he drops the dart he took off the girl. He waits as falling snow drifts over it, until only the red fletching remains. When that's gone, too, he zigzags westward again, cutting through more pitch and white pine, snapping branches as he goes.

He's moving down now, toward Alpena Gap, or at least that's what anyone with a GPS would assume. From the Gap you can pick up a fair number of hiking and logging roads, and eventually make your way to US Route 33. It's a reasonable path off the mountain, if that's what you're trying to do.

Deep beneath the trees now, Walton finds the small pond he was searching for, frozen over now, a slick, beautiful unblemished surface, so white it almost hurts the eye. In summer this is little more than a thumbprint in the mountain, a mossy wellspring of cave water.

He and Kellan swam here now and then, fiery sun on their backs, dappled angel light through the trees, the water so cold and fresh and clear it made their teeth ache. Kell found Indian points below the surface, bones too. Most graves on Black Mountain aren't marked by headstones.

Walton hunkers down and slowly starts working free one of the butterfly bandages from his wounds.

He took a beating from that . . . thing . . . worse than he wanted to let on to either Maggie or Marcus. Despite the cold, he's still bleeding bad, like the proverbial stuck pig. His core temperature's dropping fast, too, so he'll just as likely freeze to death before these wounds kill him or a clot stops his heart.

Even in the cold, the stink of chilly blood will carry far.

He sticks the stained bandage to a pine and lets it wave there like a tiny, crimson flag.

He then unsheathes his Jackal Pup and crouches as quietly as he can, watching the snow-flecked woods. His little blade's not got anywhere near the heft or length of Maggie's, but it did the trick before. It'll do it again.

But as sure as he was that the thing tracked him away from the cabin, he's not so sure it followed him down from the cemetery. It called out for Luna before, certainly seems drawn to her, but of the four of them, he's the most wounded, the easiest kill, if this man or thing reasons that way. If nothing else, Walton is also the one who hurt it, hurt it *bad*, and even animals remember that. Sometimes, anger and vengeance are enough.

Either he's lured it away or he hasn't, but he's also given Graham and his men a merry trail to follow, if they're smart enough to look, and Walton's betting they are.

A trail far from Lost Hill.

He fights to keep his eyes open, tries not to shake and rattle from the cold. You lose body heat about twenty-five times faster in water than in the air. If he cracked the ice on the pond and slipped in, he'd be dead in twenty minutes or less. If he doesn't get moving soon, get his heart and blood flowing again, he'll still be dead in an hour.

It's going to get bad for the others soon too. He didn't want to tell them just *how* bad.

But still, he waits.

Cold. Patient. Dying.

Kell could sit up in a hunting blind or deer stand for days like this, mostly just watching the world go by. He'd pass up good shot after good shot, one excuse after another, so as not to pull the trigger, not rush the moment. His boy was infinitely patient; seemingly the only thing he was ever eager to get away from was Walton.

Oh, Kell, I hear birds coming to carry me away . . .

He doesn't know what that means, but he likes it.

Walton watches the storm breathe in and out all around him until he can't feel the knife in his hand or even his hands or feet at all and each breath is like broken glass in his chest, piercing his heart.

51

She likes the new man, Marcus.

He doesn't say much to her, just keeps a hand on her shoulder or small of her back, helping her along, willing to touch her in a way the old man wouldn't.

Marcus and Maggie don't talk much, but they constantly check on each other. Maggie is up ahead, leading the way, and often slows and stops and looks back and waits.

She can feel all the unspoken thoughts and fears and unanswered questions between the two winging their way over her head, a feathered flurry of dread and worry.

Marcus's thoughts are angrier, a constant war of dark sparks and flickers inside him. The cold can't do anything to cool or calm that down. Maggie's emotions are naturally chillier. But below that ice, black things lurk and move.

Neither expects to live long, but neither *fears* it, and she wonders at that. When the plane went down, she nearly exploded with anger and fear, not just her own, but from all those around her.

She couldn't take it all in.

When she's scared or hurt, when she can't cage her own dark birds or keep everyone else's at bay and out of her mind, she lashes out, just like she did on the plane, like she did again at the cabin. And when that happens, all of Dr. Jewell's techniques aren't enough to hold back the murmuration in her head. Dr. Jewell once told her maybe nothing in the world can.

The old man is too far away for her, as are the others from the cabin, those who survived. When she woke up from being drugged—not the first time for her—Roach's frantic thoughts were just taking flight again, too, but now he's either too far away or he's mastered masking them. He was never very good at it before, but it's not just him, it's this *place* too.

The mountain.

All around her, heavy, weighing at her, pulling her down.

Not just that bat-winged presence from before, but more than that. Not alive in any way she can understand, but not necessarily dead either. More like an old house, haunted by a hundred ghosts, a thousand spirits, and the spirits on this mountain don't fear anything.

She wants to be more like Maggie and Marcus.

She wants to be more like the mountain.

52

"Tell me," Ekker says, "how they get off this mountain."

Martin Feiser, loudly chewing peppermint gum, spins the tablet around on his lap, starts pointing out roads and trails and campgrounds on the brightly illuminated screen. "Not easily, and not fast," he says. "Maybe never if they're on foot."

Ekker watches fresh snow collect on Feiser's windshield, the world beyond as white as TV static. Outside, he was barely able to see his hand in front of his face. "Assume they are."

Feiser taps at his tablet, and Ekker glances back at Bisek, staring wordlessly out the windshield, hands folded in his lap like a child. They've moved over to Feiser's SUV, stifling since Feiser never left it during the raid and he's had the heater blowing for hours. It's one of the two Ekker's team positioned in the woods near Landry's cabin before the shooting started. The other is supplied with more practical, tactical gear, but this one is like Feiser's personal lair, fetid and cloying like the man himself, full of his laptops and tablets and his mobile comms array and Wi-Fi network.

Feiser taps again, *here, here, here.*

"They're going to want to find major blacktop if they can," Feiser explains. "Best chance to get help, right? That's US Route 33, same way we got to *The Hills Have Eyes* up here. But . . . there are dozens of trails and logging and forestry roads they could take. This mapping software is as up to date as you'll find, but we're still in a maze. State Road 91 will take you up to Bickle Knob; all these other little county roads wind you around to campgrounds or whatever. If they do go to ground, hole up somewhere, the only towns of any size they could reasonably make for are"—Feiser squints, pops his gum—"Bowden, Wymer, Alpena Gap. Harman."

"The largest of those?"

"Harman." Feiser pops again. "Population 143."

"Did you run geospatial?" Ekker asks. "Can you give me a search grid based on foot speed?"

"I ran everything," Feiser says, "but it's a statistical mess. The inputs are thin. We're not sure if they're all still together, or even still alive. This storm dirties up the data so bad the algorithm is merely guessing, which, you know, fucks the whole data and metrics thing—"

He fixes Feiser with a cold look. "Then *you* guess."

Feiser stops popping his gum, eyes wide and white and bleary behind his glasses. Ekker's never liked him but uses him even though he's useless in an evolving, dynamic situation like this, because he's generally good at keeping a situation from ever going dynamic in the first place.

Feiser swallows. "Who's the slowest? This mysterious young girl you didn't factor?"

"*We* didn't factor, and no. Likely the sheriff."

Feiser snaps his fingers, remembering. "The cripple."

Ekker leans close. "He's not crippled, and don't make that mistake. Porter and Mosley did, and now they aren't alive to make it again."

Feiser blinks, nods, then bends back over his tablet. Ekker can almost make out the gears, diodes, or synapses firing behind the man's glasses, whatever systems make him tick. He has this sudden strong image of Feiser, only filled with lighted points like his map, otherwise dark and empty. "Alpena Gap."

Ekker takes Feiser's tablet without asking, finds Alpena Gap. "Assess."

"Smaller than Harman, if they're still trying to stay out of our sight line. Mining town, remote, but multiple points of egress and ingress. If Walton Landry is alive, he's likely to know someone there. On the numbers alone, the algorithm likes it. If you call it a coin toss between, let's say, Wymer and the Gap . . ." Feiser trails off, shrugs. "My guess is the latter."

Ekker tosses the tablet back at Feiser and taps at the frosted window with a scarred knuckle. "My guess is neither."

Feiser looks down at his tablet, unwilling to meet Ekker's gaze.

"Landry's too smart for that," Ekker explains, "and Mia Rade is too prepared. No, she had a grander plan, a very specific purpose, up here."

Feiser says, "So she abandons them now? Heads out on her own again. She is one cold, cold bitch."

"Possible," he concedes. "Or Landry forces the split, dividing our attention and assets. But I don't care about either now . . . I only want the girl."

Feiser taps on his tablet some more. "Brooking—"

"Not your concern."

Feiser pushes anyway. "The girl is a nonfactor . . . if there even is a girl. She's a literal nobody. And she's not the payday."

"And don't make *that* mistake again either. I decide. I pay." And Ekker's very much decided there is a girl. The staging in the cabin, the blankets, and the mugs are clear to him.

Feiser's lips go thin, the closest thing he's ever come to demonstrating anger, or any emotion other than complaining, in front of Ekker. "Okay. But there are only three of us now. Pascal back there still doesn't seem too dialed in, and . . . *this* . . . this isn't what I do."

"It is now . . . because there are only three of us."

"I don't even have a *gun*," Feiser whines.

Ekker smiles. "Those we have plenty of."

Feiser sighs, chews that thin lip of his. "Look, more of Sheriff Austin's deputies will be on the way. Someone will figure out they're missing and come looking. Meanwhile, we're still blind out here, and I'm not just talking this blizzard falling on us. Rade's smart, she's kept zero digital footprint for almost two months now, and that's both impressive and near impossible nowadays. I don't know how Theroux tracked her this far, and we saw what that got him. Even with a gun, a hundred guns, I'm not a whole lot of good to you. But without data, without intel, without anything more than our own fucking educated *guesses*, I'm useless."

On that, Feiser isn't wrong. "Then make yourself useful. Fast." Ekker taps the window again, the glass so cold it numbs his whole hand, despite the heater blasting high across from him. "What about the White Rabbit?"

Feiser chuckles. "Not in this, even with its self-heating batteries and all the modifications I've made. Wind is too strong, and wet snow will play havoc with it. If we get a break in the weather, sure. I can have it up and running in ten minutes." Feiser clicks off his tablet and fishes out a new piece of gum. He doesn't offer any to Ekker. "What now?"

Ekker rubs at a spot between his eyes, his angel still blessedly quiet, as quiet as Bisek in the seat behind him. Ekker looks at Walton Landry's cabin, nearly lost to the snow, trying to decide if it holds any more answers as to where the man might go, where the others might be. Trying to decide if he should just go ahead and burn it to the ground, to hide whatever evidence of his team's extraction attempt remains.

If Feiser has an opinion, he doesn't offer it.

Ekker says, "I'm going back into the cabin for one more look. Ten minutes at most."

"And then?" Feiser asks.

"We stage at Alpena Gap until we get a break." Ekker pushes the ruined papers at Feiser. "When you get a signal, run these names, and get me some intel. Hard intel." Ekker opens the door, letting the storm in. "And get the Rabbit ready anyway."

53

Twenty-four miles.

That's how far Walton told them they needed to go to get to Lost Hill, Maggie's alleged escape route.

The last time Marcus hiked anywhere close to that was in Khost, Afghanistan. He and his unit were stationed at Forward Operating Base Yukon, a major CIA hub. After a suicide bomber detonated himself inside Yukon's wires, killing twelve, Marcus led a counterstrike against the insurgent group responsible to Obasta Tsukai, over the border in Pakistan.

Obasta Tsukai was a mountainous peak like Black Mountain, although more than twice as tall, at a full twelve thousand feet. He summitted it, but he had both legs then. Now he's hobbled by his Genesis bionic, the snow getting thicker, the drifts deeper, and the icy wind is like getting punched in the face again and again.

Twenty-four miles.

Given distance and elevation, and the ground they've covered so far, it'll take them another six hours, and that's moving as fast as they can.

They'll never make it.

No, Marcus, you'll never make it . . .

☾

They find another quiet hole in the storm and rest.

Even Marcus admits to himself it's beautiful up here, dusk sunlight glittering like diamonds on the snow, trees draped in pearl and crystal, dressed up for a night on the town, an enchanted forest for a fairy princess. Night is coming fast, but before Walton disappeared, he assured them they'd have a place to bed down, to get a fire going. They're going to need it to stave off freezing to death. Already Marcus's hands and foot feel bad. His heart beating slower, his blood retreating deeper, trying to keep him warm enough to keep him alive, barely.

The girl's stayed close to him, mostly silent, but now she asks him about his leg.

She asks him if it hurts.

He pulls up his sodden pant leg and taps at the carbon fiber frame. "You mean now . . . or then?"

"Both," she says, sitting on a downed tree. Maggie kneels between them, watching the exchange, but one eye behind, still on the lookout for Walton.

"It doesn't hurt now. I'm used to it. And it's amazing what this thing allows me to do. If we weren't hiking through all this snow, you might not have even noticed it, right? It's strong and waterproof, to protect the electronics. A technological marvel. Still, this is hard terrain."

"Hard on any legs," Maggie adds.

"True," he agrees. "But did it hurt *then*? Yeah, it hurt a lot." He drops his pant leg, wonders about the things Maggie told him about Luna, the weird vibe Maggie alleged the girl can give off. But Marcus hasn't felt anything strange since the cabin, and almost nothing from Luna at all. Despite her mostly outward calm, she must be scared out of her skull, though, and he knows that even hardened, well-trained soldiers can still break down in terror in the throes of combat. Fear is a powerful predator that way, relentless, merciless, unforgiving. Everyone faces it down differently, some with a scream, others with little more than a smile. He has no idea what's going on below the surface of those eyes of hers, but he admires the resolve she's shown so far. "I lost most of it in an explosion. That happened so quick, so sudden, I don't know that I felt anything, really." But he knows that's not exactly true; he was burning, screaming. "But it was all the surgeries after that, doctors trying to save my life, trying to help me get better, that were really painful." He tries a smile: all he can offer. "They sucked."

"I've had surgeries," Luna says. "So many I lost count."

"They hurt too?" he asks, flicking a glance to Maggie.

Luna nods. "Worse than anything."

The wind pulls at the girl's burned hair, and for the first time, he notices that Maggie and Luna could almost be sisters. Except for the eyes: those are Luna's alone. As bright as Maggie's are, they're nothing like the girl's. Hers are magical, hypnotic. "Can you tell me about them? Can you tell me why?"

Luna thinks. "To make me better too."

"Well," he says, "I guess we have that in common. And we both have scars now, right?"

Maggie waves at them to get moving again. "You have something else in common too."

"What's that?" Marcus asks her.

"You both survived and you're still here."

$$\smile$$

They're moving slow along a small ridge, moving over tumbled rocks, protected from the worst of the wind by knotted trees, when Marcus finally asks Maggie what she did.

"Graham said you and your husband owned a company, stole a bunch of money from some drug cartels."

"Something like that," she calls over her shoulder.

Both breathing heavy, really blowing hard, neither in a condition to hash this out—Marcus most of all—but he wants to have this conversation before Walton returns, if he does. "He told me innocent people lost money as well. People who trusted you, who invested their life savings with you. And you took it. Took it all."

Maggie doesn't look back at him. "That's true too."

"Why?"

Maggie keeps moving, picking her way carefully forward, always upward. "Why is it important? Like, right this minute."

He stops. "Because I'm trapped on this mountain with you, and like I said earlier, I'm relying on you to get us off it. Because we're *all* trusting you now."

Maggie finally stops, too, hands on her knees, and Luna stops a little behind them. "Okay," Maggie says, "you're right. I did all those things. Graham, or whoever he was, wasn't lying about that." She takes a few steps back toward him, so they're not shouting at each other, so her words aren't lost in the wind or fluttering snow. "My husband Vann and I first set up a digital currency venture in Saint Kitts and Nevis, then another in Condado, Puerto Rico, where we laundered money for drug cartels, human traffickers, offshore betting concerns, pornographers, and a variety of high-yield investment plans."

Maggie looks to Luna.

"All Ponzi schemes," she finally continues. "At its height, we had about three million user accounts, seventy million transactions, more than eight billion dollars on the move. Once global law enforcement agencies started taking a hard look at us, we closed shop, even as I refined and updated our model. It was my idea to create our very own crypto-currency exchange. I called it CambionXCG, and through Cambion we did thousands of fundamentally legal transactions a day, on behalf of more than eighty thousand unwitting small investor accounts . . . as well as the blood money we were still funneling around the world on behalf of Vann's clients."

"Vann's clients?"

"Mine too. Look, I'm not absolving myself of this, none of it. But Vann dealt with that side, meeting people, making the connections. I am, I was, all about the numbers." She blinks as sun blinds her off the snow before the sky clouds up again. "And the numbers were good. Cryptocurrency is still the Wild West, a black box, and CambionXCG itself was nothing but smoke and mirrors, a full-blown Ponzi sandcastle built on fraudulent accounts, false identities, and nonexistent trades."

Maggie pauses, gathers herself, watches the snow lift and swirl between them. "No offense, but it's incredibly baroque to explain. Just know that for someone like me, it was also very lucrative. We bought the obligatory yacht, a couple of houses on both coasts. Vann got himself a plane he couldn't even fly. We traveled to more than fifty countries, living the high life. Then the crypto bubble burst, for about the fourth or fifth time, and the authorities caught onto us again, and the whole castle started to tumble down around our ears. A software glitch, *my* software, cost us ten million. Not long after, another fifteen mil in Cambion funds was frozen for suspicious activity. Then, $480 million in so-called *cold wallets*—external hard drives disconnected from Cambion's virtual exchange that functioned like high-tech safes or vaults—up and vanished."

"Before or after your husband was killed?" he asks. When Maggie doesn't answer, he presses. "More to the point, Graham told me he might've been murdered . . . that maybe you murdered him."

"Vann died in a boating accident, Sheriff Austin."

"Sure, and conveniently he was the only one who had the electronic codes to unlock those wallets," he says. "So, no wallets, no codes, and all that money might as well not even exist. Lost at sea . . . like your husband."

"I'm telling you it's gone," Maggie says. "All of it."

Marcus shrugs. "But that's not entirely true, is it? I know it's really complicated and all, but I understand enough to know that money still *does* exist. Like I said, it's just . . . lost . . . one more pirate's treasure. All you need is a good map." He looks pointedly at Maggie's pack, where he knows there are at least two maps: Maggie's trail map, and the hand-drawn one she claimed Walton gave her. Now he gets to the question he's wanted to ask all along. "What's really waiting for us at Lost Hill? Who's waiting for us there? Vann?"

"He's at the bottom of the Atlantic," Maggie says, with such finality he almost believes her. "Everyone thought Vann grabbed the money and ran, assumed the boating accident was a bullshit cover story, some-thing Vann planned alone or something we dreamed up together. I was watched for months by the real FBI, Sheriff, as well as certain individ-uals like your fake agent Graham, who were hired by our very upset foreign clients."

"They still believe you have these wallets, these codes or whatever, right? They're still after the money." He looks to the girl, who has her back to them, watching the storm gather strength again. "That explains Graham . . . how his ambush went down at the cabin. Those darts too. They're trying to bring you in alive."

"Sure, only so they can torture me, find out something I don't know." Maggie stares down at her gloved hands. "But you're wrong: it's not only about the money. Not entirely."

"Then what?"

"Three months before Vann died, I *did* meet with the FBI. The real FBI. I finally wanted out. Out of the lies, the schemes, the web we'd spun around ourselves. I just wanted it to stop."

"You were going to flip on everybody?"

"Myself most of all. But yes, everyone. Vann too. My own husband. But those early conversations with my FBI handlers didn't go well, and I became less convinced they would or could protect me once my coop-eration came to light. I should've known better. A part of me did know better. I've dealt with the FBI before." If Maggie is inclined to elaborate on that, she doesn't, and Marcus lets her go on. "Months and months of testimony and trials, shuttling between one out-of-the-way place or another, forever hiding, always worried about cars I didn't recognize and faces I didn't know. Honestly, that existence didn't sound any safer than what I was trying to escape from. That's why these men are after me. They want to know who and what I've compromised."

"Because you know where the bodies are buried. You helped bury them." He adds, "And that might be something we can use if it comes down to it."

Maggie laughs at him, shakes her head. "And that sounds just like something Vann would've said."

He tries not to flash his anger. "But your dead husband isn't with us on this mountain. You are. And these men out there? They're after all of us because of *you*. No matter their reasons. Don't forget that."

"Vann was violent and abusive. I can't begin to truly describe what he was like, and maybe I deserved that. We were both a mess, all the drugs, alcohol, the money. We had too much of everything and not enough sense to recognize the danger we were in or the danger we posed to others until it was too late. But in the end, I did all those things. All of them. And I don't *ever* forget it." She shakes her head. "Do you know what a *cambion* is?"

"No."

"A cambion is a changeling, like a demon or faerie child exchanged for a human one."

"Like a monster?" he asks.

"Yes, out of myths and legends. A monster that can pass as human, Sheriff, at least for a while. But a monster all the same."

Marcus doesn't know what to say to that but doesn't even get a chance because as he's making ready to start hiking again, Luna falls off the mountain.

54

He finds the old man's blood and smiles.

Appreciates the effort, the cunning.

It's been slow going for him with the wounds the man gave him, and the strength the mountain gives him can be capricious, fleeting.

He's been falling in and out of consciousness, adrift in old memories and pain, untethered in a hazy, gray purgatory that's neither safe nor comforting, but long as he's awake, he's moving.

He lost the girl at the ancient cemetery, in that dead place. For reasons he can't explain—and he knows he's losing the ability to reason at all, everything about him slipping through his fingers—he couldn't sense her there, didn't have that itch or those birdlike rustlings inside his head. It was like those frozen gravestones had closed ranks, conspiring to hide her. There were spirits hovering over that ground that had nothing to do with the mountain, and they warned him away. It hurt to even be close, a deep ache like a bad tooth, or just the accumulated pain of all his soul sufferings. He had to retreat, pull back, lick his wounds. By the time he was alert again, or awake again, they were gone.

She was gone too.

So, he scented and tracked the old man instead, trailing him to the torn medicine wrapper and the strange dart and this frozen pond, this tree, this bloody bandage frozen to it. Clever. No doubt just like the old man wanted.

It'll take him some time to find their scent again, her scent, to close in on their trail, and by then they'll have miles on him.

But the snowy silence is suddenly broken by a new serrated noise, a sharp, scuttling whine, high pitched, and annoying to his sensitive ears now.

For once, it's not in his head.

He bounds from the pond, looks skyward, and starts to follow it.

55

Walton finds Austin facedown.

Maggie's holding on to his legs, straining to keep Austin from slid-ing over the lip of the embankment to a rocky, snow-shadowed ledge down below, where the girl is curled in on herself about thirty feet below.

"What the hell?" Walton calls out, threading his way to them.

"Snow gave way. She slipped, fell," Maggie calls, her face twisted with the effort. "We thought she was gone. We thought *you* were gone."

"Both of you hold still," Walton says. "All that kicking and strug-gling, you'll bring half the mountain down on top of us. Give me a few minutes, I'll get her back safe."

Maggie nods and Austin rolls over, face crusted in snow. "No way I was going to be able to get down there, Walton. Just no way. Not on this leg."

Walton can see the despair, the frustration on Austin's face.

"It's okay, son, I got it. Just . . . keep a lookout." Walton also reads the question in Austin's eyes. "And no, I didn't see nothing," he says, starting to pick his way down to the girl. "Doesn't mean nothing's not there, though."

☾

It takes him a slow, tedious half hour to crawl and climb down to her ledge, the storm quivering ominously in the sky just over his shoulder the whole time, darkening, darkening, along with the coming night.

At one point, the rock and snow give way beneath him, too, and he finds himself grabbing desperately at cold, empty air, feeling that peculiar magical weightlessness that comes with falling, and there are no birds to carry him away.

It takes everything he has not to yell, but he lunges and scrabbles and begs the mountain not to let him die like this.

You can have me . . . you will have me . . . but not now . . . not yet . . .

And then he does find a handhold, and his boots reclaim their purchase, and instead of pinwheeling deeper down the embankment and into the hollows below, he's suddenly hugging a knot of frozen tree roots and cracked granite for dear life, but least he's alive.

By the time he gets to her, she's sitting up, knees drawn to her chest, watching him. Her lips are blue, cheeks sunken. She was little more than a shadow before, and now she's not even that. She's been fading away right in front of him these last twelve hours.

"Sun going down, it's a pretty view up here," he says, sitting down next to her—almost collapsing—and relieved to have a reason to. "Looks like we're almost above the clouds, don't it?"

She doesn't answer but gives a short head nod.

"Who here has all the bad luck? You or me? 'Cause it sure seems from the moment the two of us met, it's been one bad thing after another. I'm starting to think one of us is a real bad penny." He chuckles, and even that leaves his chest, his heart, hurting. He left blood on the rocks above them. "I reckon we got off on the wrong foot, you and me, and hell, that's mostly my fault." As he talks, he eyes her, doesn't see anything broken, just a few more bruises than she started with. "Truth be told, you scare me, girl, and I'm not used to that. Thought I was too old to be scared by much of anything, and then my boy disappeared,

and that put all kinds of fright in me. And then you show up, and it's
been a fright of a different kind."

. . . i know what happened to your son . . .

She blinks at him.

"But you know all that, right? All about fear. Because that's one of
the things that triggers it, isn't it? That thing you do. Those episodes or
seizures or spells or whatever you call them. You get scared, and then
things really get scary, right?"

He takes her silence as agreement. "You scared now?" he asks.

She hesitates, then nods.

"Yeah, I know. Me too. But I'm going to need you to be brave enough
to start walking again, to start climbing back up with me. I'm going
to need you to dig deep and find the sort of courage you've never had
before, because if you get scared and do that scary thing, we're going to
be in a world of hurt. I promise I can get us both off this ledge, back up
to Maggie and Sheriff Austin, where we'll get a fire going and finally get
warm. But I can't carry you on my own. I will be with you every step of
the way . . . unless you're magical enough to fly us both up there. Or fly
us away from here."

She shakes her head.

"Then we walk." He breathes deep. "Once upon a time, there were
wolves all over these mountains. They weren't scared of anything, they
owned it all. My boy loved that idea, wild wolves running loose up here,
and he tried to get them reintroduced to these woods. Tough thing to
do, lots of red tape, lots of folks don't like the idea of 'em being around.
In the end, he got frustrated and nothing much came of it, and that's
kind of the way it was with him. Big heart, big ideas, so big they'd
swallow him whole sometimes. He kind of had spells of his own, too,
like you, but he also had an imagination as big as this mountain, and he
wasn't scared of anything. He just wanted to be wild and free as a wolf,
and that's what you're going to do now. For the next hour or so, as we
crawl off this ledge, you're not going to be Luna anymore, or whatever

your real name is. You're going to be like Kell, like my son. You're going to be a wolf, and you're going to be *fearless*."

She turns those amazing wolflike eyes on him, almost gleaming again, and he smiles. "Just one step at a time, okay? That's all. Easy. Just one step forward, and don't look down." He winks at her, helps her up. "Just look at me."

56

They got as far as they could, and Feiser did get the White Rabbit aloft—one of a pair of rebuilt Loki Mk2 drones he keeps stowed and curled in on itself like an insect in the back of the SUV—for about thirty minutes of coverage, but they ended up shuttered in Alpena Gap for the coming night, with still no sign of the girl or Mia Rade or the rest.

Ekker commandeered a cabin on the outskirts of the small town, a launching pad for the morning. He knifed the two occupants, an old man and a woman, and tossed them out in the snow and had Bisek and Feiser loosely cover them until the falling flakes could do the rest.

The couple didn't even put up a fight, just held on to each other as they bled out in front of their tiny natural Christmas tree, their faces lit by blue and white bulbs laced among the pine needles. The old man with the rheumy eyes and liver-spotted hands kissed the dying woman's forehead, then her hair. He stroked her gray strands until she breathed her last and followed suit not long after.

Ekker watched it all, and if there was a moment when their souls finally left their bodies, he didn't see it.

☽

Now—

Feiser's drinking the pot of coffee the dead couple had brewing and is rewatching and reviewing the White Rabbit footage frame by frame as Bisek sits post by a window and stares at the accumulating snow.

Ekker's going through the handmade maps and drawings he pulled out of Walton Landry's cabin, impressed by the intimate, precise detail. Most of it is useless, though, except for two recurring images that catch his eye: an old lookout station, covered in kudzu, and an even older cemetery, a kind of family graveyard.

Scanning through Feiser's workups, he finds the lookout, Buckner Fire Lookout. It sits near the top of the mountain, high ground giving a good view all around. There'd be no reason for anyone to go there other than sightseeing, and in this weather, you wouldn't see much of anything at all. But it's a familiar landmark in a place that has few of them, and well known to Landry.

Unlike Buckner Lookout, the cemetery doesn't appear on any local map or database, no public record or local reference. But Ekker's sure it exists too. Another landmark, again, if you know where to look.

He's already ordered Feiser to check for it on the Rabbit's recordings. Maybe they got lucky.

The information on the girl is a mixed bag as well. There's plenty of readily open-source information about Leo Stier, a tech genius who's made and lost two or three fortunes in artificial intelligence—architect of the same algorithms Feiser himself is running—but whose most recent focus has been biotech, an Atlanta-based research company and hospital called Tesseract.

Most of Tesseract's holdings appear to be medical-related, cutting-edge, and experimental stuff, and Stier himself has given several talks about biohacking, which, as Ekker understands it, is little more than gene editing and biological experimentation without regard for any accepted medical practices. It's easy enough to file with all the other faddish, trendy, silly things that current semifamous CEOs espouse, like shamanism, periodic fasting, and silent retreats. But Stier appears to be a true believer, and more than one article suggests he's even been willing to biohack himself. But like Landry's secret cemetery, there's nothing in either Kornblue's scraps or Feiser's research about the strange girl. She might as well not exist, either, and there's no obvious connection between her and Landry or either of them or the Rade woman. Nothing to indicate Stier has a daughter or any family at all.

That leaves Conrad Stoll . . . a.k.a. Colm Roach.

Registered owner of a Glock handgun, and Ekker assumes it's the same Glock that Landry assaulted him with. Roach has a felony stalking charge out of California from his twenties, now more than fifteen years ago. Did a stint in the military, was dishonorably discharged, slipped into overseas protective detail and contract work for two years. Returned stateside after something bloody in Ukraine and bounced around several private West Coast security firms, each more discreet and less reputable than the last.

Ekker's crossed paths with a few of them.

And currently employed by Cadmus + Gray, a shadowy subsidiary of Tesseract Inc., also out of Atlanta.

Ekker doesn't need Feiser's algorithms to form an educated guess about all this.

Roach was private security on a Tesseract-chartered plane that went down on the mountain, and that plane was a life flight, the girl an invaluable, still-beating heart, a living *transplant*—one of Stier's closely guarded medical advances or black-market biohacking procedures—which is why the plane wasn't registered anywhere or a public search initiated.

That's why the girl and everything about her is a seeming black hole.

What he doesn't know is if she can permanently help him, heal him. That hellish black light hasn't returned full force yet, his vision not blurred by that horrible, encroaching glow.

But it's coming, just at the edge of sight. His dark angel will return.

The girl is valuable to someone. To Stier, to Tesseract. And that someone will have the answers he wants.

Feiser claps his hands and calls over to him, "Hey, take a look at this . . ."

57

Landry gets Luna off the ledge, and then finds them the cave.

Maggie balks, remembering the hole beneath Landry's cabin, but Landry tells her he's been in there before, a dozen times.

"It's not too deep," he says. "But it'll be warm, dry enough."

But even he seems surprised by all the bones they find inside, a pale scattering of osseous shards and fragments stretching wall to wall.

Like a warning.

☾

An hour later they have a small, smoky fire going. It glitters and shines off the rough-hewn walls, drawing fantastical shapes in the air, casting all their faces in flame and shadow.

Maggie found a thirty-hour light stick in the MyFAK, and it glows, too, on the floor at the back of the cave, casting an emerald ambience on the ceiling.

Marcus sits closest to the cave entrance, the rifle in his arms. He leans his head against the stones, and Maggie can't tell if he's awake or dozing. Luna is curled by the fire, eyes open, fluttering.

She's sitting closest to Landry now, wrapped up in a space blanket Maggie also dug out of the med kit, and she's barely left Landry's side since he pulled her off that rocky, snow-strewn ledge.

Landry picks through a few of the bones—pitted, gnawed, savaged—turning them over in his hands.

"What could do that?" she asks. "What was it?"

Landry shakes his head. "Bear or coyote, but I can't be sure. Wolves once upon a time roamed these woods plenty, but not anymore. Kell would've known, I guess." Landry tosses the bones away, wipes his hands on his jeans. "Most appear to be bird bones, some other small critters."

"Great," Maggie says. "A good chance we can still get eaten then."

"Sure," Landry says, "if the mountain or those men out there don't get us first."

"Do you really think they're still looking?"

Landry gestures silently at Luna, then Maggie herself. "Seems they do have some incentive."

She stands, tries to stretch, careful not to brain herself against the cave's low ceiling. Wonders if bats roost in the dark corners. "What are the chances we make it to Lost Hill?" she asks.

"What are the odds everything you put in place is still there to spirit us away if we do?" he asks back.

Maggie shrugs, retrieves one of the bones Landry tossed away.

"Exactly," he says, answering himself, as he dry-chews more Cetafen. They're almost out.

"You going to be okay?" she asks.

"No, I'm going to die before too long. Just being stubborn about it." When he sees her face, Luna's face, too, he shakes his head, smiles. "Bad joke. No, I'm fine. Promise."

She mouths a silent *fuck you* and studies the bone in her fingers. It's cold, smooth in some spots, rough and pockmarked in others. If she didn't know better, and thankfully, she has no way of knowing, some of the blemishes and striations even look like teeth marks. She has no idea what it was once connected to, what its function was, can't imagine it ever being part of a living thing.

Dust and bones . . . this is how we all end up . . .

She tosses the piece down, too, unwilling to touch it anymore, and pushes at the fire with a wet branch, stirring up wet smoke and dying embers. They had a devil of a time getting it started, even with her fire kit, and she's afraid if she closes her eyes, it'll go out, and she'll wake up in the pitch-black dark, all alone.

They're all suffering hypothermia; Landry was subtly slurring his words earlier, and Marcus's hands won't stop shaking. Maggie forgot Vann's name and couldn't remember her dad's face for a bit. The fire is doing everything it can to keep them alive, but they're dying slowly all the same, and tomorrow they'll go back out again into that killing cold. It was starting to snow thick and furious again even before they retreated to the cave.

"Will you tell me about your son?" she asks.

Landry emphatically shakes his head. "No."

But now Marcus speaks up, too, awake this whole time, his voice deep and echoing. "I want to hear as well, Walton." Marcus slides a few feet closer to the fire but keeps himself firmly between the rest of them and the cave entrance. Out there, the wind and the snow are whipping around, blowing sideways, the night falling hard. "Donnie said some things about him, others around town did too. I figure I might as well hear it from you."

"Glad to know I'm all about gossip and rumors."

"Jesus, Walton. It wasn't like that. Nothing like that at all. People cared about you. Still do. Hell, half of them still wish you were the sheriff." Maggie can't tell how much that bothers Marcus to admit that, but the earlier tension between the two isn't as palpable as it was before. The hard hike up to the caves, the stress of getting Luna off the ledge, their shared grief over Donnie Kornblue, has finally dulled their sharp anger. "Seems they cared just as much about Kellan too."

Just hearing his son's name seems to soften Landry further . . . at least a little. He leans back against the rocks, stares into the fire. The red and orange flames, none bigger than one of Maggie's hands, hold each other tight, like intertwined fingers.

"My boy loved these woods, this mountain," Landry finally says, "couldn't keep him off it. As much as I've always loved it, too, I wanted more for him than this place . . . all these old bones . . . old stories." He picks up a bone shard and tosses it at the flames. "Blood is a burden. And ghosts are heavy chains." Landry smiles at Luna, who is watching him fiercely. "Anyway, he was diagnosed with anxiety and depression when he was around twelve. Now, that wasn't anything I knew much about, nothing I truly understood, not in any clinical way. Way I was raised up, you get mad, or sad, or whatever, then you get over it . . . and you keep it to yourself." Landry looks at the cave walls. "That's the way it's always been up here."

Maggie can understand that.

"But, you know, he had his good spells . . . and bad. Sometimes it was like living with a wild wolf, quick to bite. There was just this . . . darkness . . . inside him. It would swallow him up, and then you better watch out. And it got worse the older he got. We went to specialists and all that, or Lottie did. She handled that stuff, all the therapy and medicines and whatnot. I wasn't ready for any of that. Didn't want to admit what he was struggling with . . . what we were all struggling with as a family." Landry can't hide his embarrassment, even now. "Didn't want anyone to know about *my* own struggles that way . . . and the guilt I felt for passing it all down to Kellan. That dark burden I gave him."

"No guilt or shame in that," Marcus says. "Depression is its own kind of monster, worse than any of your backwoods legends." And Maggie gets the feeling Marcus is speaking from experience.

Landry reluctantly nods. "Kell was way too smart for his own good but struggled in school. Was forever running or moving away, forever coming home. Always something holding him back, something always pushing him away again. I did both." Landry now seems mesmerized by the fire. "I made everything harder, and the only thing that did come easy for us both was this mountain . . . these woods, these rocks, these caves . . . there wasn't a place here Kell was scared or worried or anxious over. Out here, he was free of all that." Landry pauses. "I guess I was too. And then he was gone."

Landry tosses more twigs into the fire.

"Everyone said it must've been a freak accident. Fell while hiking, like the girl here did earlier. Or he got lost caving and got himself hurt, couldn't crawl out, couldn't get help. My whole life this mountain's been taking people like that, and there's never any rhyme or reason to it. No explanation, no answers. Just mystery . . . just grief and tears. Folks would sometimes tell themselves it was monsters or ghosts, like the White Things, by way of some kind of explanation. Or maybe that was just a way to make all the grief easier to take, but it didn't for me. There wasn't any mystery about what happened to Kellan."

Luna suddenly reaches out, puts a hand on Landry's leg.

"He didn't have to leave me that note," he continues, "but I couldn't hurt his mother that way . . . didn't want anyone to know what he truly thought of me . . . didn't want anyone to know how little he cared for himself. I wanted to honor him more than that."

Marcus says, "Wait, a note? A *suicide* note?"

Landry won't look at any of them. "A few lines. But enough for me to know. And I knew my son." Landry grabs up Luna's hand, squeezes. "Not like I hadn't thought about it a hundred times myself. Walking off a cliff. Driving into a ravine. Putting my gun in my mouth. The dark thoughts come, and sometimes those things feel like the only thing that'll make them go away."

Marcus again, "You knew all along he was dead then. All those searches, everything, it was—"

"*My* grief . . . my shame," Landry finishes for him, the hurt and anger as bright as the fire between them. "This mountain didn't take my boy. He *gave* himself to it. And if it wasn't a White Thing, it was his dark thoughts, those coal-black feelings. That's what I told myself when

I started hearing things out here too . . . when I started wondering if I was finally going full-on crazy as well. My guilty conscience, or . . ."

"The same darkness that overtook your son," Maggie offers to him, "coming to take you."

"It's just fear in the end, though," Landry says. "When you're too afraid to face the truth about yourself, too afraid to admit and fix it. Or too afraid you're going to succumb to it." Then he falls silent, leaving the cave filled with the crackling of the fire, their collective breathing.

"Fear is vicious, it's unforgiving," Marcus says.

"I dream sometimes about Vann, my husband," Maggie adds. "I dream about the things he did to me, but mostly about all the people we hurt, those we stole from. The dreams are different, but they're all steeped in guilt and grief and shame. Over all the things I did, over the things it took me far too long to do."

"Aren't we a pair?" Landry asks.

Maggie laughs, fights back tears, and grabs his hand the way he grabbed up Luna's. His grasp is warm and comforting. "We're an absolute mess . . . and we deserve each other, I guess."

"What about *her*?" Marcus asks, gesturing to Luna.

"What about *you*?" Landry asks back.

Marcus shakes his head, smiles. "Oh, trust me, I'm a fucking mess too."

Maggie laughs again, and now Landry joins her. "Okay then," Landry says. "We got that all cleared up. Anyone got any more stories they want to tell, secrets they want to share?"

"I do," Luna says, sitting up. "I do."

58

It's not Landry's cemetery, but better.

The angle is bad, and the resolution is a grainy, static mess from the snow and the moisture eating at the White Rabbit's internals, but the image is clear enough—

A creature.

No, a man . . . maybe. Staring up at the drone through a stand of trees, as if puzzled or surprised, like a rainforest tribesman seeing a plane for the first time. A smoky, tenebrous form where no one should be.

"Could be something," Feiser offers. "Hard to tell. Harder to imagine it's just someone out for a stroll, though."

Ekker stares at the figure . . . hunched . . . wounded . . . watching the drone, using the trees for partial cover. Or it's just small . . . like a woman or a young girl. "You have coordinates on this?" he asks.

"Yeah," Feiser replies, loudly sipping the dead couple's coffee. "Rabbit One is down for the count, but I've got a spare in the morning if we get another break in this soup."

"Where?"

Feiser shows Ekker the plot on his tablet. Says, "About six miles from our current."

"Grid it."

Feiser blinks. "Grid what? What's the reference?"

Ekker looks at the drawings he took from Landry's, the neatly penned charcoal maps. "Landry's cabin." He points at a drawing. "This place here, Buckner Lookout."

Feiser nods, taps, and slides and rotates his screen. His fingers dance, about the only thing that ever moves fast on the man. "That works." He taps harder. "Here."

"They're crossing *over* the mountain," Ekker says, his eyes following Feiser's grid. "There will be trails up to that lookout—"

"And down the other side," Feiser finishes for him. "Both directions."

"Our former sheriff wouldn't need a marked trail, not up here, but the others . . ." Ekker turns the idea over. "Rade might be following a prescouted route."

"In this weather, in the dark, how does anyone find or follow anything?"

Ekker studies the hand-drawn maps again. "She had time to prepare for this. This was her plan all along. The rest of it . . . the storm, Landry, the girl . . . they were just unforeseen complications."

"Disappear into the woods. That's some Grimms' fairy-tale Hansel and Gretel–level shit right there." Feiser smiles, impressed. "She's no doubt prepped another new name, a new identity. She's got a dead drop somewhere on the other side, and a car or RV or something tucked away over there, all gassed and ready to go." Feiser studies his screen. "Maybe *Mr.* Rade is still alive, too, waiting for her over Gumdrop Candy Mountain."

Brooking and his people were convinced Vann Rade was alive and well, but, in his short time reviewing the woman's file, Ekker less so. He read Mia Rade as someone who'd have more than enough foresight and fortitude to kill her husband and go it alone, and the willingness to do it. He saw it in those eyes of hers.

Feiser continues to stare at his screen. "If that is our lady, she's also got the advantage of that silly National Quiet Zone, almost all the way back into Virginia." He draws a line with his finger. "No coverage of any sort. We'll still be blind."

"But no unwanted eyes either. No one to see *us*," Ekker says.

"Yeah," Feiser agrees halfheartedly, casting a side-eye of his own out the window, where the dead couple lies buried. He puts their coffee mug down. "There is that."

Ekker calls over to Bisek. "Sweep the perimeter and warm the truck. We move again in ten."

If Bisek hears the order, he doesn't acknowledge it, but after a few long moments, he hefts his rifle and opens the door, letting in a frigid blast of air.

Snow swirls and eddies around his feet.

"Damn," Feiser says. "We can't get clear in this. He's going to have to dig the truck out."

Ekker draws his own SIG and puts it against the side of Feiser's head and gives the man's temple two light taps with it, one for each body out in the snow.

Should be a sufficient reminder.

"Then find a shovel," Ekker orders. "And if there isn't one . . . use your hands."

59

The girl tells them a story.

Tells Marcus and the others about Dr. Jewell, and how this so-called doctor, an older Chinese woman with kind, quiet eyes and steady hands, cut her time and time again.

Her face . . . her chest . . . her heart.

Tells them how she remembers waking up screaming, begging for someone, anyone, to make it stop. Tells them that Dr. Jewell would simply say the work was just too important . . . that *she* was just too important, and that she was sorry.

Only to start cutting again.

Marcus doesn't know whether to laugh at how absurd it all sounds, or cry because of how horrifying it is. But in many ways, nothing she says surprises him. He's seen too much, done too much himself, to be shocked at just how awful the world is and how barbaric people can be to each other in the name of some belief, some cause, some so-called greater good. By the time he was discharged, his leg gone, his body racked with wounds and his (mostly) sleepless nights a patchwork of pain pills and nightmares and bad memories and shaking hands, his heart was little more than scar tissue too.

But *this* . . . this is something else altogether.

The girl leans close to their small fire like she wants to scoop it up in her hands, hold it close. Staring into those strange eyes of hers as she shares her horrible secrets, even Marcus struggles to imagine what someone might be capable of, what someone would be willing to do, to make that kind of pain stop.

To never feel that helpless again.

She tells them the mountain all around them is full of ghosts.

Then she tells them about the birds.

☾

Now Marcus sits in the cave mouth, wondering if the snow will ever stop, as Maggie sits down next to him, shoulder to shoulder, both their backs against the wall.

The wind is fierce outside, but just inside the cave it's quiet, little more than their own breathing. The world is a black-and-white photograph, brief snapshots of white frost and dark night.

"She's asleep," Maggie says, "all curled up next to Landry. They're good friends now."

"They weren't before?" Marcus asks.

"Not so much. Guess pulling her off that ledge back there broke the ice."

"You pulled her out of that plane crash. Saved her life too."

Maggie shakes her head. "I'm not so sure about that. And I still think she saved all of us back at the cabin." Maggie closes her eyes. "Maybe she can do it again?"

"I'm not sure I even know what *it* is. Headaches, bright lights . . . a bad hangover? Ghost stories and a creepy sound like birds? So, no . . . I'm not waiting for her to blink her eyes or wave her hands and make all this go away."

"She knows. She *feels*. She knows and feels everything. And remembers."

But to Marcus, that doesn't feel very helpful. "Just remember that right now she's a highly traumatized young girl, and that's all she is."

"It's more than that. You heard her. You felt it . . . her . . . back at the cabin too . . . we all did. And Landry and I felt it when we were with her before. I don't understand how or why, but whatever this thing is, I got to believe she's too important to just be left out here, abandoned and alone. Someone should be coming for her."

That he can't argue with. "Then it should just be a matter of time to see who gets us first." He grips the long gun tight. "Did you see her scars?"

Maggie opens her eyes. "I did. And they were just as horrible as she described."

"Hmm," he says, still not sure how much real credence he wants to give any of this, or how much he wants to fuel Maggie's fantasy that some cavalry will come for Luna and save them all too. But he does have a thought. "The military debated about planting biological implant trackers or microchips in soldiers. I mean, it was real sci-fi stuff, and nothing came of it, for all the obvious reasons."

"Could someone do that to Luna?"

"Given what she claims they did? Sure. If you're any kind of right, she is extremely valuable, a powerful asset. So, if someone *could* do it, they might. They'd have every incentive to. But it might also explain why they're not beating the bushes for her. They already know where she is, know that she's still alive and on the move, and now they're just waiting for the weather to clear or the right moment to make their own move."

"I guess I'm also valuable to the men chasing us. If I give myself up, maybe they'll give up too. You suggested that."

He did suggest it, but it was foolish then, and a desperate, foolhardy idea even now. He makes sure Maggie is looking at him when he tells her this next thing; he needs her to hear him and understand it. "And after you tell them what they want to know, give them whatever they want, they'll kill you anyway because you're still too dangerous to live, or just on principle, for all the inconvenience and effort you've caused.

Then they'll kill the rest of us to tie off the remaining loose ends. This is triage for them now, like when those doctors took the rest of my leg, to save my life."

"Think so?"

"It's what I would do. Close to the very kind of thing I used to do. Difference is I told myself I was the good guy, that it was for all the right reasons." He stops, squints into the storm and black. "Probably no different than those people experimenting on that girl in there. Make no mistake, Maggie, they're going to kill us too. To get her back, to hide what they've done, to protect their investment. And all because in a world where we even think we know what the right thing is, we were just in the wrong fucking place at the wrong time."

"Are we going to do that? Are we really going to let them just take her if they come for her?"

Marcus doesn't answer; instead, he gives Maggie the big rifle, charging it for her. He makes sure the safety is off. Says quietly, "Trade you for that knife."

Before she can ask why, he turns her head to follow his gaze beyond the cave mouth, whispers, "Keep your eyes up and scanning. Scoot back a couple of feet. Go prone. Use the cave floor to brace the rifle because it will kick. If someone approaches and doesn't say the word *Donnie* out loud three times, open fire, then displace, shift back another foot or so to where the tunnel bends. You have what we call a *fatal funnel* here, one way in, one way out. You can hold off a dozen men with this one rifle and all these cave walls around you, least for a while."

Maggie slips him the big knife, the two of them almost holding hands for a moment. "What is it?"

He says, "I saw someone . . ."

60

Maggie starts to truly panic after Marcus has been gone twenty minutes.

He fell off this mountain, she thinks. Just like Luna.

Or worse . . . one of Landry's White Things got him.

The night storm is impenetrable and she's freezing, barely feels the big rifle in her arms resting on the cave floor—nothing like the hunting Weatherby she had before—and she's not sure she can pull the trigger even if something leaps out of the darkness at her.

Despite everything, she still can't explain to herself around how she ended up curled in a cave on the side of a West Virginia mountain, trying to fend off a band of mercenary killers, protecting herself and a young girl from their pursuers. If she'd just turned her back on that wreck, she might be in Lost Hill by now.

Are we going to do that? Are we really going to let them just take her if they come for her?

That's what she asked Sheriff Austin twenty minutes ago, and that same question could've been just as easily posed to Walton Landry about Maggie.

Are you going to do that? Are you going to let them take her if they come for her?

His answer is Deputy Kornblue lying dead back out at the cabin. It's Marcus now, lost in this blizzard. It's Landry himself, wounded and dying.

His answer has cost him everything.

She almost leaps out of her skin when Landry himself suddenly slides up behind her and joins her on the ground. He asks, "Where's Austin? Taking a piss?"

"No . . . thought he saw something."

Even Landry can't hide his alarm. "He went out there *looking*?"

"Not like he was going to let me stop him." She runs down Marcus's instructions for Landry, their signal. Donnie. Donnie. Donnie. "It's been twenty minutes."

No, Maggie, it's been twenty-five minutes, almost thirty . . .

Landry narrows his eyes, like he's trying to stare *between* the snowflakes. His stare seems to last another thirty minutes.

"He's not coming back, is he?" she asks.

Landry slips the rifle from her arms and settles into a similar prone stance. If Marcus thought she and that one gun could hold off a dozen men at the cave mouth, Landry looks like he can hold off the whole world.

She asks, "But you're not going out there to look for him, are you?"

"No. Can't risk it now, not in this. Fool should've stayed put here with you."

"With us," she corrects him.

"Yes," Landry says. "Now, go on back to the girl and get *us* ready to move on my say-so."

But she doesn't move. "Thank you," she says. "For sharing all that about your son."

"None of that old stuff about my son helps this situation we're in . . . at all."

"No, but it's important anyway, I think. I'm glad you did."

Landry sights down the rifle's barrel, still trying to see through the snow. "For a few years, starting when Kell was around twelve or so, he got into this thing called geocaching."

"I've heard of that."

"He would hide all these little boxes all over Black Mountain here, filled with a bunch of nonsense. Pretty rocks, bird skulls, quarters, candy, or even his drawings. Once he hid away a bottle of the meds he was supposed to be taking. Anyway, it was like a big ole treasure hunt, and I was expected to find all this stuff. Wasn't fair to use GPS, though, just had to recognize the natural clues or puzzle out the codes he'd give me. For the longest time I thought he enjoyed outsmarting me, you know, showing up his old man. I thought that was the whole point of the game, making a fool out of me. But just before he disappeared"— Landry pauses, pushing the words out—"before he killed himself, he told me the best part of it was me finding his treasures. That's what made it all worthwhile to him."

"Landry—"

Landry lays the rifle down. "My wife is buried over in that cemetery, but my son is buried all over this mountain. There's a dozen of his treasure boxes still out here, and I'm gonna spend the last bit of life I have left looking for them. I'm never leaving here, Maggie, and you need to understand that."

She reaches out and touches his shoulder, his face. He's so cold. "I do."

Landry looks at her. "I was a pretty shitty father in so many ways . . . but I loved my son every way I knew how."

"I know," she says. "And I want you to know something, I want to—"

But before she can finish, there's frantic, shadowy movement at the cave's mouth, a figure tumbling forward out of the darkness.

Landry grabs up the rifle and settles it into his shoulder and is about to shoot when—

Donnie . . . Donnie . . . Donnie . . .

And Marcus falls forward into the cave, encrusted in ice and snow.

He still has her knife clutched in his hand, but if it's bloody, the snow masks that as well.

☾

Both Maggie and Landry abandon the cave mouth and drag Marcus deeper into the warren, back toward the fire. They all but throw him into the smoky embers to warm him up.

Luna helps, too, grabbing from their pile of drying tinder and twigs to feed the flames.

"Find anyone?" Maggie asks. "See anything?"

Marcus fights to catch his breath, to get his frozen lungs thawed and working. The wind scoured him, and like Landry warned, his eyelids are almost frozen together. "No, if something was there, it stayed beyond my reach. It's fast." He coughs, struggles. His hands are shaking. "Too hard to move around out there."

"That's good," she says, meaning the men pursuing them are snowed in and fighting the elements as well. But Marcus shakes his head and smacks the prosthetic leg with her knife.

"No, too hard for *me*. This damn thing is fucked . . . somehow . . . something's wrong. Knee joint locked. Not sure if it's the ice or the cold or what . . ." Marcus scoots backward on the floor, and the leg is literal deadweight below the knee. "Supposed to be state of the art." Marcus's frustration is evident, tangible. "Guess I'm the one not so state of the art anymore."

"It's okay," Landry says, "we're not going anywhere for a while, particularly if that storm is walloping us the way it looks out there. Still a few hours before sunup anyway. We'll figure it then." He crouches, recovers the rifle. "Warm up here, son, grab an hour of sleep. I'll take the watch."

When Luna looks like she's going to go to the cave mouth with him, Maggie assumes Landry is going to tell her to stay put, but he doesn't. Instead, he makes sure she's bundled up tight, space blanket drawn around her shoulders, and the two of them disappear around the bend.

Marcus watches them go. "Some war hero I am. I'm going to get us killed."

"We're already dead without you," she says. She tosses through the MyFAK and finds a last pouch of Cetafen and some more Proprinal. She's not sure he's in any actual pain, but taking a few couldn't hurt. He swallows them without argument, and pokes at the fire.

She asks, "Really think there was something out there?"

"Could've been a coyote, I guess . . . ," Marcus says, trailing off. "Something seeking shelter in this cave the way we did." He looks around at the midden, all the broken bones extending as far as he can see, glowing a ghastly green beneath the light stick. "But there was something. And whatever it was, it could've taken me out easily if it had wanted. But it didn't."

"That's good, right?"

Marcus glares. "No, not really. Because that means it wasn't scared of me either. I wasn't a threat." Marcus tosses his stick into the fire. "And if I'm not a threat, then I'm not much use to anyone . . ."

61

As she sits with Landry at the cave mouth, she finally understands how hurt he is.

She didn't realize it when he pulled her off the ledge, or when they hiked up here to this place so high above the world, or even when they were sitting close together inside by the fire. But she knows it now.

She knows what it's like to hurt like that, how that pain reflects in your eyes, in every small movement. How you try to keep your movements small, so it won't hurt as bad. How you make yourself small, too, so they'll stop hurting you.

He can barely keep his eyes open in front of her, so he doesn't even try. Instead, he tells her to look hard, to be *his* eyes, and if she sees anything, anything at all, to poke him awake.

He reminds her she's still a wolf . . .

But he doesn't go right to sleep, though.

He talks with her awhile, eyes closed. He tells her more about his son, as if talking about him earlier has brought back a flood of memories.

She doesn't have many memories of her own. She doesn't dream when she sleeps.

He tells her about his wife, Lottie. About Deputy Kornblue too. He tells her about cathead biscuits and a pond he used to swim in, and treasures buried on the mountain and a story about another kind of wolf, something terrible called a *smoke wolf*, and wonders out loud if that's what tore him up so bad.

Sorry, he says, I'm tore up so bad . . . so sorry . . .

She wonders, too, if that's what Roach has become, and if the mountain has claimed him in its own way.

He shares his dark thoughts and feelings, and for once these things don't frighten her. They don't hurt, and she can't explain why it's different with him, or if she's the one who's changing.

. . . *donnie* . . . *snow is high now* . . . *kell* . . . *hear birds coming to carry me away* . . .

When he finally does fall into a deep slumber, she opens herself up just a bit, lets *both* their birds free, and finds his sleep is dreamless too. Then she touches the scars on her chest, even beneath the borrowed layers she wears.

. . . *sorry i'm so tore up bad too* . . .

She doesn't want or need to be the mountain anymore; instead she's going to forever be a *wolf*, just like he showed her.

She does what he asked and stays wide awake and stares furiously into the dark, searching for other smoke wolves or anything else that might want to hurt them . . .

Later, when the red glimmer appears, she thinks it's men approaching.

She's about to push Landry awake when she realizes it's neither men nor monsters.

It's the first feeble light of the sun.

62

They get lucky with the weather in the morning, the storm pulling back just after dawn, leaving the world clean and white and cold.

The sun dances on the snowpack, trees crystallized in ice, and they gleam shiny and sharp. Everything is in high-def, brighter, like the world's resolution has been turned way, way up, a spotlight turned on them. But it's still slow going, excruciating, even with a combination of Walton and Maggie helping Austin. Walton would kill to have one of his carbon trekking poles, and he did his best to crudely fashion something from a ridge pine limb, but it's not enough. Walton knows it'll take them a lifetime to get down the other side of the mountain at this rate.

Austin knows it too. He's thrown a dozen hard looks at Walton all but yelling at him to leave him behind, but Walton won't do it. Neither will Maggie.

When they finally draw up to Buckner Lookout and get Austin settled at the base of the tower, the long hand-over-hand climb up to the observation deck gives Walton a chance to decide if Marcus is right.

☾

"They call it a lookout or observation tower now," he says, as Maggie joins him fifty feet up above the snow. "But it was built for fire watch back in the twenties. There used to be a whole group of forest guards and fire wardens who manned towers like these, always keeping an eye out for wildfires. They do all that from planes now. Or even satellites, I guess."

Maggie looks around the small, wood-framed cabin with a wrap-around porch. The windows, long glassless, let cold air whip through. Cracked ice, dead leaves, bird droppings litter the floor. "Someone used to live up here?"

"One of my great-great uncles did. Used to tell me how these towers would sway in high wind, felt like you were standing on the deck of a ship in a storm." He shifts to the center of the cabin. "This one is the oldest, but thirteen others were put up in the thirties and forties across the Monongahela. Some wood like this one, others prefab metal kits." He spreads out his hands, gesturing to the floor. "Each one had something called an alidade so you could make azimuth and distance readings. There'd be a topo map on a table right about here, marked like a compass. You'd have to look through these apertures and crosshairs, note the degrees, and triangulate the fire from there. Then call it out to the next tower, and so on."

Maggie circles around the room. "My dad would've loved to have seen this. He loved old things."

"I saw that sextant in your pack, so I guess you like real old stuff too." He smiles. "I get it, you like being hands on, being able to figure out where you're going, where you are, where you've been, without all these high-tech devices. Just the sky and some numbers and *this*." Walton taps his head. "Kellan loved that too. Spent an entire summer in this lookout right here. I came up once or twice to check on him, bring him some stuff; otherwise, he was out here alone. Lottie worried something fierce he'd get bit by a black widow or a copperhead, straight fall off this old thing, or it'd fall on him."

"I worried the same thing when we were climbing it," Maggie says.

"This is good wood, Maggie. Like certain old things, it'll still be here long after we're gone."

She looks at him. "You didn't just bring me up here to show off the view."

"I didn't, although I did want to get a good look and see if I could make out anyone on our tail." He walks to one of the empty windows and takes in all the rolling white, the occasional green flash of a pine that's shouldered off its coat of snow. "We're about to make a hard choice here."

"You don't want to make it alone?"

"Not sure it's all mine to make," he admits, "and I already know his thoughts on it." Walton points down below, where Austin and the girl wait. "I'm not doing well, dragging us down by the mile. Austin's even worse. We can't move this slow and not have the cold kill us, even if those men don't. We're set to lose some fingers and toes anyway."

"You want Luna and me to leave you behind."

He knew he wouldn't have to explain it. "No, leave us *both* behind. You two still got a chance if we give you some more layers and—"

"Steal us some more time. A few more moments."

He won't deny it. "Something's gotta give here, Maggie."

But she only shakes her head. "No, we're going to keep trying, just like we are. All of us."

That's the second time she's talked about them all that way, like they're a kind of family. But his family is dead and gone. "Yesterday I could barely keep you from running out on us; now I can't get rid of you."

"Should've let me go then," she says. "But then I'd be dead. And you all back at the cabin would be too." She joins him at the window, her face raw and red, windburned. But her eyes are clear. "We're alive because we're together."

"You can't believe that," he snorts, "and I don't. And I already told you I'm not leaving. We're alive because we've been getting damn lucky."

"And you know Sheriff Austin feels the same way?"

"In every way that matters."

"Sure, the only way," she says, shaking her head, and saying it for him, so he doesn't have to. "He thinks it's just luck too. Even after all this, that's all either of you are willing to believe."

"Why are you so willing to believe in something more?"

Maggie looks out at the sky, the distant sun. "Because I saw that girl standing alive in the middle of that plane crash, and although I can't begin to explain it, and probably never will, I know that was more than luck." Maggie shakes her head. "You promised us you'd get us off this mountain. You promised *her*."

"I did. And I am. But I never said *I* was."

But he can tell that Maggie's suddenly not listening anymore, distracted instead by something outside the tower. He follows her intense gaze. "What's that?" she asks, pointing at a tiny black dot winging its way toward them high above the trees. "Some kind of bird?"

But it doesn't move herky jerky like any kind of bird that Walton's ever seen, and it's not wayward circling, either, borne aloft on the wind, the way eagles and vultures sail the sky. This thing's movement is all perfect right angles. Up, down. Right, left.

This movement is geometric, smooth, calculated, controlled . . . like it's skating in the sky, three hundred feet up or more. If they weren't up in the tower at this precise moment, they might never have spotted it.

"Not a bird," Walton says. "That's one of those damn *drone* things . . . looking for us."

Maggie squints. "You've got to be kidding me."

"No," Walton says, pushing her toward the ladder, trying to figure out how much time they have before the thing is on top of them. "Looks like our luck's just run out."

63

Marcus can't see the drone, not yet, but knows he'll hear it soon enough, that unmistakably angry, insect-like whine.

He got familiar with them overseas, used all make and manner of the things.

They'll never outrun it, never fully hide from it if the weather doesn't ground it or ruin it or if the operator's any good at all. And Marcus is going to guess the operator is probably *very* good; otherwise it wouldn't even be airborne.

Imagines the cold-eyed Graham himself working the controls, searching for them.

We're screwed now . . .

Maggie and Walton have been arguing ever since they climbed down from the tower, and every one of those seconds counts as the drone angles in on them. The girl seems to understand there's something dangerous in the sky, even if the word *drone* itself doesn't mean anything to her. She stares up at the cloud-hidden sun, searching too.

How does anyone this day and age not know what a drone is?

Chalk it up to one more mystery about the young woman that Marcus knows he won't live long enough to unravel.

The only advantage they still have, perversely enough, is the drone's superiority itself.

"Even if it flies right over us," he says, interrupting Maggie and Walton's argument, "the controller could still be up to four or five miles away. Serious drones have serious range, and I imagine whatever you saw up there is more than a toy. It might see us long before anyone can get to us."

"There could be more up there," Walton counters, "even more men on the ground than what we saw yesterday."

"Sure," Marcus agrees. "They also could've blown the whole top of this mountain off, but they haven't. They didn't." He points at Maggie. "Remember, they still want her alive."

Maggie glances at Luna. "Or maybe someone's finally come looking for Luna."

"Possible," Marcus concedes, but the drone still feels like Graham's handiwork, and Walton seems to agree. He only shakes his head at Maggie, still staring into the sun. "Think I can track back to whoever's flying it?"

"Maybe. FAA requires a drone operator to keep it within line of sight for recreational flying, so as not to fly it into the side of a building or fall and crash onto people on the ground. LOS for a small to midsize drone is what, two thousand feet?" Marcus tries to recall his briefings. "Any farther and you wouldn't be able to tell the difference between it and a bird. But none of that matters out here. If our pilot is flying it only on the camera rig at max range, seeing everything real time, that's likely too far for you to run him down."

"Seeing all of *us*," Walton corrects, "and if it is Graham, we're not gonna get all that far away as long as that thing is up there."

Marcus doesn't argue. Their little group will stick out against the white snow like red blood. They may bob and weave for a while, but not forever. For the first time, Marcus wishes the blizzard would punch them again.

Maggie asks, "How long can it stay up?"

"Forty-five minutes max, maybe," he says. "But who knows how they might have modified it."

Walton stares down the tree line opposite of where they saw the drone approaching. "Assume it's got another twenty minutes of flight time and that it'll be on us in ten." Walton points to the far trees. "Start moving that way." Looks at Maggie. "You know where to go."

"And you?" Maggie asks.

"I'm going to give that thing a merry chase . . . and then I'm gonna hunt down the sonofabitch flying it and stab him in the heart."

"No, you're not," Marcus says. "You're going to get those two off this mountain. I'm going to end this here." Before Walton can protest, he grabs the old man's coat. "And don't give me all that *I'm a hunter and this is my mountain* bullshit. This is what I did, Walton, for years and years. This is what I was trained to do. Kill boxes and ambushes. Applied assault techniques in a combat theater. You might be a hunter . . . but I was a killer."

"No, you're the law now," Walton says.

Marcus wrestles off his own coat, takes off his badge, tosses it to Landry. "Not anymore. Guess you're Wolfe County sheriff again."

Walton turns the badge over in his hands, then tosses it right back at him. "That leg gonna hold up?"

Walton holds his gaze, gives him a gentle head nod, a small, subtle smile.

He appreciates the old man's bluntness and appreciates more the fact he's not trying to talk Marcus out of this. Walton knows what needs to be done, and knows, too, one way or another, Marcus isn't walking off this mountain any more than he is. They're both hunters now, and this is *their* mountain. Marcus is already diagramming in his head the dark trees circling them, the wide expanse of white around them, the tower looming over them. "For this, the leg will be fine. Trust me."

Maggie says, "It's sweet you two arguing over the right to get yourselves killed." But she says it without humor and doesn't mean it as a joke.

Walton ignores her. "You got a plan?" he asks Marcus.

"Yeah," Marcus says. "The start of one. I'm going to need your belt, though . . ."

"Good, that's fine," Walton says, already yanking at his thick belt. "Let's hear it, son . . . and let's finish it . . ."

64

"Got 'em," Feiser calls out to Ekker.

Feiser gives a small, tired fist pump in Ekker's direction, but Ekker ignores him. Feiser is trailing ten yards behind Ekker, stumbling along, weighed down with his pack and other gear he needs to keep the Rabbit aloft.

Bisek is a full fifteen yards ahead, almost invisible beneath the trees. He's switched to a three-color pattern snowdrift camo and found some white tape in the dead couple's house, so even his guns match the snow now. He's otherwise remained enigmatic as a sphinx since the girl did whatever she did to him. Responsive, but just barely.

They've been moving since before dawn after abandoning their SUV when the roads gave out, working their way on foot toward Buckner Lookout, where it appears Ekker's gamble has paid off.

He whistles at Bisek to stop and drops back to Feiser, who unhooks the Rabbit's control tablet from a chest harness and hands it to him as he tumbles to a breathless heap on the ground.

This hike is killing the man.

But Ekker ignores him, scans the screen for what caught Feiser's attention, a flash of movement.

Landry climbing down the lookout's ladder, less than two miles away.

No sign of the girl or the others.

"Probably camped up there last night," Ekker says. "Probably looking for us."

He doesn't know for sure that Landry and the others have made the drone, but better to assume they did. Bad luck, but not fatal. He loses the element of surprise but gains the strategic value of knowing where they are and that they're still on the move. They're alive and they're not far.

"I've got eight minutes of battery left. Got to bring it down and swap it out." Feiser fights to get each word out too. He's thrown up once this morning with the pace. "I'll get it back up and stay put here, be your eyes in the air."

"I need you up there with him," Ekker says, pointing toward Bisek, who is still a shadow beneath the trees. "I need you closer in case they try to circle back around us."

Feiser struggles to stand as Ekker watches Landry on the screen. He's climbed down from the tower and moved closer to the trees, something in his arms. He's digging at the snow with it.

Feiser breathes hard over Ekker's shoulder. "What's he doing?" Then, "What's that in his hands?"

Ekker hands the tablet and controls back to Feiser. "Show me."

Using the twin thumb sticks, Feiser expertly rotates the Rabbit a few degrees, pushing it a few yards ahead, higher in the winter sky, wherever it's currently hovering unseen. He dials the drone's four forward cameras in for a better look. Feiser almost laughs. "That's Marcus Austin's prosthetic leg. Landry's *burying* it, like he's hiding it." Feiser dials the cameras again, as if changing the resolution might change what he's seeing. "Fuck me. Why?" A moment later. "And where's Austin then?"

Ekker whistles again at Bisek. Holds two fingers up high, points them forward, and sweeps them left.

Bisek disappears.

Ekker says, "That's exactly what they want us to be asking ourselves."

65

A mile away, he eyes the dark spot in the sky.

He's been shadowing it all morning, keeping it over his left shoulder and between himself and the men following it.

Somewhere ahead of the black blemish waits the girl and those with her.

He's still not close enough to feel her in his head or smell the blood of the man he almost killed, but it's just a matter of time now.

He saw that stain in the sky yesterday—reminding him not pleasantly of a hovering knot of birds—and followed it until it disappeared, just as the storm roared in again in full throat. His efforts to crawl forward in the howling dark were slowed enough by the savage wind and blowing snow he had to abandon his chase and bed down in a thicket.

He came to this morning crusted in thick ice, frozen to the ground itself. Pulling himself free was excruciating, more torture, and he left behind blackened skin and blood still frosted to the grass. Then he spied that buzzing, unlit spot again, and tracked it as cleanly as one might track a trail of blood.

It hovers now, like an animal scenting prey, like *him*, and then it turns, turns, turns . . . and drops below the trees.

66

Pascal Bisek still doesn't know what the girl with the magical eyes did to him.

One second, he and Tancredi had the Rade woman dead to rights and were about to put a couple of 10 cc darts in her neck, and the next he was covered in blood.

Tancredi's blood . . . and his own.

In between those seconds, the whole world went black, a blast of dark-purple UV light like every memory in his head fired off at one time, like he was on fire, and then, just like that, he was twelve years old again, when Uncle Stepan—although he wasn't truly Bisek's uncle, just what everyone called him—used to get drunk on Pabst and Jameson and then slide into young Pascal's room while everyone else was out or partying and slip into Pascal's bed and say, *You got this comin'* . . .

Bisek's spent the years since trying to hash all that out; to understand that he didn't have that abuse coming to him, that he didn't deserve it, that he isn't a bad person.

But I am a bad person . . . I've done so many bad things . . .

But in that lost, black second outside the cabin, all those horrible things came flooding back to him. Every shitty thing he'd ever done flew by like a flock of black birds, and then he was twelve all over again and Uncle Stepan was leering at him in the dark, pressing against him, and he could smell, practically taste the Pabst and Jameson, and then he shot Uncle Stepan in the heart, which is exactly what he should've done twenty-three years ago.

It wasn't Uncle Stepan, though, who in fact died painfully from lung cancer when Bisek was still in high school, and Bisek showed up at the hospital long enough to fire up a Camel and put it out on the old bastard's bare skin and then drink a Pabst to celebrate.

It was Tancredi.

And by the time Bisek snapped out of it, he was already covered in blood—

Tancredi's blood . . . and his own.

☾

Bisek eyes the lookout tower from beneath the cover of the trees and tries to hear Ekker in his ear.

They're using their Silynx earbuds and radios, but the constant rising and falling wind makes even that high-end system dicey, and Bisek must admit he's not 100 percent recovered from whatever the girl did to him outside the cabin, or the drugs Ekker's been fueling him with. He's not all totally together.

He knows it, and he's pretty sure Ekker knows it. He doesn't care what Feiser does or doesn't know, since he never liked that little prick anyway. But it's like a part of him has permanently flown back to that old bedroom of his, the one that leaked in the Philly winters, with the posters on the wall and that Menlo's fish tank he could never keep anything alive in.

A part of him is still *there*, right now, which means not all of him is *here*.

And even the part of him that is here has got those birds let loose in his brain, a constant chirping and chattering, his thoughts flapping around wildly and incoherently inside his skull, behind his eyes.

Yeah, I'm pretty fucked up . . .

But Ekker is not the sort of man to accept "fucked up" as any kind of excuse and will expect Bisek to keep going until this is done. Until either he drops dead or Ekker kills him, something Ekker will have no compunction about doing. That's why, even though Bisek can barely think, can barely make sense out of whatever Ekker's jabbering on and on about in his ear, he's going to go through with this thing and kill that old man and that sheriff and—now—it seems their original mark, the Rade woman too.

Kill them all . . . including the girl.

Ekker desperately wants her alive, but if Bisek could just organize his thoughts a little better, if he could just get a moment of calm and silence, he'd explain to Ekker that no, the girl is exactly the one they should be killing, because she's the real danger up here on this fucking mountain.

I'm a bad person . . . I've done so many bad things . . .

Killing one young girl isn't even the worst of them.

He stares at the tower and the last known location where the old man was seen. That's at his two o'clock, about twenty to thirty yards away, a little north of the tower's base. The old man isn't there now, but he couldn't have gotten far.

He's drawing us in . . .

Of course he is. It's a perfect killing field, and the lookout tower is the highest point, and even Bisek can think clearly enough to see the danger in that, and so can Ekker, which is why Ekker wants Feiser to first sweep the tower with the drone before they commit to crossing through all those overlapping fields of fire. But that's wasting precious time, time for the others to bury in and get ready, time for them to put even more distance between themselves and Ekker.

Time enough for the girl to find him and unleash those things in his head a second time, and Bisek can't take that again.

He can't go back to that old bedroom of his forever.

He clicks off the earpiece, turns off the radio, and starts to move toward the tower on his own.

67

Maggie and Luna are crossing a pine thicket, moving downward, when Maggie stops.

She hunches over, hands on her knees, breathing hard. She's so frozen, tired, and sore. Despite her layered clothes, the punishing, unforgiving cold has worked its way deep inside her, but that's not all. "I just don't know if I can do this," she says. "I don't know that I can leave them like this."

Luna fixes her with bicolor eyes. They look even less natural outside like this. "They're going to die, aren't they?"

"Yes, they're going to die trying to save us. You deserve that chance, that gift, but I don't. You don't know how close I was to leaving you at the crashed plane. How close I've been to running out on you and Landry from the moment we met. But now—"

"Now it's different?"

"No . . . I'm different. And maybe I have been from the moment I saw your fingers dance in the air like they were playing a piano, like they'd plucked that thought right out of my mind." Maggie fights back tears before they can freeze on her face, can't keep any of her thoughts straight again, the cold and her guilt and her grief conspiring against her. "Can you help them?" Luna looks blank, confused. "The birds," Maggie presses. "Dr. Jewell and those tests. Everything you did at the cabin. Whatever you did on that plane. Can you . . . let it go . . . free it . . . whenever you want?"

"No . . . I don't know, it's—"

"Dangerous. Scary. I get that. I know I'm asking something huge of you, so big you can't see over it, like this mountain." Maggie smiles despite herself, remembering Walton saying something very similar to her. "And maybe you can't control it, and we'll just be killing them anyway . . ." She grabs up the girl's hands and pulls off her oversize gloves. The tips of Luna's fingers are bluish white, the skin waxy. She doesn't want to know if the girl's toes are turning black yet, or her own. "But we're so close to dead already. And if they're risking everything to give us a *chance* . . . maybe we can give them one too."

Now that they're holding hands, it's Luna's turn to grab on to hers. "Close your eyes," she says. "Don't push me away. It's . . . easier like this." And somehow, Maggie understands Luna doesn't just mean physically, but something more than that.

The young girl's grip is strong, and like the cold, unforgiving too.

"Dr. Jewell always says, *Let me tell you a story . . .*"

And Maggie does, as a sound like a flock of birds soars free in her head.

68

The first time Marcus nearly died was in Barisha Idlib, in Syria, just a few miles from the Turkish border.

It was during the joint Task Force 8-14 raid that killed terrorist mastermind Abu Bakr al-Baghdadi, when the team encountered surprisingly fierce ISIS resistance at the remote compound.

Their heliborne assault force—including drone and jet fighters for air support—took heavy fire during landing, and after Marcus and the others explosively breached the booby-trapped compound, they found themselves fighting door to door, tunnel to tunnel, until they cornered a suicide-vest-wearing al-Baghdadi, who blew himself up as well as two of his own children, both believed to be under the age of twelve.

Two of al-Baghdadi's wives were similarly cornered, both wearing vests too. Marcus was less than five feet away from one of those women as she frantically tried to detonate the explosives wired around her chest. Close enough to see her wide, scared eyes . . . even in the darkened room. Close enough to hear her breathing . . . her prayers.

He expected to be blown apart then and there, but when the vest miraculously failed, he shot the woman dead. Two to the chest, one to the head.

The raid in Barisha made the news, or at least one version of it did. Not the version he remembered, all that glowing-hot tracer fire and the buzz of the drones and the barking of the military dogs and the chatter of small arms fire, that praying woman staring at him as she tried to blow them both sky high.

But for some luck, a miracle maybe, Marcus should've been dead. Instead, he was called a hero and given a medal.

He ran out of miracles less than six months later, though, when that IED in Ghazni Province, Afghanistan, took his leg.

The explosives in Ghazni did detonate as designed and—frankly— should've killed him too. That event never made the news, but he got another medal for also surviving that, even though two of his fellow soldiers, two of his best friends, both less than three feet from him, were instantly immolated.

Even as the doctors were taking the last shreds of leg, they were telling him how lucky, how fortunate he was, to be alive.

That was when Marcus decided that most times, being a hero, getting a medal, surviving, or dying simply comes down to dumb luck, a twist of silly fate, a bit of either good fortune or bad.

And no one really deserves it, either way.

☾

He breathes shallowly now, listening.

He's so cold he can't feel anything anymore.

He knows how Graham and his men *should* approach, knows what he would do if he was out there looking for himself, so he's going to give them the benefit of his own experience.

Going to assume Graham is just as smart and capable as Marcus fears he is.

But . . . he's also going to assume that Graham is tired and cold too. That he and his men have been humping all over this mountain most of the night, that they're frustrated if not outright pissed off, and that they want this to be over just as much as Marcus does. That their first order is still to capture Maggie, and that constrains some of what Graham might truly *want* to do, what he might bring to bear on them.

Marcus is praying his own luck or fortune holds out just a few minutes longer.

So—

He breathes shallowly now, listening . . .

Trying not to move. Trying to make himself as small as possible. Trying not to freeze to death.

He won't hear Graham or one of his men approach until they're almost on top of him, but he's betting everything he's got on hearing that drone before that, and fortunately, he does.

A low-pitched whine coming in fast over the tower and the mostly open ground surrounding it. It Dopplers around him, spiraling Buckner Lookout, giving the pilot/operator a real eyeful through those open wood windows, where even a half-ass shot with plenty enough ammo could post up and take out an approaching brigade, where a trained sniper—like Marcus—could defend the whole crown of Black Mountain.

Clearing the lookout is what Marcus would do and what Graham *should* do if he's really looked through Marcus's file.

How long until he's satisfied? How long until he commits?

Marcus counts in his head, the same length of time that young woman in those tunnels beneath Barisha—she couldn't have been more than twenty—frantically tried to detonate those explosives pressed against her small breasts.

One . . .

When Marcus was at his worst, Deidre used to tell him he'd lost all patience. But the kind of killing he was so good at overseas was oftentimes predicated on nothing but patience.

Two . . .

The whine drops . . . a little . . .

Three . . .

Marcus almost can't remember how he got here, in this white place. Can't remember the last thing he said to Deidre before she left. Or the last thing he said to Donnie Kornblue, who's lying dead in the snow somewhere on the mountain below him.

Four . . .

The whine recedes . . . replaced by the icy crunch of footsteps . . .

Five . . .

Marcus says a final prayer of his own and pulls himself up . . .

69

Of course, Feiser sees it all before he hears it, watching in real time through the White Rabbit's glassy optic eyes.

He's just spinning the Rabbit around the top edge of the lookout tower, confirming—no doubt to Ekker's surprise too—that no one's hiding up in the lookout's raised cabin, when Bisek starts moving from his tree line cover to the tower itself.

Not the plan at all, way too soon, but there's Bisek all decked out in white, on the move.

He gets fifteen yards across that pale expanse when the snow and a tangle of dead winter undergrowth *beneath* the tower suddenly explodes. When something crawls like a zombie out of a grave in the horror movies Feiser likes so much.

A man . . . cleverly concealed . . . buried in a pile of snow . . . right under the lookout tower's spindly legs and tucked deep in one of the Rabbit's few blind spots.

Marcus Austin, Wolfe County sheriff, armed with one of their own team's SPEARs.

As Austin pulls himself up, still covered in packed snow and dead leaves and twigs—using something tied to one of the tower's legs like a pulley to aid him—he leans the heavy gun against that tower's leg for support and starts firing.

Feiser counts the muzzle-flash flare on the Rabbit's small screen as Bisek responds in kind. Hears the reports of both men's rifles a half second later as they echo through the woods.

Tricky, Feiser thinks. We were all convinced the best place for a one-legged man to post up would be at the top of the tower, not under it.

Now he can also hear Ekker in his Silynx earbud, realization dawning on him too. He's barking even louder than Austin's gunshots, ordering him to help Bisek, ordering him forward again.

Fuck that. I'm not getting one step closer to a bullet in the head . . .

He's too close out here in the cold, out in these desolate woods. He's not a field guy, never has been. Feiser's so exhausted from all this hiking he can barely lift a leg, so sore he feels like he's suffering the bends—or how he imagines the bends might feel, if he'd ever been scuba diving in anything deeper than a resort pool—and his hands are so cold and red and swollen he can barely grip the Rabbit's control tablet.

He couldn't accurately manipulate the Rabbit's twin joysticks with the super-thick and warm Northstar gloves he brought, so he's been reduced to much thinner tactical gloves he swiped from dead Tancredi's kit. He can't imagine how Austin and Landry and the rest have survived this.

But he can still give Bisek a hand, in his own unique way.

The Rabbit's got a few minutes of charge left—3:23, to be exact, according to the digital timer blinking in front of his face—but more than enough to do what Feiser needs it to.

The White Rabbit is primarily a surveillance platform, but Martin C. Feiser III is an inveterate tinkerer, and when he's not surfing internet porn, investing hours in his favorite online MMO game, *Siege Perilous III*, or working his sideline spam and ransomware business, he enjoys MacGyvering things together. Taking a cue from the Ukrainian Territorial Defense Forces, who once affixed Molotov cocktails—gas-filled beer bottles—onto DJI cinematic drones, he's stashed a plastic explosive payload on the Rabbit equal to a 40mm grenade, and he's going to dive-bomb that sucker right onto Sheriff Austin's head and bring the fucking lights down, once and for all.

He just wants to go home.

He arms the payload, and a red light on his tablet winks at him as he pulls the Rabbit up high and banks it left, circling it back around the lookout tower, coming at Austin from his six o'clock. Focused on his O. K. Corral shoot-out with Bisek, the sheriff will never see it swoop down on him. With his prosthetic leg gone, dug in there in his hidey-hole between the tower's ancient wooden supports, he's a sitting duck, sitting in the center of a bull's-eye.

But as Feiser spins the Rabbit in the bluish sky, his high-def camera captures more unexpected movement, *another* figure on foot down below, slipping in and out of white-capped trees. A wraithlike black figure moving toward Feiser himself.

What the—?

It's neither the mysterious girl Ekker's become so distracted by, or even their original target, Mia Rade. Feiser's not totally convinced it's Landry either.

Who is that?

And for one stomach-churning moment, he imagines it's that old man Ekker murdered in front of his own Christmas tree, that Feiser reluctantly helped toss in the snow outside the cottage in Alpena Gap.

Oh no, another zombie crawling out of the grave . . .

Flashing a weird, glitchy grace, a herky-jerky dance like all its parts don't fit together right, like it's barely holding itself together at all. But Feiser loses it just as fast and now he's only got a handful of seconds to either reacquire it with the Rabbit, kamikaze the Rabbit into Austin, or just drop everything and run like hell.

Unfortunately, he doesn't even have that long.

He's just glancing up from his screen, scanning the ominous trees around him with squinting eyes for that horrible scarecrow figure, when Landry descends on him.

The old man—looking like the walking dead too—appears out of a sudden swirl of windblown snow and before Feiser can apologize or beg or say anything at all Landry growls *got you* and then stabs Feiser in the heart.

70

The explosion jolts Maggie, and she breaks free from Luna's grasp, still crying cold tears from the things Luna's shown her, all the things Maggie herself has revealed again.

. . . vann . . . a boat . . . water like blood . . .

"Oh my God," Maggie gasps as an oily fireball lights up the sky at their backs, ugly black smoke smudging the sky.

"What is it?" Luna asks, but Maggie can only shake her head, stunned by that dark ink stain.

"I don't know," she answers, peering up through the trees, where it looks like there's nothing but smoke where the top of the tower used to be. Marcus was down below somewhere, and the reality of what's happening back there hits her now as hard as that explosion.

Even if Marcus survived that, he's trapped, pinned . . .

Those men will capture him, torture him.

She pushes Luna close to a tree, pushes her down to her knees. "Stay here, don't dare move." She slips off all her gear and her pack and piles it next to Luna. She doesn't want to be weighed down at all, except for the knife in the small of her back.

"Give it ten minutes, and then if you don't see me or Marcus or Landry again, you run. Just run. You know where to go, what to do. You know everything . . ."

Maggie then turns and starts running herself . . . back toward the spreading smoke.

71

After the initial burst of gunfire, Ekker hears two other things in quick succession—

A man's high-pitched scream off and to his right . . . presumably Feiser, dying badly.

Then the bass thump of an explosion, by the lookout tower . . .

Reflexively, Ekker takes a knee by a heavy pine, makes himself a smaller target, even as a thick knot of smoke roils skyward. For the last several minutes, he's been working up the mountaintop along the tower's left flank, intending to entirely skirt the rickety structure and the killing ground below it, hoping to pick up his quarry's trail in the surrounding woods.

The former sheriff knew the drone would spy him burying Austin's prosthetic, knew there was no way Ekker and his team could ignore it. They'd be forced to check out the tower, with no easy way to do so without exposing themselves to the tower itself, the most logical place to stage an ambush. He's going to assume it was Austin who set the trap and felled Bisek. Landry must've gotten Feiser, who, based on that scream, is assuredly dead too.

If Mia Rade and the mysterious girl are still alive, that means it's four to one now, yet Ekker still likes his odds.

Austin and the others are handicapped by their desire to keep each other alive, while Ekker was always more than willing to sacrifice Bisek and Feiser to spring their trap and flush them out. Now that it's done, now that Ekker knows how many adversaries he's facing and roughly where they are, he can pick them off one at a time on his terms until only the girl remains.

Then he can get his answers.

What did you do to me?

That black light in his eye is starting to return, and metal filings fill his mouth. He'd love to exercise infinite patience, let the cold and exhaustion and panic prove better assets than either Bisek or Feiser, but he doesn't have forever.

His time is running out again.

So, he's surprised, even irritated, when he spies *another* figure cutting through the trees to his left. Someone—or something—again unaccounted for. Neither Austin nor Landry, it's too fast, too low to the ground. Not Rade or the girl, either, it's too purposeful, too predatory. It *wanted* Ekker to see it.

Another trap?

He tries to draw a bead on it with his rifle but loses it just as quickly as it appeared, slipping into the gloom beneath the canopy, daring him to follow. The thing was stalking him, the way he's been stalking Austin and the others.

The girl . . .

Whatever or whoever it is, it must be drawn here for her, too, the same way he is. He doesn't know how he's intuited this, but predators know predators and he knows he's right, just like he knew Austin and Landry would try to turn the snowy ground below the lookout tower into a killing field.

Now keeping one eye to his left, he zigzags tree to tree, always keeping some measure of cover and concealment to that side of him.

Flakes start to fall again, the sky through the branches grim.

Below, in the thick of the trees, he's the one disadvantaged now, since the thing has spotted him. Even with his superior firepower, it'll slowly work in closer and closer, come at him from some unexpected angle, the same way he was planning on picking off Austin and the others.

But closer to the lookout tower, where the trees thin and give way to more open ground—

A killing field.

72

Walton doesn't know if Marcus is alive.

He saw and heard the explosion just after he descended on the man with the drone, so he assumes the man he just killed had something to do with it.

Damn thing was armed with explosives.

But at least Walton is armed now, too, with the dead man's guns. Two Glocks, four extra mags. The bastard died without much of a fight, as if he was surprised to find Walton in this desolate place among the trees and snow, stabbing him again and again. But he can't assume Graham or whoever else is out here with him will go down so easily.

The gunfire's already receded from the tower, and now that the echoes of that explosion and the dead man's screams have rolled off the mountain, too, the woods are ominously quiet again.

Only his own labored breathing, his crunching footsteps, as he searches for Graham.

No one is more surprised than Walton himself when he finds him.

☾

Graham is leapfrogging tree to tree, too intent on something to his left, when Walton catches up to him.

He's twenty yards out, lots of brush and low branches between them, and although it's not the best shot to take—and Walton's not in the best shape to take it—he's not going to get many chances even half as good as this, and probably none where Graham isn't furiously shooting back at him. He doesn't want to rush it but doesn't want to lose it.

He drops to a knee, puts the Glock muzzle a hair in front of the moving man, and empties it downrange.

For as long as Walton's been handling and shooting guns, the big pistol is still surprising, almost deafening, in the snowy silence. It leaps and recoils in his hands like a living thing.

His first shot badly clips the closest tree in front of him, spinning wood chips into the air and into his face.

The second goes high and wide.

The others peel off bark, shred leaves, kick up snow, close around Graham.

Closer . . . closer . . . closer . . .

But not quite. The man reacts snake quick again, just like he did at the cabin, spinning, falling, firing in Walton's direction all in one smooth motion. Goddamn, he thinks as a bullet digs deep into a tree by his head, dusting him with snow and pine needles. I truly, truly hope I hit that sonofabitch. Because there's no way he's going to fend or fight off Graham for long, and clearly not going to outshoot him either.

He doesn't even bother reloading the empty Glock, just tosses it down and instead draws the second and starts running to his right, keeping eyes up for Graham, as another unseen round furrows the air by his ear and nearly takes the top of his head clean off.

He throws rounds downrange, all scared instinct now. He can't see Graham, has no idea where he is. But that's okay.

This is it, Kell, I'm coming . . .

He fires wildly back over his shoulder and runs like hell.

73

Marcus was disappointed that he didn't straight up kill that bastard with his first shot.

The old Marcus would have.

But he gave himself a little grace, given the circumstances.

The other man got off two shots of his own before Marcus put his second right through the man's forehead, blowing brains, blood, and bone out onto the snow. He died still pulling his trigger, emptying his own rifle into the ground at his feet. He never even knew where Marcus was lying in hiding, never had an inkling of where the kill shot came from.

But Marcus never had much of a chance to celebrate either.

Suddenly that drone came spiraling in and smashed into the tower's cabin far above Marcus's head and the whole tower shook, shuddered, and groaned and everything over Marcus turned into flame and smoke before it turned black.

☾

Now he's conscious again . . . still alive . . . covered in burning wood and debris.

The tower's cabin is mostly gone, though, blasted into smoky black char, still dropping embers merrily down on him. Least the bulk of the tower itself is still upright, still standing.

It didn't come down completely on his head, but he's pinned between the tower leg he braced himself against and a pile of the fallen cabin's heavy plank flooring.

The part of him that Deidre never understood is content to lie here and let either the fire or the cold take him. But that other part of him, the part that refused to die when his fellow soldiers were injured or endangered, whenever there was still a battle to fight or a war to win, pulls himself upright again using his and Landry's belts tied together and scans for more shooters in the trees.

He doesn't see anyone, but it's not long before the cold silence is broken by fresh gunfire deep in the woods, a lone handgun trading shots with the uglier rattle of one of those SPEARs like the one in his hand.

Walton . . . got himself armed . . .

Marcus silently pleads with the old man to bring his quarry back into Marcus's line of sight. It was Marcus's plan all along to use the tower and Marcus himself as bait to draw in Graham's men as Walton worked the perimeter and tried to take them down one by one, arming himself if he could. There was nothing creative or innovative about the plan, and Marcus bet Graham was trying a similar gambit, but the kill Marcus claimed right from the jump suggests it was working. Marcus just didn't expect the drone to turn into a missile, or Walton now running off script, heading the opposite way, deeper into the woods, alone.

Marcus scans and scans. Then fires off one round after another, anything to draw Walton's attention or the men chasing him.

Walton . . . please . . . please come back . . .

But the running gun battle recedes, gets farther and farther away from where he lies trapped, and then falls quieter and quieter, too, until it stops altogether.

74

I wish you could see this one more time, Kell, Walton thinks, staring off the side of Black Mountain. Still pretty enough to hurt your heart, to take your breath away . . .

Another break in the storm and the blue sky churning with leaden clouds has revealed the partially exposed granite flanks of the mountain's lower reaches shimmering with ice, quartz, and mica, the darker trees rolling out below him into the distance, shrouded in white.

Although it has no official name, he and Kell named the path up here the Larkspur Trail, for the blue-purple dwarf larkspur that grows in the summer. Kell liked to call it the Black Eye Trail, too, since the late-season larkspur was mottled so dark it reminded him of the colors of a bruise.

The full trail, two miles long, winds up from below, and in the spring, water from this ledge mists down in a gentle waterfall. Kell called this outcropping Take Wing Rock, a spectacular exposed knuckle of granite visible from across the gorge but otherwise hidden from view.

From down below, Walton thought it looked like Black Mountain was secretly giving the finger to the world. Standing up here now, it's like he's flying.

He has no way of knowing for sure but has always imagined this was Kell's last sight on earth. Imagined his boy stepping off this rock out into that infinite sky. Not falling but flying instead, up, up, and away on feathered wings of his own.

Gone.

Just another story or legend or myth Walton tells himself, one he's never shared and never will.

This one is his alone.

C

He doesn't turn when Graham finally slides to a stop somewhere behind him.

There's a dangerous crack in Take Wing Rock, and if you don't know it's there, you're likely to stumble or trip, break a leg or worse, slide right off the mountain.

He hoped the snow and ice might make it even more treacherous, that in Graham's haste to get to Walton, he would fall of his own accord. But Graham is not the sort of man who gets sped up often. He knew all along, just like Walton did, there was nowhere for Walton to go.

Walton's content now to take this one last look over the side of his mountain, breathe the frigid air, let the little bit of distant sun touch his face.

"Where are they?" Graham calls out. "Where's the girl?"

"The girl? You mean Maggie? Mia?" He turns to find Graham, legs spread solidly apart to brace himself on the rocky outcropping, his long gun aimed somewhere at Walton's chest.

"No. Not Rade. The other girl. Who is she?"

"Who is she to you?"

"*What's* she to you?" Graham hurls at him, almost a scream. "Or even Rade for that matter?" Graham is still wearing Walton's kick; one side of his face is a spectacular nightfall of blues and blacks. He's earned the Black Eye Trail. "Why get involved in any of this at all?"

Walton nods out to the clouds. "I don't know, I truly don't. I guess it's like they just fell out of the sky. What else was I gonna do?"

Graham raises the rifle higher. "You're going to tell me where they are."

"No, no, I'm not. Each step you chased me out here to ask me those silly questions has already put you three steps farther from them. By now, they're *gone*. Gone for good."

Graham blinks over his rifle's long barrel. "Think that's true? You don't think I'll hunt them to the ends of the earth?"

Walton tosses the empty Glock over the ledge, watches it drop until it's gone too. "You're looking at it, as far as either of us are concerned."

Graham almost smiles. "One more time, what do you know about the girl?"

"Hardly a thing at all, and that is the God's honest truth." A gust of wind shakes the rock, like the whole mountain is watching, waiting, trembling. Graham takes a step back.

Graham says, "I might let Rade go if you prove a little more helpful here."

"No, you won't. And that young girl's a mystery you're never going to live long enough to solve. She's a handful, that one. A wolf." Now it's Walton's turn to smile. "They both are. Out here, we're all wolves now."

Now that Walton's getting a good look at Graham's face, Graham truly doesn't look good at all. It's not just the dark bruises, but the fish-belly pale beneath that. His eyes are oddly bloodshot, blinking furiously, and his face and throat speckled with bright-red blood turning black to match his shiner. He's sick, dying, but he's not going to die fast enough. "Almost put you in the ground back there, didn't I?"

"Almost," Graham agrees, reluctantly. "Took off my ear. Half an inch more and you might've taken off my head."

"Goddamn, life's a game of inches sometimes," Walton says, and sighs. Although the snow had stopped for a bit, now it's starting to drift down again. It's delicate and white and reminds him of Lottie's hair at the end, so white it was see through, so fragile it would fall apart in his hand. It's so beautiful way up here . . . the sky so goddamn close. If there is a heaven, he can almost touch it. He wishes he could see Marcus one more time, wishes he'd told him all the things he should've when Marcus first became the sheriff. Marcus would've proven to be a good one, eventually.

Walton takes one last look at the snow, at the mountain, at his *home* . . . and then launches himself at Graham, flashing the Jackal Pup concealed in his off hand.

Graham drops to a knee and fires once, twice, three times. The first shot blows through his shoulder, the next goes high over his head, the third hits him center mass, close to his heart.

He doesn't feel any of it. He just keeps coming.

Just a few more inches . . .

He falls into Graham, not wasting the effort to wrestle for the gun, instead letting his weight and momentum roll them both toward the ledge, letting the slippery snow and ice do the hard work and accelerate them toward the sky.

Too late, Graham finally understands Walton's true intention and he kicks and scrabbles furiously as Walton holds on for dear life, stabbing when he can. He's gone numb and it has nothing to do with the cold. Still, Walton won't let the sonofabitch go and Graham is screaming in his ear and all Walton knows is—

Kell, they're coming to carry me away . . . carry me to you . . .

He begs, begs, begs the mountain to take him, and it does.

The rocky ground gives way to empty sky, and then he's weightless and then he's falling, falling, falling, gentle as the snow itself . . .

But if Walton Landry was expecting wings, there aren't any.

75

Maggie is shocked to find the dead man dressed all in white sprawled in the snow, the lookout tower still smoking and burning.

Still standing, though, just like Landry said—

This is good wood, Maggie. Like certain old things, it'll still be here long after we're gone . . .

The scorched pine reminds her of a campfire, a big old winter fire in a snug log cabin, like the last fire burning at Landry's place, where she was drinking coffee a lifetime ago. But there's no sign of Landry, no immediate sign of Marcus, either, leaving her to stand there alone as the snow starts to come down again. She knows she's exposed, that everything Marcus and Landry sacrificed for her means nothing if she gets taken now, that she needs to get back to Luna and they both just need to keep on running. Still, she hesitates, until she hears a voice calling out for her from the debris beneath the tower.

Marcus.

Even after she runs over to him, struggling to throw aside smoking planks to reveal his body twisted in the wreckage, Maggie can't believe he's alive. Marcus can't seem to believe it, either, yet still doesn't seem happy to see her.

"Grab that dead guy's guns," Marcus says. "Get whatever he's got on him and go." Marcus doesn't work with her to help free him. "He might have a cell or a radio, some way they're communicating. You can listen in on them, even call for help."

"Let me get you out of here."

"No," Marcus orders, grabbing her arm. "There are more out there."

"Where's Landry?" she asks, shaking off his grasp, still grabbing at planks.

"Where's Luna?" Marcus throws back. His face is bruised and bloody, covered in ash. His eyes dark hollows. "Maggie . . . Mia . . . you need to listen to me right now."

Hearing her old name stops her, the way he obviously intended. "No," she says, furious. "I'm trying to get you free."

But he grabs her arm again, shakes her. "Walton is dead. He led them on one hell of a chase, but make no mistake, he is dead. We've done all we can, and it's probably more than we could've ever wished for." He squeezes her arm, but there's little strength in it. "Take my gun too. It's still got two rounds in it. Only two, if it comes to that." Those dark eyes trap her. "But it won't . . . if you just go now."

She holds the charred piece of wood in her hand, smoke tendrils curling skyward, embers falling and dying onto the ground at her feet. Luna's back there waiting for you, she thinks. Alone. She relents and lets the board slip through her fingers and fall to the ground at her feet too. "She showed me, Marcus. She *showed* me . . ."

"And?"

She hesitates. "A miracle."

Marcus says, "That word's been getting thrown around a lot. Not sure I believe it."

"It's a miracle we were ever even here, the four of us, on this mountain. What are the odds?"

"Graham said you were a numbers person. You tell me."

"Infinite," she replies. "Infinite." Then, quieter, "What are you going to do?"

He sighs, smiles. "Figure I'll just hang out here a bit and watch the next storm roll in. See who passes by."

She throws a quick glance back toward the trees, then to the dead man's body, where the bright-red blood all around looks like blooming flowers. "I'll see what he has on him. We'll split whatever he's armed with, and then I'll go. I promise."

Even Marcus can't argue that with her. "Just be quick then."

She starts to make her way toward the body, haloed in blood, when a cracked voice stops her—

"Not another step, Mia."

76

Landry nearly drug Ekker right off the mountain with him.

A game of inches is one of the last things the old man said, and that's what it came down to, as Ekker clawed, scrambled, and held on to the rocks as Walton fell toward the sky and dropped from sight.

It wasn't just Landry, though.

It felt to Ekker like there was at least one other ghostly set of hands grabbing him, pushing, pulling him toward that icy ledge. Closing around his throat, gouging his eyes.

It was the angel in his head taking hold of him again, like the dark light and the metal in his mouth and the missing words. Just another symptom like all the others the girl was able to quiet and still, least for a while.

But it sure felt real.

☾

"Not another step, Mia," he calls out to Rade, from behind the safety of a large pine. "Although I will admit, you've truly impressed me every step of the way." Ekker keeps his SIG semiauto pistol—his "Agent Graham" duty gun—aimed at her windburned face, since his SPEAR went over the mountain with Landry. "Theroux, Brooking, all underestimated you. It's possible I did too. But I also always respected your tenacity, your will."

Ekker is careful not to expose too much of himself from behind his tree cover. He's not convinced Austin is alive but won't take that unnecessary risk.

Rade raises her hands. "I'm no threat to you."

"Doubtful," he says. "You killed Theroux in Pullens." Ekker uses his gun muzzle to acknowledge Bisek's corpse between them. "You handled him too . . . or was that Austin?"

She ignores his question. "Is Walton Landry dead?"

"Yes," Ekker says without emotion. "He fell . . . tried to take me with him."

"No, you killed him."

"A little late to start assessing blame here, Mia."

"Don't call me *that*," she screams.

"Oh, you prefer Maggie now? Or *Melissa*? Or something else. I know all about you, about your father. I know how meaningless a name can be because a million names don't change who or what you are. And we are not that different. It's somehow fitting that the only one who didn't underestimate you was Landry, and he didn't know anything about you at all." Ekker looks at Black Mountain all around them. "He warned me you're all wolves now."

She keeps her hands up, takes a step back. "I'll go with you. Right now. Take me."

"I don't want you, Mia."

"Then whatever those men are paying you, I'll pay more. I'm set up in Lost Hill, just down the mountain. Everything is there, waiting for me. I'll pay anything if you just walk away." She takes another step back. "You know I *can*."

"Ahh, the money," Ekker says. "The fortune you swore was gone, that only your husband could ever retrieve."

"No," she says. "Vann never had those codes, never even had access. He never had the fucking *brains*."

"A generous offer then," Ekker says. "And to another man it might mean something, might even sway the dynamic of what's going to happen here." He leans into his pistol. "But I'm not that man . . . and your money means nothing to me. Nothing is going to change what happens here now." Dark light blooms in his eye, his knees go weak. He doesn't just taste metal in his mouth; his fingers also go heavy as lead. He needs to end this. "Bring the girl to me."

He can see that Rade is suddenly so confused she can't help herself. So cold and tired she can't make sense of his demand. "Luna?"

"Luna," Ekker repeats. "I didn't know her name. Thank you." And he truly means that. "Now I do."

77

Marcus can hear some but not all of it.

He can't get Agent Graham in his sights, either, can't even truly see him he's so hidden in the trees, although Marcus knows that's who Maggie must be talking to, pleading with.

Also knows how hard it is for Maggie to talk and talk some more, even as she's taking one slow, agonizing step backward at a time, trying to pull the man out so Marcus can get a clear shot. But when Marcus hears Graham say he doesn't care about the money, when he demands the girl instead, Marcus realizes that if Graham isn't here for Maggie or her knowledge or even the fortune she might've stolen—if the only thing that will buy her way off this mountain is Luna herself—then Maggie's got nothing left to offer the killer in front of her.

She's alone, exposed, and useless, and Graham's going to kill her where she stands unless Marcus does the last thing left to either of them.

He calls out Graham's name, yells at Maggie to run, and then he fires.

78

It all happens fast for Ekker, but exactly how he envisioned it.

Austin calls out to him, challenges him, finally revealing his position in the smoking, broken planks beneath the tower.

Ekker knows the shot's coming long before he hears it, and although he doesn't believe Austin has a clear line of sight, he drops low anyway, taking cover behind another tree, before putting a tight three-round group into the wreckage even as Austin's lone wayward round goes high overhead.

Austin yells at Rade to run but she hesitates, and it's clear to Ekker she can't decide whether to run from Ekker, run at him, or even go for Bisek's abandoned weapons, which is impressive. After everything she's been through, everything she's lost and can still lose, she's still a fighter at heart.

Walton Landry warned him—

We're all wolves now . . .

By the time she finally decides to run the opposite way, beyond the lookout tower, it's all the tell he needs. She's not running to save her own life, the one she was so willing to sacrifice a second ago; she's running to the girl. To Luna.

The girl can't be far away, and with Landry dead and both Austin and Rade *here*, she's alone, out in the woods.

She's his.

Austin's immobile, trapped, useless. And Ekker simply doesn't need Rade anymore. He leads her just a bit as she runs, struggling through snowdrift as even more snow illuminates her. She's beautiful in a way, although Ekker's long past that sort of physical attraction for either a woman or a man.

He doesn't want to give her hope.

He's a violent man, but not always a cruel one. There was no other way this could end, and a part of her always had to know it. Landry knew it as he fell to his death and Austin knows it now—pinned, wounded, alone—futilely yelling out Ekker's false name again and again.

Hope is such a delicate, dangerous thing, and that's exactly what this girl Luna has given him.

He'll do anything to hold on to it, just like they did.

Ekker lets Mia Rade run and counts out her heartbeats and just before she disappears into the far trees, he guns her down.

She spins, turns, and falls without sound.

79

He comes for her out of the trees, almost crawling.

Broken and burnt, frostbitten blue-black, most of his skin peeled back or gone altogether. He looks like he's been torn apart and put together again.

He looks like one of Dr. Jewell's experiments, fresh off the table, so unrecognizable he doesn't even look human anymore. He's a monster, one of Walton's White Things, one of his *smoke wolves*.

But those eyes are his eyes, and she knows them—

Roach.

He shambles inexorably over the snow, leaving blood and ash footprints behind him, and she's still too weakened from the moment she shared with Maggie to escape his grasp.

He tries to speak but words don't come, just a horrible squawking— almost cawing—like her dark birds. But she doesn't need to hear him out loud or peek at what's at work behind those horrible, all-too-human eyes, to know he's saying her name over again.

He reaches for her, lunges for her, and as she turns to run, shots ring out.

The snow at his feet erupts. He whiplashes from one or more bullets, and then he screams. And that's all too human too. She knows that pain. And although she'll never feel sympathy for the monster he was or whatever monster he is now, she doesn't want anyone to hurt like that. Never wants anyone to feel that.

She runs toward the man with the gun, and by the time she gets to him, Roach is gone again, leaving only slick blood where he was last standing.

"It's okay," the man says, tossing the gun aside where it lands in the snow ten feet from them. "I have you now."

She doesn't recognize him, and although he must be one of the men who's been chasing them, he kneels with his hands raised, empty and unthreatening.

"I know you're scared," he says quietly. "I am too. I have no idea who that was . . . *what* that was. But I won't let it hurt you, and I won't hurt you either. I promise. I'll do everything I can to help you."

He smiles, and it's such a normal, simple smile it takes her aback. Reminds her of the plane's pilot, blond, unassuming, unremarkable. He smiled at her, too, just like that, before they took off, not long before she crashed the plane and killed them all.

This man's smile disappears beneath a mask of horrible bruises and blood. Only his eyes remain, dark and huge, staring at her from behind those wounds.

"You're safe, Luna," he says. "I'm here to save you."

When Cooper entered Tunny's Tavern he was slicked in blood.

His face bore rake marks, one eye blackened, one arm swinging useless at his side. He and Rory and two other men had ridden from Tunny's on horses down to Warden's Creek for yet another wasted search for the White Thing, but that had been a day before, and only Cooper had returned . . . and returned alone.

Even a heavy draught of liquor could not summon Cooper's tongue. For half an hour he sat and stared into the licking fire as others ran for his family and yet still others called for a search for Rory and those who had vanished with him.

Only Rufus Strange would dare approach and put hard questions to Cooper about the lost men, the same Rufus

Strange who would disappear himself five years hence into the very woods he mocked.

But Cooper Landry would speak little of it, would barely acknowledge Rufus looming over him.

All would say later, too, that not all the blood on Cooper was his own, that some of it was stinking and black as a midden cave.

They would say alabaster hairs dusted his torn coat like newly fallen snow.

They would say his eyes were as haunted as the West Virginia woods, hills, and mountains.

"There are things we can never know and never answer," he finally whispered to Rufus through clenched and bloody teeth and tears in his eyes. "And there are things out there we should never disturb . . ."

The White Things:
Tall Tales of West Virginia's White Monsters
Jim Collymore

Dark and Stormy Books
Pullens, West Virginia
2006

FOUR

80

Eighty-two hours, twelve minutes before—

Anika Jewell doesn't understand why Luna is being moved and doesn't understand why she isn't going with her. To say that Luna has been her life's work, her life, for more than six years is an understatement.

Anika almost doesn't recognize herself in the mirror anymore. She's gone gray, gotten unpleasantly thin. She carries the death pallor of those closeted Atlanta labs; her skin has the sickly incandescent-green sheen of the complex's overhead lights, like they've permanently scorched her, a forensic sunburn.

She doesn't date anymore, doesn't have any hobbies, doesn't take vacations.

It's been Luna—all Luna, all the time—and now she's being taken from her.

Stier won't see her in person, committing only to these video calls, where he's otherwise preoccupied, and she's reduced to pleading.

"You always knew this day was coming, Anika. It's not personal," he says. But she knows that with Leo Stier, it's *always* personal, even the professional decisions.

"There's still so much work to do," she says. "And she's not ready for this kind of adjustment. If you've seen my reports—"

Stier's now muted her, speaking to someone else, off screen. Whoever it is must have sufficient clearance to even know that Leo Stier and Anika Jewell are speaking, and she wonders if it's Leo's personal, resident sociopath, Colm Roach.

Stier clicks back in. "I have. I've read them all. Including what's *not* in them."

Anika purses her lips. They're so thin, too, like the rest of her. She's fading away, and if they take Luna from her, she'll lose all meaning and disappear altogether.

"Meaning?" she asks.

"Progress," Stier says. "You've stalled. You're orbiting, going in endless circles. The measurables were impressive, but now they're hardly measurables at all."

"We expected plateauing. I warned you about this." She's provided so many warnings about Luna, both in her written reports and presentations. "It's her age."

"Understood," Leo says, making some note to himself on a tablet. "But I expected something more . . . seismic . . . by now."

Anika wants to laugh . . . *seismic* is Stier's latest word. He fixates on a word or phrase for weeks or months on end, finding a way to use them. Sometimes they get picked up internally, but they always get picked up externally, by the press, the media.

Seismic. Triage. Triangulate. Scale. Spectrum. Burn rate. First mover's advantage. Hyperpersonalization. Bioharmonizing. Biosynergizing.

Eustress. Empath.

Bloodless.

Stier is a genius on the spectrum, but he's a closed loop, a circuit with finite inputs, incapable of truly understanding her work, much less Luna herself. Luna is the universe.

Some who've experienced the side effects of her telempathy liken it to the sound of bird wings, or even birdsong, those amazing syrinx vocalizations. To Anika it was always the sound of stars singing.

But now she can tell Stier is getting bored, this conversation almost over. He granted it as a mere courtesy, and he doesn't do courtesies.

"Please. Don't do this. You'll unwind all the systemic progress I've made."

"Or we'll shock the system itself," he counters. "Get things moving again."

"Luna doesn't like shocks, Leo," she says, risking the informality. "Her empathic resonance is dialed into the stratosphere. And you need to keep that Roach at a distance. She absolutely doesn't like *him*."

Stier takes off his expensive glasses, an affectation because his vision has been perfect since his surgery. "My understanding is she doesn't like *you* either, Anika. That's why she's not responding anymore. It's just not working."

"She's not a computer. Not a machine."

"Then you're not working hard enough or smart enough." Stier replaces his glasses. "And we're all just machines, Anika. Blood, bone, electrical impulses. We're a collection of biological processes that can be reiterated and duplicated, manipulated, and modified and improved. Our work here is predicated on that. As a doctor, you should know that as well as anyone."

But she hasn't felt like a doctor in a long time.

"You're going to have a problem on your hands," she says, "if you don't manage this expertly, delicately."

"That sounds ominously like a threat."

"No, not at all. Just a reality. Just let me help you."

"It'll be a quick flight. She'll see it as an adventure, a welcome change of scenery. And she'll be moderately sedated. We can handle it."

Anika tries to imagine all the things . . . everything . . . that can go wrong with even a sedated Luna in the tight confines of a small jet, forty thousand feet above the earth, moving at more than five hundred miles an hour. But she also knows it's been decided. There's no more she can say or do to change Stier's mind. She has no seismic rejoinders.

It's done.

"They'll take good care of her in DC. You'll be kept in the loop. You'll have visibility on the team's work there."

No, I won't, she thinks. What she worries now is that she'll wake up sometime in the next month to find Roach in her bedroom, tasked with closing the Anika Jewell loop, once and for all, and it won't be bloodless.

She recalls the books on her nightstand she hasn't made the time to read. The clothes that don't fit her anymore. The things she ordered that she never opened, boxes still untouched. She got so lost inside Luna's universe, among her stars, that she doesn't know how to make her way home again.

Stier says something to someone off screen again.

He looks at her but doesn't see her anymore.

Just before he kills the call, he says, "Enjoy the holidays. Really, if there are any problems, Dr. Jewell, I'll let you know."

81

Maggie is warm but that's impossible.

She's lying in the snow.

But she is warm, everywhere, all over her body, just like she's sitting again in front of Landry's stone fireplace, the last place she remembers being warm.

But Landry is dead. And she's dying.

She remembers that now, too, running for the trees, running for Luna, with that man Graham gunning for her. He shot her in the back, and she fell, and now she's bleeding out spectacularly and she can't even complain, because once upon a time, not all that long ago, this was what she wanted, just for everything to be finally, mercifully over.

I'll just fade away . . . let the snow cover me.

To lie here in the snow and let it cover her, just like she imagined a day ago.

No more memories . . . no more nightmares . . . just that black and welcoming silence.

She's sad about Luna, about Marcus, about Landry, but they aren't her problems anymore, and for that she's truly grateful. But as she lies there, a figure falls over her, a shadow. A hand reaches down to pull back her hair, to touch her face.

It's gentle.

It's Landry.

He doesn't try to help her up, just holds her hand.

He's squinting into the sun, and there's something hazy, indistinct about him. He's like that old photograph of his son, Kellan, blurred by lens flare.

He's not injured, either, not all cut up and bruised the way he was. He even looks younger, like Kellan. In this weird light, he almost looks like her dad too. But when he speaks, it's all Landry. "Really thought you were gonna make those trees," he says. "I truly did."

"Me too," she says through tears. "Me too."

He squeezes her hand, and it's both so strong and so gentle at the same time. "You're not done yet, though, Maggie. Oh, I know you feel like you are. I know you can't draw a good breath without pain shooting all the way through you, like you've been hit by a truck. Before long you're gonna wish you were dead all over again, but you aren't. Not yet. The cold won't stop the bleeding, and no bullshit here, it's bad, real bad, but that bastard didn't hit anything right-off fatal."

"Yet," she echoes.

Landry squints, squeezes. "Right. So, no, I'm not gonna lie, it's not good. But you're a fighter and you still have just enough fight in you and that young girl is out there on her own and that sonofabitch who shot you is still after her. Don't know why and might never know. But there's another out there too . . . that man or thing that attacked me back at my cabin, the White Thing, and those two are gonna tear each other up over that girl, like two hungry wolves. And you know what that means."

"But we're all wolves now," she says. "That's what Graham said."

"That's what *I* said. And we are. You are. So, you gotta be that wolf now, Maggie. You got to. For Luna's sake."

"Where are they?" she asks. "How do I find them?"

He winks at her. "The only place that makes any sense now. Graham is stuck out here, and he's hurt too. Not as bad as you, but bad enough.

I made sure of that. He ain't got many options either. Oh, and his real name is Ekker. Or as real as it gets."

"How do you know all this?" she asks, now really feeling the pain Landry's been warning her about. It almost takes her breath away.

"My boy told me," he says, with something like a smile, washed out by the sun.

"He's dead," she says. "You're dead, too, right?" And she doesn't want to hurt him that way, but needs to know what's going on here, needs to understand.

"Sure," he says. "I know. But we had a long walk, worked some things out. We crossed the mountain, Maggie." And now she can see that he's crying. Crying and smiling. That's when she realizes he's not alone in the place, over the mountain. "And it's all good now. We're both better. Better than we've ever been. God, I'd missed him." Landry squeezes her hand a third and final time and starts to pull her up, the pain enough she almost throws up. "But it's time for you to go. Time for you to finish crossing the mountain too."

Now it's her turn to start crying, or she's just been crying all along too. "No, I'm not ready. I thought I was, but I'm not."

Landry says, "We never are."

Then he shakes her awake.

☾

But it's not Landry, it's Marcus.

Shaking her, slapping her conscious.

It was all bullshit, all that stuff about Landry, just some sort of death dream or hallucination or her imagination dying from the cold and the pain.

Except for her tears. Those are real, frozen on her face.

"You're hurt," Marcus says. "Hurt bad. And the—"

"Cold won't slow the bleeding," she says. "It just makes it worse, I know."

Marcus starts at that, puzzled. "Graham is gone," he continues.

"No, his name is Ekker." And maybe that's all her imagination, too, or Ekker revealed it while they were standing there talking in the snow, just before he shot her. She can't remember, doesn't know how, and the look on Marcus's face suggests he doesn't know either.

"He went for Luna. I heard yelling, commotion. I heard gunshots, Maggie, and we need to assume he's got her now."

That realization forces Maggie to drag herself upright, where she discovers that Marcus crawled across the snow to her from the tower, hand over fist, leaving an ugly trail of broken wood, ashes, and even blood in the snow, all of which more snow and wind will soon wipe away.

"They're going to Lost Hill," she says, with a surprising certainty, although her head is still fuzzy and warm, like it's filled with late-afternoon sunlight. "Hey, you know it's almost Christmas?"

Marcus doesn't answer that and doesn't argue her assertion about Lost Hill, doesn't even bother to question how she knows. "We take whatever we can off him," Marcus says, referring to the dead body behind them, "and track them down. Not sure how far they could've gotten."

"How are we going to do that?" she asks, trying to shake off the sunlight in her head, Landry's voice. "How are we going to do anything? Look at us."

"First," he says, "you're going to help me find where Walton buried my damn leg . . ."

82

Ekker doesn't know what to make of the girl as she trudges in the snow next to him.

Despite the remarkable circumstances, she seems so ordinary, so *unremarkable*. He's not sure exactly what he was expecting.

Bright lights . . . a choir of angels?

Instead, she's stayed mostly silent, her answers two words or less and sometimes not even that. She hasn't asked him anything at all, not even about the fates of the others.

She hasn't asked about him, either, even though he said he was an FBI agent and showed her his badge and his credentials. Before they started hiking, he went through everything in Rade's pack, impressed again with her thoroughness and preparation, and used the med kit to dress the worst of his wounds. He told the girl then he was going to get them to Lost Hill, where they could ride out the last of the storm, but if she already knew that's where Rade herself was originally headed, she didn't acknowledge it.

At least she's not resisting.

She just stares at him now with those wonderful, awful, alien eyes of hers.

It's the eyes . . .

The lamp of the body is the eye . . .

He wonders and worries if she can see his darkness, all of it, in a way no one else ever has. If so, it doesn't frighten her. Conversely, he can't see a thing about her at all. Her eyes are mirrors, and that's never happened before. He has no idea what's lurking behind that gaze, and that both amazes and terrifies him, an unusual occurrence for someone who rarely feels fear or surprise.

Worse, the horrible dying light in his left eye is so dark now he's lost all vision in it, and that metallic taste in his mouth is inescapable, choking him. He wants to spit, constantly, but although his mouth is caked and dry, he's sweating profusely. He's losing the occasional word again and his train of thought, and he doesn't know if it's the cold and exposure, the wounds and blood loss he's suffered, or the killing angel in his head extending her wings a final time.

The relief, the reprieve, the girl gifted him at Landry's cabin has fully worn off, and he needs her to do it again if he's going to get them both safely down the mountain.

And if she can't, or won't, then there is no need to bother with that charade anymore.

☾

They're crossing a frozen stream, a serpentine icicle in the snow broken by the occasional toothlike rock, when he finally asks her about the man or thing he drove off.

She says one word, "Roach."

Ekker remembers that name, the registered firearm from the crash that the deputy was tracing for Landry. Conrad Stoll, a.k.a. Colm Roach. Cadmus + Gray private security. Another mercenary. Like him. "Are you telling me that . . . thing . . . is, was, a man named Colm Roach?"

She doesn't respond as he helps her over the stream, finding her balance on the rocks, trying to stay off the ice itself. The wind buffets and scrapes them both, sharp as sandpaper on skin. It's been snowing on and off since the lookout tower, the skies increasingly dark again.

"I find that hard to believe," he says aloud. That thing was beyond terminal, little more than a cadaver. Sinew holding a mess of bloody bones together, and barely that.

The pain must be . . . unimaginable. Which leads Ekker to wonder if the Roach apparition might experience some measure of psychic relief in the girl's presence, too, some sort of respite from that agony. If so, it will continue to pursue them until it no longer can. Or until Ekker stops it once and for all.

"You're the same," the girl says, eyes down, still marching forward.

"How so?" he asks, although she's only echoing his own thoughts from a moment ago. Despite his wounds and wrecked face, he still wants to believe he's a long way from turning into that kind of ravaged monstrosity.

"You want something from me," she says. "You *need* me."

"We need each other now," Ekker corrects. "I said I don't want to hurt you, and I mean that."

"But you will," she says. "If I don't give you what you want."

Ekker stops and stops her, too, but not roughly. He's careful with her. "And what is it I want?"

She stares at him with those eyes, just as sharp as the wind. "To take it away. The pain. The hurt. The *want*. You want me to take the want away. And so did he."

"Can you do that?" Those eyes again, impenetrable, unreadable. "Can you?" he presses, trying not to sound desperate.

She says, "I can take anything I want . . ."

And then she starts walking again.

83

He had her.

Close enough for the second time to smell her, touch her, almost taste her.

She was right there, too stunned, too tired, too cold to resist him.

The others either too occupied or dead. He finally had her all to himself.

Right there . . . until that man appeared.

Now he's hurt again, hurt worse, curled in a thick white drift, and despite the mountain giving him so much, he doesn't know if he has any strength left to pursue them. But also knows if he doesn't, that man who grabbed her will hurt her, and that makes him howl in anguish.

Not that she doesn't deserve to hurt, not that he isn't going to hurt her, too, but because that's his sole right, his alone.

She is destined for him and no one else.

All this pain is a *promise*.

And on the mountain, pain isn't what kills you: it's the only thing that keeps you alive.

He crawls to his bare feet and starts after them again.

84

A rundown of the man Marcus killed reveals he was carrying one of those SIG Sauer SPEARs and four mags, a SIG 226 semiauto pistol with four clips, ATN night vision goggles in a small belt pouch, a set of those crimson-fletched darts, an M13 thermobaric device, an M67 baseball grenade, and a Silynx earbud and radio rig, not much different from what Marcus himself used overseas.

They also find a tactical communications device. The TCD is the same slim, black phone-like device Marcus saw Graham, now Ekker, use after they left Pullens. A high-tech amalgam of radio, phone, and satellite device. Marcus deployed with them before but has no idea how to unlock this one.

More importantly, the dead man was carrying a regular iPhone still holding on to a hint of a charge, although no coverage bars.

They strip his snow camo, including his boots and wool watch cap.

Marcus keeps the SPEAR, the NVGs, the TCD, and the grenade and thermobaric for himself and gives Maggie the phone and 226. Then he has Maggie do a quick concentric scout for Luna or anyone or anything else, and they get lucky: a second body, the drone operator Walton must've ambushed. She pulls another Silynx earbud and radio rig from him and, amazingly, a NewBeeDrone tool kit: screwdrivers, soldering irons, hex drivers, pliers, tweezers, wire cutters.

Marcus still hates using the word *miracle*, but the tools are a godsend.

Marcus gets his Genesis reset and, using the drone tool kit, works some functionality back into the bionic, ratcheting it into a flexed position that approximates a normal gait, like Marcus is forever taking a small step up an invisible stair. Enough so he's not dragging an iron I beam around behind him anymore, but not enough to truly move a whole lot better. He's not running anywhere.

Least he can move without Maggie constantly holding him upright.

When they make their way to where Maggie left Luna, there's no sign of the girl.

Just fast-disappearing prints in the snow—

Two sets of boots or shoes heading north and east, down the mountain.

A lone set of bare prints heading back into the woods.

☾

He makes her take off her layers so he can get to the bullet, see how bad it is.

They huddle beneath a pine as she strips bare from the waist up, her skin as alabaster as the snow around them.

Ekker's lone bullet passed through the meat and muscle of her left shoulder. A couple of inches down and to the right and he would have blown out her heart, likely where he was aiming. Marcus doesn't tell Maggie about all the significant blood vessels in the shoulder, the kind that could leave her bleeding out quick. Or the very real danger that arterial blood drowns her lungs.

It's bad.

Without Maggie's gear, he binds her up as best he can—which isn't good at all—fingers working hard over her freezing skin. If she feels his unsteady hands, or the wound itself, she doesn't flinch.

Now that she's exposed, he finds a small tattoo on her right shoulder, a tiny winking dragon with ruby wings, curled in on itself in the shape of a compass or cartouche.

It's bright, impossibly whimsical, against her frostbitten skin.

"You don't seem the type," he says, rubbing a thumb over the tiny creature as he helps her get her merino pullover and her jacket back on. They've divided the dead men's clothes between them as well, and for the first time since he left Pullens yesterday, warmth seeps into his bones. Now they just need to stave off dehydration.

She winces, glances over her shoulder. "I was young once. A kid, just like Luna. I know it's hard to believe."

"You two kind of look alike. Notice that? Could be sisters." When Maggie doesn't say anything, he asks, "Does it mean anything? Your ink?"

She zips up, wincing again. She's in pain, a world of pain, but there's nothing more he can do for her. "No."

"I have one too." He taps a spot above his heart. "Names of the men I served with. Those that didn't come back. And it means everything."

She looks at him. "Is it a long list?"

"Yeah," he says as they pull each other to standing. "Too long."

☾

An hour later they've made slow progress, but they've long lost the tracks.

"We push on to Lost Hill," she tells him.

"You sure?"

"Yes." Then she adds without any hint of a joke, "Landry told me." And a part of him almost wants to believe that, although he doesn't want to talk about Walton, the old man's sudden death—his missing presence—an open wound they're both trying to live with or not die from. Maggie continues, "Ekker has Luna and all my gear; he'll figure it out."

"Why is this Ekker so interested in the girl now?" he asks.

"That I don't know. He didn't get around to telling me before he put a bullet in me." Now she does gift him a grim smile. "Maybe he sees the same thing I saw in her that moment I pulled her from that crash. A kind of magic, I guess, a fearlessness. A rage. She's kind of impossible to ignore." Maggie smiles. "A dragon. That's what it is. Those magical eyes of hers. She's a dragon, despite all of Landry's and Ekker's talk about wolves."

"Yeah, but dragons aren't real," he says.

"And maybe neither is she. Maybe none of this is." Maggie waves at the mountain. "But we're still not letting that bastard have her."

"No," Marcus says, pushing them both forward. "We are not."

85

She knows what he wants—

Her.

Like Roach, he's drawn to her, a moth flying into a light. Back at the cabin, when she screamed and *released*, she broke something inside him. Dr. Jewell used to call it *unmooring*, and although the doctor rarely had to cope with that awful sensation or its lingering effects herself, they both understood she affected some people differently than others.

Some more powerfully, a few for the worse.

Even fewer who were already so sick, bad, or evil, their psyches or minds or brains already so damaged or warped, there was never any telling what truly might happen.

Sometimes when she releases the dark birds, the worst thoughts and desires and fears and dread don't just take flight; they multiply—*infinitely*—leaving a million black birds loose in their wounded heads, crowding everything else out, until no other rational thoughts or even memories exist at all.

She doesn't yet know how to cage them back up again, or if she can. Doesn't know how to fully keep her own dark thoughts tamed, when they fly free with all the others.

It happened with Roach, and it's happening now with this man.

I know what you want . . .

The way he looks at her or *tries* not to look at her. The way he recoils when she looks at him. The way he hovers close, always close enough to touch her, to grab her if she tries to run. Despite his cloying presence, though, she knows now that she's alone in all the ways that matter. No one is going to come for her other than Roach, and if her choices are Roach or this man, both broken and dangerous and desperate in their own ways, then she really doesn't have any choice at all.

Walton told her she's a wolf . . .

Be a wolf . . .

And a wolf has teeth and fangs.

She stops and turns to Ekker—

"Do you want to tell me a story?"

And he does.

☾

They find shelter, two trees intertwined like two lovers embracing.

It's not much, but it keeps the wind off them, if not the snow. It's everywhere now again, thick, wet, and heavy.

They kneel together, and the man says something about an angel in his left eye, a dark light he can't unsee. He says he can't see at all now and tells her she made it all go away at the cabin and she needs to make it all go away again, and she tells him it's okay; he just needs to relax and let her in. Open himself up to her, don't resist.

Such openness doesn't come naturally to him, the way it did with Dr. Jewell, or even Maggie back at the watchtower. And although this man can't draw on any special techniques or mindfulness meditation, he's practiced enough at hiding everything about himself. His whole life blank walls and empty rooms.

But the harder someone resists her, the harder she can push, like rattling a cage or banging on a wall, and that sometimes happens all on its own when she gets truly scared or surprised. She can't control herself, and so far, no walls, real or imagined, have ever been able to keep her out then.

He tries to relax, and she tells him to hold her hand, since physical contact helps, makes her stronger. And so, they sit like that, holding hands, as she wanders his mostly empty rooms, as she relives . . . *releases* . . . all the moments, feelings, and impressions she can find in this man's head, and they circle her like black motes or shadowy stars or dark birds, their eyes just as shiny and sable, reflecting her over and over again.

Do you want to tell me a story?

Although she used to find some small comfort in a handful of Dr. Jewell's shared memories, simple moments she never imagined she'd experience herself—driving in warm rain or gently touching a man's face or snuggling with a nuzzling dog—there's nothing warm or safe or comforting inside this man . . . this Ekker.

If she thought Roach was horrible, no words can describe the cold void inside Ekker.

If she stays too long in here, goes too deep, there's no telling what things she will release, no way for her to make her own way out again. A part of Ekker seems to understand that, too, gets an inkling of what she might be doing there inside his head—the magnitude of what she's truly capable of and what he might reveal—because now he starts furiously resisting, trying to throw her out of his memories.

That's okay because that prompts her to push onward harder, deeper, darker. Because this was never about helping him at all.

She feels, experiences, and relives all the things he's done, all the people he's hurt, his infinite capacity for pain.

The moment he killed Marcus's and Walton's friend Donnie.

The moment he killed an old loving couple in front of their last Christmas tree.

The very last moment Ekker pushed Walton off the side of this mountain.

She relives that again and again, and so does Ekker.

And even though Walton wouldn't want this for her, wouldn't wish these kinds of memories on anyone, she won't let it go. She holds this awful one tight until it grows its own pair of wings. Bat wings, monstrous wings. Then she screams inside Ekker's head, releasing all his dark birds and hers too.

No, she howls . . . like a wolf . . .

And all those birds turn into wolves, running wild and free.

Snapping and biting at what's left of Ekker's sanity.

86

Ekker comes to with blood freezing in his eyes, his ears, his mouth.

A ringing in his ears too . . . first a horrible cawing, then a howling . . . inside his head.

. . . *we're all wolves now* . . .

He's trembling, spastic, and it has nothing to do with the hypothermia and frostbite eating away at him.

The girl is gone.

Rade's pack and gear are gone.

His weapons are gone, too, flung away. Buried or taken.

He has no idea what she did to him, still can't see out of his left eye, and worse, now his right eye is horribly eclipsed by that black light too. His vision is permanently occluded, opaque, all shifting shadows and satin ink. He doesn't taste metal anymore, but something far worse, rotten feathers and rancid fur.

The black cancer in his brain growing by the second, eating him from the inside.

She didn't heal him; she didn't even help him. She tried to fucking *kill* him by unwiring him one nerve and synapse at a time. Before he may have had months, weeks; now he's down to days.

Hours.

The last thing the girl Luna said to him was, *Do you want to tell me a story.* And he thinks he remembers telling someone else a hundred years ago, *Tell me a story . . . the whole story . . . and I decide if there's anything next at all . . .*

But there's nothing now. Nothing. The pain is Richter scale bad, and those earlier dark cigarette burns in his vision are smoldering holes all the way through his head, dark spots where his memories used to be.

The lamp of the body is the eye . . .

She's taken *everything* from him.

He has no idea how long he's been just kneeling in the snow like this, but he's dusted thick with it like an exposed gravestone, a weeping cemetery angel, and the sun's already moved overhead and arced lower, not that its waning light means anything to him anymore.

All this time not moving at all, the cold's come for him and it won't let go.

It won't ever let go.

And neither will he.

87

Maggie doesn't know how they do it, all but slipping and sliding and falling their way down the icy ledges and rock-strewn gullies.

They don't speak much because there's nothing much to say anymore, and they both need to conserve their waning energy. Just the occasional *give me a minute* or *hold on* or *take my hand.*

They carry each other down Black Mountain.

Keeping their eyes up, looking for any sign of Luna, Ekker, or anyone or anything else.

Most of the way down it's just the two of them and the cold and the snow and the trees. The storm comes and goes, buffeting them again and again, like the mountain itself is breathing, a cadence of stillness followed by racking wind, spinning flurries, icy sleet.

There's one moment when there's something else under the trees with them, a pale creature, like a big wolf or a dog.

She's about to get Marcus's attention to check if he sees it, too, but he's too intent, too locked in on the path ahead of them. So, she just watches alone this lonely thing watching them, remembers Landry's stories, that old book back in Pullens, all the missing and the monsters that have made this mountain their home.

Landry told her—

Sometimes things do get lost up here forever, Maggie, no matter how goddamn hard we look . . .

As she stares at it, the creature slowly rises to its feet, and stands just like a man.

Watches her with baleful eyes but makes no sound.

Now she really wants to get Marcus's attention, so she calls out to him to *stop, look*, and points to where the thing is standing.

But by the time Marcus turns, she's pointing at empty space, at cold, dead air, and it's like there was nothing there at all.

☾

Night is just falling when they see the first lights of Lost Hill.

It's a remote, small town on the Virginia side of Black Mountain, although it's still technically part of West Virginia. The population is barely five hundred.

Maggie remembers her dad telling her about the place when she was fifteen or sixteen, and when she was planning her vanishing trick, she rediscovered it through an extensive Google search at the Yorkville Library, East Seventy-Ninth Street, in New York. She chose Lost Hill not only for its isolated location and diminutive size but because of the East Bradford Self-Storage Company, a single row of low-slung, red-roofed, roll-door units with twenty-four-hour access, no gates, and no cameras.

Each unit secured with a simple renter-provided padlock.

The other thing that fascinated her was the local legend her dad recounted to her about an eighteenth-century pioneer settler who went missing in the area when this whole region was nothing but thick woods, bears and wolves, and Indians.

The settler was never found, but some years later a mess of bones and a ruined Charleville musket were recovered by a beech tree and a small creek, although the creek was no longer identifiable. Her dad couldn't, and it doesn't help that Lost Hill is crisscrossed with dozens and dozens of identical nameless small streams, like veins under the land's skin.

But the most interesting thing about the legend was not the bones or the guns, but the weird couplet etched into that beech tree, allegedly marking the dead man's passing.

Strange is my name and I'm on strange ground, and strange that it is that I can't be found . . .

Maggie appreciated the joke, even if she'd be the only one to ever get it.

☾

"When were you last here?" Marcus asks as she guides them through the snowy streets to East Bradford.

Although Lost Hill's few streets and houses are quiet, fewer still draped in bright Christmas lights, and the tiny main street itself is deserted, she's trying to keep them to the edge of town, skirting side streets and lawns.

There's a quaint, bright-red post office, a pharmacy, a bank, a church, and a general store with one gas pump and a half dozen flashing neon signs advertising beer and lottery tickets.

Under the cover of snowfall, it's picture perfect as any postcard.

"Thirteen months," she says.

"You've been planning all this that long?"

"Longer." She stops them, staring down Main. They're in a sparse field adjacent to the small Baptist church, not far down from the general store. Its bright lights and obvious warmth beckon, but she wants to watch a few moments longer before deciding if it's safe to approach, or if they should. "Started putting bits and pieces into place a couple of years ago. Vann and I always had exit strategies—couldn't do the things we did and not plan to run. But I also started to set up one of my own, just in case."

"In case you decided to leave his ass behind . . . or he met an untimely but convenient end, all on his own."

"Still want to know if I killed him?"

Marcus seems transfixed, too, by the bright lights and the neon pooling in the general store's parking lot, glowing acid-electric green and yellow and red. "No," he says. "I don't."

"Anyway, my dad was always into puzzles and mysteries and adventures, that sort of thing. He traveled when I was a little kid, always came back with these great stories and gifts from all these places he'd been to. Lost Hill was one, for reasons I can't remember. I believed him for years and years."

They lean together against the icy bricks of the church, clinging to the shadows, as an old Ford F-150 turns down Main, headlights picking out individual snowflakes. The roads are mostly unplowed here, the snowfall thick.

"Are you saying he didn't go on all those trips?"

"A few . . . maybe. Mostly he ordered those gifts and trinkets online, probably where he got all those stories too."

The truck turns into the general store—JT's—and passes the pump and parks by the front door, where it sits idling, smoke curling from the exhaust.

"My dad was a drug dealer," she says. "A kind of one, anyway. At first, it was these rogue online pharmacies, shipping non-FDA-approved meds across the country. Stuff that wasn't necessarily illegal, just hard to obtain domestically. He thought he was doing good, like Robin Hood. He'd open one for a few months, shut it down, do it all over again. But eventually he moved onto the dark web, started selling illicit drugs . . . the real stuff . . . meth, opioids, fentanyl. You name it. He was thoroughly anti-government, anti-establishment, *anti* a lot of things, yet by all outward appearances, we had a normal, solid, middle-class existence. But he was juggling the money, investing in this and that, investing badly, losing it all and trying to get it back again. A gambler by nature. He told people he was into stocks and equities, claimed he was into imports and exports. Had all these websites faked up, faked these neat or exotic trips, yet every day we were one step ahead of jail or the poorhouse. It was all a lie. All of it. I was a few months away from heading off to college when it all came tumbling down after an FBI online sting operation. A knock on the door, and then it was all over."

"You really didn't know?"

Maggie hesitates, suddenly weary of confessing. "He shielded me. We didn't have the same last name, and part of his plea deal was a guarantee they'd keep me out of it. So, of course, I didn't know . . . and I did. He never came out and told me, but I learned not to ask. An unattractive trait I carried on when I first met Vann."

The truck continues to idle, but otherwise the street is empty, quiet. If they do decide to approach the store, they need to wait until the lone customer in the lot leaves. She wonders what would drive anyone out on a night like this.

"He still locked up?"

"No. Died of pancreatic cancer, two years before he would've been first eligible for parole."

"I'm sorry," Marcus says. "Your mom?"

"Gone . . . just . . . gone. Let's just say she was anti-family." That's a whole other story she doesn't want to get into. "My dad was all I ever had."

Marcus uses the church to keep himself upright but slumps low against it. "You helped him with those websites, didn't you? You didn't know exactly what was going on, not at first, but you had your suspicions, right? And later, enough knowledge to set up a similar scheme with your husband."

"Like father like daughter. And like I said, I was always the brains." Maggie settles against the church, too, so exhausted she might fall asleep right here, in so much pain she might die right here. It's been getting harder and harder to breathe, but Marcus has been pushing and pushing them onward, barely willing to let either of them stop, probably because he doesn't want her to dwell on just how badly hurt she truly is. "My dad was in prison, and suddenly I was on my own. Left to fend for myself for years . . . or try to. Until Vann came along, and then it didn't have to be just me anymore . . . and I needed that. Despite how horrible Vann was, despite how he treated me and the things he did to me. I hated *us*, but I hated being alone with myself even more. I'm not proud of it, but it's the truth."

"No need to apologize to me."

"I'm a bad person, I think. Just . . . a bad, bad person."

"A crook and a liar? Absolutely. Emotionally fucked up? No doubt. But bad?" She can't see much of Marcus's face in the dark. "I don't know about that. Ekker's bad, he's . . . *wrong* . . . in ways I can't explain or even comprehend. You're nothing like him." Marcus pauses. "A truly bad person wouldn't even think about helping this girl. But here you are, freezing, bleeding out, still trying to do the *right* thing."

"I'm going to die, aren't I? Ekker's bullet."

"Hey, we all do, sooner or later. So, let's make it later. And not on my watch." Marcus laughs, quiet and gentle. "That sounds like something Walton would say, right?" Marcus pulls himself up and her too. "Why will Ekker and Luna go to this specific storage place?"

"It's his best way out of here. It was my way out. And she knows all about it now. She knows everything, although I can't explain how. That's where she'll go, with or without him." She doesn't want to say *if she got away . . . if she got this far . . . if she's still alive.*

Marcus suddenly gets tense, goes on high alert, and puts a hand to her lips. She follows his silent, hard gaze down the street, to the brightly lit general store, where a garish paper Santa waves at them from a window. "Sonofabitch," Marcus whispers, and Maggie sees why.

Ekker.

Getting out of that idling F-150.

Maggie is stunned, Marcus just as shocked. All their effort to find the man, and here he appears miraculously out of the darkness in front of them, just like that.

Maybe they just got lucky.

Ekker stands oddly by the truck for a moment, almost hunched, shaking his head as if trying to clear it, and peering into the dark as if searching the night. But if he spots them, he doesn't give it away. He goes inside and leaves the truck door open . . .

"Where is she?" she asks. "Where's Luna?"

But before Marcus answers, the dead man's cell phone stowed beneath her coat starts to buzz.

88

Ekker stumbled onto the road before he found Lost Hill.

He flagged down the truck slowly making its way toward him, and when it stopped and the driver rolled down the window and said, *"Holy shit, man, what are you doing out here? Have an accident?"* Ekker grabbed him by the head and gouged his eyes out with his thumbs.

He rolled the body out of the cab into the snow, frisked it for ID, cell phone, keys, anything useful—although honestly, he wasn't sure what would be useful to him anymore, given his current state—and then hopped in.

The man had been listening to some soft, sorrowful country station, turned down low, but the noise was so loud, like the blast of a thousand trumpets or more of those howling wolves right behind his eyes, that he used his fist to smash the radio again and again until that sound finally stopped, and he broke three bones in his right hand.

He started driving, slumped over the wheel, barely able to see, sitting in the man's still-warm blood.

☾

The general store is bright and loud, louder even than the wild menagerie in his head. So bright it blinds him, even though he is mostly already blind.

Like lit cigarettes are being put to his eyes.

Nothing is working right. He issues his arms and legs commands, and they follow them, eventually. But there's a natural latency in everything he does, a two- to three-second delay that throws off his well-honed timing, his movements, his instincts.

The general store is a burning fun house, but at least it's empty . . . except for a lone man behind the counter, eyeing Ekker's every move.

The man is thin, his chin scruffy with a long gray beard, his equally gray hair pulled in a loose ponytail that hangs down past his shoulder. He's wearing two layers of mismatched flannel shirts, and a (real) dying cigarette burns in an ashtray at his elbow. He's got one bony hand resting on the counter, the other beneath the counter, gripping a gun.

For a moment his face looks like Bisek's, then Feiser's.

Then he's Jon Brooking reflected in colored glass, until he opens his mouth.

The man says, "Friend, you don't look so good." He makes a loose circular gesture with his free hand, indicating Ekker's face. "Matter of fact, you look like someone took a goddamn lawnmower to your face. That there's a shitload of blood . . . getting all over my floor."

Then Ekker understands it's not just the blood of the man he just killed out in the truck, but his own as well, from the things the girl did to him. The panoply of Landry's bruises and the mountain's frostbite too. He looks as bad now as that creature out in the snow—or even worse.

"What the shit happened to you?" Ponytail asks.

Ekker tries not to let his ruined face slide onto the floor. "An accident. A crash."

But Ponytail isn't completely buying it. He glances over Ekker's shoulder to the truck parked outside. "That's Delroy's truck. I'd know that rolling rust bucket anywhere." Even in his weakened, wounded state, Ekker catches the other man's shoulder and arm tense, veins popping, gripping tight the gun he can't see. "And, brother, you ain't Delroy."

"I'm not," Ekker rasps, and even the sound of his own voice is torturous. He raises his hands, slow. "Just let me reach for my ID, and I'll clear this up. But we don't have much time. I'm looking for a young girl."

That gives Ponytail pause. "A girl? Now?"

Ekker nods. "As I said. There's been a crash. A plane. In the mountains." He pulls out his creds and his badge and puts the latter on the counter, where it gleams so bright it's like a stiletto in his brain. "I'm Special Agent Carl Graham, FBI."

89

Marcus decides they're not going to use the phone.

It's flashing a signal at last—one bar, but enough—and showing multiple unanswered text messages, which is what set it off beneath Maggie's stolen coat. But he reminds her they still can't unlock it, leaving their only recourse the Emergency SOS function.

"And who is going to come first?" he asks. "If anyone comes at all?" He takes the phone from Maggie. "It'll be some deputy like Donnie, someone like me or Walton. I won't throw anyone else in front of that killer. I won't turn this street into a war zone."

"What then? How'd he get that truck? Where's Luna?"

"Don't know," he admits as he pulls out the night vision goggles and other gear they recovered from Black Mountain. He'd run various scenarios in his head on the way down, but finding Ekker shopping alone in a mini mart wasn't one of them. "He could've sedated her with one of those darts and has her all trussed up in the back of the cab, but I'm not convinced, not the way he pulled up and got out so casually. He hardly glanced back, didn't even shut the door. But only way to know for sure is to get in close and get a look."

"Let's go then," Maggie says, hefting her gun.

"No." He powers up the NVGs and slips them around his neck, even though the general store is too bright for them, all those overhead incandescent and neon lights threatening to just bloom out the lenses.

"If Luna's not in that truck, if she somehow escaped and she's out here on her own, even if he's stashed her somewhere else, he'll never tell us that. *Never.* We finally got him outgunned, Maggie, but we only get one shot at him here. One. He's too good, and we're both too injured. And if we both end up dead, Luna is left all alone. Again."

The struggle plays vividly out on Maggie's raw, peeling face. She cuts her eyes back and forth between him and the general store across the street, where Ekker disappeared only moments before. Marcus still can't see him inside, lost in the aisles and light.

Maggie says, "We found him, Marcus. He's right here."

"But Luna isn't, not for certain," he says. "And we need to find her. We're all she's got. And none of this matters if we don't."

Maggie says, "I don't know what you're asking me to do."

"Ekker thinks we're already dead, back up there on the mountain." He starts divvying up the things they have in the snow. "So, let's stay dead just a little bit longer."

90

He has their scent now, all of them down below.

A small town cloaked in darkness settled in deep beneath the snow.

He can hear, feel, all their frantic beating hearts.

And he descends on them.

91

The storage place is just as Maggie remembers it.

It sits off the road bracketed by a couple of dying trees, and if it wasn't blanketed and blurred out by snow, she could make out the cracked weedy lot that fronts it, the handwritten WE STILL DON'T TAKE CHECKS notice beneath the company sign. There's one light on a utility pole on the eastern corner that shines a yellowish sodium light, filled with snow flurries, but it barely illuminates anything.

Still, she crouches across the street and watches and waits.

Nothing moves, the old building looming quiet in the dark like a crouched dog or wolf, wreathed in a miasma of frost and fog.

After several minutes, she escapes the shadows and crosses the street.

☾

The lock is a Brinks Stainless Steel Combination Discus Padlock.

Polished steel lock body with a steel four-pin resettable cylinder.

Just four digits, but Maggie used a computer algorithm to choose them so she wouldn't pick a date or some other number that was inadvertently familiar to her.

She bought the lock with cash at a hardware store in Rochester three months before she reset the lock and never wrote the number down after she did. The risky part of it all was getting the lock on this innocuous red roll-up door in Lost Hill. But like she told Marcus, she and Vann were planning their joint exit strategies for some time, and she was planning her own longer than that.

Everything she's done, every step, was leading up to this very moment, back in front of this red door, where, after rolling it open and walking through it for the second and final time, she was supposed to be walking into a brand-new life, one finally unfettered by the weight and chains of all the things she's done, all the people she's been.

She had to reinvent herself after her dad died, again in college, then again when she and Vann got together. She's been a *Maggie* and a *Mia*, but even before that she was a *Melissa Hanover* (and briefly, a *Melissa Dennon*), and after she goes through that door, she'll come out another someone else altogether—

Lily Shane.

That was the plan, carefully and artfully constructed over years. The plan since even before she emptied out Cambion's coffers and pushed her husband into the cold Atlantic after he'd hit her one too many times.

Still want to know if I killed him?

But almost nothing has gone to plan since Vann dropped unconscious beneath those cold waves. Since she pulled into Pullens, West Virginia, three days ago. Since she met Luna and Landry and Sheriff Marcus Austin.

So, she isn't angry or even much surprised when she finds that the Brinks Stainless Steel Combination Discus Padlock's already been removed from her long-hidden storage unit.

She just holds the dead man's gun higher and raises the door.

92

Stars.

Of course, Marcus can't see any from where he's huddled. He was never much interested in stars anyway, heaven, either, for that matter. But he does wonder now if he missed out, not paying attention to certain things. Missed out on some important things altogether.

Like stars.

The way the sand moved in the African desert.

The way the sun rises over Pullens.

The sound of wind in the pines in summer.

He was overseas when his daddy died, and he missed that too. His mama sent him a video she recorded of the burial, but he never watched it.

He deleted it a month after he received it.

He keeps falling back to a moment in those last months he and Deidre were together. It was a Saturday, maybe a Sunday, and she was curled on the couch in that way she sometimes did, her slim legs tucked underneath her, her hair loose and spilling over her shoulders. Wearing one of his old green Army Ranger T-shirts two sizes too big, and drinking . . . something . . . he can't remember now, coffee or tea, and it was raining lightly, so light it sounded more like breath against the windows than actual rain. He was channel surfing, and he caught her looking at him, could see there was . . . something . . . right on the edge of her lips, a question or a thought or *I love you*. And one hand was wrapped protectively around her belly the way he'd seen some pregnant women do it, and there she was just looking at him with those dark eyes of hers beautiful and immeasurable and that question or thought or whatever it was or whatever it was supposed to be right there . . . right on the edge of her lips he'd kissed a thousand times . . . but it never came, and all he had to do was ask, just say . . . something . . . and he didn't.

He didn't, never did, and even now he doesn't know why. He missed his chance, let another important moment slip through his fingers like so much else in his life.

You never know what's too important until it's too late.

Likely it wouldn't have changed anything—he'd let far too many of those moments pass by—and doesn't know why he's even reliving it now, until the old truck starts up underneath him, loud and rough, and he realizes he's fallen into one of those fugue states again.

Slipped into a dream.

The truck is finally moving, rolling along, and Marcus tries not to roll around too much in the open bed, barely concealed by the tarp he found there.

He grips the SPEAR and watches the snow and dark overhead, but even the powerful NVGs hiding his eyes aren't strong enough to pick out the stars above, if there are any at all.

☾

It's slow going, the roads snow choked and bad, and the old truck isn't built for them. But after tiny Lost Hill falls away several miles behind them, Marcus concludes that Ekker isn't taking them to wherever he's hiding Luna.

Ekker's just heading for the hills . . . escaping.

That means either the girl's already escaped him or she's already dead, and Marcus is going to believe it's the former. He finally got

Maggie to believe that, too, which is the only reason she agreed to splitting up and didn't rush across the street to the general store and try to finish off Ekker all on her own.

We only get one shot at him here. One. He's too good, and we're both too injured. And if we both end up dead, Luna is left all alone. Again.

We're all she's got . . .

Either way, Ekker is a dead man.

He wishes he could tell Maggie, but she's too far away. He truly hopes she finds Luna, hopes whatever bond they shared on the mountain is still strong enough to draw them together, a bright-enough beacon or light to both follow.

A star.

He hopes they get the hell out of this place and never look back.

It's just him and Ekker now.

Marcus lets another mile roll by before he makes his move and then rolls to sitting in the back of the truck bed and puts the big rifle's electro-optics on the back of Ekker's head and is about to blow that sonofabitch's brains right through the front windshield when he realizes it's not Ekker at all.

His NVGs reveal it's just some long-haired guy who now spies him looming in the truck bed and yanks the wheel in terror and nearly drives them both off the road and into a tree.

Goddamn, Marcus thinks. Goddamn, he got us again . . .

☾

The man is Dillon Paul Fuente, and he really regrets keeping his general store open in the middle of a storm, given the shitty night and the total lack of business, and the two apparent psychopaths he's now had to deal with.

"It's Christmas Eve, man," Fuente says. "Christmas fucking Eve."

Marcus sympathizes, but still won't let Fuente go.

Fuente says, "Guy told me he was an FBI agent and that there was a plane crash. Said he was looking for a little girl. Asked me if I had seen her . . . or really, anyone out of place." Fuente gets defensive. "And he had an actual *badge*, motherfucker, and that's more than I can say for you."

Marcus admires Fuente for cursing at a man with a rifle pointed at his head. Fuente's opened the sliding rear window between the cab and the bed, and they're talking to each other through it, both men freezing, snow turning to sleet, both figuring Fuente's not going to be able to make a run for it before Marcus shoots him dead in his tracks. Least that's what Marcus wants him to believe.

"He was all jacked up, hurt bad," Fuente continues. "Face an awful mess. Bled all over Delroy's seats, all over my store. Looked like he'd been the one in a plane crash."

"What'd he say?"

"Told me to haul ass out toward Curley, where I'd meet the rest of his 'team.'" Fuente makes air quotes around the last word. "Said Delroy was hurt something fierce, too, but his men needed someone local to show them the trail routes up to the crash site. Said I could also help get Delroy to the hospital."

"How far is that?"

Fuente thinks. "Berkeley Medical Center, but in this shit show of a storm, no one's going much of anywhere. Told him that too."

Marcus knows that hospital. "What was he going to do?"

"FBI guy? Look, I'm not saying I believed any of this, just that he had a legit badge, and I have some outstanding legal issues I'd prefer to keep that way. I also wanted to check on Delroy. He's got a mean wife and some ugly kids, but still . . ." Fuente eyes the gun in his face, like he might be working up some courage, and Marcus admires that too. Fuente reminds him of SPC Lionel Mathers, who died in the same IED explosion that took Marcus's leg. "Seems like the guy was intent on tossing the town for that girl he kept asking about. But, like I said, he didn't look so good, should've drug his ass to Berkeley himself, and Lost Hill ain't that big. Trust me, you can't hide a stolen TV or an eight ball of crank in that place, much less some missing kid or an RV." Fuente stares at the NVGs still draped on Marcus's neck. "He wanted my ride, though, piece of shit Dodge I had parked round back. But you know, whatever."

"That it?"

Fuente breathes into his thin hands as the ice and snow falls and falls. "Said he lost his gun, and took the piece I keep stowed beneath the store counter in case anyone gets rowdy, or my ex-wife shows up angry. Old Remington scatter gun. Unlicensed, unregistered, and fully loaded. Twelve-gauge buckshot."

Marcus doesn't have time to piece together what's happened to Ekker since they last saw him on the mountain; the only thing that matters is he doesn't have Luna and doesn't know where she is. If Fuente is right about him being hurt, he might even be suffering the lasting effects of something the girl's done to him. She somehow got away. But they're all suffering the effects of exposure, exhaustion, dehydration, and hypothermia. Yet Ekker's still moving, plotting, operating. Still has enough wits about him to send this man out as a stalking horse in case anyone was looking for him or the truck he murdered for.

Ekker is still very fucking dangerous.

He asks, "Hey, what's that you said about an RV?"

Fuente replies, "Yeah, Mr. FBI wanted to know all about nearby barns and farms, rental houses, storage places. Small airstrips. Anything like that. Anyplace where someone might be able to store a plane or a van or RV for a while."

93

There's only one thing crowding the inside of the storage unit.

An older Honda Accord, which at any given time comprises more than 3 percent of all cars on the road in America, making it one of the most popular, recognizable, and unobtrusive vehicles in the country.

This one is snow white—Platinum White Pearl—which is also the most popular car color in America, at more than 20 percent.

After extensive research, Maggie couldn't find a vehicle *less* interesting, any vehicle *more* likely to fade into the background and disappear than the Honda. And it's all stock. All she did was top off the fuel and add a fuel stabilizer and disconnect the negative battery cable so it wouldn't run dry while it was sitting here waiting for her.

She left it covered with a seven-layer spunbonded polypropylene cover to protect it from the cold, since the unit isn't heated, but that's been dragged off and left piled on the floor.

She keeps her gun up and moves to the driver's side door and finds Luna asleep in the frigid back seat.

☾

Luna knew the warehouse that until an hour ago existed only inside Maggie's head.

The combination to the lock that no one other than she knew or could ever know.

The girl knows everything about her now, and although Maggie still has no idea how that's possible, after everything that's happened and those few moments holding Luna's hands in the snow, she also knows better than to doubt it.

She doesn't recall much of what happened out there, other than sensations, electricity in the air and on her skin, galvanic pressure, a touch like fingers on her brain.

All she remembers is a sound like birds, a thousand beating wings, carrying her aloft.

☽

Luna is okay, mostly unhurt.

Not hurt outwardly, anyway. But there is fresh blood on her face, her eyes.

The crimson tears she cries when the hurt *inside* gets to be too much.

It takes Maggie a few minutes to get the battery connected, and using the keys Walton found in her bag—Luna was using her backpack as a pillow—she soon gets the engine rolled over too. As Luna warms herself by the heaters, Maggie goes to the trunk, stuffed with two mismatched suitcases, a black Adidas duffel bag, a smaller Baggallini Triple Zip Bagg, and two seventeen-gallon HDX flat-lid Tough Totes.

She takes the Triple Zip Bagg and the duffel bag back to the front seat and dumps both out on the floorboard at Luna's feet, revealing hair dye and makeup and scissors and other sundries, as well as a change of clothes and shoes, two wallets, a rubber-banded passport with a driver's license, a stack of heat-sealed bills, more small bills neatly folded together and two rolls of quarters all in a ziplock bag, two Mint Mobile phones, a spare set of Honda Accord keys, and a Colt handgun.

"Clean up and change out of those clothes as best you can," she tells Luna. "Take that gun and stay down. If anyone other than Marcus approaches this car, you shoot them."

She returns to the roll door and slowly raises it again, gun out in front of her, and when she doesn't see anything, doesn't hear anything—including Marcus in her ear—she retreats to the warming car.

She and Marcus are both wearing the earbuds and radios they took off the two dead men, but the range hasn't proven to be all that great, and they haven't spoken since they parted ways at the Baptist church. She radios him anyway, lets him know she's found Luna and that she's okay and safe, just in case he can hear her.

Just in case he's still okay too.

"Ready?" she asks Luna, who instead of answering, reaches over to Maggie's seat and pulls back a hand thick and sticky with fresh blood.

"I'm fine," Maggie whispers, gunning the engine. "We're getting Marcus and getting the hell out of here."

She rolls the Honda carefully out into the street, the long-unused brakes and tires protesting. There was a time when she flirted with the idea of hiding that Cessna Skyhawk Vann bought—even taught herself to fly with a laptop flight sim—and escaping into Canada or Mexico with it, but the plane would've proven too easy to track.

Never would've gotten it off the ground in weather like this.

This old car—simple, solid, dependable—several years past its prime and without any sort of onboard navigation system or LoJack, is all she and Luna and Marcus need.

As she pulls away from the storage place, the earbud crackles to life and Marcus's voice pops in—

Ekker . . . coming . . . a blue Dodge . . .

Hearing him causes Maggie to hit the brakes, to stop and look up and down the dark streets again, and likely saves her and Luna's life.

A midnight-blue Dodge Durango clips the Honda's front end rather than plowing through the driver's side door but still sends the smaller sedan spinning and sliding off the accumulated ice and snow and into the corrugated side of East Bradford Storage.

94

The shock of the collision almost throws Ekker through the Durango's windshield.

As it is, he pinballs around the vehicle's interior, catching a face full of cigarette butts, old Slurpee cups, dated newspapers, fast-food wrappers, a Budweiser bottle that slow-motion shatters into a million sparkling, spinning fragments, and a loose twelve-inch Phillips-head screwdriver that almost impales one of his unseeing eyes.

The Durango slides to a stop twenty yards past the Honda.

He falls out of the big SUV onto dark, unforgiving ice, struggling to keep the cumbersome shotgun aimed in front of him with the bleeding hand he broke against that truck's radio, his eyesight deteriorating.

Rade's white Honda, the getaway car Feiser guessed she must've hidden here some time ago, sits pinned against the storage facility itself, engine revving, exhaust still smoking.

He can't make out Rade behind the wheel, can't see the girl either.

He's moving only on instinct now, and it's only instinct that saves him as *another* big vehicle caroms down the snowy street: that truck he stole outside Lost Hill.

He should've killed that fool in the general store.

Someone is driving it right at him, shooting at him with one of his team's own guns—although he can barely see, he recognizes the unique chuffing rattle of the SPEAR—and it can only be Austin. Ekker can't fathom how both Austin and Rade are still alive.

Then again, he's not sure how he's still alive.

Ice and snow eat the rounds meant for him as the truck closes the distance, bearing down, fighting snowdrift, and fishtailing heavily on the slick street.

Old headlights reflect and refract the falling sleet, bright fleeting geometries that to his clouded gaze appear like tiny, winged birds.

He falls to a knee and wildly empties the shotgun into the coming truck, buckshot blowing up the hood, blowing out a tire, blowing through a windshield.

Sparks and snow mix and the F-150 spins three-quarters around and slams into a thick drift, throwing white powder high into the air.

Ekker takes a last rifle round through the shoulder or gut but he's already numb from the recoil of the big shotgun. The Remington's empty, too, and he's left wielding it like a bat or an axe.

Swinging it back and forth, he turns toward the white car, and hunts for the girl.

95

Marcus abandons the buckshot-riddled truck and over Ekker's slumped shoulder sees Luna fighting to get a helpless Maggie free of a wrecked, white Honda, where Maggie is either pinned against its steering wheel or unconscious.

Ekker crookedly bears down on them. He doesn't run so much as shuffle left to right, left to right, kicking up snow with each heavy-footed step, swinging Fuente's shotgun in front of him like a home run hitter taking a few practice swings or a blind man caning his way across an intersection.

Marcus tries to reload the rifle but fumbles it and drops the mag and loses his grip on the empty gun altogether. He starts after Ekker anyway, limping on his broken bionic. And although there's still no way he'll catch the man, he screams at him over the storm, "Come and get me, you prick!"

Just a few seconds more, he thinks. Need to keep him on me a little longer so Luna can get Maggie free . . .

Then Marcus runs at him.

Despite the leg. Despite the snow. Despite everything. He *runs*.

He tackles Ekker, and the baseball-bat shotgun spins away and the two tumble and roll, until suddenly Ekker's on top of him, faster than he could've imagined, standing over him now, dragging him across the icy pavement. Ekker hauls him up, and Marcus finally understands what Fuente was going on about—

Oh, what big eyes you have . . .

His face . . . Jesus, his face . . .

And then Ekker headbutts him once, twice, and Marcus can only cling to consciousness like a drowning man to driftwood.

He spits teeth shards into Ekker's blood-smeared face, taunts him, "Can't kill me, you sonofabitch, I'm already dead."

Ekker pulls him close, headbutts him again, leaving black stars spinning behind his eyes. "No, Sheriff Austin, I'm going to make you wish you were dead." But Marcus isn't focused on Ekker anymore because something else is stalking down the street now, loping toward them all.

Smoky gray and white, the color of ashen shadows, of soot and dried blood and old bone. A frantic origami of impossible arms and legs . . .

"Better turn around," he says, laughing at Ekker, but it's not a joke or even a warning.

It's a threat.

96

He goes for the girl and is about to grab her when something strikes him from behind and sends him sprawling.

He howls, turns, to find the man who drove him away from the girl on the mountain.

But that man is already badly hurt, he smells the death clinging to him like grave dirt, and the man has no gun now, no weapon of any kind.

Just feeble human hands, small teeth.

And *he* has *claws* and *fangs* . . .

97

Maggie comes to with Luna pulling her from the car and two men, or what used to be men, tearing at each other scant yards away from them.

Like two wild animals, two wolves going at each other. Tooth and claw.

Ekker and Roach—Luna's other crash survivor—or one of Walton's White Things.

Whatever the latter is, it's looking even less human than the badly injured Ekker as it works bare teeth into Ekker's throat, one savage predator taking down another.

Ekker screams as hot blood sprays skyward and Maggie finally crawls free from the car.

Marcus lays sprawled behind the two men, barely moving, barely conscious or not at all.

Maggie struggles to standing and pushes Luna behind her and searches for both their guns, but they've been tossed around by the accident, and Roach or the White Thing or whatever it is now howls over Ekker, kicking and squirming beneath it.

The creature's call is an eerie, unearthly sound, made only worse by the dozen or hundred or thousand answering calls from Black Mountain.

The creature cracks Ekker's skull against the pavement again and again and rips at the man's face and eyes until he's a broken, bloody, shattered heap, then turns a haunted, very human eye . . . his eyes are blue . . . toward Maggie and Luna even as Marcus finally rises to his own knees and fumbles with something and then tosses it overhand at the thing.

That thermobaric device, one of those flash-bang things, they took off the dead man on the mountain.

It detonates in the air above the thing's head, sending a million starlike sparks everywhere, sucking all the oxygen out of Maggie's lungs and the whole world, too, leaving only heat and fire, but the creature leaps anyway, backlit by the corona of a black star.

It flies at them on fire.

Maggie unsheathes the Tracker from the small of her back—same six-inch blade Walton warned her wouldn't do them any good buried in her pack—and cuts the monster's throat in one smooth, perfect swing.

It falls before her on its knees, human eyes wide and dying, mouth open, hands still reaching, still clawing, a blackened silver watch on its bony wrist.

Blood pools and freezes all around Maggie, and before she rams the blade in one last time, Luna puts two bullets into the monster's heart.

She stands next to Maggie, gripping the gun Maggie gave her with both hands, muzzle smoke drifting into the night.

No magic now, no supernatural aura or weird energy or phantom sound of invisible birds. Just a young girl with a gun and a dead man at her feet.

But . . . but . . . in the final, fading spark light, before Maggie's own concussion overwhelms her, she gets one last good look at Ekker sprawled in the snow behind the dead man, and thinks she spies something break free from his cracked skull—

Something wet and slick and feathered . . . that takes to the night sky and soon disappears.

98

Marcus takes the still-warm gun from her hand, and then she and Marcus help Maggie sit up, get her conscious, pull her into the cover of the open door of the storage unit as the sleet turns back to gentler snow.

Maggie asks them both, "Are we alive?"

Marcus spits blood and a tooth. "Oh, we're just great." He huddles next to Maggie. "Listen, guy from the mini mart made a call for me. This place is going to be swarming with sheriff's deputies and state police, even the real FBI, hell, maybe the National Guard, too, soon as they can make their way up here."

Both Maggie and Marcus glance her way, but it's only Maggie who says, "What do we do? How do we explain all this?"

Marcus replies, "I don't know. The truth, I guess? But . . . I know you're not big on that." He grins a bloody grin and pulls things from his coat and presses one of them into Maggie's hands. "This is that tactical communications device we got off that guy on the mountain, and it got me wondering. It's a phone, sure, but it's more than that. It's a GPS tracker too. A very, very good one, probably allowing Ekker to monitor his team's movements in real time. He likely knew every second where they were, and they would've known where he was. That's how they got to Walton's cabin so fast."

There's a conversation going on between the two of them she doesn't understand, but she knows it's about her. But she can't take her eyes off Roach through the open roll door, still slumped forward on his knees, head nearly touching the snow.

The blood all around him reminds her of wings.

Maggie says, "But Luna doesn't have a phone or anything like that. That all got destroyed in the crash."

"No, but the *tracker*, Maggie. The chip or whatever it might be. The surgeries. The *scars*." Marcus hesitates. "I'll have to look."

"And then?" Maggie asks.

Marcus shows them both the other thing in his hand: a clear case holding red-feathered darts.

He looks at her now, drawing her attention from Roach. "If this thing is inside you, Luna, I'll have to put you out, so that way . . . you know . . . nothing weird happens. I might have to poke around some, although it should be close to the surface. Probably just beneath the skin, maybe your arm or neck. No promise I'm right or that it'll even work. But you might finally be free." He puts the case in her hand. "And hey, what's one more scar to us?"

She grips it, and it doesn't feel any heavier than the gun.

"Is the Honda still drivable?" Maggie asks.

Marcus doesn't bother to look, just looks at Maggie. He doesn't take his eyes off her. "Yeah, she'll go a bit farther."

Another conversation passes between Marcus and Maggie, a decision made, but this one is silent. This one is final.

Maggie suddenly pulls her close, hugs her. "It's going to be okay, Luna. We'll take care of you if you want. But it's your decision. All yours. You can just lie back and sleep for a bit, and when you wake up, this will all be over. Over forever. Nothing more than a dream."

She hugs Maggie back to hide her own tears, and then opens the case and returns it to Marcus . . .

Maggie says, "I feel like I should tell you a bedtime story, the way my dad used to do for me, but you already know all mine. And frankly, mine all suck." Maggie laughs weakly, buries her face in her ruined hair. Whispers, "But I'll try."

Luna feels the sting of the dart, but for once, it doesn't hurt.

Feels Maggie's heartbeat, too, soft and feathery, against her own.

"Once upon a time . . ."

99

The blue Dodge Durango sits in the snow on the side of the road, occupied by two people, a male driver, a girl passenger.

Anika Jewell's team catches them seventy-eight miles outside Culpeper, Virginia.

She was relieved Stier brought her back in after the plane crashed in the storm, after the Tesseract biometric array and GPS web Anika sewed into Luna a year ago indicated she was injured but alive.

Given the girl's physical and mental state, no one knew for sure what sort of shape she'd be in, how she'd respond.

No one wanted to get close to her.

The call Stier made to Anika was reluctant but unapologetic.

Anika was thrilled to get it.

☾

Anika uses the Ts'ao-tung meditation techniques she's practiced for years to clear her mind as she and her team move toward the Dodge, but still she's scared.

They've set up a twenty-yard perimeter with the road blocked in both directions with a phalanx of SUVs.

She races up to the passenger side, and although one of her men is there to shatter the window with a window punch and unlock the door for her, both doors open easily.

Anika doesn't recognize the driver, clearly deceased, a ravaged corpse whose hands have been zip-tied to the steering wheel to keep him upright.

A mannequin, she thinks, despite her efforts to keep her mind silent, still, empty.

A prop . . .

The other person in the front passenger seat is about Luna's height and has similar hair, but when her eyes flutter open at the first touch of the cold air and swirling flakes, they aren't Luna's. This mysterious woman says, "I've been waiting, thought you'd never come." Then starts mumbling to herself, barely a whisper, something like a nursery rhyme—

Strange is my name and I'm on strange ground, and strange that it is that I can't be found . . .

The woman has two objects in her hand, the still-bloody biometric GPS web someone cut free from Luna's neck, and a small, metal spherical object like a baseball.

Dr. Anika Jewell's fear overwhelms her, her mind far from empty now.

Oh no, oh my God, that's a—

The woman smiles up at her and says, "Time to cross over the mountain . . ."

And then the grenade explodes, enveloping everyone and everything in white light.

BLACK MOUNTAIN

C

Nineteen months later—

Carl parks the white Honda in a dusty lot of the Hanging Rock Trailhead.

It's early but already hot, the bright spring sun shimmering and sparking through the green trees, and it'll be a bit of a hike.

Fortunately, Lily knows the way.

C

After they drove out of West Virginia that Christmas, they went to Deidre's and stayed for three days, anxiously watching the news.

Hiding out with his ex wasn't ideal, and he didn't want to put Deidre in danger that way, but he truly didn't know where else to go. There was no one else he could trust, not after the mountain. But those three days came and went quietly, without incident. Nothing on the news. Nothing about the crash, or the dead men on Black Mountain, or those in Lost Hill.

Nothing about Luna or even Maggie.

Nothing about him.

That's when he understood what they were truly up against. Not something supernatural, but something immeasurably powerful all the same. Forces that couldn't make a whole mountain disappear but might as well have.

He did just enough research, put just enough of Luna's secrets together to learn about a man named Stier and a medical company called Tesseract, and he knew from his own shadowy military experiences that this Tesseract was neither a hospital nor a true company; it was a *program*.

And shadowy, secret programs never just end.

Deidre got the Honda repaired, and despite her protests they got on the road again before New Year's, when they surprisingly discovered that Ekker's fake IDs, as well as Maggie's, were real enough.

Sure, he didn't look like Graham, but no one paid any attention to the photo itself, not when he paired it with a flashing badge. And it wasn't a problem for Luna. The photo on the license might as well have always been her, they looked so much alike.

He forced them to practice their new names again and again—

Carl Graham. Lily Shane.

Until the names rolled off their tongues. Until they felt normal, natural, real too. There was *before the mountain* and *after the mountain*, and after they adopted those new names and identities, they didn't talk about *before the mountain* anymore. They disappeared.

Those people didn't exist anymore either.

☾

They find Walton's cabin burned to the ground.

They think about leaving flowers, but they don't have to. Flowers already bloom everywhere, a riot of beautiful color, so bright they hurt the eyes.

Saxifrage. Indian paintbrush. Guyandotte beauty. Dwarf larkspur.

Another year or so, and the cabin will be nothing but flowers, nothing but a memory.

☾

It's the only time they've been up here together, the only time he's ever been here at all, but it amazes him how much the damage from the crash site is already grown over.

The wreckage is gone, every single piece, but scars do remain, visible in the damaged trees and plowed earth.

It amazes him how quickly the world moves on, how it forgets, how it heals, and to some extent, how quickly some people heal too.

Lily has her scars; she lost two fingers to frostbite—she jokes together they make a whole person—but swears she doesn't remember much of their time on the mountain. She's grown five inches since they were last up here, and although he'll never say this to her, she looks more and more like Maggie every day.

Lily dreads the home-school curriculum Deidre sends them but loves current pop music and tolerates even some of the classic rap, rock, and blues he likes. She favors thick black eyeliner and old band T-shirts and occasionally rolls out a West Virginia twang and is a whiz at any kind of math and despite her missing fingers wants to learn to play the classical piano and enjoys crappy reality TV and mint Oreo milkshakes and is always threatening to sneak off and get tattoos like his, maybe a bird or a wolf or even a dragon, and he tells her she can if she still wants to when she's older.

She's a healthy teenager in almost every way, and in the ways that matter most she's 100 percent normal. Beyond occasionally finishing a sentence for him, or seemingly being able to pick a stray thought out of his mind or know exactly what he's feeling when it rains, there's been no more magic since Black Mountain.

So, maybe none of that happened.

Or maybe, maybe, she's just growing up . . . and learning that most fairy tales aren't real.

☽

She leads him from the plane crash to a white pine about a half mile away, where she shows him a collapsible shovel, abandoned in the kudzu.

In all these woods, on the side of this mountain, there's no way in a million years he'd ever find this spot, but she walked right to it.

She says Maggie saw the plane fall from here.

He digs where she tells him to, and a foot down he strikes a hard object wrapped in a tarp. It's a beautiful antique snow globe, a little girl with a red scarf ice dancing away from a black wolf.

But then Lily takes the shovel from him and digs down deeper . . . until she finds a black plastic Pelican case.

She tells him Maggie was burying both the globe and the case the winter night of the crash, planning to come back sometime in the future to recover them, long after anyone had forgotten about her.

Least that's what she'd dared hope.

They open the case together to see it holds two ELLIPAL Titan air-gapped cold wallets, Maggie's true long-buried treasure at last. But there was never any real map. Maggie used a compass and that old sextant to calculate the latitude and longitude and then memorized the coordinates, so she could eventually make her way back here. Maggie herself was the only map. Until Lily.

Even with the fluctuation in cryptocurrency, the boom/bust cycles, whatever's on those wallets is still worth a fortune. Fortunately, Lily knows the sixteen-digit code to unlock them too.

She knows all this and more because once upon a time Maggie stood here in the falling snow and watched her fall from the sky, like a shooting star.

Tell me a story . . .

She knows it by heart.

AUTHOR'S NOTE

Now a quick note about the beautiful geography of West Virginia.

For a myriad of reasons, some aesthetic, some structural, I played fast and loose with my West Virginia locales. I extended and condensed distances and mixed and matched real places with more than a few fictional ones. I apologize and hope it doesn't detract from this story or the reality that West Virginia is a wild, wonderful state. I urge you to (safely) hike the Monongahela yourself.

JTS
September 2022

ACKNOWLEDGMENTS

I need to credit the usual suspects: my amazing team at Thomas & Mercer, my agents, my family, and particularly Delcia, who had to suffer through this one with me.

I've said that books are journeys, that some take longer than others, and some are ones you're eager to take again, albeit on a whole new path. In many ways, this book is a companion piece to *The Flock*, although it's not technically a sequel. But it does touch on a handful of similar themes, the same amalgam of magical realism or paranormal horror I was exploring in that earlier story.

I'm glad I took the trip a second time, and I hope you've enjoyed it too.

ABOUT THE AUTHOR

Photo © 2018 Marie Feutrier

J. Todd Scott was born in rural Kentucky and attended college and law school in Virginia, where he set aside an early ambition to write to pursue a career as a federal agent. His assignments have taken him all over the United States and the world, but a gun and a badge never replaced his passion for stories and writing.

His previous books include *The Far Empty, High White Sun*, and *This Side of Night* in the Chris Cherry / Big Bend Series, as well as the Appalachian crime novel *Lost River* and the thriller *The Flock*.

For more information, visit www.jtoddscott.com.